Jemez Hijinks
A Death in the Core of the Valles Caldera

DAVID HOEKENGA

This is a work of fiction. Names, characters, places and incidents either are the product of the author's imagination or are used fictitiously, and any resemblance to any actual persons, living or dead, events, or locales is entirely coincidental.

This book was printed in the United States of America.

ISBN: 1463612737
ISBN-13: 978-1463612733

To order additional copies of the book, contact:

David Hoekenga

1-505-644-2080

www.DavidHoekenga.com

I HOPE YOU ENJOY THE SCENES

DEDICATION

To the mentoring aunts, Mae, Blanche, and Marian

SET IN LIBERAL AMSTERDAM, ONE OF MY FAVORITE CITIES AND HOME TO THE BEST CAFE IN EUROPE! (GREAT PEA SOUP)

DAVID H.

WINTER 2015

ALSO BY DAVID HOEKENGA

Santa Fe Solo:

A Death in the Shadow of the Sangre de Cristo Mountains

Placitas Particular:

A Death in the Rind of the Sandia Mountains

The Hampton Court Murders:

Death by Design

That is part of the mystery of sex, it is a flow onwards. Sexless people transmit nothing.

From *We Are Transmitters*

By D. H. Lawrence

PART 1

CHAPTER 1

An intense orange and yellow twisted-ribbon sunrise filled the sky over Santa Fe, New Mexico. The May dawn crept in slowly delayed only by the Sangre de Cristo Mountains that loomed over the eastern edge of the city. The town itself, at over seven thousand feet was experiencing a late, cool spring. Signe Sorenson, homicide detective, was enjoying a walk through the upper, older part of the city encumbered only by a very large cup of strong, hot coffee.

Universally called 'Seena,' by her friends and acquaintances, she had been on loan from the Copenhagen Metropolitan Police Department for a year before recently becoming a permanent member of the Santa Fe Police Department. Her rumpled, chain smoking, Chief Gerald Hartford, had become her confidant and mentor. Hartford wore frayed shirts and ties of mismatched color. His main goal was to retire without scandal, but he never failed to stick his neck out for his young Detectives. Signe often thought that detectives, like professional basketball players, learned most of their skills outside of school. She had learned a great deal from Hartford and from her first mentor, Thor Nielsen, Chief of Detectives in Copenhagen. Nielsen had encouraged her intuition and her quirky tangential way of approaching cases.

Most homicide detectives were partnered with another detective for a partner. Signe had always worked that way in Denmark. In Santa Fe, Signe's sidekick was a mere patrolman, Jack Gallegos. He was six feet tall with jet black hair and a rugged face softened by large brown eyes. He lifted weights and walked in a way that told you instantly that he was proud of his physique. Although not a detective, Signe's testosterone-driven partner had helped her through some tough scrapes over the past eight months. Chief Hartford was convinced that Signe didn't partner with another detective because she always wanted to be the boss. He didn't mean it in a derogatory way, but Signe didn't think that was the real reason. Truth be told, she did like picking her own direction in an investigation without having to consult anyone. Jack followed her lead well due in part to the fact that he was in love with her. As she walked, the streets gradually brightened. Her mind was centered on work. She was not focused on the local surroundings.

A black Suburban with tinted windows stopped suddenly at the curb beside her. A man in a blue suit pointed a pistol at Signe's head through the open front window.

"Get in, now!" he shouted as the back door flew open.

Signe moved slowly in the direction of the car while her eyes surveyed the scene without turning her head. If she decided to run, a large shrub next to the sidewalk would provide some cover while she unholstered the .38 caliber Smith and Wesson located under her left arm pit, if she decided to run. However, she had a more immediate problem—the large caliber pistol pointing at her head. As she moved toward the car she extended her coffee toward the man with the pistol as if wanting him to take it from her before she docilely climbed into the back seat. Instead, when the coffee was six inches from him she threw the large, full cup in his face after first squeezing the base to make sure that the lid came free.

She considered rolling under the car and firing up into the cabin with her .38 and then with her .32 caliber backup pistol, but if there were four men in the suburban and they jumped out quickly, they would have her surrounded. Instead, as the man screamed in pain, she used the open back door to shield herself as she somersaulted toward the shrub. Once behind the dense foliage she pointed both of her guns at the suburban and waited. A leather wallet with something shiny attached was thrown into the bush in her direction.

Someone in the vehicle shouted, "FBI!" as the vehicle pulled forward a few feet and then came to a stop. A man wearing a gray suit and a white shirt and narrow tie got out of the driver's door and walked toward the shrub with his hands over his head.

"I'm special agent Farrell of the FBI," the man said as he started around the bush. "I need to ask you some questions."

"Stop right where you are," Signe shouted. "What was the drawn gun about?"

"I just wanted to get you off the street quickly so that I could explain what we wanted. We found a body and I need your help."

"You have an 'unusual' way of getting someone cooperation. Why didn't you just come to my office?" Signe asked as she came from behind the bushes brushing off her walking attire.

"Our meeting can't be made public," Farrell replied. "But I apologize for frightening you."

"I wasn't frightened, Farrell," Signe spat back. "I was and still am angry about your ham-handed approach. It's very likely that I might have ended up shooting you or one of your not very bright accomplices. I would have responded a lot more rationally to the badge first rather than the pistol. You just weren't thinking straight. You government guys think you can do whatever you want without any consequences. You see yourself as above the law and you enjoy pushing local law enforcement around. "

"I don't usually apologize for what I do but, again, I am sorry," Farrell replied in a contrite voice. "Could you get in the vehicle so we can continue this conversation in private?"

The two walked to the suburban and Signe climbed into the back seat. Two other agents were in the vehicle's front seat.

"Tell me about the body," Signe began in an angry tone without preamble.

"We found a body yesterday west of town," Farrell began. "From the look of it he has been dead for two or three weeks. He was wearing hiking clothes and so far it seems he died of natural causes."

"What does any of this have to do with me?" Signe asked in an exasperated tone.

"We have reason to believe that you knew this man," Farrell replied.

"Based on what?"

"When we searched his office in Los Alamos yesterday," Farrell replied. "We found a sealed envelope with several dozen black and white pictures of you inside."

One of the other agents, a redheaded man named Boyle handed Signe a large brown packet. Signe undid the clasp and spilled a stack of eight by ten photos into her lap. The photos clearly had been taken surreptitiously. Some were of her alone while others were taken when she was talking with a friend or colleague. A few photos showed her undressing or toweling off after a shower. She concealed her surprise by studying each photo carefully before she put them very deliberately back in the envelope. Signe held onto the few pictures that showed her disrobed and placed them face down on the seat.

"You can't keep those," Boyle said vehemently as he reached for the photos.

"Those very personal pictures of me are not critical to your investigation, agent," Signe spat back. "They are just something that you will put up on the office bulletin board and forward to your friends so everyone can leer at them."

Farrell raised his hand toward the agent indicating that he shouldn't say any more. Signe knew that the FBI had already made copies of the photos, but she wanted to assert as much control as she could.

"Who is the victim?" Signe finally asked.

"Dr. Lawrence Abramowitz," Farrell replied. "Do you know him?"

"I'm sure you already know that yes, I did know him. He was an exceptionally bright man, full of vigor and very engaged in life. I am very sad to hear that he is dead. He was a good and true colleague, and I'll miss him," Signe replied. "We met shortly after I moved to Santa Fe and had dinner together two or three times. Later he helped me identify a strange chemical, hydrazine, which came up during a murder I investigated at the State Fair."

"Had you seen him recently?" Farrell asked.

"No. Unfortunately, I hadn't seen or heard from him for a few months, but I have always considered him an ally."

"So, you didn't know that he took pictures of you?" Farrell asked.

"Absolutely not. Although, if he had asked me, I would have let him shoot almost all of the photographs you showed me."

"He had thousands of photos and hundreds of them were of you," Boyle volunteered.

"How very strange," Signe replied. "Why is the FBI investigating this case rather than the local police? Larry always told me he worked for the University of California at Livermore even though he was assigned to Los Alamos. Why are you involved?"

"He had security clearances," Farrell replied.

The car was getting warm inside so Boyle opened one of the windows. Farrell suggested they drive during the rest of their talk. Signe agreed and the third agent pulled the large black vehicle into the light morning traffic.

"What Dr. Abramowitz said was true as far as it went," Agent Farrell continued. "However, everyone working at the National Lab was also a US government employee in the Department of Energy. Because of his work in the area of nuclear physics, he had the highest government clearance usually restricted to members of the President's cabinet or higher. Among ourselves we call the clearance

YW which is short for Yankee white. Several other levels of clearance are named after other colors, but white is the highest. Abramowitz could, for example, walk into CIA headquarters in Langley unannounced and look at unedited intelligence received that day from our agents in the old Soviet Union."

"Why did he have such an extraordinary level of clearance?" Signe asked.

"I'm just learning about his career but we believe he may have designed the trigger for the first hydrogen bomb which was exploded sometime in the early 1950s," Farrell replied. "Over the following decades he worked on a variety of designs for making hydrogen bombs more powerful and smaller. To do that work he had to know everything about the strengths and weaknesses of our entire defensive posture. I suspect he had enough information in his head to make any third world country into a major nuclear power."

"With all your connections and high powered investigating tools, how exactly do you think I can help you with your investigation?" Signe asked.

"Unlike any of us, you actually knew the man, Detective Sorensen," Farrell answered. "Even though we got off to a bad start, I think you might have a lot to contribute. Do you want to see where we found him?"

"Yes. Is the body still there?"

"Yes, it is. We just found it yesterday and, as I said, it appears to have been lying there for two or three weeks. I left two men with high powered lights there overnight to begin collecting samples. Shall we go?"

CHAPTER 2

The suburban sped west out of town and then north of Santa Fe on US 84. They raced past the Santa Fe Opera soaring skyward on a ridge among rolling hills and piñon trees and then past Camel Rock. At the small village of Pojoaque the driver turned west on NM 4. Despite the narrowness and sudden curves in the road the agent drove just as fast, screeching around corners and accelerating on every straightaway. Signe was still angry about the pistol that had served as her introduction to these three men so she didn't make small talk.

Just before climbing the mesa where Los Alamos was located, the road dipped and then crossed the Rio Grande Bridge at Otowi Crossing. Signe remembered that she and her partner, Jack, had been ambushed here just a few months ago. As the road straightened, the Suburban sped along the south side of the small town and into the Ponderosa pine covered hills. The road climbed again and continued west.

About ten miles outside of Los Alamos the pines opened up to reveal a huge shallow grass covered bowl that stretched far to the north. This huge depression, called Valle Grande, was left after a volcano exploded millions of years ago. When Signe first saw it, with her Danish sense of small spaces limited horizon she thought the caldera looked like any other large field. Then she realized that the very, very tiny specks she saw in the bottom of the caldera were actually cattle. The scale of the landscape was overwhelming. The driver turned the Suburban off the narrow, two-laned, blacktop road and stopped at a barbed wire fence. One of the agents looking out of place in his suit and tie jumped out of the car and opened the gate, closing it again once the vehicle had passed through.

The high speed travel resumed on the narrow dirt lane. Most of the road was packed dirt with a strip of grass growing down the middle. However, an occasional pothole sent Signe flying. Twice she hit her head on the roof.

"Isn't the poor man we are going to see already dead?" Signe asked Farrell sarcastically.

"Yes."

"Then slow this damn vehicle before my bones are broken," Signe demanded of the driver.

The Suburban's speed dropped noticeably. It bounced and swayed more gently for the next five miles. As the grassland gave way to a Ponderosa pine forest the vehicle came to a halt. The four occupants disembarked and continued on two ATVs with large knobby tires. Signe much preferred this slower travel in the open vehicle. The day had become warm and comfortable and the trail twisted through the woods with puddles and fallen branches. The two ATVs traveled north and slightly east eventually driving between two large hills named Cerro San Luis and Cerro de Trasquilar. The sputter of their unmuffled engines echoed off of the slopes of the hills. Signe had explored Valle Grande one weekend with her son, Axel, before he returned to Denmark, but they hadn't gone this far into the back country.

They continued on through the valley between the hills. It was open country with sparse vegetation and towering Ponderosa pines. As they drove further, the flat land along the trail widened and they came to a small river, the Rio San Antonio. Along the shore of the river were two more ATVs and two more investigators. At least they are not wearing suits and ties Signe thought to herself. She stepped off of the vehicle first and went to examine what appeared to be a small campsite surrounded by the FBI's equipment.

"Please don't touch anything!" Agent Farrell yelled after her.

Signe stopped in her tracks, turned and glared at him with a mixture of disdain and annoyance in her eyes. After replacing her walking shoes with paper booties she walked into the camp. A small old fashioned orange tent was staked out along the edge of the river with the tent fly pointing toward the churning water. A burned out campfire ringed with river rocks was close by. A collapsible chair and table stood between the fire circle and the tent. Camp silverware, an aluminum plate and condiments occupied one corner of the table. Nearby was the body of a man long dead.

"Poor Larry," Signe murmured almost inaudibly.

She approached the body and knelt down. The weather must have been dry for the past three weeks because the corpse was dried, like jerky, rather than swollen and rotten. Animals had nibbled the hands and something had eaten one of the thighs, but for some reason the face was untouched. Signe recognized the face of her friend immediately despite the desiccation and bronzing of the skin. He was wearing a brimmed hat, a blue chambray shirt, khaki shorts with many pockets and hiking boots with heavy wool socks. She studied the body silently for quite a time. Everything she saw looked like a death by natural causes. Nothing was out of place or incongruous. Finally it was the very perfection of the scene that made her suspicious.

She stood and moved slowly around the camp, in wider and wider circles, just observing and trying not to form any impression. She had not completed studying about an acre of ground around the campsite when one of the agents called Signe over to a nearby area where the FBI had set up camp. She had to admire their preparation. She hadn't eaten all day and quickly devoured a sandwich and a large bowl of soup. One of agents, who had spent the night at the scene, sat down across from her with a cup of coffee. Signe eyed it covetously. Without saying a word, the agent got up and returned with a large aluminum cup full of steaming coffee.

"Thanks for the java," Signe said as she took a long swallow. "I don't know about you, but to me this looks like a death due to natural causes."

"Yeah. I've been here for thirty some hours now and I haven't found anything that makes me think otherwise."

"Larry must be pretty important to generate this kind of response from your agency."

"I don't know all the details, but apparently he knew as much as any living person about our military abilities."

"I had dinner with him a few times and never detected a hint of that," Signe mused.

"He had been concealing that from almost everybody for decades," the agent replied. "I'm sure it became second nature to him."

Signe cleared her dishes and walked back over to the body. Farrell's men were placing the corpse in a body bag and securing it to the back of one of the ATVs.

"Have you seen enough, Detective?" Farrell asked.

"No. Doesn't this whole tableau seem a little too perfect to you?" Signe replied in a confidential tone.

"I guess not," Farrell replied without a pause. "However, if it does to you, you had better find the missing clues quickly. We are planning on pulling out in thirty minutes."

Suddenly, Signe felt very unsatisfied about the death of her good friend.

"It took us three hours to get here from Santa Fe, and I'm just not satisfied yet," Signe reflected. "I'd like to spend the night and work the scene again tomorrow. Just leave me a tent, one of the ATVs and a Nikon. I'll return everything in a couple of days."

"Okay," conceded Farrell. "I could leave one of my men to make sure you are safe."

"That won't be necessary, Farrell. I'm a big girl."

He walked toward the other agents giving them instructions as he went. A half an hour later three ATVs and five agents left the camp in a cloud of exhaust and engine noise. Signe made herself another cup of coffee and sat down by Larry's tent. The woods were still except for the occasional call of a canyon towhee high in the Ponderosa pines. Signe searched her memory for conversations she had had with Larry over the past two years. She knew he had come to Los Alamos in the nineteen fifties fresh out of graduate school and never left. He liked good wine, photography and bird watching in the canyons and river beds around the Jémez. He went to the Santa Fe Opera every year. She reflected that obviously she didn't know very much about the man. She would have to learn a great deal more.

She got up with her large borrowed camera and worked around the camp again in narrow circles but in the opposite direction taking pictures as she went. Nothing turned up. She didn't find a random piece fiber, scrap of paper or strand of hair. It was as if the area around the campground had been staged and then ten technicians in white scrub suits and sterile gloves had gone over every inch along the San Antonio River. She recalled the case of the Dutch ballerina that died between acts of *Giselle* in Copenhagen. It had taken her twenty months to find the small cut in the ballerina's toe, where the powerfully fatal strychnine had been introduced. She decided to search the crime scene again until the light became too dim to see.

As darkness descended, Signe lit a Coleman stove on the small aluminum table the FBI had left. She made a not very tasty dinner of canned beef stew, white bread and canned peaches in overly sweet syrup. The agents had left some decent coffee so Signe made a small pot saving most of the aromatic grounds for the morning. She took a full cup and walked over to the river, sitting on a large boulder. There was no moon and the sky was filled with thousands and thousands of stars so bright they looked like diamonds cast across the heavens by a carelessly rich god. In Denmark the sky was often overcast at night and lights from the many cities and towns reflected yellow light off the underside of the clouds. So seeing stars was rare.

Even the moon had trouble casting its reflected light on the little kingdom where she was born.

Signe hadn't seen stars like tonight since she rode across the Pampas of Argentina with Inspector Juan Vivendi. Signe threw the dregs of the coffee in the river, walked back to her tent, and crawled into the sleeping bag. With bands of coyotes creating a polyphonous choir in the background Signe was sound asleep in minutes.

CHAPTER 3

The sun was up at five thirty the next morning and the light shining through the khaki colored tent woke Signe. It was a chilly morning and she could see her breath as she pulled on her clothes and heated water for her coffee. Then she went back to sleuthing. Unfortunately, even in the heavy morning dew she was unable to find anything amiss. After searching the area around the camp for two hours, she came back to the place where the body had been lying before the FBI removed the body. She was surprised to see that she could still make out the outline of her friend in the dirt. At first she thought that perhaps fluid had leaked out of his body over the three weeks that he lay there and that it had changed the composition of the soil. She couldn't image what it might be, so after she took pictures of the body's outline, she collected samples of the soil under and beside the body. Then she climbed both hills. First she ascended Cerro San Luis, the smaller of the two hills and took several panoramic shots. Cerro de Trasquilar was both taller and steeper. She had to stop twice on the way up to catch her breath. Again, she took panoramic shots in each direction but particularly toward the campsite. Taking her last picture toward the southwest, the sun glinted off a metal object. She marked the nearest tree in her mind's eye and set off for it when she reached the bottom. After a little searching she found a stainless steel sleeve with numbers and letters on it that she slipped into her pocket.

When she got to the agents camp she packed their camping gear onto the ATV and drove out of the camp. She drove back over the hills of the Valle San Luis and cut into the Valle Jaramillo. She startled a bear eating strawberries and then surprised a large herd of elk that had been grazing in a meadow. They moved out of her way on long spindly legs. She loved being out in the backcountry on her own. The only distracting factor was the noise of her ATV. As she entered Valle Grande she pulled off the trail and shut the motor down. Signe sat back on the driver's seat and took out the FBI's binoculars. She scanned the thousands of acres of green meadow that made up the valley and stretched toward the south. She spotted some elk but mostly cattle. Beyond Valle Grande she saw the blue colored Jémez Mountains. She couldn't imagine a prettier or more majestic scene.

She had told Farrell yesterday afternoon when he departed to call her partner, and have Jack meet her at the Valle Grande gate with his pickup truck at one p.m. When she got to the gate Jack had already opened it, and as she went through he bowed in mock formality.

"Thanks for coming, Jack," Signe called out as she stopped the ATV behind Jack's pickup truck.

He closed the gate before coming over and giving Signe a bear hug.

"I wouldn't have missed it for the world partner!" Jack sang out. "Your new boyfriend has a strange sense of the romantic."

"Actually, this is a spectacularly beautiful place," Signe replied. "I hadn't been in the back country before. Last night was pure magic, dazzling stars and coyote symphonies. I'm sorry I couldn't have had you camp with me for the night."

"I would rather have spent the night across a campfire from you, than in the curvaceous warm hold of Rhonda," Jack replied as he drove the ATV up into the bed of his truck.

"You must find something there that you like, Jack," Signe replied. "You keep going back for more."

"Let's not talk about her, partner," Jack retorted sarcastically. "I want to hear about your new squeeze."

"His name is Liam Farrell and he wears a suit, even in the back country. He has curly brown hair and sexy dark green eyes."

"A suit? A space suit? If so, why aren't I picking you up in Roswell?"

"No. A nice single breasted wool suit with a button down white shirt."

"Oh! So, he was one of those. What did he want from you except to bend you over and ravish you?"

"He wanted my help with a death. He had found the body of poor Larry Abramowitz. Do you remember him?"

"Yes. You introduced me to him at The Pink Adobe one night when we were investigating Chloe Patterson's death. He helped you solve that case, didn't he?"

"You're right. I never could have solved it without him and he was also a good friend."

"If the feds are investigating his death they must be pretty damn sure he was murdered, Signe," Jack remarked.

Signe had climbed into the passenger seat and Jack was driving back toward Los Alamos.

"I stayed an extra day because the campsite was so strange."

"In what way?"

"It was perfect, Jack. Everything was perfectly tidy. No fiber or scrap was out of place. It was like the Dutch ballerina that I told you about without the tiny cut that killed her."

After they had gone through Los Alamos, Jack turned north to Española. They had agreed to eat at El Paragua. By the time they arrived the stone wall along the road was packed with old pickup trucks just inches from the stones. Sometimes, Signe would drive for two hours to eat the flautas there. Long strands of tender beef wrapped in a corn tortilla and then fried. After a large cold margarita, a large platter of beef flautas arrived. In many restaurants the tortilla on the outside was greasy or cooked so long that they couldn't be bitten. At El Paragua the wrapping was hot and crispy followed by a soft center. The beef inside was tender and aromatic. Signe polished off one of the seven inch batons quickly and grabbed for another. Jack and Signe polished off two platters quickly and were half way through a third when suddenly both of them were full. Signe had tried taking the leftovers home once but found that they didn't taste nearly as good the next day.

Jack drove Signe back to her apartment in Santa Fe and promised to return the ATV and camping equipment to the FBI office on Federal Way in Santa Fe the next morning. After a hot bath, Signe fell into bed.

After a long uninterrupted slumber, Signe awoke early feeling renewed. She went for an early walk, this time without a black Suburban, men in suits or even a pistol. Once back in her apartment, she changed quickly and went to work. Her mentor and boss, Gerald Hartford was already at his desk. Signe ground coffee beans and then brewed a pot of thick, rich nearly black java. She poured two large cups and then walked into her boss's office and sat down.

She had been told by Agent Farrell to mention nothing about the Abramowitz case to anyone until the scientist's death was proved to be of natural causes.

"What have you been up to, Signe?" Hartford asked in an avuncular tone.

"I was captured by the *faddens* FBI at gun point and abducted, Chief."

"What did those incompetent, arrogant bunglers want?"

"They found the body of Dr. Larry Abramowitz in Valle Grande and they thought I might be of assistance."

"Isn't he the nuclear physicist that helped you with the Patterson case?" Hartford replied.

"Yes. He knew so much and he was also my good friend."

"I'm sorry, Signe. I understand you spent the night out there alone. Did you find anything?"

"No, I didn't. Neither did the feds."

"Perhaps it was just a birdwatcher's perfect death. He was in a beautiful spot, deep in the wilderness, when he spotted his first Bullock's oriole and as he raised his binoculars toward the bird's bright orange belly his heart just stopped," Chief Hartford offered.

"You are not that much of a romantic, Chief," Signe replied in disbelief. "You've been in law enforcement for thirty nine years. You've seen everything. Don't go soft on me now."

"Okay. Here's my other theory, your friend was killed by diabolically clever rogue Stasi agents that are still working for GDR even though East Germany doesn't exist anymore."

"That's more like it!" Signe remarked enthusiastically as she took a large sip if coffee.

"Next you are going to ask me if I will let you work on the death of your friend," Hartford replied.

"You know me very well, Chief," Signe replied. "My gut tells me this is a murder even though I don't have a single piece of evidence."

"You are a very good Detective, Signe," Hartford replied after a large swallow of coffee. "I'm willing to let you follow your instincts as long as things remain this quiet in the department. Right now, as you know homicide is dead. No pun intended. I suppose the alternative is to have you write parking tickets."

"Given the hopelessness of parking in the capital, it's probably the hardest job in the department."

"I had lunch yesterday with the vice president of the Chamber of Commerce. She said she heard about a blog from some tourists from Rhode Island who wanted to visit Santa Fe. They claimed that to save time, they parked in Pojoaque and walked to the plaza."

"Larry told me he always parked at Museum Hill and then took a taxi to a restaurant or museum."

"That is definitely a PhD approach to our very narrow seventeenth century streets."

"He had his own unique way of looking at things," Signe mused. "I need one more favor from you, Chief."

"Shoot."

"May I have Jack help me with this investigation, if it turns out to be a murder?" Signe queried.

"Yes," Hartford replied without pausing. "You know I think you are an odd couple, but I've come to see that you two have real synergy. Have at it."

CHAPTER 4

After thanking her boss, Signe went in search of her partner, Jack. She walked across the 'bullpen' where all of the detectives had desks, greeting each one as she went by. She refilled her coffee cup and walked into the conference room. Jack had just returned from the FBI office where he had returned the ATV.

"Any problems with the suits?" Signe queried.

"No. Farrell stopped to quiz me about what I knew about his case," Jack replied.

"He was just trying to find out if I blabbed everything to you," Signe said.

"I just did my dumb patrolman routine with a lot of 'yes sirs' thrown in," Jack responded. "But I'm not sure he bought it."

"That's okay," Signe said. "The good news is that the Chief is going to let the two of us work on the case. So let's get started."

She took the stainless steel sleeve she had found in Valle Grande out of her pocket and handed it to Jack.

What do you think this is?" Signe asked.

Jack turned it over in his hand before saying, "This is a piece off of a large high tech gadget that wasn't made in China."

"What makes you think so?"

"It was carefully machined out of high grade material, and the numbers stamped on it would let a repairman order another one if it started to wear out."

"I agree. I don't think it belongs in the wilderness. Let's see if Valerie can figure it out for us."

They walked through the double doors into the crime lab. Valerie was bent over a spectrometer. As they approached she sat up quickly.

"Hi. You two are up to something. I can see it in your eyes," Valerie noted as she gave Signe a warm smile and rested a hand on her forearm.

"See what you can tell us about this fitting, if you please," Signe said as she placed the sleeve on the counter.

"Case number?" Valerie replied as she reached for a manila tag.

Valerie was the best CSI Signe had ever worked with, and she used her for all of her cases, especially ones that were outside the Santa Fe district. Valerie had puzzled out several impossible clues.

"Well it isn't exactly an official case," Signe said. "Perhaps we could just give it a random number."

"Okay," Valerie replied without missing a beat. "How about 092266."

"It's not very random, Valerie," Signe remarked. "It's my birthday."

"I know, but at least we can both remember it," Valerie shot back.

"I also have two soil samples. One is from under the body and one is from nearby," Signe remarked as she handed over two small baggies filled with earth. "For some reason the color and reflectance of the two samples was different. It was really more the latter than the former. The sunlight shone off the soil under Larry's body so that I could clearly see the outline of his form after his body had been removed. I don't think I'm explaining what I mean very well."

"Let me start by analyzing both samples and looking for differences," Valerie offered. "And I'll see if anything turns up."

Signe thanked Valerie and walked with Jack over to her desk to check for messages. The only recent one was from Liam Farrell thanking her for her help with the Abramowitz case and offering to take her to lunch.

"I think we need to check out Larry's house first," Signe suggested. "Would you like to take a ride up to Los Alamos?"

"Sure, partner," Jack shot back. "Don't you think the FBI will have collected everything and shipped it to Washington?"

"No. They don't believe this is a murder yet and they didn't find anything at the campsite. They are also a lazy crew as evidenced by their attempt to scoop me up quickly with a pistol instead of following protocol. Let's go."

Jack pulled an unmarked car around to the front door, and the two started on the thirty four mile trip up the hill to Los Alamos. During the last two murder cases; Signe and Jack had been ambushed and shot at frequently. They rode around in an armored black and white with bulletproof windows that Signe called C Vicky. She was actually the second fortified Crown Victoria the two had adopted. Their first model, called the Crown Vic, was blown up in front of their eyes at the entrance to the police station. Today they didn't want to be obvious.

The drive to Los Alamos took forty minutes in light traffic and Signe directed Jack to Larry's house. The neighborhood was tidy and quiet except for an occasional barking dog. The house was surrounded by the obligatory yellow crime scene tape. Jack drove on past the house without pausing before parking under a Ponderosa pine tree. By Los Alamos standards it was an old house. It was a one and half story tall brown shingled house with a darker shingle roof and a wide covered porch across the front supported by columns nearly thirty inches wide. It reminded Signe of California bungalows built in the 1920s she had seen on a trip. The house was in a settled neighborhood on a surprisingly big lot for a government town. The lawn was sparse and untidy with large cedars growing on both sides of the porch.

Jack and Signe walked furtively along the side of the house to the back door which was locked. Jack picked up a rock and was about to smash one of the six panes of glass in the wooden door when Signe dangled a key on a brass chain in front of him.

"Where did you get that?" Jack asked in an incredulous voice.

Signe slid the key into the lock as she said, "Larry gave it to me."

"I had no frigging notion that you two were that good friends, Signe."

"I met him in a great old fashioned bookstore just off the plaza in Santa Fe called Collected Works," Signe said as she went into the house and up three stairs into the kitchen. "I was looking for a bird book for northern New Mexico and he offered to help."

Signe noted the stale, stuffy smell of the kitchen. Unwashed dishes sat in the sink, but no food lay about. The room was dark so Signe turned the light on. Jack placed the evidence bags, tape, flashlights and chemical test kits they had brought with them on the kitchen table.

"You were right, Signe, because of laziness or disinterest the FBI hasn't even been in here yet!" Jack said enthusiastically.

"I wish we had brought Valerie and more lab materials," Signe said in a regretful voice.

"She can be up here in an hour," Jack replied as he stepped outside to call her.

Signe put on gloves and started rifling through the kitchen drawers. She didn't find anything out of the ordinary. Jack walked back in.

"She's on her way," Jack replied. "I told her to bring some sleeping bags and food, in case we don't finish this evening."

"What a great idea," Signe shot back as she pulled another clattering draw of silverware open.

Signe was heartily tired of the kitchen. She hadn't expected to find much there and she hadn't. She skipped the dining room which had heavy old oak furniture and looked to her as though it had been little used. She brushed through the living room which looked more inhabited. An old TV set sat in one corner and uneven stacks of books were present on all of the end tables. She had Jack catalogue each book title and check every volume for loose pieces of paper and notes.

Signe moved on to the library where piles of papers and manuscripts were tottering on every horizontal surface. Investigating her first murder in Santa Fe during the previous fall at the New Mexico State Fair, Signe had been disappointed by the paucity of clues around the body of a beautiful young woman. Now she was confronted with so much material that for a few minutes she wasn't even sure how to proceed. She decided to sit down at the desk and turn the computer on first. It was a very sophisticated instrument not at all like the laptop or desk top that Signe had had experience with. Several thick cables ran from the monitor and keyboard to a stack of processors nearly four feet tall. As the blue screen of the monitor lit up it asked for a password before Signe could proceed. Signe knew that the password would be complicated not the pet name or reversed birthday numerals that most amateur nonsecure users employed.

Larry was an employee of the University of California and of the Department of Defense who knew the nation's highest level secrets. His password had to be very sophisticated and uncrackable. Signe wondered if there even was such a word as 'uncrackable.' However, she also recognized that if it was that complicated or lengthy even a theoretical physicist would have trouble memorizing it. She thought that Dr. Abramowitz had probably been forced to write it down and that was the Achilles' heel of such a sophisticated system. She began to rifle through Larry's desk in a careful and systematic fashion. She found old pencils, pens, scraps of paper and ticket stubs in the various drawers.

A worn paper with rows and columns of numbers caught her eye. When she was a young student in Odense, Denmark her teachers had suspected that because of her intelligence and fascination with counting that she was a polymath. She fell a little short of all the classic characteristics especially in the area of playing music. Next they tested her to see if she had obsessive compulsive disorder because of her concerns about symmetry, but her rituals never became endlessly repetitive or more complex. Her final diagnosis was mild OCD largely manifest by 'counting'. She told no one how excited she became when she saw a string of numbers that might contain a clue. In the case of the German Banker back in Copenhagen, Signe had pasted a list of seven numbers on her mirror which she looked at daily for fourteen months before she broke the code and solved the case sending the felonious German financier to prison.

CHAPTER 5

Signe had Jack catalogue the stacks of papers in the office and photograph each with the Nikon while she puzzled over the paper covered with numbers. She hadn't made much progress when Valerie arrived with more lab equipment and red chili meat burritos. Signe felt better after she ate. She showed the paper of random numbers she had found to Valerie.

"I agree. I think the password is probably on that paper," Valerie remarked as she looked carefully at the paper. First, let me hook up a gadget that may detect his password in another way."

She plugged a small console into a USB port. Valerie rested a hand on Signe's shoulder or brushed her very sensitive lower arm every chance she got. Valerie was gay and attracted to Signe. Last fall, Signe was surprised by a woman friend one night and ended up kissing and fondling her. A patrolman tapped on the steamy window of their BMW and unfortunately recognized Signe. The rumor that the Danish detective was a lesbian spread through the Police Department like wildfire. Signe was pretty sure she wasn't.

"I'll try a personal attack first," Valerie suggested. "Just give me his full name, phone number and social. Users often use these names and numbers because they are easy to remember"

She quickly typed in the information.

"If that fails I'll try a dictionary attack. This little box can check three thousand words a second."

She punched two buttons.

"Wow. That's 180,000 words a minute. At that rate it can look at the one million words in the English language in six minutes!"

"Yes, but your brainy physicist isn't restricted to English."

"True. I know he spoke German, Italian and Russian fluently."

"Did you ever watch him use a computer keyboard? Did he use touch typing or some funky one finger method?"

"I did watch him access a bird watching report here once," Signe replied. "As smart as he was he only used two fingers."

"Then he probably put his finger below the first number of the password to hold his place while he started typing in the password. Let me dust the paper for fingerprints."

Valerie dusted the paper with a dry black ink and then dispersed it with repeated circular motions of a fine squirrel hair brush. A smudge developed below a 2 in the center of the page.

"It looks to me like he usually rested his finger here before he started typing," Valerie suggested.

"Good. Now all we have to do is figure out which direction he went in and where he stopped," Signe remarked in a discouraged voice.

"He could just count, but if it was long, which I suspect it was, it would have been easy for him to lose his place. Look the sheet over for some small mark or pinhole."

Signe picked the paper up and studied with a magnifying glass.

After several minutes of study she said, "I think there is a faint pencil line under the last seven."

"I agree that must be the last number," Valerie replied.

"Just think of all the ways to get from the 2 to the 7," Signe replied with delight.

"I will leave that puzzle to you," Valerie replied.

While Signe manipulated her numbers, Valerie checked on Jack's progress with the photography.

"How goes the picture taking?" Valerie asked.

"It's a damn lot of papers," Jack replied in an irritated voice. "I just can't believe the FBI left this to our despised and incompetent police officers."

"Signe says they're lazy," Valerie replied.

Signe called Valerie back over to the computer. Signe had drawn four pathways from the 2 to the 7.

"These are the only simple pathways I can see," Signe said. "Can we try them all?"

"Sure," Valerie said as she sat down at the console.

Her fingers began flying over the keyboard. Suddenly the screen lit up with the seal of the Department of Defense seal with a dark blue background.

"We are in!" Valerie exclaimed. "It was the clockwise spiral that worked. Jot the numbers down on a piece of paper, Detective. I believe it is only eighteen numbers."

Valerie attached an external hard drive to the computer and began downloading the contents of the scientist's computer. Valerie suspected that she would be trying to crack a big computer when she left Santa Fe so she brought extra peripherals. The external hard drive was quickly full. She labeled it and then connected another hard drive. Signe made a quick inventory of all the rooms in the house and then came back to the library to make a sketch listing all the dimensions. She found two little used bedrooms upstairs and a living room, dining room, kitchen and larger bedroom on the first floor. She sent Jack outside to measure the outside of the house to eliminate the possibility of a hidden room. He found no discrepancy.

By late afternoon, Signe felt the search of the Larry's house was going well. She thought if there weren't any surprises they would be finished by late evening. As the afternoon wore on she became less and less worried that some of Farrell's louts would show up. She had mentally practiced a dumb blond excuse with a lot of batting of her eyelids for being there if they had confronted her. She thought everyone needed a break so she suggested dinner at a restaurant in nearby Pojoaque. Jack drove. The restaurant was nearly deserted. They each ordered a combination plate of Mexican food. Since they were returning to work no one had a drink and the dinner went quickly.

On the way back each one of them reported what they had found and what other things they hoped to discover. After hearing Jack and Valerie give their summaries, Signe realized how lucky they had been to accomplish so much.

"Larry was a spook and an inventor of doomsday paraphernalia for all of his adult life," Signe began. "He would want an easily accessible place where he could try out an idea. I think he has a secret room or a laboratory somewhere around the house, you two, that we haven't discovered. When we get back Valerie and I will check the basement. Would you give the yard a once over, Jack?"

"Of course. There are an old unused garage and a garden house that is falling down," Jack replied. "I'll investigate both."

When they got back to the house Valerie and Signe took their flashlights and went down into the basement. The cellar had a strong musty smell and boxes of old tools and broken yard implements were covered with dust. The basement was smaller than the house and was made of round cobblestones. Valerie began studying the floor while Signe tested the walls. After a few minutes Valerie called Signe over to the back wall.

"This very dirty floor hasn't been swept in years," Valerie said. "But notice that there is a clean path from the bottom of the stairs that ends abruptly at this wall as if Larry walked from there to here frequently."

"I see what you mean," Signe replied as she got down on her hands and knees and shown her light across the floor.

Both women began tapping the wall and trying to twist or move the stones. After twenty minutes with no success, both of them were frustrated. Valerie sat down on a dusty old school desk.

"Larry was clever but also very impatient," Signe mused. "If he installed an apparatus to move that wall, it would operate slowly because of the weight. He wouldn't want to wait in front of the masonry while the door slid open. He was always in a hurry. I think the switch was either on the stairs or in the kitchen. Let's look for some conduit that goes from that wall to the other side of the basement. For the first time, Valerie and Signe turned their flashlights on the dark brown wooden joists that formed the ceiling.

"This might be it," Valerie remarked as she shown her light on a shiny tube of silvery conduit.

The cylinder was tucked along the side of a joist and went to the top of the stairs. Signe was up the stairs first and just inside the door to the basement found a switch disguised as a knot in the wood. As soon as she depressed it she heard a grinding sound from the back wall of the basement and a section of cobblestones opened to reveal a large, brightly lit and very modern laboratory. It was a marked contrast to the dark, dirty cellar. Large yellow signs with a rose colored trefoil in the center and 'radiation danger' written across the top were posted everywhere. The lights were on and the machines were running even though Larry hadn't been in the facility for at least three weeks. Signe and Valerie set about listing the names and model numbers of all the machines.

"I don't know these particular instruments but I do know the manufacturers in Germany, Great Britain and the US. These are the finest instruments made. Signe, we may be looking at ten to fifteen million dollars of equipment," Valerie remarked in astonishment.

Ten minutes later Jack appeared from the back of the laboratory.

"Where did you come from?" Valerie asked.

"I found a hidden trapdoor under the potting table in the garden house," Jack replied. "There was a rusty iron spiral staircase like you would find in a U-boat."

"Can you believe this lab?" Valerie said to no one in particular. "It's bigger and better equipped than my lab at the station house."

The three spent the rest of the evening cataloguing their find. Signe realized they would need an expert to explain just exactly what Larry was doing in his laboratory. She wondered if his research here was sanctioned by the Department of Energy or if her friend was doing rogue experiments that led to his murder. By the time each finished listing the high tech gadgetry in their third of the lab it was one a.m. While Jack stretched out in the master bedroom, Valerie and Signe spread sleeping bags in the upstairs bedrooms. Once Signe was settled naked in her down bag, Valerie came into her room equally naked and knelt by her bed. She kissed Signe very softly on the lips.

"May I sleep with you tonight?" Valerie asked.

"Not tonight. Mostly because I feel like I'm still on duty," Signe replied as she gave Valerie a warm good night kiss.

CHAPTER 6

When she awoke at first light, Signe found Valerie's warm, naked form snuggled against her side. Signe tousled her bedmates hair gently as she slid out of the sleeping bag and stood barefooted on the cold wooden floor. She stretched her hands over her head and noticed a reflection of herself in a mirror atop and old oak chiffonier. She was five feet ten inches tall with a slender figure. Her face was longer than it was wide with pretty, regular features. She had peerless pale Danish skin that drove men crazy and beautifully shaped gray-blue eyes. She was a natural blond with small high breasts and a flat stomach. Her lips turned down ever so slightly at the corners, but few noticed as she was almost always smiling. Her legs were long and shapely and often men and women said it was her best feature. She grabbed her bra and panties and walked into the other room to put them on.

By the time she got down stairs Jack was cooking some bacon and eggs that Valerie had brought. Signe found the aroma of the bacon irresistible. It made her stomach rumble.

"Good morning, partner," Signe said as she took a mug of coffee that Jack handed her. "We've made ourselves right at home here. I hope Agent Farrell doesn't have insomnia and pay us a surprise visit. I'll give him a friendly call in a bit so I can nail down his location."

"I moved Valerie's van around to the back door and started loading our evidence about an hour ago," Jack volunteered as he pushed bacon, eggs and toast onto Signe's plate.

Signe sat down and began eating. She was ravenous. Valerie had thought to bring a bottle of fiery hot salsa which Signe scooped onto her eggs. Valerie wandered into the kitchen just then in a pair of loose sweats, stretching as she walked. As she raised her hands over her head she exposed an expanse of bare belly that drew Jack's admiring eye.

"After you've eaten Valerie, I want you and Jack to drive the van to Santa Fe," Signe instructed. "I'll stay and try to make it look like we were never here."

The three interlopers ate quickly. Valerie washed the dishes while Jack put the remaining boxes of evidence in the van. Jack counted twenty six boxes. Signe called Farrell and caught him on the way into the office.

"Any new developments on my friend's death?" Signe asked.

"We haven't turned up a thing," Farrell replied. "After the autopsy we will declare Abramowitz's death due to natural causes. Just as a formality, we are going to Los Alamos to search his house today. I don't think we will find anything. Would you like to come along?"

"When are you heading up there?" Signe asked disingenuously.

"In about twenty minutes," Farrell replied. "But we could wait for you."

"That's okay. I need to see a judge this morning about another case," Signe replied. "I appreciate the offer."

Signe pushed the end button on her phone. She turned to Valerie and Jack.

"The FBI will be here in an hour," Signe said as she picked up a file box to put in the van.

In fifteen minutes Valerie's van was loaded and she and Jack pulled out slowly from behind the house, once they were sure there was no traffic, Signe watched them pull onto Forty Ninth Street and then turn left onto Trinity Way.

After she was gloved Signe went from room to room straightening furniture and wiping her compadres fingerprints from all smooth surfaces. She took the time to straighten the beds upstairs and flush all the toilets once again when she remembered she had left the list of random numbers used to find the computer password in Larry's desk. She raced into the library and retrieved it. As she started down the basement stairs she heard the sound of broken glass as someone broke a pain in the back door window. It seemed too soon, but she was sure it was them. She hit the switch to open the secret door to the lab as she bounded down the stairs. Covering her tracks with a dust mop she stepped into the shiny white glare of the lab and hit the switch to close the door. The cobbled wall rumbled slowly into place. Signe felt sure that the FBI wouldn't find the lab, but she quickly rubbed the counter tops and prominent glassware of possible prints.

In the back corner of the lab she found the rusty iron spiral staircase that Jack had described. She ascended slowly and then pushed her head up slowly under the potting table to be sure no one was around. When she was sure the coast was clear she climbed out of the garden shed and hid behind it before crouching low as she walked away from the house and then back to her unmarked car. She drove the other way so she wouldn't have to pass the house and then turned onto Sandia Drive. On the way back to the station house she called Jack.

"They were in the house before I left," Signe said.

"Did Farrell see you?" Jack asked in an anxious voice.

"No I went out that escape route that you found," Signe replied. "When I arrive at the station house I want to prioritize the evidence we found otherwise we may miss some important material for weeks."

"Roger, that, partner."

When Signe got to the station house Valerie was already sorting and cataloguing the stacks of evidence the three had collected. Signe looked at a long list of items Valerie had already entered into a file organized by date and also subject.

"First, I want to study any letters and also diaries," Signe said. "Before we move on to the scientific papers that Larry wrote."

"At first blush, I believe we may have collected in excess of five thousand items," Valerie offered in a discouraging tone.

"It's a lot of ore to mine even if it is very low grade, but we <u>must</u> find a nugget in it that will help us unravel this case," Signe replied emphatically.

"We also have need of a theoretical physicist to help us unravel that sophisticated laboratory in Dr. Abramowitz's basement," Valerie volunteered.

"I thought about that problem driving in from Los Alamos today, and I think I know a person who can help us," Signe remarked. "Larry had a dear friend, Dr. Pieter van der Waals, who worked with him at Los Alamos for several decades. He is a courtly old Dutchman who took road trips with Larry. I'll call him this evening. I'll have to go and see him though. The very existence of the laboratory is potentially explosive. It may be the reason for Larry's death."

"He didn't build that exquisite laboratory on his government salary," Valerie observed.

"That is what frightens me," Signe replied.

"When will the autopsy be done on your friend?" Jack asked.

"The feds weren't suspicious enough about the case to pay for the body to be sent to their special necropsy facility in Maryland," Signe commented. "They're having it done locally."

"Will it be done by your pathologist friend, Dr. Bernadette Gilchrist?" Valerie asked.

"I suppose so."

"When will it be done?" Jack interjected.

"Would you call for me and find out?" Signe asked. "As you know, Bernadette was held in prison for five days by the authorities without being charged. They were trying to get her to reveal the members of her anti-rape group called Violence against the Violators. The feminist group identified and then viciously beat possible rapists. You helped crack the group in Santa Fe wide open, but the group in Albuquerque was much more secretive and militant. So Bernadette isn't very compliant anymore with the government. If I had to guess, I would bet she strings them along a bit. Today is Friday so she has a good reason to hold it off until Monday at least. I know her well and she can be very stubborn."

"I'll call the Office of the Medical Investigator right now," Jack said as he left the lab.

Signe turned to Valerie and said, "Show me what you have so far."

"There are dozens of books, but none of them have any notes or stray papers in them," Valerie began. "I'm looking for a diary or journal but so far I haven't found anything. He saved stacks of letters but unfortunately half of them are in German and a quarter or so are in Dutch."

"I can read those without any difficulty, just copy them and put them on my desk. I'd like the most recent ones first, please," Signe remarked.

"I analyzed the soil samples you gave me by running them through the spectrometer," Valerie said. "The soil under Dr. Abramowitz was rich in mica, feldspar and river sand. The other sample, which I suspect is the usual Valle Grande soil, is full of organic material and volcanic tuff from the last gigantic volcanic eruption that occurred one million years ago. So I think the earth under the body was brought in from elsewhere for reasons that are unclear to me. I will see if I can find a match for that soil sample someplace nearby."

"Thanks for helping me with this case, Valerie," Signe said as she walked out of the laboratory.

"Thanks for letting me sleep with you," Valerie replied cheerily.
"I didn't," Signe remarked.

CHAPTER 7

Mateo Romero, a Cochiti Pueblo medicine man, arrived at the station and sought out Signe. This seventy year old man, in Indian dress, wore his long gray hair in a pony tail tied at the back of his head by brightly colored red, blue and green yarn. He played the Dr. Watson role to Signe's Sherlock Holmes. Signe met Mateo when she was investigating her first murder in Santa Fe. Mateo's son and Chloe Patterson, the murder victim had been in drug rehab together. Chloe's parents didn't visit her during her expensive incarcerations and Mateo became her surrogate family. On family weekends Mateo took Chloe and his son on picnics and trips to zoos and museums. After the pointless death of Mateo Romero's son, Chloe came to the Indian medicine man for help when she was strung out and destitute and had no one else to turn to. After she got clean Mateo taught the beautiful, young white girl the Indian way. Mateo didn't take advantage of Chloe in anyway. He was the one true friend that Chloe had.

Once the case was solved, Mateo began to teach Signe about animal spirits and herbs and help her with her second murder case. She in turn gave him books by Arthur Conan Doyle to read and instructed him in crime solving methods. During the second murder investigation he proved invaluable as a dogged auxiliary interviewer and investigator.

"I'm sorry I couldn't join you at Valle Grande, *el poco sabio,*" Mateo began. "I was at a meeting of the Pueblo Indian tribes at Santa Domingo. The Valles are sacred to us and I could have shown you some of our worship sites in the Caldera."

"I would have loved your company and your wise eyes," Signe replied. "But it occurred with no notice. I got to thinking that I was only a few miles from where that pea green Oldsmobile got dropped right in front of C Vicky when we were driving back to Santa Fe."

"Yes. It is only six or seven miles as the hawk flies," Mateo calculated.

"And Tim Monroe, the young man who pulled that caper for a few hundred dollars ended up dead for no good reason," Signe reflected.

"Tell me about your newest case."

"My friend Dr. Larry Abramowitz was found dead at a campsite in Valles Grande, and I believe he was murdered. I want to find out who did it."

"So, no one else agrees with you?"

"That's about the size of it."

"How can I help?"

"We collected boxes and boxes of material from his house. Perhaps after lunch you could help Valerie catalogue it."

Signe took Mateo to The Shed, located in an ancient abode building to the east of the plaza. She had a favorite, fiery hot red enchiladas with blue corn tortillas while Mateo had a gigantic bowl of posolé. Signe was fanatical about well prepared New Mexican food. After sipping Mateo's soup she noted with pleasure that it contained only six ingredients, water, pork shoulder, hominy, coarse red chili, garlic and oregano with lime juice squeezed in at table side. During lunch Signe told an embellished story of finding the Star Wars lab in Larry's basement. Portraying herself as a bumbling small town cop made Mateo laugh. After lunch they went back to the station house and Signe called Dr. van der Waals while Mateo began processing evidence. Mateo bridled a bit at working with Valerie. He found her a little dictatorial given her age and background. He hid his displeasure behind frequent smiles.

Signe agreed to meet Larry's friend at El Nido, a wonderful restaurant located half way between them. It was located in the sleepy little town of Tesuque. Signe left early and turned off the main highway near the town of Nambe. She wanted to checkout the restaurant and fond a quiet corner where she could talk privately. A table in the back dining room seemed perfect.

Pieter van der Waals walked over to Signe and greeted her. He was in a rumpled suit suggesting that he had just left work at the lab. Signe had decided to probe her dinner companion very gently. Van der Waals was one of her few entrees into Larry Abramowitz' life and she didn't want to frighten him off. He had been close friends with the dead man for years. He was also terrifyingly smart and would quickly pick up any clumsy probing by Signe.

"Thank you for meeting me so promptly, Sir," Signe said as she sat back down at the table.

"It is entirely my pleasure young lady," van der Waals replied. "And please call me Pieter."

"I hadn't seen Larry for months, and we hadn't talked for weeks but I was very surprised at his death," Signe remarked. "He always made me feel like a dear friend, even though we didn't spend that much time together. I never thought of him as old."

"Yet he was born in 1934," van den Waals remarked. "That made him sixty-nine."

"I would have missed his age by fifteen years," Signe replied in amazement. "His curly brown hair didn't have a bit of gray in it."

"His parents were from Poland and didn't live long lives but that was probably due to the Nazis," Pieter said thoughtfully. "I guess like you I thought he would always be around. He was my closest friend and I miss him terribly."

"Did he have any health issues?"

"He had a touch of diabetes and about five years ago he had a mild heart attack, but he was only in St. Vincent's for four days. He went back to work very quickly. It didn't seem to slow him down. I always thought of him as the picture of health."

"The FBI talked with me about him this week," Signe volunteered. "Did they speak with you also?"

"Yes, they came by my office today."

"It gave me a shudder when they told me the news. Do you think someone might have killed him?"

"He certainly knew decade's worth of the most top secret information about our military defenses. It made him truly invaluable, but I would think he was worth much more alive than dead."

"Do you know what he was working on recently?"

"Yes. He was trying to develop a new method for detecting thermonuclear weapons. I'm sure you know his early brilliant work was on the switch the US used for their hydrogen bombs for almost a decade. Then he worked for almost fifteen years on miniaturizing the H bomb. I always thought that this was a misguided effort. We were the first nuclear power and were never likely to use 'little' weapons which are only good for acts of terrorism. What always worried me was that we invent a suitcase bomb and then suppose some petty Arab fanatic steals it, takes a train to the central station in Amsterdam and blows the whole lovely metropolis off the map."

"So I take it, you didn't work on that program?" Signe asked.

"I most certainly did not," van der Waals replied. "And I told them exactly what I thought of it."

"Did Larry ever do research outside the lab?"

"Yes, of course. He collaborated more than the rest of us with other theoretical nuclear physicists. He was always doing experiments with scientists in other NATO countries, particularly the British, the French and the Swiss. He traveled to Europe six or eight times per year and often stayed for two weeks."

"He told me about some of those collaborations, but did he ever perform any experiments away from the lab and totally on his own?"

"Not that I'm aware of. Plus how would he do that? He would need a lot of very expensive equipment that he couldn't afford, plus some very dangerous isotopes."

An excellent smoked salmon appetizer, made at the restaurant, arrived that Signe had ordered for both of them. They ate quietly for a few minutes and both sipped a chardonnay that Pieter had ordered. Once the plates were cleared, Signe continued.

"I don't mean to ask so many nosy questions, Dr. van der Walls,"

Signe said in a soft voice. "However, if there is even a small chance that our mutual friend was murdered, I will pursue that person to the ends of the earth."

"Do you really think that is a possibility?" van der Waals asked aghast.

"Probably not," Signe replied in a soothing tone as their entrees arrived.

Pieter had a crusted Chilean sea bass and Signe dug into a large rare rib eye steak. Signe decided not to push Dr. van der Waal any harder since she was just getting to know him. She talked about Denmark, and van der Waal talked about the northern part of the Netherlands where his family originated.

"Did you get a notice about the funeral tomorrow?" van der Waal asked.

"Yes. I believe it's at the Bahai Temple in Santa Fe," Signe replied. "I never discussed religion with him, but I would never have guessed he was a congregant of that amalgam of faiths."

Crème Brulee with a beautiful even brown crust arrived.

"Will any family be present at the service?" Signe asked.

"Larry didn't have much family, as you know," Pieter answered. "His wife left him in the early sixties and returned to her home in Minsk. She died a few years later. They had three pretty daughters who would be in their forties now. But I don't think he heard from them regularly. Maybe a phone call on his birthday."

"If they are there tomorrow would you introduce me?"

"Of course," Pieter replied promptly.

The two walked out of the restaurant and said their goodbyes.

CHAPTER 8

Signe jumped into her BMW and raced home. What had she learned? Even Larry's closest friend didn't know about the extensive secret laboratory she had found. Signe would have to approach that important discovery from a unique angle outside the national lab. Also, Larry wasn't close to his family. Apparently, his wife left him. Why? Before she did, she moved back to Poland which would make talking with her friends and relatives difficult, at best. Signe's best bet today would be to get some information from the three daughters. She had learned nothing about Larry's sexual orientation and habits from her talk. When she was dating him they kissed and petted, suggesting he was a heterosexual. They hadn't had intercourse although Larry had suggested it. Signe had demurred, despite liking him. She found him too short, too disheveled, and too curly headed for her taste.

When she got home she sat in front of her painting by Claude Monet and immersed herself in it for the better part of an hour. Signe appreciated art, and her lover, Brian Hagen, had loaned her the original, painted in 1907. Signe had met Brian when he was considering giving his families' collection of twelve oils by Georgia O' Keeffe to a museum in Santa Fe. She hung her clothes up padded into her bedroom in bare feet, and put in a call to Brian once she was in bed. He called her back promptly as he always did. They had a pleasant conversation about when they might get together again. With her head full of pleasant thoughts about art and Brian, Signe went to sleep. Signe had a dream about Larry gamboling through the Swiss Alps with seven young boys. In the morning, she decided to file the dream for further reference.

In the morning, Signe met Jack at Tante Maria's for a breakfast of huevos ranchero before going to the service at the Bahai Temple. The narrow, little restaurant was packed with patrons; many were police officers who had just finished working the night shift. Signe ordered Christmas tree huevos which was shorthand for a mixture of red and green chili sauce on the eggs. After they had eaten Jack drove them to the seven sided Baha'i Temple.

"I was raised a Catholic, but I haven't been to mass in years," Jack said as he navigated through the light Saturday morning traffic. "I'm not even sure I believe in religion. There was an article in *The New Mexican* yesterday about a woman in San Angelo who saw the face of the Virgin Mary in a trashcan liner. She charged the townspeople three dollars to view it. At one point the line was seventy people long."

"I'm not bringing you to this funeral for your religious edification, Jack," Signe replied in a slightly irritated voice. "I need your eyes and ears."

As they arrived at the edifice, Jack parked in the no parking zone at the front without giving it a thought. Groups of mourners wearing suits and dresses were entering through the large wooden doors. On the way in Signe saw a guest list by the entrance to the sanctuary. She planned to take a picture of it on the way out. Signe and Jack sat at the back of the hall so they could observe the people attending the service. Pieter van der Walls and his well-fed Dutch family filed in and sat in the first pew on the right. Just before the service began, three blond women, obviously sisters, accompanied by a man filed into the first row on the left. Those are Larry's three children Signe thought.

The service was very bland and overly long. It didn't do justice to Larry's intelligence and good humor in Signe's opinion. On the way out she took photos of every page of the guest register. While she was taking pictures, Liam Farrell gently grasped her elbow.

"Lunch?" Liam asked.

"Yes, after the grave side ceremony," Signe answered thinking that she could pump him for information.

Signe followed the mourners to the cemetery. Jack pulled their car into the long processional through town. The graveside ceremony was luckily brief. Signe approached the oldest of the three sisters after the ceremony and showed her one of her cards.

"I'm Detective Signe Sorenson, and I was a good friend of your father," Signe began. "I'm sorry for your loss."

"I suppose you slept with my father while he was still married to my mother," Magdalena, the oldest sister, said bitterly.

"Your father and I went to dinner and did some bird watching," Signe replied. "Do I really look old enough to have slept with him during the seventies when he was married to your mother?"

"I suppose not," Magdalena answered.

Albina, the middle sister, came to her sister's defense by saying," Forgive us, Detective, but all of us were hurt by our father's outside relationships."

"And we're also upset by his death," Katarzyna, the youngest sister, replied.

"I apologize to all three of you," Signe began. "I know this is a bad time, but I was just afraid that I might never see any of you again and I believe that your father was murdered."

"That's horrible. Why do you say that?" Magdalena asked quickly.

"I have some circumstantial evidence," Signe replied. "That someone killed your father for something he knew and wouldn't tell."

"None of us live around here, and we all need to get back to our homes, Detective," Magdalena said forcefully. "Give us a call if you come up with something more substantial. Otherwise this is the end of a sad chapter in all of our lives. We didn't deserve a father like him."

Jack collected email addresses from each sister before they walked away. Signe followed Liam Farrell to his car, and he drove her to Rancho Encantada for lunch. Liam opened the car door for her, and Signe made sure to show a lot of her very shapely legs as she slid across the seat. Liam ordered an expensive bottle of 1996 Chateau Margaux Bordeaux. They chatted over a Caesar salad, made tableside, and rare tenderloin topped with Béarnaise sauce, before discussing the case. Signe thought that Liam was trying to impress her by ordering the most expensive items on the menu

"I was surprised to see you at the funeral," Signe said.

"I'm ready to close the case if there aren't any surprises at the autopsy tomorrow," Liam replied. "I was just looking over the congregation in case someone of interest in another case was foolish enough to show up."

"Did anyone?"

"No. And you were attending because Abramowitz was a close friend, I suppose?"

"Yes. I believe you told me you were going to search his house. Did you find anything?"

"Not really. For some reason the house smelled strongly of bacon. We found a lot of obscure physics papers in Dutch and German. That was about it. My conclusion is that he was near the end of his career and was no longer doing cutting edge research."

"I'll bet you are right," Signe replied. "By the way, how are you going to do an autopsy on a body that's already been buried?"

"We will exhume it tonight," Liam answered. "I didn't want to raise the family's suspicions by delaying the funeral. If we declare it a national security issue, we can do it without the families consent."

They both had chocolate mousse and French roast coffee for dessert before Liam drove Signe to her apartment. When she got home she found a large pink box wrapped in a wide white ribbon on her porch. Signe smiled involuntarily as she assumed it was a gift of lingerie or clothing from her boyfriend, Brian. He had perfect taste, she thought. She hurried into the apartment and tore it open. Instead of the beautiful gift she expected, when she opened the package four bats flew out and one brushed Signe's face. She recoiled at first and then out of curiosity, leaned in for a closer look. Signe thought that bats were amazing monogamous mammals so they inspired no fear in her. She found a hank of straight brown hair, a piece of bone that looked like a rib and a half of a lower jaw bone with some teeth attached. Some dried tissue was attached to the bone, and maggots were busy chewing on it. She definitely didn't like maggots. Signe quickly ran through a list of people who hated her and might have sent her such a revolting gift. She knew right away that this collection wasn't about her friend Larry Abramowitz as he had very curly hair.

Signe called Valerie and Jack and asked them both to come over after she told them what she had found. Both arrived in record time. Valerie took samples of the hair and bones for DNA analysis. She also collected the maggots so she could extract the human DNA from their digestive tracts. Valerie also checked the samples for gun shot residue and found none. Jack checked the porch and yard for clues and found a partial boot print.

When he came back into the house Jack said, "I found a partial print outside but it is very small, at most a woman's size seven. I didn't find anything else except a small sample of latex."

"My list of possible perpetrators included Tony 'The Squid' Squitero, Wanda De Berneres, and Janphen Palawat," Signe began. "But now that you tell me about the small print of a woman's boot and the piece of latex, I'm sure this little gift is from Svelty Patterson. I can't imagine why she is back in play. I suspect the hair and bone came from her husband, Dirk Wilkes Patterson. She must still blame me for his death. Please compare the samples you collected to his DNA first, Valerie."

Signe didn't feel comfortable at her apartment, so she invited Jack and Valerie to the Coyote Café. After a few drinks, Signe felt better. The three law enforcement officers took turns telling about their most bizarre cases. Jack told about a burglary he was sent to investigate his first week on the job. The thieves broke into an appliance store but only took toasters, mixers and a toaster oven. All the big-ticket items stereos, radios and TVs were untouched. Jack's partner decided the theft was committed by three women who were outfitting their new apartment. The college semester had just begun, and he thought they wouldn't need TVs or stereos because they would be studying. Jack went to the College of Santa Fe and found the stolen items in the third room they searched. The coeds were in their robes with their hair in curlers.

"I cuffed each one of them," Jack concluded. "But as I pulled their arms behind their back the front of their robes kept falling open."

"Poor things," Valerie remarked.

Valerie told about the precious sword found buried in a church during Signe's last case.

"It had a gold handle and was encrusted with diamonds and sapphires," Valerie remarked. "A $30,000 sword that belonged to the Duke Domenico Pugliese from the Piedmont region of Italy had found its way to the impoverished soil of northern New Mexico."

Jack ordered another round of drinks for everyone. Before Signe could launch into her most bizarre case, her phone rang. It was a patrolman calling to say that someone had broken into her apartment.

CHAPTER 9

Jack drove the two women to the apartment with lights flashing and siren blaring. Signe knew he had had at least three drinks and shouldn't be driving, but she didn't feel she was any less impaired, and she was in a hurry to get there. She had moved to a gated apartment complex during the investigation of the Chloe Patterson murder for her own protection. Signe's Jetta had been forced off I-25 at high speed one night and then a sniper had fired on the department's Suburban near Wagon Mounding killing her friend Art Johnson who was sitting just behind her.

As they approached the complex, Signe noted that the gate was barely hanging by a hinge. Someone had driven through it at high speed. The tire tracks led across the lawn to the porch of her apartment. Her front door had been ripped from its hinges. Signe's main concern was the Monet. When she entered the living room she noticed it was missing from its place on the wall. The floor was littered with books, paper and clothing that had been torn from shelves, closets and cupboards. Some of her Indian pots had been smashed on the floor. The only thing that Signe cared about was the Monet.

"Damn that Svelty," Signe cursed.

"You had her in your sights that night she stopped you on the freeway," Jack replied without having been asked. "You should have blown her away then."

"I almost wish I had," Signe replied.

Once all the evidence was collected Signe went to bed. Her front door couldn't be fixed so a patrolman spent the night on her porch to protect her. Signe didn't sleep well. She got up early and drove to Mateo Romero's adobe in Cochiti Pueblo. Signe enjoyed the drive in her BMW. It was a cool spring morning and the purplish Sandia Mountains loomed ahead. She sped down La Bajada hill and turned onto the dirt road to the Pueblo. Mateo's adobe was located on the square and was larger than most of the dwelling presumably because he was a medicine man and former mayor. Signe knocked gently on the bright blue door before walking in. Mateo invited Signe into his cluttered office and offered her a cup of herbal tea.

"I was robbed last night, Mateo, and they took Brian's Monet!" Signe wailed.

Mateo reached up and put his arm around Signe before saying, "I know how special that revered painting was to you. May I help you get it back?"

"I wouldn't think of doing it without you, partner," Signe replied. "But I don't want that to spoil our day."

"It won't. I will rustle you some breakfast while you study our language."

Mateo went into the kitchen. Signe had embarked on a study of the Cochiti Way with the wise medicine man. She had to study traditional dances, fetishes, history of the Pueblo, famous members and the traditional Cochiti language. Mateo had instructed her to study Keres, the traditional Cochiti language, first because he knew that she disliked it the most. She went through her alphabet and then began saying and writing the words she had learned. Mateo arrived soon with a stoneware plate of eggs from the medicine man's chickens, homemade salsa and warm flour tortillas.

Mateo sat across from her and said, "I will start tracking our burglar tomorrow."

"I think the thief was Svelty Patterson," Signe replied.

"Jack told me. She stands out in a crowd. I bet we can find her."

Mateo cleared the plates, and Signe went back to the study of Keres. A couple of hours later her mentor took her language books away and placed a jumble of carved fetishes in front of Signe. Bear, moles, eagles and coyotes stood out. Some were carved in black obsidian, some in a bright red stone, but Signe's favorites were carved from bright blue blocks of turquoise with flecks of gold in them. The Hopis and Navajo carved large kachinas that represented the myriad of dancers in their festivals, but the Pueblo Indians focused more on small fetishes that could be carried in a small pouch on one's person. Signe was expected to learn them all, and to understand what kind of evil was warded off by each one.

After studying the fetishes, Signe's eyes were blurry. Mateo suggested a walk around the Pueblo. Many members of the two hundred families were out planting vegetables and flowers in garden areas that were held in common. Corn, chiles and beans were the favored crops. Signe knew the average last frost wasn't until May 6th at that altitude. She hoped the Pueblo's fetishes would keep the guy Americans called 'Jack Frost' away. When they got back to Mateo's house they ate red enchiladas and both drank a cold bottle of beer. Mateo went into his darkened living room and stretched out on an old green sofa, taking his moccasins off for a nap. Signe pulled down the volume entitled *History of the Cochiti Pueblo* which fortunately was in English. Had it been in Keres or Spanish her mentor would have had to read it to her. The Pueblo was founded in 1250 CE. Signe recollected that Copenhagen was founded in that century. It had its first King, Christopher I and about fourteen hundred inhabitants, just two hundred more than the present day Pueblo.

Like the other Pueblo peoples, the Cochitis traced their origin to the underworld. They emerged through an opening called Shipapu. Over time they drifted slowly south to the Rio Grande. For many generations they lived in the Rito de los Frijoles and constructed cliff dwelling in the friable volcanic tufa. Long before the coming of the Europeans, the Indians abandoned the Rito and moved further south separating into a number of autonomous villages.

Signe was tired of studying and Mateo had awakened from his nap. He stabled two of his horses and they rode to the south along the banks of the Rio Grande. The river was full from melting snow in Colorado. Signe remembered her long pleasant ride across the sea of grass called the Argentinean Pampas in search of a missing Lipizzaner. When they got tired of the shoreline they galloped into the river splashing the horses and themselves. They both started laughing.

When they got back to Mateo's old abode they ate bowls of lamb stew with warm chunks of potato and carrot mixed in the thick aromatic broth. It was one of Signe's favorite meals. They spent the evening by the fireplace where aromatic piñon logs were burning. Mateo read stories of Cochiti heroes to the young detective until she drifted off. Signe planned to go on to Albuquerque in the morning for Larry's autopsy so she spent the night in her host's extra bedroom.

After a light breakfast, Signe drove south to the Office of the Medical Investigator on the campus of the University of New Mexico medical center. Her assistant, Mateo Romero rode along. The OMI was located in an unimaginative low slung building probably built in the 1970's and sat below most of the other buildings on campus. A congested parking lot with five different categories of 'No Parking' signs out front left several cars milling around in circles hoping for a stall like wasps around a crowded nest. Signe pulled up front and parked in an 'Authorized Parking Only' spot where the penalty for disobedience was towing and a $500 fine. She walked inside and after showing her badge was buzzed through Plexiglas walls and reinforced doors worthy of Fort Knox. All they have inside, Signe thought was dead bodies and a dozen MDs who had labored their whole live without saving even one patient. Signe had Mateo wait in the reception area.

Signe found her former friend, Dr. Bernadette Gilchrist, in the locker room pulling on a pair of pink scrubs that were two sizes too small. The two women had met in Santa Fe and found they enjoyed the same art, food and music which was mostly Brahms. Bernadette had initiated an intimate relationship between them, and they had made love a couple of times. Signe had found it pleasurable but more confusing than completely satisfying. Bernadette turned out to be the capo of the local Violence against the Violator chapter. The VaV had ferreted out unpunished rapists and then jumped and beaten them with cudgels. The beatings were raw with unrestrained violence sending the victims to prolonged rehab and occasionally to a cemetery. Signe had fought with Bernadette over the lawless vigilantism of the group's method.

"Well, look what the morning tide washed in," Bernadette said in a voice dripping with sarcasm.

"Just here about the Abramowitz autopsy," Signe replied softly.

"It looks like it won't be for several hours," Bernadette replied in a nonconciliatory tone.

"I told Jack that now that you were an enemy of the government, you'd make the FBI cool its heels."

"I just don't have an available room. There were a lot if shootings and knifings in the south valley this weekend."

"Come on, Bernadette. I just walked by three empty theaters. Can't we just bury the hatchet, agree to disagree, and move on?"

"Let me think that over."

Signe walked over and put a hand on Bernadette's shoulder and said, "I can remember a lot of good times we had together. Let's focus on that.

Bernadette slumped and then put her hand over Signe's. She stood up and turned toward her old friend putting her arms around Signe in a warm, affectionate hug. When she pulled away Signe noticed that Bernadette had tears in her eyes.

"Okay. I have missed you and your intrusive ways. Walk back to the desk and tell Marie to set up Abramowitz in autopsy two."

CHAPTER 10

Signe found Mateo, got some execrable coffee in the pathologist's lounge changed into some surgical scrubs and then went into autopsy two. Liam Farrell and one of his assistants in a suit that was a little too tight were already there looking uncomfortable. Signe greeted both of them and then walked to the head of the table near Bernadette. Bernadette was examining the exterior of Larry's body and dictating as she made observations.

"This sixty-nine year old white male is of average height and weight and without major external abnormality," Bernadette said into the small microphone no larger than a grain of rice that curved down in front of her mouth from her ear.

She went on to describe the unblemished nature of the victim's skin and lack of *rigor mortis*. As her assistant turned the body over, Bernadette ran her gloved fingers over the victim's back. She made a small incision out of view of her observers and extracted a small object which she hid in her palm until she could slip it surreptitiously into one of Signe's pockets. She noted some slight skin abrasions on the dorsum of both forearms consistent with camping and two small punctures in the right antecubital area. On the underside of the right forearm she also found an old faded tattoo. Her assistant focused a bright light on it and took multiple pictures. Bernadette took a large magnifying glass and read the faded old blue numbers, A 17836.

"I'm almost certain that this is a sad reminder from a German concentration camp during World War II. Many of the Jewish, Soviet, and Polish prisoners were given identification tattoos at some of the camps," Bernadette remarked after turning her recorder off. "I will give Detective Sorensen a book that should identify its origin."

"I'm sure there is some mistake, Dr. Gilchrist," Liam Farrell remarked. Certainly, Dr. Abramowitz wasn't old enough to be caught up in World War II."

"Actually he was born in 1934 so he would have been ten years old in 1944 which was a year before the war ended," Bernadette replied. "Jewish children by the thousands were sent to concentration camps. Young children along with the old and disabled were gassed as soon as their rail cars arrived at a camp like Auschwitz. There was no need to tattoo them, but able-bodied men and women were put to work building munitions, and most received a tattoo first on their left breast and later on their forearm."

Bernadette turned her dictation machine back on and made her usual Y shaped incision from the point of each shoulder meeting over the sternum and then straight down to the pubic bone. Signe usually left the room for this part of the exam; she found it made her a little queasy. However, the FBI was present and Signe didn't want to lose face so she looked across the body and unfocused her eyes. Dr. Gilchrist and her assistant worked efficiently as they had performed hundred of autopsies together. Soon the internal organs were laid out on the table and each one was weighed.

"Lungs are a normal blue gray in color with no signs of heart failure, emphysema or infection," Bernadette noted.

She went on to describe the orange-red liver, pancreas, intestines. In the back of the abdominal cavity was a large quantity of clotted blood. When she removed the spleen, hidden away in the upper left part of the abdomen she noted a tear in the capsule and showed it to everyone present.

"This may be the cause of death," she said holding the purplish, bean shaped organ in her hand.

Next she turned her attention to the heart freeing it deftly from its connections to major blood vessels, the aorta and inferior vena cava.

"The heart is enlarged and there is a scar on the bottom wall of the left ventricle. It is a moderately large heart attack, but I won't know whether it is old or new until we do the histology." Farrell gave her a quizzical look. "I'm sorry. That is, I won't know until microscopic slides are made in about a week."

She carefully identified the right coronary artery and sliced it open in several places.

"In the inside of the artery you can see extensive yellow deposits of atheroma and right here," she pointed with the tip of the scalpel. "This is the dark red clot that caused the heart attack. A normal heart weighs 350 grams and this one weighs 510. He had some heart failure, either acute or chronic."

"That's about all, gentlemen," Dr. Gilchrist replied. "I have yet to exam the brain, but I don't expect any surprises."

The two FBI agents filed dutifully out of the room. The autopsy assistant cut the scalp at the base of the neck and pulled the decedent's hair down over the victim's face and began cutting the cranium with a power saw. Signe felt this masking of the face was the most disrespectful part of the autopsy. Bernadette's assistant popped the top of the skull off like rounded top of a pressure cooker. The soft pink brain was easily cut from the spinal cord and weighed. Then Bernadette picked it up and examined it closely.

"I believe you said he was the smartest man you ever knew," Bernadette said as she turned toward Signe.

"Yes. That's correct," Signe replied. "Can you tell that from looking at his brain?"

"Not really. Some scientists think that smart people have a more convoluted white matter than people with a lower IQ, but most scientists disagree. Larry's brain weighs over 1500 grams which is unusually heavy for a brain. The top weight is usually 1400 grams. But a recent paper about Einstein, perhaps the smartest person since Leonardo da Vinci, reported that his brain only weighed only 1230 grams."

Where do you come up with facts like that Bernadette?" Signe asked in amazement.

"It's my job as a forensic pathologist," Dr. Gilchrist remarked as she walked out of the autopsy room motioning Signe and Mateo to follow.

She walked down the hall with Signe and Mateo right behind her. She opened a door marked Dr. Bernadette Gilchrist, M.D., FACP. Signe noticed that American physicians had multiple clumps of initials after their names which she regarded as pompous. The small office was cluttered with piles of charts, scientific papers and trays of microscope slides. Bernadette sat down in an old wooden chair after clearing the seats of two other chairs for her guests.

"Let me see that chip that I slipped you," Bernadette said without preamble.

Signe retrieved a small titanium lozenge from her pocket and passed it to her.

"Someone planted a chip in your friend so they could track his movements," Dr. Gilchrist observed.

"Did he know about it?" Mateo asked.

"I doubt it very much," Bernadette replied. "I imagine that they caught him sleeping in a hotel one night perhaps after slipping him a doctored drink then gave him a short acting sedative, like the Ketamine the Russian use. On the street it is known as 'Special K.' Then they probably made a small incision, inserted the chip and closed the skin with a self-absorbing subcutaneous stitch. As long as it healed without sepsis our subject might have a little itch there and never be any the wiser."

Bernadette put the chip on the stage of a low power microscope that sat next to her desk.

"There is writing on one side. I believe it is in Cyrillic," Dr. Gilchrist observed as she handed the chip back to Mateo.

"I read of a Bulgarian diplomat that was killed in London using a poison tipped umbrella," Mateo remarked. "Perhaps something like that happened to Dr. Abramowitz."

"We studied that case at the Police Academy in Copenhagen," Signe replied. "They delivered a pinhead sized capsule of platinum filled with ricin to his calf. The poison was held in place by some sugar that melted at body temperature. The diplomat, Markov, was dead in three days. This chip was many times bigger."

"I will check Dr. Abramowitz for all the usual poisons," Bernadette remarked. "But also for ricin, hydrazine, that poisonous rocket fuel that you two studied, and any other substances that have been used in spy related murders."

"Thanks for your help, Bernadette," Signe said as she rose from her seat and headed toward the door. "You really hate the FBI, don't you?"

"My government held me in jail for six days without charging me in an effort to get me to talk about my righteous sisters. I don't find them any more just than Hitler or Stalin. Give me two or three weeks to get you some results."

Signe and Mateo walked out to her car and found it plastered with warnings about parking in that spot. Signe tore them up and threw them on the ground. Mateo suggested they begin tracking down Svelty Patterson, the presumed robber of Signe's Monet. They went first to the old Patterson house on stately Rio Grande Boulevard. The house was still unoccupied and the lawn had gone to weeds with large branches scattered about that had fallen from the large cottonwoods and elms. Mateo broke into the empty house easily. The furniture had been removed. Scraps of paper and old envelopes lay scattered on the dirty floor. A blood stain remained on the wooden floor of the library. In the corner guest bedroom upstairs they found a sleeping bag and in an adjacent bathroom some ladies toiletries.

"I think she has been here recently," Signe said picking up an expensive bottle of wrinkle cream that contained colloidal gold and whale sperm.

"Let me stake it out for two or three days and see if I can catch her scent," Mateo said as he hunkered down by the sleeping bag to search for hair or nails that would contain DNA.

PART 2

CHAPTER 11

Signe gave Mateo a hundred dollars to pay for some of his expenses while he stayed in Albuquerque. She sped back to Santa Fe. It was a warm spring night and she drove with her windows down. Having been forced off I-25 at high speed the previous fall she had been apprehensive on the highway for months, but recently the feeling had waned. She saw emergency lights as she approached the Sandia reservation, and all the old feelings quickly returned. She pulled into the left hand lane and slowed as a solid line of vehicles, all with their brake lights on, blocked her progress. She inched along at two miles per hour until she came to a large trailer that had turned over on the shoulder. No one seemed to be hurt and once past the police and fire vehicles, she accelerated. Soon she was back in Santa Fe.

The gate to her apartment complex had been replaced and reinforced. She was pleased to see that her front door had been rebuilt and freshly painted. The minute she got in the door she called Brian. They talked for an hour and a half. Signe told Brian all about the murder of her friend and Bryan told her about his efforts to get a new arthritis drug approved by the FDA. He was CEO of a family owned drug company since his older brother was kidnapped and murdered. Brain suggested they finish with some phone sex since they hadn't seen each other since they were in Caracas on April 24th. Signe had never done phone sex and she was horny, but she suggested Brian fly over the next morning in his Gulfstream and spend the day with her. He looked at his calendar, decided his appointments weren't very pressing and agreed.

"I will meet you at Bishop's Lodge at nine-thirty, my love," Brian said in a soft voice before hanging up.

Previously, Brian had arranged a trip to Paris for a night at the opera. They had seen a startlingly modern production of *Lucia de Lammermoor*, and now, whenever she heard the aria from the second act, *Spargi d'amoro pianto*, she felt a warmth between her legs. Brian had also arranged a romantic fantasy at the Banyan Tree in Phuket for the two of them. She wanted to return the favor, so she packed a suitcase and drove up to Bishop's Lodge and got the chef and maître de out of bed at midnight. They planned a breakfast of Eggs Benedict, Brian's favorite for his arrival. However, it would be served in their large bedroom and she would be dressed only in some elegant under things. She intended to lure him into a long bubble bath in their tub to follow.

She outlined a lunch in the dining room featuring a slender Japanese girl with sushi and sashimi artfully placed on her barely clad body. The Japanese girl sent the maître de scurrying for his cell phone. For the afternoon, she planned a nap together after a Beethoven trio was piped into their bedroom. She knew that her lover would have to arise at four this morning to arrive at the Lodge on time. When he awoke, she planned to make love to him again before they had cocktails and *hors d'oeuvres* and he flew home. Signe was done with her arrangements by two-thirty and decided to stay at Bishop's Lodge for the rest of the short night.

Signe awoke early and spent a little more time than usual showering. She then put on silk stockings, a bright green garter belt and a semitransparent matching green bra. After ordering coffee she got back into bed to read her current book, *The Other Boleyn Girl*.

Brian burst through the door a few minutes early and kissed Signe without saying a word. While he caressed her under the covers, she pulled at his clothing until they lay in a heap on the floor. She tossed him a large fluffy robe and led him into the living room where their breakfast awaited. Signe thought that the bowl of yellow daffodils she had asked for matched the yellow of the hollandaise sauce on the eggs perfectly. Between bites, Brian announced with pride that his new drug had been approved by the government.

When they were finished eating, Signe took Brian's hand, and led him back to bed. She had read that scent memories were more persistent than any others, so she always wore Shalimar with its vanilla, amber scent when she was with Brian. She went over every inch of his body with the soft pads of her fingers and then with her mouth. By the end, he was insistently pulling her on top of him. When they were finished, they lay side by side, panting. Gradually their breathing slowed, and they slipped into a soapy hot tub for some prolonged kissing while Signe sat astride her lover. They toweled each other off gently, and Signe led the way to the living room. Sprawled on a wooly rug with scents of sage and sweet grass flowing on a slight breeze through high windows, they talked of Albert Pinkham Ryder, the pottery collection she and Axel had collected, and Monet's haystack paintings.

After an hour or so of quiet napping, the table was decorated with sprigs of white flowers, and in the center lay a slender Japanese girl covered in artfully designed sushi and sashimi with some strategically placed leaves. The living table was perfectly still.

"I have read about things like this, darling," Brian said. "But I had no idea it could be this beautiful."

After grasping ivory chopsticks, they fed each other for the next hour with lots of pauses for kisses and caresses. When they were finished, they thanked their sensuous table decoration and then bowed toward her with hands prayerfully before their faces. They slipped back into bed, and Brian was snoring peacefully within two minutes. Signe lay next to him with an arm across his body and thought about her murder case.

She decided she needed to understand what Larry was making or studying in his secret laboratory before she could deduce why he was killed. She needed a topnotch scientist. Los Alamos was full of them, but it was also a very small scientific community and she was afraid of idle talk. An official enquire into the clandestine lab would thwart her investigation. Surprisingly, she had heard that there was another atomic weapons lab, called Sandia, nearby. She decided to talk to Chief Hartford about it.

Signe let Brian sleep a little longer than planned. When he awoke they made love once more. Brian lay behind Signe like nesting spoons in one of her favorite positions for making love. Once they were coupled Brian reached down and grasped her ankle raising it toward the ceiling. Suddenly he was much deeper inside of her. She exploded with waves of pleasure like stately combers crashing lazily on a long curving shore. They had a hurried cocktail in bed. Signe had a gin martini with three olives. One olive was for love, one for money and one for wisdom, Signe thought to herself. Brain dressed quickly and Signe kissed him good by at the door.

"Now, wasn't that better than phone sex?" Signe whispered into his ear.

Brain simply nodded his head.

Signe thanked the staff of Bishop's Lodge for the magical day and drove to work. It was four-thirty when she arrived but Chief Hartford was still in his office. She ground and brewed fresh coffee and took two large cups into his office.

"You look very pleased with yourself, Signe," Hartford began. "Why is that?"

"I'm not completely sure," Signe replied with a large smile on her face.

She never lied to her boss, but she didn't want to tell him about the release that made her so in harmony with the world.

"I'm not making much progress with the murder investigation," Signe said, completely changing the subject.

"Maybe that is because it wasn't a murder."

"No. I'm sure that it was. I just can't get his friends or his family to talk."

"Where else can you look?"

"I think I need a few days to figure out what Larry was making or discovering in that beautiful white and chrome laboratory that he had spent so much time and money assembling."

"I'll bet there are fifty people on the hill who would understand it immediately."

"I thought of that, Chief, but every one of them will talk and once the administration and security hear about it, I will be barred from further access."

"You are right. You'll have to get someone from outside to analyze it for you."

"I believe there is another atomic research lab, Sandia National Labs only sixty miles away. Do you know anyone there?"

"Actually one of the assistant directors at Sandia is big in the Archdiocese. We are on a committee together and he is an acquaintance. I'll give him a call."

"My next problem is how to pay him for his expertise."

"I certainly don't have money to use on the investigation of a possible murder of a man who is way outside our jurisdiction."

"I know. Brian would give me the money in a heart beat but it doesn't seem fair. Perhaps I could trick Farrell out of it."

"I don't even want to know what you are planning, but I can loan you a thousand dollars until you get the money from the Feds," Hartford replied.

Signe decided to put in a call to Liam Farrell right then before she lost her nerve. He had given her his private cell phone when they had lunch together.

"Hey, Signe. "I'm glad you called," Liam said in a cheery voice. "Do you want to get a margarita? It's Cinco de Mayo you know."

"I'm sorry I can't," Signe replied. "I'm going over to my partner, Jack Gallegos house for dinner, but thank you. The reason I called, is that Chief Hartford is upset about the two days I spent helping your agency with the Abramowitz case. Could you possibly reimburse him for my salary?"

"I believe I could do that. You were invaluable in helping us close that case quickly. How much do you make per day?"

"He says it's $457.36 which seems high to me. Most of it must be benefits."

"I'll submit an invoice for two days salary as soon as I get to work tomorrow."

"Thanks, Liam," Signe said as she hung up.

CHAPTER 12

Signe called her friend Terecita Armijo and invited her out to dinner. They started at the Coyote Café for drinks.

"I'm glad you called," Terecita commented as she took a sip of a Cosmopolitan. "I was planning another night alone in my robe and curlers with a Lean Cuisine for company."

"That doesn't sound very exciting," Signe replied sympathetically.

"I spoke with you before about being a judge. It was what I dreamed of being since I was a little girl growing up in Española. I got appointed to District Court at least the years sooner than I had dared to hope. I'm rendering opinions almost every day but then I spend the next few days and nights wondering if my sentence was correct, and I still miss Manny."

"Wow. That doesn't sound very healthy to me," Signe remarked.

Manny Ramirez was another young Santa Fe Judge who had been brutally murdered in February. Manny and Terecita had been colleagues and then lovers before his death. Signe gathered Terecita up and drove her to The Pink Adobe for dinner. It was one of Signe's favorite restaurants, cozy and welcoming. On the way across town Signe tried to come up with a plan for her friend. When they were settled, Signe ordered Chicken Marengo for them both. Signe cared a great deal about food and one of her rules along with never eating from a buffet was to never eat chicken at a restaurant. Her one exception was the dish created by Napoleon's chef after his great victory at Marengo in 1800 that sealed the success of his Italian campaign. Signe found the combination of tomato, mushrooms, garlic, wine and tarragon with the chicken a soothing combination.

"Perhaps you need a leave of absence or a lighter load of cases," Signe suggested as the dinner dishes were being taken away.

"I've only been on the district bench for twenty-0ne months," Terecita replied. "It would be easier for the chief justice to replace me than to grant such a request."

Signe took a bite of chocolate mousse and then said, "In that case you need to see my friend Dr. Vivian Goldiamond right away. She's a very bright and practical counselor. I'm sure she can get you back on track."

Signe drove Terecita back to her car and gave her a warm hug. Back at her apartment, Signe parked near her door. A patrol car sat on the street by the steel gates to protect her. Signe had difficulty going to sleep. She was thinking about her delicious time with Brian and her friend's murder. She awoke early and read several chapters in the book she was reading about Anne Boleyn.

Signe drove to work early through the quiet streets of Santa Fe and found Chief Hartford already at his desk. He gave her the name of three physicists at Sandia National Laboratories. She called the first name on the list.

"This is Detective Signe Sorensen and I'm calling for Dr. Pushpa Chatterjee," Signe said to soft female voice that answered the phone.

"Speaking," Dr. Chatterjee replied.

Signe was very surprised that the theoretical physicist she was speaking with was a woman. She made a quick recovery.

"I'm investigating a crime that involves a clandestine laboratory in Los Alamos. The lab contains a large amount of very sophisticated equipment and I need to know what purpose it might have served."

"You believe that if you understand the purpose of the lab you will know the motive for commission of the crime?"

"That is very succinctly put, Dr. Chatterjee. Can you help me?" Signe queried.

"I would be very happy to," Dr. Chatterjee said immediately in a soft voice.

"Thank you. I can pay you for your time," Signe replied gratefully.

"That won't be necessary, but it is most kind."

"When may I drive down and meet you?" Signe asked.

"You said this secret lab is in Los Alamos?"

"Yes, it is."

"Then there is no need for you to come here," Dr. Chatterjee answered. "May I meet you in Santa Fe today? I'm between projects right now. Then you can show me."

"That would be excellent," Signe replied in an excited voice. "I'll meet you at the La Fonda Hotel on the Plaza at noon."

Signe checked on Mateo. He had been shadowing the house on Rio Grande Boulevard but hadn't even caught a glimpse of Svelty.

"I've been lurking around the house at night when I think she would be most active," Mateo reported. "I haven't seen any sign of her. Perhaps she has moved on."

Next she went to the lab and got all of Valerie's notes about the equipment in the lab before driving to La Fonda. She got to the hotel early so she could talk with her good friend, Jefferson Barclay, the concierge. Jefferson knew everyone and everything that was happening in Santa Fe.

"Greetings, sweet lady," Jefferson said as his friend approached for a hug.

"How is everything, compadre?" Signe replied.

"Exceptional. I'm having a fabulous spring. How about you, Signe?"

"I lost my friend Dr. Larry Abramowitz about two weeks ago, and I'm afraid he was murdered. What have you heard?"

"Your friend has lived here for decades, but he did most of his playing and vacationing elsewhere."

"So you don't know anything about him?" Signe replied in a discouraged tone.

"I most certainly didn't say that, dear. Even if that were true I wouldn't admit it. It could tarnish my image. He brought women to the hotel several years ago. I keep a diary of interesting people who visit the hotel and I'm sure some of his companion's names are listed there. Three weeks ago a middle aged man stayed here. Larry picked him up every morning in his car. The man wore an old fashioned overcoat and spoke with an eastern European accent. I can get the information on him while you are eating lunch."

Dr. Chatterjee had walked up in a traditional sari draped over her shoulder. Signe made the introductions before the two women sat down in the colorful La Plazuela. They sat near the center of the high ceilinged room which had a tree in the middle. The walls were made of small window panes painted in colorful patterns with a distinctive turquoise border around each pane. Both ordered the sopa de tortilla and then chatted amicably. Signe pulled out a list of the equipment found in Larry's extensive modern lab. Dr. Chatterjee studied it for several minutes.

"These are the latest models of all of this equipment," Dr. Chatterjee remarked. "It is better than the instruments we have at Sandia Labs."

"Would a physicist employed by the government be able to buy this equipment?"

"Absolutely not," Dr. Chatterjee replied without hesitation.

When then finished eating, Jefferson handed Signe an envelop as she walked past the concierge's desk. Signe drove Dr. Chatterjee to Larry's house in Los Alamos. The California bungalow had a deserted look and most of the yellow crime scene tape had blown away. Signe parked out of sight and used the key Larry had given her to open the back door. She led Dr. Chatterjee down the basement stairs and hit the lever that opened the door to the laboratory.

"Chal Chaiyya," Dr. Chatterjee exclaimed in Hindi. "What a glorious laboratory."

"Is this enough to murder someone over?" Signe asked.

"Indubitably," Dr. Chatterjee replied. "I'm a pacifist, but I might murder for this."

"Can you deduce what it was meant to study or manufacture?"

"But of course. The location of the machines and their settings would be of great importance. It can be determined. It will just take some time. It may take four or five hours, but it will go faster if you write for me."

Dr. Chatterjee had brought a laptop computer in her briefcase. She plugged it in and set it up for Signe. She helped Signe draw a diagram of the lab so each piece of equipment could be accurately placed. Then Dr. Chatterjee started in one corner and worked her way around the lab. She found isotopes of plutonium, polonium, and uranium, isotope counters, centrifuges and milling machines for making fine metal components. There were bins of mercury switches, computer boards and spools of colored wiring.

"I know that one man cannot build a hydrogen bomb," Dr. Chatterjee remarked as she opened the sample compartment of one of the Nuclear-Chicago instruments. "It took ninety scientists and hundreds of enlisted men to make the first atom bomb in this mountain town in 1945. Unfortunately, diagrams and specifications for crude nuclear devices are everywhere on the internet now. Sixty years ago only one country had nuclear weapons. Now at least eight do, including my home country of India."

"Do think Larry was building something for one of members of the nuclear club or perhaps for some rogue country that was trying to join?" Signe asked.

"More likely the latter. The eight nuclear powers are very open about having weapons, except for Israel," Dr. Chatterjee remarked.

"They could buy what they wanted on the open market unless it was something new that the US had invented and didn't want to share."

"If there were such a thing Larry would know about it?"

It was nearly seven o'clock.

Dr. Chatterjee set a small instrument back on the counter and said, "I think I'm done for tonight."

Signe helped her pack up her computer and notebooks and they drove into Santa Fe.

"I would still like to pay you for your time, Dr. Chatterjee," Signe remarked as they drove past the Opera.

"That won't be necessary and please call me Pushpa."

"May I at least buy you dinner?"

"That would be lovely."

Dr. Chatterjee suggested the India Palace near downtown. Pushpa ordered lamb jaffrazi, pea's pallao, and prawns vindaloo and baingan bhartha. The latter, an eggplant dish baked in tandoor with herbs was Signe's favorite. They chatted like long lost friends about their upbringings in Denmark and India while they ate. Signe dropped Pushpa off at her car which was parked by La Fonda. Pushpa handed her brief case to Signe just as she was getting out of the car.

"I don't want the Department of Energy snoops finding this information in my office or apartment," Pushpa said. "Perhaps you can keep it safe for me."

"I will. Goodnight."

CHAPTER 13

As she drove home, Signe felt lucky that she had found such a knowledgeable and helpful physicist. Helpful wasn't one of the qualities she ascribed to very bright scientific people. Pushpa had said that she would have some answers in a couple of days, but Signe suspected she would also have some questions that might require another trip to the hill. Signe's apartment seemed in complete without the Monet in her living room. Brian had sent over a Matisse which was now hung in its place. It was a colorful painting of woman looking out a window at Mediterranean street scene. The long session Signe had spent with Dr. Chatterjee at the Abramowitz house had tired her. While thinking about reasons for making nuclear triggers, she fell fast asleep.

In the morning Signe went first to Valerie's laboratory. As she walked in Valerie was holding up a stainless steel sleeve.

"You will never guess where this came from," Valerie said in a smug voice.

"I think that is part of a vertical landing plane that was manufactured in Vladivostok," Signe replied after a moment's hesitation.

"What a great imagination and surprisingly close," Valerie conceded.

"It's part of the landing gear of a 1980's vintage Polish SM-1 helicopter called the 'hare.'"

"What was it doing in Valles Grande?" Signe asked.

"Some of these small, old helicopters are still used in eastern Europe and Asia according to *Jane's All the World's Aircraft*," Valerie replied. "You may have found the only piece of evidence that proves that campsite was a crime scene. It certainly eluded the four FBI agents."

"But why go to the trouble of importing a foreign aircraft when the murderers could rent a chopper in Albuquerque or Santa Fe?" Signe wondered out loud.

"First this tiny aluminum eggbeater would be invisible on radar if it flew low," Valerie suggested. "Secondly, there wouldn't be any paperwork for nosy FBI agents or small town detectives to stumble across."

"Your second reason is compelling. See if you can find the range of that little chopper and we will get out some maps and try to confirm where it was fueled before dropping into Valles Grande."

While she was waiting, Signe went to her messy desk. She threw several things away in frustration and then saw a recent message from Mateo. She gave him a call.

"I've staked the house out for the last five days and I haven't seen a sign of Svelty Patterson or any one else suspicious," Mateo said.

"Don't waste anymore time there, partner," Signe replied. "Come back here and check on the places we know that she goes-Houston, Oklahoma, and Bernalillo."

"I'm on it, Chief."

Signe wandered back over to the lab after grabbing a fresh cup of coffee.

"That little whirlybird only has a range of 600 kilometers," Valerie said as Signe came through the door.

"Three-hundred and sixty miles isn't much range."

"It's much worse than that, Detective," Valerie replied. "They had to fly in and out on one tank of gas. That cuts their range to one hundred and eighty miles even if they didn't allow for bad weather or any other problems."

"Let's get out some maps and see if you can discover where they came from," Signe suggested.

Valerie soon had a topographical maps and highway maps spread allover the surface of a large table. She marked the location of the body with a red circle and handed Signe a pair of calipers.

"Albuquerque's close enough to the south but it is bristling with radar and military personnel," Signe began. "It wouldn't be my pick for departure of a chunky Polish helicopter. Las Vegas and Santa Rosa are the right distances to the east, but the criminals would have to fly right over the Sangre de Cristo Mountains at up to 13,000 feet. I'd come in from the unpopulated north." As she swung her calipers around she continued, "Durango, Alamosa or Trinidad."

"They each look like they have a small airport," Valerie offered.

"I'll call Mateo right now," Signe suggested. "If he isn't too far out of Albuquerque he can turn off at Bernalillo to Durango. You can fax the pictures that we have to the Durango Police Station and he can pick them up there. I think I'll have you go to Trinidad and Jack and I can go to Alamosa. I'll make up some packets of information."

"I'll start working on it right now," Valerie said.

Within a half an hour Jack was driving Signe north. The picked up a sack of flautas at El Paragua and then Jack took US 285 north out of Española. The countryside was rolling as sparsely wooded at first. Then they went through the small town of Ojo Caliente and past the lovely territorial style resort, Rancho de San Juan set against warm tan bluffs. Signe had spent some magical time there with her Swedish friend Sven Torvaldson. Jack kicked the speed of their crown Victoria up to one hundred miles per hour on the sparsely traveled road. Next they went through the village of Tres Piedras which Jack translated as three rocks and soon they were at the

Colorado border. They slowed for the small town of Antonito where the narrow gauge railroad for New Mexico terminated and then drove through miles and miles of fields planted with potatoes. When they pulled into the San Luis Valley Regional Airport a small commuter plane was taking off to the west. They went to the small terminal building and showed a photo of the Polish helicopter to the flight attendants. Neither of them had seen anything like the distinctive lumpy chopper.

"You should talk to the manager of general aviation," one attendant remarked. "He usually is in that building across the runway."

Jack drove them across the tarmac but found no one there. A note on his desk said that he was harvesting potatoes but could be reached on his cell phone. Signe called. Joe Montoya gave them directions to the farm. The drive to the west was through clouds of gray, brown dust from the harvesting and from huge trucks hauling tons of potatoes along the dirt road. When they arrived, both were choking on the dust. Joe Montoya climbed down from a large tractor that was harvesting a twelve foot wide swath of tubers. He pulled a red bandanna off of his nose and mouth.

"You folks come a long way," he said. "How can I help you'se?"

"We are looking for an old Polish helicopter that may have refueled here," Signe said as Jack pulled out a photograph.

"Yeah. A chopper like that stopped here about four weeks ago," Montoya replied. "I had never seen anything like it. I called it the pregnant guppy. They loaded up on gasoline and strapped a dozen jerry cans full of fuel in the cargo bay."

"Can you tell us exactly when this happened?" Signe asked.

"Sure, I wrote it all down. Let me shut the tractor down first."

Jack gave Montoya a ride to his car, and Jack and Signe followed him back to the general aviation shed. On the way Signe called Valerie and Mateo and told them they had found the departure point for the Polish chopper. Once inside, Montoya pulled down a large leather-bound journal and leafed through the pages. He paged back and forth several times.

"A page's been torn out of my log book!" Montoya remarked.

"The one that pertained to the Polish helicopter?" Jack asked.

"Yes."

"Tell us what you can remember," Signe replied.

"I can remember everything except the identification numbers on the side of the craft," Montoya replied as he began to write.

"It looks to me like you write with a heavy hand. Perhaps we can lift an impression of the numbers off of the next page," Jack commented.

He took a pencil and shaded the area where the call letters had been written on the preceding page.

"I think its ID number is PXCH239," Jack said after a few minutes work.

"I only have one other question, Mr. Montoya. Where did they say they came from?" Signe asked.

"They said Ft. Collins," Mr. Montoya replied. "But I thought they were lying then. I don't think that pregnant guppy had that much range."

Jack and Signe thanked Mr. Montoya for his help and began driving south.

Just after the two left Colorado, Signe noticed a roadblock up ahead with a row of cars and trucks waiting to run the gauntlet. Normally, Jack and Signe wouldn't have given the minor delay a second thought, but having experienced being shot at, forced off the road, and having had a squad car bombed, Signe was more suspicious.

"When you get a little closer, pull over Jack," Signe instructed. "There are few flashing lights for an official roadblock. I'd like to glass the vehicles."

"I'll get on the radio and see what's going on," Jack replied as he pulled to the side of the road.

After several minutes of looking through her binoculars Signe said, "The roadblock is made up of farm trucks. Most of them have American Minuteman, Death to Communists and Don't Tread on Me! stickers."

"I think that is that prick, Sergio Garcia, standing in the bed of that truck on the left," Jack remarked.

"The guy that precipitated that shootout in March at the Rocking G Ranch?" Signe replied.

"The very guy and now he's pointing a rifle at us," Jack said as he slid down in the seat.

Signe grabbed the rearview mirror and pushed it violently to the right catching the afternoon sun and then directing it right in Garcia's eyes. The slug pinged into the dirt beside the car.

"Let's get out of here!" Signe shouted.

Jack slammed the car into reverse, spinning around as he gained speed and slid from the shoulder onto the highway, accelerating as his tires gripped the blacktop.

"Let's go back to Alamosa, drive east to Fort Garland. Then we can head south on NM 522 to Taos," Jack suggested.

Once they were miles from the border, Jack asked Signe, "Where did you learn that trick with the mirror?"

"I didn't. It just seemed like a good idea at the time. I'm sure he would have missed anyway."

"I'm not as confident. Those survivalists did some pretty straight shooting when we were at the Rocking G Ranch."

"How did Sergio Garcia get out of jail anyway?" Signe enquired.

"'Viva la Raza!' and all that crap," Jack replied. "Northern New Mexico judges are soft on the lawless, downtrodden Hispanics."

CHAPTER 14

Arriving in Taos at seven thirty, Jack turned into the parking lot of Lambert's restaurant on Paseo Del Pueblo Sur. Without asking he knew it was one of Signe's favorite places to eat. Signe ordered roasted corn chowder, a warm spinach salad, and pepper crusted lamb Colorado, served rare. Part of the dining room was closed off for Julia Roberts who had come in from her nearby ranch and was dining with friends. Jack ordered a rib eye but seemed more interested in sneaking peeks through the curtain at his favorite movie star. He didn't have the nerve to ask her for an autograph, but he came back to the table whistling "Pretty Woman."

"I have never seen you act like this, Jack," Signe remarked between spoonfuls of soup. "You seem as nervous as a teenage girl."

"Give me a break, Signe," Jack replied petulantly. "You know I've watched *Steel Magnolias* twenty times even though *The Pelican Brief* with Denzel Washington is actually my favorite Julia Robert's movie."

"It just a side of you I don't get to see much," Signe reflected. "I like it."

Signe ran into Ms. Roberts in the ladies room. Julia opened the conversation.

"I cook most nights and it is really a treat for me to go out like this," Julia began as she put on some lip gloss.

"Lambert's has the very best food," Signe replied. "I stop here whenever I can."

"Where are you from?"

"I'm a detective in Santa Fe. My partner and I were in Alamosa investigating a murder."

"Did you have any success?" Julia asked as she applied some mascara.

"Not as much as you did in *The Pelican Brief,*" Signe replied.

"Yes, but Sam Shepard and John Heard both died during the investigation and it was just a work of fiction," Julia replied as she folded up a small black purse. "I trust you haven't lost anyone in real life?"

"No we haven't, but we did get shot at today," Signe remarked in a resigned tone.

"If you are done eating, would you and your partner have coffee with us?"

"I wouldn't want to intrude, but my partner, Jack Gallegos, would be just elated."

Signe collected her partner and directed him to two extra chairs that had been pulled up to the table. Ms. Roberts made the introductions. Signe told the group about their murder investigation embellishing a little as she progressed. Julia talked about her soon to be released movie, *Mona Lisa Smile.* After a delicious cup of coffee, Signe and Jack excused themselves, not wanting to overstay their welcome. As they left Julia gave Signe a leather bound menu she had autographed for Jack. Jack had a birthday in two weeks and Signe decided to give him the menu then.

Jack babbled excitedly on the way to the car.

"You know. When you analyze Ms. Robert's face up close her mouth is way too big and she has a ski-slide nose, but when you put it all together it is just perfect."

Jack's talking made Signe sleepy and she drifted off during part of the ride home. Jack said he would check on Sergio Garcia's record as he walked Signe to her apartment door.

In the morning, Signe decided to bring Chief Hartford up to date on her investigation. She carried the usual two large steaming cups of coffee into his office.

"After the FBI left Valle Grande, I found a stainless steel sleeve that ended up belonging to an outdated Polish helicopter," Signe began.

"That would support your theory that this was a murder and suggests that a foreign government was involved," Chief Hartford replied.

"Jack and I discovered that the chopper refueled in Alamosa but that is as far as we have gotten."

"Maybe it's time to turn this over to the NSA or the FBI."

"Well, the FBI would be logical. They have a local office, but I am not very impressed by their diligence or focus. Let me at least get a report from Dr. Chatterjee about Larry's clandestine lab. By the way, thanks for hooking me up with her. She is knowledgeable and fun to work with."

"I had never met her, but my friend sang her praises."

"Are you willing to keep a murder of possible international significance a secret from the US government, Chief?"

"Yes, I suppose I am. I think you and Dr. Chatterjee will do a faster and better job of solving it than those bunglers with the fancy initials."

Signe said, "Thanks, Chief," as she grabbed her coffee cup and left.

Valerie had been out late the night before and was just getting in as Signe entered the lab.

"Did you find anything in Trinidad?" Signe asked.

"I'm pretty sure that antiquated chopper stopped in Trinidad on the way out," Valerie began. "There is an almost illegible entry in the airport flight log two days after the entry you discovered in

Alamosa. The landing occurred late at night, in the rain, and the attendant did not pay much attention. He was just trying to stay dry. He did remember the sound of the craft's piston engine which isn't common in whirlybirds anymore."

"Was this our helicopter?" Signe asked.

"I'm ninety percent certain it was."

"Where did it go from there?"

"Even though it was dark and rainy he thought that it headed north toward Pueblo or Colorado Springs."

"Good work, Valerie. Call the Pueblo and Colorado Spring's airports and see if you can track the pregnant guppy any further."

Signe went to her desk and put in a call to Jefferson Barclay.

"I've got some information for you," Jefferson said. "It's fairly extensive or I would give it to you over the phone."

"I'll meet you at the Shed for lunch," Signe suggested. "And we can talk about it then."

Signe drove to the plaza and was surprised to find a nearby parking place. The Shed was in an old adobe house built in the 1690s. She always noticed the rickety blue and purple wooden door. Today though, she noticed the five rows of irregular brick that topped the abode wall. She knew that branded the building as territorial style even though New Mexico didn't become a territory until 1848. Signe was seated at a small table near the street so she could watch the passersby. She ordered a margarita while she waited for her friend.

Jefferson placed a manila envelope on the table before he sat down.

"Larry came to the La Fonda quite often," Jefferson said after giving Signe a hug. He used to meet women there for the weekend. I don't know how much luck you will have tracking them down, but at least they were considerably younger than he was."

"I hope that the women were local," Signe asked hopefully.

"Not exactly, Signe," Jefferson replied, "But most were from the Southwest, Phoenix, Las Vegas and LA. Here are their last known addresses, but many are probably bogus."

After thinking for a moment Signe said, "I'll have Mateo see if he can track any of them down."

Signe ordered gazpacho followed by blue corn red enchiladas and Jefferson ordered carne adovada.

"What about the unstylish gentleman with the wide lapels that met him there weeks ago?" Signe continued

"I gave you his registration form the day you had lunch with Dr. Chatterjee. He listed himself as a Polish business man." Jefferson replied.

"Did anything else turn up on him?"

"No. Except for his meetings with Larry, he kept to himself while he was here. He did some sight seeing but I had the feeling he was just killing time. He liked the Museum of International Folk Art, which I've always just seen as a bunch of tschoskes. I heard him talking about reversed religious paintings on glass from Poland."

"I wonder if he didn't meet someone at the museum," Signe remarked.

"You'll never know," Jefferson suggested as he finished his carne adovada.

"Perhaps they have surveillance cameras. I'll have Mateo check."

"Thanks for lunch," Jefferson said as he stood up and kissed Signe's cheek.

Signe went back to the police station and sat at her cluttered desk. She now had an Eastern European suspect and an old fashioned Polish helicopter involved in her murder case. As a Danish citizen, Signe kept track of politics in Western Europe, but she knew she was woefully ignorant about Eastern Europe. She thought about getting on the department's antiquated computer and reading about Poland and its neighbors, but she decided she would get more information from talking with a knowledgeable human. She had met some of the local priests during her previous murder investigation, and several of them had come from the old iron curtain countries. Signe called the Archdiocesan office and told the secretary what she wanted.

"You remember Father Edward?" the secretary said. "He is the Archbishop's assistant. His last name is Wisniewski and he has relatives all over Poland and Byelorussia."

The secretary rang Edward's office, and he and Signe agreed to meet that evening. He suggested meeting at The Compound on Canyon Road. Signe let Edward order for her. He picked a Caesar salad and a chateaubriand for two. While Edward was picking Bordeaux, Signe explained the reason for her call.

"I have a murder case that involved a Polish businessman and an eastern European and I'm woefully ignorant about modern Poland," Signe said. "I hope you can enlighten me."

"I write to my relatives in Poland every month and try to send them some money," Edward remarked. "They send me letters with news about the economy and local politics. Did you know that Poland joined NATO in 1997?"

"That must have made Josef Stalin turn over in his grave," Signe remarked.

"Probably not as much as the fact that Poland is joining the European Union next year," Edward replied as the Caesar salad was served.

"Are there any dissident Generals or politicos?"

"Of course. They were raised in the Soviet system before perestroika. Many of them have retreated to the southwest part of the country. I can make some contacts for you. They are hostile toward western governments but enjoy telling their stories to individuals, even ones from America."

Signe took her first tender bite of the Chateaubriand that had been prepared at their table. All talking stopped. When they finished their meal Signe asked that Edward make some enquires for her.

CHAPTER 15

When Signe returned to her apartment, she studied the Matisse that Brian had loaned her for the first time. The woman had a green nose! At first, Signe was offended, but now she decided it fit with the purple window frame and the yellow flowers outside. She missed her Monet and was angry again that Svelty took it. She decided to meet with Dr. Goldiamond in the morning and get some clues for catching her female sociopath. Signe slept soundly although see dreamed again about her dead friend Larry. In the dream they were dating again.

In the morning, Signe went to Dr. Vivian Goldiamond's office at nine. The office was decorated with small statues of figures, carefully arranged books and heavy drapes. Signe always felt calmer when she stepped into the office. The department required all officers to get a psychological evaluation after each incident that involved shooting. Unfortunately, Signe had had many visits during her last two cases. Dr. Goldiamond was writing at her desk and Signe sat down on a long purple couch. When Vivian finished writing, Signe explained her latest interaction with Svelty Patterson in minute detail, just the way Vivian liked it. Them they sat in silence for several minutes while Vivian mulled over the information.

"Svelty was one of the two so called *hetaerae* we worried about last fall," Dr. Goldiamond began. "You remember you are the one that named them after the Greek word for courtesan."

"I remember well. I suppose Wanda De Bernares is still in Venezuela."

"She was the less scary of the two," Vivian replied. "She was the rescuer that had been physically and sexually abused as a child. That Mafia boss, h Bacechi burned her chest with a lit cigarette. Wanda saw everything as black and white. I was always afraid she was going to flip on you."

"Yes, but she never did."

"You are enquiring about the second one, Svelty Patterson," Dr. Goldiamond remarked. "She had that early triad of pyromania, bed wetting and animal cruelty."

"Svelty always told me that the only thing she burned down was an old garage in Oklahoma and that that didn't count," Signe rejoined.

"That's like Lee Harvey Oswald saying, 'I only shot the President once.' I'm sorry. Svelty has the triad. Then she spent her adult life being deceitful, irresponsible and disregarding others. Fore most of that time her husband, Dirk Patterson did all these things for her. Therefore, she was a sociopath by proxy if you will. However, now that he is dead she is acting out her own bad behavior."

"She has accosted me on the highway and threatened me with a gun," Signe recalled. "She broke into my apartment and stole Brian's Monet which, in addition to being worth several hundred thousand dollars was my favorite possession! I have no idea what she will do next or where I can find her."

"Sociopaths have a certain rigidity of character that will take her back to the same place over and over again," Vivian suggested. "What do you know about her haunts?"

"She hails from Oklahoma. When she was a stewardess she was stationed in Dallas. She lived with Dirk in Albuquerque. After he died, she ended up in Taormina, Sicily. I have no idea of how she got there."

"Where was she happiest?"

"Probably when Dirk was flush and she went on shopping sprees to New York. She told me she could spend $35,000 in a weekend."

"I believe I would start looking for her there."

"Why do you think she is still after me?"

"Dirk was her ticket out of poverty and even though he tried to kill her for a bundle of insurance money—I believe you said $2,000,000—he gave her the power to act out her fantasies. She loved him as much as she can love anybody. In some strange way she must still hold you responsible for his death."

"I told you that I felt guilty because I didn't investigate his torture and murder thoroughly when it occurred. I didn't approve of him or what he stood for, so I thought it was poetic justice. Of course, he deserved a thorough investigation just like any victim. I didn't treat him fairly."

"You are only human, Signe," Vivian replied. "You don't always have to be perfect."

"I suppose you are right," Signe said after reflecting for a moment. "Tony Squitero fingered his girlfriend, Wanda De Berneres, as Dirk's killer and I told Svelty all about it. However, maybe that is not the real story. Tony 'The Squid' and Wanda are both pretty slippery. On the other hand, perhaps Svelty just doesn't want to believe it. In any case, I have some contacts in New York and I'll have them look out for her," Signe said as she got up from the purple sofa.

Signe went back to her office and put in a call to Dr. Chatterjee. She hoped that Pushpa would have some ideas about the clandestine lab that Larry had built. As Signe suspected, Pushpa wanted to see the lab again and offered to pick Signe up in an hour. Signe ordered some burritos so they could eat in the car during the drive. Dr. Chatterjee picked Signe up in a gray-green Jaguar sedan and they headed up the hill. The lab was undisturbed. Pushpa checked her list against several items on the tables in the lab. She pulled down one long heavy gray chassis that wasn't labeled.

"I need to know what this item is and I believe I know someone who can help me," Pushpa said while Signe grabbed the other end.

"We can't question any of the authorities," Signe reminded her.

"You don't have to worry about this person," Pushpa replied. "His name is Edward Grothus. He was a bomb maker, but now he has turned into a peace activist. He has a warehouse in an old grocery store called the Black Hole. He has thermocouples, oscilloscopes, Geiger counters and lots of other castoffs from the national laboratory. He would never tip our hand to anyone of importance."

The two women loaded the heavy instrument into Pushpa's car and headed off to the Black Hole. Grothus was at the counter haggling over the price of a cryogen storage device with a disheveled old man.

It's called the Black Hole," Pushpa remarked, "Because everything goes in and nothing comes out."

Signe and Pushpa fiddled with the stacks of old equipment while they waited for the haggling to stop. The old man left without the item he had wanted to purchase, Signe noted.

Ed Grothus turned his attention to the two women and said, "How can I help you pretty ladies?"

"We need to know what this piece of equipment is," Pushpa said as she pushed the gray chassis toward him.

He unscrewed the cover quickly and shined a flashlight into the back of the instrument. Then he turned to a shelf of dusty manuals behind him and pulled down a large manual.

"That is a Milliken high voltage power supply," Grothus replied. "I'll give you twenty bucks for it."

"It's not for sale," Signe replied. "But thanks for the info."

"You ladies need to attend the First Church of High Technology this Sunday. I'm going to perform a critical mass."

Pushpa chuckled and Signe laughed out loud as they carried their power supply out of the Black Hole. As Pushpa drove down the hill Signe enjoyed the mesas and occasional Ponderosa and Piñon pines. The New Mexico sky was a spectacular cerulean blue totally unlike the blue-gray of the moisture laden sky of Denmark. Just at the turnoff for Bandelier Park she saw a long pole blowing in the wind. On leather thong tied to the end of the stick Signe spotted three eagle feathers.

"Stop the car!" Signe shouted.

Pushpa skidded the car to a halt. Signe knew that possession, let alone display, of eagle feathers was a federal offense for non Indians, and she knew Mateo had three golden eagle feathers. She got out of the car and found a scrap of paper tied to the pole. She untied it and read, 'come to Tyuonyi now.' It was unsigned but written in Mateo's hand. Signe collected the prized feathers.

She pointed down the road to Bandelier and said, "My associates in trouble. Let's go."

Without asking any questions, Pushpa accelerated along the twisty road to the south. She had a natural instinct about how fast she could go and drifted through curves effortlessly. Signe flashed her badge at the entrance station and they barreled on to the headquarters. It was just time to close and Signe showed her badge to the ranger. He recognized Signe from her many visits with Mateo. She collected two powerful flashlights and headed into the monument with two rangers close behind. They walked across the grassy floor in front of the mesa and then started into the cliff dwellings. Mateo had been allowed to write clues as to his whereabouts, but in Keresan, his native language. Signe was sure that was a little twist from Svelty, and Signe was glad she was studying the Cochiti language so diligently.

Due to the altitude, the night was cool but not cold. If it took all night to find Mateo Romero, he would not suffer from exposure. The cliff dwellings were one to four stories tall and carved out of the soft sandstone. Adobe walls completed the small rooms that were usually only four feet tall. The two rangers explored the west end of the cliff dwelling while Pushpa and Signe worked on the higher east end. As it got darker the climbing and searching took longer. About eleven p.m. the two groups gathered below the dwellings and studied a map the rangers had brought.

The only unexplored area was a series of eight rooms in the center top of the cliff dwellings. The area wasn't open to the public or even to Indian people who had special permission to go into more areas of the ancient ruin. Pushpa, Signe and one of the rangers took some wooden ladders from other areas and put them against the walls to the fourth floor. Against one of the back walls they found Mateo Romero naked and bound with a Kevlar rope that the rangers couldn't cut. Signe and Pushpa spent thirty minutes laboriously untying the rope. Once free, Mateo brushed himself off after he stood up.

"Are you all right?" Signe asked.

"Of course," Mateo replied. "She was going to torture me until I answered her questions. I just looked at her like, are you crazy? I'm Indian. I'm not answering your questions, white woman."

"But she beat you?" Pushpa answered.

"Yes," Mateo said, as he showed her his bruised back. "But it is nothing."

CHAPTER 16

The two Rangers wrapped Mateo in a blanket and carried him down the ladder with difficulty. He was short but quite stocky. Once they got him to headquarters, he seemed more responsive.

"Can we call an ambulance for you, Mr. Romero?" One of the rangers asked.

"No. I will be fine," Mateo replied in a strong, sonorous voice. "I'm sure my partner and her friend will take me home."

Signe and Pushpa loaded Mateo, wrapped only in a blanket, into the small back seat of the Jaguar and drove to Cochiti Pueblo as quickly as they could. On the way Signe asked about his abduction.

"How did Svelty get her hands on you?"

"I went back to check on the Patterson house in Albuquerque and she was waiting for me. When I went into the library, she sprang out from behind the door and injected something in my neck before I could turn around. My muscles got weak almost immediately, and soon I was lying on the floor totally paralyzed but fully awake. A large man helped her put me in the backseat of her car and drove me to Bandelier. They questioned me all the way."

"Did you recognize the man?" Signe asked.

"No. He had oily hair and was heavy set and tan. He wore a lot of gold jewelry. I thought he looked like the Mafia bosses I've seen in the movies."

"Did he have an accent?"

"Yes either New York or New Jersey."

"What else?"

"He had a large tattoo of the Virgin Mary on his forearm with the initials CNF underneath it in a fancy script."

"That shouldn't be too hard to find."

"Why didn't you tell Svelty what you knew?"

"I am not helping her. You helped her through that almost fatal overdose when no one else cared if she lived or died, and this is how she repays you?"

"She's just mentally ill, Mateo," Signe replied. "She can't really help how she behaves."

"Just like those perverted priests they have warehoused at the Servants of the Parakeet. We Indians are not so forgiving or understanding. A person and their spirit have to make their own way through life. They are responsible for the trajectory of their own lives."

"I understand what you are saying. I'm just glad we found you as quickly as we did."

When they got to Mateo's house the two women helped him out of the car. Signe thought he looked like his knees hurt. She tucked him into his bed. Signe built a fire and instructed one of the neighbors to look in on him. Signe ruminated on the death of Larry while Pushpa drove her back to Santa Fe. She was sure that Svelty had nothing to do with the murder of her friend, and Signe decided to talk with each of Larry's three daughters about their father's life.

The oldest daughter seemed the most unwilling so Signe decided to talk with the youngest daughter Katarzyna first. Dr. Katarzyna Abramowitz was an assistant professor of microbiologist at Tulane University. Signe decided to get a cheap ticket on Southwest Airlines to the Crescent City and pay for it out of her own pocket. When she got home, she booked a flight for the next morning, and then she slept for four hours.

In the morning, Jack drove Signe to the Sunport in Albuquerque. He was still talking about meeting Julia Roberts, which made her chuckle. She was thinking about her trip to Louisiana.

"Have you ever been to New Orleans?" Signe asked her partner.

"No. I always wanted to go for Mardi gras but so far I haven't made it. By the way people call it Nawlin's and they say it's like another country."

"I tried to get Brian to go, but he had a large pharmaceutical meeting in Philadelphia that he had to attend," Signe remarked somberly. "He's having one of his managers show me around."

As the plane approached the New Orleans airport, she could see the curve in the broad café au lait river with the city nestling inside the arc. She understood instantly why it is called the Crescent City. As Signe stepped out into the muggy heat, her underarms got wet. Brian's manager, Tanya Peterson, greeted her and helped her into a limousine. They drove to the Provincial Hotel where Signe was staying and she changed into some lighter clothes. Tanya took her guest to the cramped Acme Oyster house for platters of raw oysters served on trays of ice and washed down with cold beer, following which she suggested an orientation tour of the city. Tanya then suggested an orientation tour of the city. She had the driver take them through the Vieux Carré, or old square, and then through the garden district. Tanya had arranged a quick stop at the Audubon Zoo so that Signe could see the rare white tigers and white alligators. Signe wondered how they would survive in the wild. Next, they stopped at Pat O'Brien's in the French Quarter.

"The popular drink here is a fruit punch in a shapely glass with rum called a hurricane and it will give you one in your head," Tanya remarked. "Let me order you a French seventy-five which will get you just as tipsy without the headache."

Both women drank a couple quickly then Tanya ordered a pitcher to take with them in the limo. Signe thought she tasted gin and champagne in the drink. Tanya seemed to like to party, Signe thought. They drove to the market near Jackson's Square.

Signe looked over at the levee and remarked, "This Square seems to be about twelve feet below the Mississippi River."

"Fifteen feet to be exact," Tanya remarked in a slurry voice. "Every drop of rain that falls in this swampy city has to be pumped out."

Tanya took her to another bar in the Royal Sonesta Hotel that she seemed familiar with and greeted the bartender by his first name. She ordered two drinks and got one for Signe. Tanya's speech was getting slurry, but she continued to drink. The next stop was a grand old restaurant in the Garden District called Commander's Palace. When they stopped for a streetlight, Tanya opened the back door, stuck her head out and vomited. Somehow, she seemed less drunk after that. Several of Brian's pharmaceutical sales representatives who were joining them for dinner met them at the restaurant. They were shown to a second floor room with a tall ceiling and pink paisley wallpaper. Everyone in the group ordered cocktails and appetizers. Most of the appetizers featured oysters, shrimp or crayfish, served by tuxedoed waiters. The ten diners asked Signe rafts of questions about both New Mexico and Denmark. Before ordering their entrée each diner had to pick a desert of either bread pudding or strawberries on just-from-the-oven shortcake. Signe picked her favorite berry. She had soft-shelled crab for dinner with a side of the best dirty rice she had ever tasted. Signe asked about Dr. Katarzyna Abramowitz. It turned out that one of the reps had met her at a reception at Tulane.

"She is a very serious young scientist," Jennifer, the young rep began. "She was educated in Europe, and told me her father was a leading theoretical physicist at the Los Alamos National Laboratory. I got the impression she was very attached to her dad, but also that she had a real sadness about him. I know a secret about her, but I can't tell you about it."

"Her father died recently and I'm here to interview her," Signe replied.

"Does that mean he was murdered?" Jennifer answered.

"Not necessarily," Signe lied. "I'm going to interview her tomorrow after her morning microbiology class."

All the diners turned their attention back to the delicious food. Tanya had ordered several bottles of a rich French wine with hints of blackberries and currants to accompany the gourmet victuals. The strawberry shortcake was tasty with a soft warm flaky biscuit covered with large strawberries sweetened and crushed just enough to release the berry flavor. Signe savored every mouthful.

When they finished eating, Tanya led the group on a pub-crawl to four jazz clubs followed by three strip clubs. As the night wore on, the drug reps dropped away one by one. They were replaced with *bon vivants* attracted to the group by Tanya, like a moth speeding toward a bare, back-porch light bulb. A young blond club owner named Roger joined the group and attached himself to Signe. Despite his mundane job, Roger had a degree in medieval history from Duke and was a good conversationalist. Signe had stopped drinking hours before. A French seventy-five sat in front of her place but she barely sipped it. Tanya directed the limo onto the free ferryboat across the Mississippi River. They landed in the grimy and dilapidated neighborhood of Algiers. Large pieces of waste paper blew down the deserted streets. Roger observed the look of concern on Signe's face.

"Don't worry," Roger said softly in Signe's ear. "Tipitina's is a well-known afterhours drinking place and doesn't look like much, but usually it is safe."

Roger guided Signe through a weatherworn wooden door into a small club lit by red lights. A jazz quintet played on a small stage. Signe thought it was the best music she had heard in New Orleans.

The group listened to several spectacularly complex sets, before a loud argument broke out at the other end of their table. As fists were raised, Roger hustled Signe out the backdoor. A shiny black sedan was waiting with a stream of gray exhaust pulsing out of the exhaust pipe.

Once safely in the car, Roger looked sheepish and said, "I said it was usually safe," by way of apology.

"You weren't very confident of that or this car wouldn't have been waiting," Signe said barely suppressing a laugh. "Thanks for saving me."

"You would have been fine without me," Roger said as he took Signe's hand in his.

The driver drove west through the deserted streets at high speed seldom stopping for red lights. He turned onto the Huey P. Long Parkway over the Mississippi River. At the bridge's apogee several hundred feet above the middle of the river, the driver stopped. Roger and Signe got out and looked out at the sharp curves of the river with the city held in its grasp. Once back in the car, the driver sped Signe to the Provincial Hotel. Roger walked her to the door and gave her a gentle kiss. Signe felt a brief wave of pleasure as she walked across the lobby.

CHAPTER 17

It was five a.m. and Signe was so tired that her back ached from all the dilapidated chairs she had sat in. She barely nodded at the desk clerk before climbing the stairs to her room. After two large glasses of water to ward off a hangover, she shed her clothing on the floor and fell into bed. She awoke at eight, having forgotten to close the blinds, and realized she wouldn't be going back to sleep. She showered and dressed for the heat before walking west on Chartres Street into the heart of the French Quarter.

Few people were about, and most were delivery men with their huge trucks blocking the narrow old streets. She went to Café du Monde just off Jackson Square for strong coffee and two plates of sugary beignets. The pastry without the sugar reminded her of the warm sopapillas she ate with honey for dessert in New Mexico. When she was finished, she cut across the square and tried walking down the famed Bourbon Street. This morning it was littered with trash. Faded pictures of overweight strippers filled the grimy establishment windows, and worst of all, the air smelled of garbage.

She quickly cut over one block to Royal Street. Signe felt like she was on another planet as she walked past tidy antique shops and art galleries with spotless windows. For the next two hours, Signe lost herself in Louis XIV furniture, Reconstruction tables and

Plantation armoires. Next, she looked at paintings by Chagall, Dali and Joan Miró. As the afternoon started, and the heat began to sap her energy her, she walked nearly to Canal Street and stepped into the sleek interior of Deanie's Seafood restaurant. Signe ordered seafood and okra gumbo and then crayfish etouffe with a large glass of chardonnay. She caught a cab to Tulane University. The microbiology department was located in the basement of a beautiful brick building on the tree-lined campus. Signe found the right office whose door was covered with colorful brochures about meetings and symposia regarding salmonella, malaria and Chagas' disease. Dr. Abramowitz wasn't in her office. Signe sat down in an old wooden chair to wait. She felt sleepy from the rich food and closed her eyes for just a second.

Dr. Abramowitz breezed by in a gray lab coat with her name over her left lapel in red letters and a tight black skirt. Katarzyna offered a hand.

"Good to see you again," Katarzyna said as she unlocked her door using a large ring of keys.

"I appreciate your taking the time to talk with me," Signe replied as she walked through the office door.

Dr. Abramowitz took a pile of journals off a chair so Signe would have a place to sit.

"No. I'm the one who's thankful that you cared enough about my dad to investigate what happened to him."

"What can you tell me about him?"

"He was a great scientist and an American patriot even though he was born in Poland. I was the last of three girls, and by the time I can remember anything, Mom and Dad were fighting constantly. He stayed at work late every night and my Mother accused him of having mistresses."

"Did he?"

"I'm sure that he did. When he came home, before he even opened his mouth, Mom would tear into him the minute he stepped through the door. He had to turn to someone for support and affection. He didn't get along with my two older sisters. I was his only solace at home."

"What sort of things did you do together?"

"When I was little he took me to the playground down the street. Later we hiked the rocky canyons around Los Alamos. He taught me bird watching, which inspired my love of biology. Later we played a spy game. He would give me small waterproof packets and I would hide them under a culvert on the next street. Albina had done that before but she got bored of it. I was only allowed to deposit the package if there was a white chalk mark on a post by the road."

"Did you ever look in the packets?"

"No. That was not allowed. I would have lost the game."

"Did your father ever discuss what was in the correspondence or who it was for?"

"No. But sometimes he used the word 'poszukujący.' When I learned Polish later I would translate that word as 'seeker.'"

"Did you ever think that perhaps your father was a spy?"

"Looking back on those parcels I innocently placed in the culvert, I did give it a thought."

"Did your father ever speak out against the west or against America?"

"He complained about inequities in pay all the time. He failed to understand why a top scientist received a modest salary and a designer of trivial dresses for women made millions. However, he never forget how much more inequitable the treatment of citizens was in his own country, Poland. He left the Nazi death camps at the end of the war alive, but for the next two years the Polish people starved on eleven hundred calories a day. He knew he was lucky to come to America as a displaced person."

Signe pushed her chair back and said, "I appreciate your talking with me. When I develop some new leads I'd like to call you back."

"That would be fine," Katarzyna said as she showed Signe to the door.

Signe needed to talk with the drug rep, Jennifer, who knew a secret about Dr. Abramowitz before Signe left town. She got contact information from Brian's office and they agreed to meet along the Mississippi by the dock for the paddle wheeler, *Natchez*. Jennifer arrived first. Signe sat next to her on a green wrought iron park bench.

"Thanks for talking with me," Signe began. "Dr. Larry Abramowitz was murdered and I'm trying to find out who did it. I need to know Katarzyna's secret."

"Can I be guaranteed anonymity?" Jennifer asked as she involuntarily looked around.

"Of course."

"While she comes across as a very conservative Tulane faculty member, she also has a dark side. She is involved with group of radical Arabs. She sleeps with the men and gives money to their radical causes."

"How could you possibly know this?" Signe asked.

"My fiancé is with the FBI, and even though he isn't supposed to tell me about his work, he does," Jennifer replied sheepishly.

"I believe the security of our country may be mixed up in this case, Jennifer," Signe began. "See if you can gently pump your boyfriend for some names. I won't misuse your confidence. Here's a number you can use to call me anytime," Signe said as she handed Jennifer her card.

Jennifer gave Signe a ride to her hotel so she could pick up her luggage and then dropped her at the airport for a flight back to Albuquerque. Jack picked her up curbside.

"What's been happening, partner?" Signe asked once she was seated in the car.

"The FBI is taking a second look at your little murder," Jack began. "Someone called in this hatchet woman, a deputy director from San Francisco and they are reviewing all of the evidence that they have."

"Did they find the clandestine lab?"

"My sources say they didn't, but it is probably just a matter of time."

"I wish I could have two more weeks before they muddy the waters."

"I don't think you'll get your wish," Jack replied.

They stopped at the Coyote Café for a late supper before Jack drove Signe to her apartment.

When she arrived at work the next morning, Signe's head was full of questions that needed to be answered. Because of what his youngest daughter had said and because of his multimillion-dollar secret lab, she suspected that Larry probably was, if not a spy, at least selling secrets. It would certainly pay for his expensive taste in women. However, if that were the case why would some foreign power or agency kill him? If he were selling secrets, and it was discovered, the US government would question and incarcerate him not have him murdered, Signe thought. She desperately needed to know exactly what Larry was making in his sleek lab and then what countries would pay exorbitant amounts to obtain the technology. Pushpa Chatterjee could tell Signe what Larry had been making. For geopolitical information, Signe was totally in the dark. She knew that her Chief, Gerald Hartford, had no interest in the area.

Signe found a secure phone in the department and called her former Chief, Thor Nielsen, in Copenhagen. It took Signe thirty minutes to tell her whole story to her sympathetic former Chief.

"I will find someone that can help you, Signe," Nielsen said when she was finished. "It's 5 p.m. here, but I will call you back in an hour."

Signe went to the crime lab and reviewed the information that had been collected from the crime scene to kill time. Nielsen called back in just over an hour.

"There is a small think tank right in your little mountain town called the Santa Fe Institute," Nielsen began. "One of its elite residents is an expert on eastern European nuclear policy named Klaus Obermeyer. He is almost ninety, very eccentric but brilliant.

Klaus has bad teeth and never combs his hair. He swears a lot, but only in Danish. He owes me a favor or two. Give him a call."

"Thanks for your help, Chief," Signe replied. "I will bounce the details of this case off of you, if I may, when I get a little further along."

"Be careful how you send it to me, Signe," Nielsen replied. "Since 9/11 NSA is monitoring all overseas traffic. Please don't let them catch either of us in their sticky web."

CHAPTER 18

Signe took Jack to the restaurant Pushpa had introduced her to, the India Palace. She ordered chicken tandoor for them both. Jack ate all his food.

"How did you like it?" Signe said.

"It's interesting," Jack replied.

Signe knew that was Jack being polite.

"Well, thanks for trying it," Signe replied as they walked back to their Crown Victoria.

When they got back to the station, Signe had a message from Dr. Bernadette Gilchrist. Signe called the OMI.

After some pleasantries, Bernadette said, "I have the results of Lawrence Abramowitz's autopsy."

"I will drive down so you can show me what you have found," Signe replied.

She drove out of Santa Fe in her BMW on the Old Pecos Trail and turned southeast on I-25. The midday traffic was light and Signe soon found herself pulling onto the medical campus at the University of New Mexico.

She found Bernadette in her cramped, messy office.

"Let me tell you about the results of the autopsy," Bernadette began. "You are the first to know."

"Which you have <u>also</u> given to the FBI?" Signe replied.

"Of course I haven't. Let the bastards call if they want it. Even then it might get lost a couple of times."

"Well, what did you find?"

"It's complicated."

"Do you know how much I hate that answer? Half the time in Denmark the pathologist solved the case for me. The last two cases I sent you, Chloe Patterson and Manuel Ramirez, were laced with suggestions, clues, and innuendos."

"This one is cut from the same piece of cloth, I'm afraid," Bernadette replied. "I found a variety of radioactive isotopes in his body including plutonium, thallium, americium and worst of all polonium. However, none was in high enough concentration to kill him. I told you about his severe coronary artery disease. I did some research and found that concentration camp survivors have three times the rate of heart disease as a normal population. It would have been a miracle if he didn't have advanced atherosclerosis."

"What else did you find?"

"He had high levels of ketamine an anesthetic developed in the sixties that is still used for human and animal anesthesia in his system. He also was taking Phenobarbital."

"So what killed him?" Signe asked.

"Again, I'm not sure I can tell you the definitive answer. I can tell you what didn't kill him. It was not the Americium, or the Thallium or the Plutonium. I suspect he was exposed to them over the years as part of his work at the lab and they would stay in his body for a long time. For example, the half-life of Americium is 432 years. The Polonium is more problematic."

"Is it named for Larry's home country of Poland?"

"Yes and it is a very bad actor. It's a quarter of a million times more poisonous than hydrogen cyanide, which doesn't even seem possible. Chronic low-dose exposure causes cancer, but in higher doses the radiation causes death, acutely. One gram of polonium is enough to poison twenty million people!"

"How high was his level?"

"It was 3300 Becquerel which is three times the allowable level, and it concentrates to even higher levels in a person's liver and spleen. The damn stuff is widely used in industry and anyone can purchase it."

"How can you say that didn't kill him?"

"I cannot be totally sure."

"If he was killed with polonium and not ketamine or simply had an old fashioned fatal heart attack it makes a huge difference in what I investigate. The trail will go cold quickly, not to mention the fact that I'm paying for the inquiry out of my own pocket."

"All you have to do is show that clandestine lab to the FBI and you'll have lots of funds."

"And no control. Thanks but no thanks. They could wreck a nocturnal masturbation as Jack says," Signe replied.

"That isn't what Jack says, but I know what he means," Bernadette replied. "And he is right. They could totally f-up a wet dream."

"I want a second opinion on your findings," Signe said as blandly.

"You pinch-faced, flat-chested, closet dyke!" Bernadette screamed as she stood up. "You haven't given me a chance since you heard about the Violence against the Violators group. I will not show my work to another pathologist, and I will tip your hand to the FBI."

Signe knew that Bernadette hated the feds more than she hated her and wouldn't give them any information. She got Bernadette's bosses name off a business card on the front desk. She would have her Chief, Dr. Thomas Tamwalt, chief pathologist, and have him render a second opinion. Signe stomped out to her car and started driving east on Lomas Avenue with no destination in mind. She thought of her friend Dr. Mark Josephson, a pulmonologist in Albuquerque, who had taken such good care of Svelty after her nearly fatal overdose. She gave him a call.

"I'm in Albuquerque; any chance I could buy you dinner?" Signe asked.

"Sure. I'm just finishing at the office. How about the usual place in forty minutes?" Mark replied.

"Great."

Signe turned her BMW around and headed for the Quarters on Yale. It was a dark place in the shape of a wine barrel that hadn't been redecorated in a couple of decades. The smell of stale beer struck her nostrils as she opened the door. She found a small table and ordered a Tuborg while she waited for Mark. Once he arrived, they ordered an impossibly large platter of barbequed ribs with a side of French fried onion rings. They talked happily about work, their friends and their plans. Signe told some Svelty stories. They splashed each other with drops of cardinal red barbeque as they ate and laughed. Signe liked Mark because he was an uncomplicated friend with no hidden agenda. When they were finished eating Mark walked Signe to the door and gave her a hug goodbye.

Signe drove up Louisiana Boulevard to Dr. Pushpa Chatterjee's apartment. Pushpa offered Signe some iced tea and sat her down at a pile of notes on her dining room table.

"The FBI told you that because of his age, they thought Dr. Abramowitz probably wasn't doing original cutting edge research anymore," Pushpa began. "My findings are that nothing could be further from the truth."

"Good for Larry," Signe replied. "Can you give me an example?"

"Indubitably," Pushpa replied with hesitation. "Look at this. The US is dependant on foreign oil, polluting coal and waning natural gas to supply its energy needs. What about nuclear power? Too dangerous the public says; look at Chalk River, Three Mile Island and Chernobyl. However, each disaster was caused by operator error. What about a reactor that is controlled by computers without human input? Larry designed such a reactor. The core is seven meters wide and eleven meters long. See this diagram? It's enclosed in a sealed armored box. It runs on thorium an abundant mildly radioactive metal. If his specs are correct one plant would produce three gigawatts of power, enough to power a city, say, the size of Las Cruces. It is a truly brilliant idea."

"That is a great innovation," Signe replied. "But why would anyone kill Larry for a peaceful nuclear application like that?"

"I don't know," Pushpa was forced to reply. "If I were to explain the idea to any nuclear physicists he could work out the details in two or three days and tell me if it would work."

"How could this concept be turned into a weapon?" Signe asked perplexed.

"Here's a scenario. India pays a third country to sell the reactor to Pakistan for use in Kashmir the province between them that is disputed. Instead of pure thorium, the sealed reactor is loaded with material from spent fuel rods and some polonium. The reactor works just as it should delivering reliable power for several months. Then the polonium begins to heat up and causes the reactor to go critical. If it was sited in Srinagar it would kill two thirds of its six hundred thousand people."

"That is a frightening enough scenario to justify a murder."

"It has one major drawback. It would take thirty scientists working for five years to make it a reality and the work would go faster if your friend were part of the team."

It was 9 p.m. and Pushpa called in an order to the nearby India Kitchen. Signe had developed a taste for Indian food and Pushpa ordered an eggplant dish and a very hot lamb vindaloo. They rode together to pick up the food along with a stack of chapattis and brought it back to Pushpa's apartment. They spread the food on Pushpa's table and ate heartily.

It's was 11:30 when Signe soaked up the last of the lamb sauce with a corner of chapatti.

"Why don't you spend the night?" Pushpa asked. "I have more to tell you about, but I don't believe I can think straight anymore."

Signe took a quick shower and went to sleep in the guest bedroom. In the morning, Signe and Pushpa sat back down at the kitchen table over tea and toast.

"I have three other ideas about what Dr. Abramowitz was working on," Pushpa began. "However, these three concepts will take some more research."

"Tell me about them," Signe replied.

"There is evidence that Larry was working on isotopes that could be used as poisons," Pushpa said thoughtfully. "A few grains of polonium could be used to kill a foreign agent and could be very hard to discover. I also see evidence from some of the machinings that what he was working on could be used in PITs. PITs stands for plutonium induced triggers and consist of beryllium balls containing plutonium that are used as the trigger in every single atom or hydrogen bomb. All the nuclear wantabees need reliable triggers."

"Was Larry really working on all these things?" Signe asked.

"Yes, and I didn't even tell you about a hydrogen bomb the size of a steamer trunk using a new isotope that he proposed," Pushpa responded.

CHAPTER 19

Signe drove back to Santa Fe and headed toward the station house. She was hoping Gerald Hartford would already be in his office so she could bring him up to date. His light was on, so she took two steaming cups of coffee into his office and sat down. She told him all of Dr. Chatterjee's ideas about the secret lab. Then she moved on to Nielsen's friend Dr. Klaus Obermeyer.

"He's at the Santa Fe Institute," Signe began. "And he is an expert on eastern European nuclear policy. It's something I don't know anything about, Chief. I hope he can give me some clues about who murdered Larry and why."

"Are you sure this was a murder?"

"Yes, but Dr. Gilchrist's autopsy wasn't definitive as to cause. A very potent poison, polonium, was present but not in sufficient dose. Also he had large doses of an anesthetic agent, ketamine in his system."

"But that can also be used recreationally, I believe."

"You are correct. This is the third important necropsy where Bernadette has equivocated and I need something definitive. Can you have her boss, Dr. Tamwalt review the findings, please?"

"Of course. You and your friend seem to have fallen on some hard times."

"Yes. Ever since I found she was the president of that vigilante group that beats possible rapists our relationship hasn't been the same. I thought I knew her pretty well. The only good news is that she is treating the FBI much worse."

"I'll call as soon as we are finished. Anything else?"

"I'm sure you heard that Svelty Patterson abducted my associate."

"Yes and he is okay?"

"He is just fine. Mateo's a tough old bird. I just can't figure out what is stirring her up again."

"I thought you investigated her husband's torture and murder, even though it was belatedly, and were satisfied that you know who did it."

"I am and I told Svelty what I had found. Perhaps she is irate about something else."

"Well, her whole family was wiped out," Hartford mused.

"Yes, but I don't think she ever cared for her step daughter, Chloe, and Svelty told me that Dirk forced her to take those barbiturates so he could get the insurance money. What possible beef can she have against me?"

"Well, first of all she is a woman and secondly you think she is crazy. Perhaps that is enough."

"That is the most unsatisfying motive you have ever suggested to me, Chief," Signe replied in a disappointed voice. "You are my mentor, for God's sake."

"You're right."

Chief Gerald Hartford was silent for several minutes.

"You have been in New Mexico for just over a year," Hartford began. "Who have you harmed?"

"This is my third high profile murder case in New Mexico, Chief," Signe reflected. "I have obviously impacted a lot of lives and some of those people were hurt."

"Janphen, Wanda, Anthony 'the quid', Bernadette and Vincent come to mind."

"That's it, Chief!" Signe ejaculated. "What if Vincent and Svelty had a relationship?"

"That is a fascinating idea that will be very hard to prove."

"Thanks for your help!" Signe replied as she jumped up and nearly sprinted out of the Chief's office.

Signe went to Valerie's laboratory and burst in upon an argon analysis of fingerprints using the department's new machine.

Without waiting to be acknowledged Signe said, "I need you to construct a time line from October 3rd of 2002 to January 2nd of 2003 and compare the locations of Svelty Patterson and Vincent Jaramillo."

"Okay," Valerie replied barely looking up.

Next, Signe sought out Jack who was working on a local Wells Fargo Bank robbery case.

"How's it going partner?" Jack asked in a cheerful voice.

"Some interesting things are starting to develop," Signe replied. "Did Svelty ever meet Vincent Jaramillo?"

"Wow! That is a very intriguing question," Jack responded. "Svelty collided with most folks."

"During the fall of 2002 did you ever see them together?"

"I don't believe so, Signe," Jack replied. "But they traveled in the same Albuquerque-Santa Fe axis during that time. Off the top of my head, I can also think of at least nine people who knew both of them. I'll go back and look through my handwritten notes."

Signe decided to call her friend, Lisa Gonzalez. She knew a lot about the players in Albuquerque during the fall of '02. Perhaps Lisa had seen Svelty and Vincent together. Lisa and Signe had worked together on the murder of Manny Ramirez. A crazed suspect had gotten loose in the Albuquerque Police Department and shot Lisa in the neck paralyzing her. She had gotten some motion back in her left arm while staying in a rehab hospital in Denver. Signe knew that Lisa was back in Albuquerque living with her mother. When she called, Lisa answered the phone.

"Hello, friend," Signe began. "How are you doing?"

"Good. I have some motion in my left arm and I can use it and my tongue to operate a computer. I'm doing data entry and statistics for the department. It helps keep my mind off my troubles."

"If I visit, can we go out to lunch?"

"Anytime. It takes hours to load me into my motorized wheelchair and I only fit in a few restaurants. "

"Can you help me with a quandary?"

"After all the help you gave me with cases? Of course."

"Do you remember the lady, Svelty Patterson that you and I visited one day at the Rehabilitation Hospital of New Mexico?"

"How could I forget? She had amazingly beautiful green eyes."

"She is stalking me now, and I don't know why. I was wondering if you ever saw her in Albuquerque with Vincent Jaramillo that handsome young State Police officer?"

"Your boyfriend?"

"Yes."

"After the visit to the hospital I saw the lady every day at Mr. Patterson's trial. Later, I saw her once with a big group of people one night at Garduño's. I was surprised to see her, but I did not pay a lot of attention to the group. I was with Hector Guaderama, a fellow officer who has an eidetic memory. I can ask him if you send me a picture of Vincent."

"I'll do it. Thanks for the help," Signe replied.

"I remember walking into that awful rehab hospital with you that winter morning and praying to the Virgin Mary. I asked her to shield me from places like that for my whole life. She didn't answer my prayer."

"No, she didn't, friend," Signe replied sadly. "I'll visit soon."

Signe was depressed after talking to her young friend. She called Jefferson Barclay and invited him to lunch. He suggested the Anasazi Inn. The two walked north from the La Fonda Hotel to the restaurant. Signe had never been there, but liked the stacked sandstone and petroglyphs painted on the walls. It reminded her of trips to Chaco Canyon she had made with her son, Axel. Jefferson had the buffalo burger and Signe had the grilled, basil-marinated moonfish with green chile risotto. As she ate, Signe felt her spirits lift.

"I want to play a game of character association with you," Signe said as they lingered over a last glass of chardonnay.

"You don't play games, my dear," Jefferson replied.

Ignoring the crack, Signe said, "Svelty Patterson and Vincent Jaramillo."

"Both play or played the edge. Both were attractive people that used others for their own ends."

"Did you ever see them together?"

"Yes."

"Where?"

"They were both at Dirk Patterson's murder trial over the death of that unfortunate young woman, Sharon something."

"Do you think they had a relationship?"

"I don't know, but they sat next to each other in about the fourth row of the gallery on the last day of the trial. If I recollect, you weren't there that day."

"You are correct. Did they speak or touch each other?"

"As you know, Vincent was very touchy. I remember him putting a hand on her shoulder."

"Are you saying you think they had a relationship outside the courtroom?" Signe asked urgently.

"I told you, you don't play games, Signe," Jefferson remarked in an exasperated tone. "The answer is I'm not sure."

"Did you ever see them anywhere else together or did anyone tell you they saw them together?"

"No."

"I am sorry to be so pushy, Jefferson," Signe said in a soft voice. "I guess being stalked is bothering me more than I'm letting on."

Signe paid for lunch and they walked companionably back to the hotel arm in arm. When she got back to the department Signe went to the lab.

"I have your time line for you, Detective," Valerie said as Signe walked in.

"That was fast."

"It went quickly because for several weeks Svelty was in a coma and then in the rehab hospital until December 20th," Valerie replied. "Next I considered all the times Vincent was in Albuquerque using his State Police log. He was in Albuquerque for a weekend after the State Fair in October and then January 16th and 17th for Dirk's trial."

"That is when Jefferson saw him sitting with Svelty at the courthouse," Signe replied.

"Did they know each other?" Valerie replied.

"Not necessarily. They may have just been sitting together by accident," Signe replied. "It could be nothing more than propinquity."

"Has anyone besides Jefferson seen them together?" Valerie asked.

"Jack is checking his notes and Lisa saw Svelty at Garduno's but isn't sure if Vincent was there."

"I'm betting they knew each other and had a relationship," Valerie said with authority.

CHAPTER 20

Signe had a quiet dinner alone at The Coyote Café. She didn't often get to do that. It gave her time to enjoy the food and think. She ordered the rotisserie pheasant with a huitlacoche (a wild-mushroom fungus that grows on sweet corn) crepe and truffle whipped cream. While her taste buds were tingling in anticipation, she reminisced about her visit to New Orleans and all the great new food she got to experience. The only distracting part was her drunken guide, Tanya.

Signe went home and called Brian. When he called back, they had a long pleasant conversation. Brian thanked her for the short but wonderful time at Bishop's Lodge. He offered to pay her back with a shopping spree in Las Vegas. Signe did not care for gambling but she did like to shop. Brian said the gulfstream would pick up at eight a.m. the next morning. Signe curled up on the sofa by her Matisse and read for a couple of hours before going to sleep.

Signe got to the Santa Fe Airport a little early and was greeted by Brian's copilot once the gleaming white Gulfstream came to a stop. He helped Signe aboard and sat her across from Brian who was on his cell phone. Once airborne the pilot came on the intercom and said the flight would take just an hour. Signe knew the distance was exactly six hundred miles. Once Brian was off the phone, they cuddled on the sofa. He gave Signe some brochures for shopping delights in Vegas. After they landed, Brian had the limo take them to the fountains by the shops at Caesar's Palace. He took her first to Harry Winton's to look at jewelry. Signe picked a simple four-carat emerald solitaire. She picked out dresses and skirts at Dolce and Gabbana and then moved on to Jimmy Choo's for one of her favorite items-shoes. Brian knew that that stop would take a couple of hours so he walked down to Casa Fuentes for a cigar and an espresso. He told Signe he enjoyed the Cuban influenced interior, skipping the part about the young attendants and there long white nearly see through dresses.

Signe bought twenty pairs of shoes. Brian took her up a level to Il Mulino of New York for lunch. They shared a buffalo mozzarella with tomato and fresh basil antipasto followed by fettuccine ragout pasta. Then after a rest, spezzatino di pollo alla romano a mélange of chicken, artichoke, asparagus and mushrooms. They drank a bottle of Far Niente chardonnay. After lunch, Brian had the limo driver take them to La Perla for some exotic lingerie picked from their black label collection. Brian picked some black vellus thongs with a patch of beige lace angling up along the left edge and a sheer stecche brief with to small oval cut outs in a line below the navel. He also picked a pizzo triangular bra of tulle that set of Signe's small breasts. Signe grabbed the lingerie in one hand and took Brian's hand with her other and led him to the commodious dressing room where she removed all her clothing slowly and modeled every item for him between kisses and caresses. They spent the rest of the afternoon at the Ghost Bar with the glass floor at the top of the Palms Hotel.

Reluctantly, Brian drove Signe to McCarran airport. He was flying to Anchorage and would take the Gulfstream for his long flight. Signe would take a quick hop back to Santa Fe on America West. Signe was shipping home all of her purchases from the day so was only carrying a small Louis Vuitton bag. She got in the short line at the check in counter, picked up her boarding pass, and hurried to security where the line of departing travelers seemed to stretch for miles. After thirty minutes, she seemed no closer to the metal detectors, and her departure time was only twenty-eight minutes away. She tapped her foot and fidgeted, but there wasn't anything else to do. Finally, some shambling TSA workers opened two more stations and the line advanced perceptibly.

Once through security Signe walked as quickly as she could toward the B concourse gates. She cut between two rows of slot machines blinking and chirping but without any suckers pouring good money after bad. Signe was just beginning to have hope that she would make her flight after all when a strong arm around her waist stopped her in her tracks. She felt the needle in her neck just before her muscles went limp. A man and a woman supporting her on both sides walked her toward the exit and put her in the back seat of a Lincoln town car. They drove out of the airport and stopped to the north where dusty wasteland waited for the next spurt of condominium growth and stuffed Signe into the trunk. Signe thought they drove for the better part of an hour with few stops. She listened for sounds but either there were none or the insulated trunk of the sedan muffled them. Signe had a superb sense of direction even with no clues and she thought they were heading west into the desert and mountains.

The car made a sudden stop and the trunk popped open. She was half dragged half-carried into a sprawling abandoned abode and duct taped to a straight-backed wooden chair. The abductress stayed out of sight but the man was heavy set and tanned, with oily hair. He had a tattoo of the Virgin Mary on his forearm with the letter CNG underneath that Mateo had described. Signe expected a barrage of questions but neither of her kidnappers said a word. She was given a drink of warm beer poured too fast so rivulets ran down her chin, and then she was left alone.

Signe slept fitfully in her uncomfortable, sitting position. When she awoke, every muscle ached and her hands were numb. She realized that she had compartmented her life into two separate boxes. She had a workbox where she studied her crime and took reasonable precautions for her and her partner's safety. She had a play box in

Paris, Phoenix, and Phuket where she went with Brain and was oblivious to safety measures. If she got out of her current situation, she realized she would have to dissolve that dichotomy. The intense desert sun shinning in her face through a dirty, broken window awakened her for good. She listened for sounds from other inhabitants but detected none.

Sitting, tantalizingly, on a table fifteen feet from her were a switchblade, a cell phone and more bottles of beer. Signe was sure Svelty was behind this abduction. First, she had robbed Signe's apartment, then she kidnapped her associate, Mateo Romero. As she started scooch her chair across the floor, she noticed that several five and six foot long western diamondback rattlesnakes were in the room. She knew they had poor eyesight but the pits in front of their eyes sensed heat from the body of a warm-blooded mammal. Waiting until after dark to move would not help protect her and she had no method to raise the heat of an area around her that would distract the snakes. She decided to take her chances and move across the floor as quickly as possible. When she reached the table, she stood with her back to it and picked up the switchblade. She opened the blade and cut the duct tape binding her hands then climbed up on the chair and activated the cell phone. It flashed 'no service.' She popped the top off a beer and drank it thirstily. Then by alternately advancing the table and the chair, she navigated through the snakes and made it to the door.

She began walking down hill from the adobe carrying the cell phone, switchblade and two warm bottles of beer. It was barely seven a.m. she guessed but the sun was already intensely hot with heat waves obscuring the city far to the east. She disciplined herself to walk fifteen hundred steps, which should have been about a mile before she checked for service. Six miles and two beers later she had one bar of service, but could not make a call. Signe decided Svelty's only goal was to torment her, not maim or kill her as she trudged on hot and tired. Why was her sociopath by proxy so bent on tormenting her? Signe came across a gas station that raised her hope when she first saw it in the desert haze. She considered the possibility of a mirage until she got close enough to realize it was real, but abandoned. It was an antiquated station as evidenced by its rounded white sign in front that consisted of a red star with Texaco written across the top. She broke in hopes of finding a functioning faucet or bottles of water or soda. Unfortunately, nothing potable was there.

As she trudged on to the east, she realized that she was getting into serious trouble because of dehydration. She recited the rules of three to herself. Death in three minutes without air, death in three hours without warmth, death in three days without water and death in three months without food. None seemed to apply exactly to her situation. If there had been any cover, she would have lain low in the shade and traveled at night. The old service station might have served if the roof hadn't collapsed.

She walked now with a listless gate. She stopped to make a sign on the ground that could be seen from the air. She picked SOS because it had fewer letters than HELP. Then above the O she scraped an arrow with her foot pointing in the direction she planned to travel. She stumbled along for several more hours realizing that she was getting more dehydrated and weaker. About seven p.m., as the sun was sinking, she sat down in the dirt. Then she heard the distant 'thwack, thwack' of a helicopter. It approached and she stood up and waved frantically. The machine dipped when the pilot spotted her and landed eighty feet away. The copilot offered cold bottled water before he started walking her to the chopper.

When the helicopter landed at the airport, Jack rushed out and gave Signe a big hug.

"I'm so glad you are safe!" Jack said not letting go of his partner.

"How did you find me?"

"Brian tipped us off last night when you didn't arrive in Santa Fe on time," Jack replied. "That gave us a leg up. The airport security tapes showed Svelty and a burly man spiriting you out of McCarran. We started searching at midnight."

PART 3

CHAPTER 21

Jack took Signe to P. F. Chang's for a quick supper. She drank three pots of tea between bites of food. Then he guided her to a room upstairs and tucked her in after she had talked with Brian.

In the morning, Signe filed a detailed report of her abduction with the Las Vegas Police Department, before heading back to the airport. The bored detectives barely listened to her answers. Signe was sure that they wouldn't really investigate Svelty's crime or search for her. That would be her job. She and Jack got on a nearly empty America West flight to Santa Fe. Signe had three seats to herself so she stretched out and slept. When they got off the plane, Jack suggested she take the rest of the day off, however her mind was racing and she knew she would be bored at her apartment. Signe checked her messy desk first for any important messages and then went into the lab for some help in tracking Svelty Patterson.

"If you had known how much trouble she was going to be, you could have put a chip in the bitch when she was in that coma," Valerie said irreverently.

"Dr. Goldiamond says that with her affliction she is likely to return to old haunts," Signe replied. "So put out an APB on her for the whole state with a special focus on Albuquerque. She also spent time in Oklahoma and Sicily."

"Will do," Valerie replied.

Signe went to check on her request for a review of Larry's autopsy.

Chief Hartford was in his office. Signe barged in without even knocking. When he got off the phone he turned to Signe and said, "That was Dr. Tamwalt. He says that your victim died from shock caused by blood loss from a ruptured spleen. He also had an overdose of ketamine. The blood loss may have caused an inferior wall myocardial infarction, whatever that is. The radioactive isotopes, especially the polonium, were just a red herring."

"That's more like it," Signe chortled.

"He also sent a full report to Liam Farrell of the FBI."

"Great. They will be all over me *lige flyver oven på honning* or as you say like flies on honey."

"I can only protect you from them a little, Signe, but I will try."

"Thanks, Chief," Signe said as she walked toward her own desk.

Signe thought she would probably only has the rest of the day to investigate without the meddling of the FBI. She called Jack and Pushpa to warn them of what would be happening. Talking about the autopsy reminded her of the titanium lozenge that Bernadette had slipped her. She took it to Valerie for processing under the same bogus number the CSI had assigned to the whole case. Then she called the Santa Fe Institute and set up a conference with Klaus Obermeyer. The Institute occupied a nondescript series of faux abode buildings in the hills above Santa Fe. Dr. Obermeyer was working on a large molecular model when Signe walked into his office.

"I'm Detective Signe Sorensen," she said in Danish as she stretched out a hand in greeting.

"My pleasure," Dr. Obermeyer replied in Danish as he took her hand and kissed it.

"First, how did a Dane like you get such a German name?"

"My family lived on the border between Denmark and Germany where there was a lot of intermixing."

Signe sat down and explained her case in detail. She emphasized the ways in which she thought Poland might be involved in the murder.

"I know you are an expert on east European nuclear policy and might be able to give me some insight," Signe suggested.

"Did you know that Poland has been a member of NATO since nineteen hundred and ninety-seven and that Poland will join the European Union in two thousand and four?"

"Actually I just learned that from Father Edward in the Archbishop's Office," Signe replied.

"Poland has been a route for armies from the east and the west for at least two thousand years. It is a flat country that separates a hostile power in the east from a hostile power in the west. Armies have marched back and forth across Poland innumerable times. Supposedly, the peaceful Polish people are now protected by the west's nuclear umbrella. However, most Poles are too realistic to think that the western countries would rain nuclear death down on the Russians to protect Poland's borders. Many citizens were alive during the second world War when death and destruction ravaged their country for six years first at the hands of the Nazi blitzkrieg and then under the oppressive and inhuman communists. I'm sure Father Edward told you that there are dissident generals from the Communist era that are still not rehabilitated."

"Do you believe that those generals are well enough organized to try and obtain hydrogen bombs for their own uses, Dr. Obermeyer?" Signe asked.

For several minutes Klaus Obermeyer said nothing and then, "Please call me Klaus."

"Could those unreconstructed generals have blackmailed my murder victim for secrets they could use to advance their cause?" Signe asked approaching her concern from another angle.

"I'm afraid that what you are suggesting is entirely possible," Klaus said as he stroked his chin. "Currently I am studying nuclear policy in Rumania and Bulgaria. The CIA allows me a little time on their geosynchronous spy satellites each week. I can have them reprogram one to concentrate on Southwest Poland and see if there is increased activity among the dissident generals."

"Thanks for your help, Klaus," Signe said as she rose to leave.

"*Faddens!* It's nothing Obermeyer replied.

Signe met her friend Terecita Armijo for supper. Terecita told Signe about her sessions with Dr. Goldiamond. Vivian was requiring Terecita to do three activities, not related to her judgeship, away from her house every week. Signe talked about her shopping spree in Las Vegas and then made her kidnapping into a long funny story.

At one point she said, "I found myself restrained in this small room with six or seven diamond back rattlesnakes as thick as my thighs. I couldn't resist thinking what an elegant set of shoes and a purse they would make."

"My heart would have stopped," Terecita replied. "I'm deathly afraid of snakes!"

"It makes a lot of sense to have that fear, Terry. Mammals evolved at a time when there were a lot more reptiles than our warm blooded cousins. So getting bitten then by a venomous creature was a very real danger," Signe replied. "I guess I didn't get the gene."

After a nightcap, Terecita drove Signe home.

In the morning, Signe sat down with Jack to plan their strategy for catching Svelty Patterson.

"Svelty usually lays a trap and we fall into it," Jack began. "Like that ambush at Otowi crossing."

"That wasn't Svelty," Signe remarked. "Remember that was that hard-scrabble rancher from Wagon Mound."

"That was a long time ago, but you are right."

"It may have been planned by Svelty. The fake road work slowed us down in an exposed place just before those strips on the road punctured our tires. Remember?"

"I sure do. My shoulder still aches when it rains where I got shot."

"Svelty was the one who shot at us from the abandoned drive in Santa Fe. She also tricked me into stopping one rainy night on I-25. She also engineered the snake infested kidnapping in Las Vegas."

"It seems like she is always laying in wait to ambush us. We need to turn the tables on her and lure her into a trap," Jack suggested."

"To do that we would need to know more about her habits. She stayed in Albuquerque for two nights according to Mateo. Otherwise we don't know where her headquarters are."

I'll put out another APB for New Mexico, Arizona and Nevada listing her as a kidnapper."

"I will call that Inspector Erice in Taormina and see if she is spending time in Sicily any more."

Signe went to the Chief's office and put in the call. Luckily, Inspector Erice was in the police station.

"Buon giorno, Inspectore," Erice began in Italian and then switched to English.

"I spoke with you a few months ago about an American citizen named Svelty Patterson. You discovered she had an apartment in Taormino and was using a small internet café. Now she has committed a kidnapping and we are looking for her even more earnestly."

"I can walk over to her apartment, Senora and now that she is accused of kidnapping I can search the premises."

"Thank you, so very much. I will call you back in an hour."
Arrivederci."

Signe went into the lab to kill some time before waiting for her call back from Sicily. Valerie was cataloguing some papers she had found in Larry's books.

"This is a detailed catalog of all of your victim's assignations," Valerie remarked. "I found it in a hollowed out book entitled, *An Atlas of Astrophysics*. It lists the location of the tryst, what positions his partners like and even how many times they came! He must have been a very thoughtful lover."

"What about their names?"

"It lists everyone."

"Even though the info is old, see if you can track any of them down," Signe replied.

Signe went back to the Chief's office and dialed Inspector Erice impatiently.

"We have found, how you say? A gold mine Detective," Erice said in English with a heavy Italian accent. "We have the detailed plans of your kidnapping. Better yet there is a meeting between your suspect and someone coming up."

"Do you know where and when?"

"Yes. It is at a place called Mesa Verde Park at 1 p.m. tomorrow."

"If you find anything else please call me," Signe said as she hung up the phone.

CHAPTER 22

Signe sent a patrolman out for some burritos so she could talk with the officers over lunch about plans to intercept Svelty the next day. She had found a stand on the plaza that made a burrito of a crispy fried chile relleno with a warm white cheese center wrapped in a soft flour tortilla. Signe's mouth was watering already just imagining the smell and taste of the burrito. While she waited she called Jack and Chief Hartford into Valerie's lab and all four sat down at a table that Valerie had cleared.

"We have been given a great lead by the Polizia Siciliana," Signe began. "They just searched Svelty's apartment in Taormina and discovered detailed plans for the Las Vegas kidnapping right down to colored pictures of the diamond backed rattlesnakes. Even better, we have some information about a meeting she is planning for tomorrow at Mesa Verde. This is our best chance to catch her."

"Do we know the precise location of the meeting?" Chief Hartford asked.

"No we don't," Signe replied. "And we don't know who she is meeting either, but it is still our best chance to capture the felon."

"I agree," Hartford replied. "Since Mesa Verde is a national park in Colorado, I will get permission both from the feds and the state for us to be in their jurisdiction."

"I would like to take some extra men also, Chief," Signe replied hopefully.

"Of course. How about four men dressed as tourists?" Hartford queried as he got up to call the authorities.

"That would be perfect," Signe replied.

Turning back to Jack and Valerie, Signe said, "I think the three of us should go up this afternoon and study the location."

"I haven't been there in years, but it's a big park. Seven people won't give us many options," Jack offered.

Signe was just ready to leave the building when she got a call on her cell. Thinking it was Jack or Valerie she answered. It was Liam Farrell of the FBI.

"We are on the way over to see you," Liam said. "We'll be there in eight minutes."

"I'm sorry, but I'm just leaving for a stakeout that is two hundred miles away," Signe replied. "I just can't meet this afternoon."

"Regional Director Blanche Baca C de Baca, from San Francisco, is with me and you don't have the option of turning down our visit."

"Any other time, Farrell," Signe replied. "I will even go to San Francisco, but I can't meet this afternoon or I might lose a dangerous felon."

"We are pulling up to your door right now," Farrell answered. "Do you remember the first time we met? Am I going to have to pull my weapon on you again?"

Signe briefly considered running out the back door before realizing that she was trapped. She went to the conference room to take her medicine. Liam swept in with two of his underlings in cheap, narrow-lapelled black suits. Director Baca C de Baca was a stylish Hispanic woman with a good figure who seemed young for a director. Signe thought she must have been lucky enough to be accidentally assigned to a big case, like a spy case, as a young agent. And that the case had gone so well that she rode its coattails up the promotion ladder. Either that or perhaps she had slept her way to the top.

"I understand you knew the victim, Dr. Larry Abramowitz, Detective Stevenson," Director Baca C de Baca said.

Signe knew that most of the native population of New Mexico came from twelve or so families that migrated north with Coronado. Therefore, names like Martinez, Gonzalez and Garcia were very common in Santa Fe. Since 'baca' meant cattle in Spanish she found Baca C de Baca the strangest of the lot. Why would anyone's name be cattle of the cattle?

"The name is Detective Sorensen," Signe replied trying not to bristle. "And yes I knew the victim."

"Did he die of natural causes?" Director Baca C de Baca inquired.

"He certainly had a list of findings at autopsy that could be deadly either alone or in combination," Signe observed blandly.

"What about the high level of that ketamine, the drug the Russians use, in his system?" the Director asked.

"It could be used as an anesthetic, but it is also used recreationally," Signe replied. "Perhaps he was just out in the wilderness bird watching and getting high."

"So you don't think he was murdered?" the Director inquired point blank.

"Your well-trained agents spent a lot more time in Valle Grande than I did, Madame Director," Signe replied. "And Agent Farrell told me that Larry died of natural causes."

"Is there anything about this case that you aren't telling me?" Director De Baca asked.

'I'm sure there is, Madame Director," Signe replied. "I just can't think what it would be at this time."

"We will be in touch," the Director said abruptly as she stood up to leave.

Signe felt lucky that she didn't have to lie anymore than she already had. As soon as Blanche was out the door, Signe raced to her apartment and packed for her trip to Mesa Verde. Jack and Valerie arrived forty-five minutes later in a department Suburban loaded with camping gear. Jack drove the two hundred and five miles to Farmington along highway US 550 without stopping. They stopped at a family run Mexican restaurant for supper and then drove north into Colorado turning west at Durango. They turned into Mesa Verde National Park at 9 p.m., showing their badges at the gate. Jack and Valerie went to set up camp while Signe met with the park director. Signe learned that the park covered sixty-three square miles, but fortunately there was only one road in or out. The Director took out a map and suggested several places where two people might have an assignation.

"Some national magazines have picked Mesa Verde as one of the top fifty tourist attractions in the world," the Superintendent said. "We've had an uptick in visits since those articles were published."

Signe got a ride to the campground, crawled into her sleeping bag laid out by the first group of officers to arrive and quickly fell asleep. A small campfire burned a dark reddish purple in front of the two tents. She awoke at 5 a.m. to the smell of bacon cooking. Jack had made a fire and cooked breakfast for everyone. Valerie had a topographic map of the park laid out on the wooden picnic table. She had marked seven places and three alternates where she thought a meeting might occur. She explained her choices to Signe.

"I think Svelty will either opt for being totally alone for her meeting or in the most crowded area of the park which is obviously the cliff dwellings themselves," Valerie remarked.

"We are in extreme southern Colorado and the Superintendent says their summer season has begun," Signe remarked. "They have over nine hundred visitors a day and they peak around 1 p.m. I think she will opt for the crowd."

"We had better concentrate on the cliff dwellings themselves then," Valerie remarked.

"When will the other agents be here, Jack?" Signe asked impatiently.

"Two came last night. The others are leaving the station at five and Anthony is a fast driver," Jack remarked. "They'll be at the gate at ten and you can position them."

"Let's go look at our sites now that the sun is up," Signe suggested as she finished her breakfast and put away her utensils.

Jack drove them deeper into the park on a narrow two-lane road that twisted up and down several mesas. The countryside consisted of scattered ponderosa pine with a large area that had been burned by a forest fire. The cliff dwellings were in a south facing canyon deep in the park. Mateo said the all the Anasazi apartments of the ancient ones faced that way to benefit from the warmth of the sun in the winter. The rock was a soft golden red and the dwellings consisted of three or four stories of rooms built in the natural caves in the rocks. Signe and Valerie marked places on the maps where the officers could station themselves. When that was done they had some spare time and the Superintendent took them on a tour of a small cliff dwelling that wasn't open to the public. The road was rough and unimproved even for the green National Park vehicle they were in and Signe hung onto the ceiling straps as tight as she could. The rooms were small with smooth regular courses of sandstone separating one from another. The floors were littered with broken pieces of pottery with a red glaze and marked with black designs.

"This dwelling is from 1000 CE during the common era when we date the tree rings from the cedar post that hold up the mud floors," the Superintendent remarked. "You are welcome to handle everything in the rooms, just make sure it isn't transferred from one room to another. The Yale University archeology department is going to excavate and catalog this ruin later in the summer."

When they were finished, the four visitors went to the cafeteria for cups of tea and coffee. Everyone began talking at once about what they had seen in the one thousand year old dwellings. Jack was impressed by the agriculture practiced below the dwellings where corn, squash, chile and beans were grown in mixed fields. Valerie focused on the long polished wooden ladders that led to the dwellings and the foot holds that could only be ascended if the Indian began with the correct foot. Signe talked about the drought that apparently drove the Anasazi out of the southwest in the 1300s.

CHAPTER 23

The four officers arrived just after ten. Jack gave each officer an assigned location in the park after checking their radios to make sure they worked and handing each a picture of Svelty. Signe wanted all the officers in place by noon. The rangers had been monitoring the entrance station for signs of the kidnapper since 9 a.m., when they opened. Signe decided to station herself near the cliff dwellings hoping that Svelty's meeting would be there. At 11:45 a ranger reported that a woman matching Svelty's description had come through the entrance gate in a red Mustang convertible with Arizona plates. At least she isn't trying to be inconspicuous, Signe thought. Svelty passed two officers as she drove toward the inner part of the park. Signe thought that she was about five miles behind Svelty and her driver closed the distance as they went.

When Signe got to the visitors center, the ranger signaled that Svelty had purchased a ticket and headed down the steep trail to Cliff Palace. Signe walked down the trail quickly, collecting the other officers from their posts so they were walking with her. At the bottom, a narrow area where a small stream flowed separated the trail from the floor of the ruin. It was clogged with a large group of tourists jabbering in German. Signe cut through the group and walked into the extensive cave where dozens of buildings were mixed with three and four story towers. Two other groups of tourists with their guides were clustered in various parts of the cave. Signe didn't see Svelty. She worked her way into the back parts of the cave where it was darker. A few stray tourists were exploring the stone work and doorways. Signe fanned her men out to explore every dark corner of the ruin. After thirty minutes, most of the tourists had moved on and Signe had still not found Svelty.

The front of the cave was a rugged cliff rising several hundred feet above the canyon floor. A radio call revealed that Svelty had not gone back up the narrow steep trail to the visitor center. Signe searched all the buildings again and only found a small tan tarp that a person Svelty's size could have hidden under. Then Signe moved to the edge of the cave where she could survey a panorama of all of the buildings. She saw slight movement far to right and started to move in that direction. A woman walked to the edge of the cave as if planning to jump. Displaying her badge, Signe rushed quickly toward the person.

"Svelty Patterson, you are under arrest for abduction and kidnapping," Signe shouted as she walked quickly toward the woman.

"You have no proof of anything!" Svelty yelled back. "And you'll never catch me!"

As Signe and four officers approached she shouted, "I've got you, you bitch!"

When Detective Sorensen got within fifteen feet Svelty walked to the very edge of the cliff as if she were going to jump. At the last minute she grabbed a thin black rope that hung from the top of the cave. She gripped it with both hands, wrapped a leg around it and was pulled quickly up and out of the cave.

Signe nearly burst into tears of frustration. She sent her men racing up the trail to get on top of the bluff, but she knew Svelty would be long gone by then. She had seen a man with the group of German tourists that looked out of place. He was wearing a long overcoat too heavy for the season. Perhaps this was the man Svelty was meeting. They could have talked in the back of the cliff dwelling. Signe sent two of her men to check up on the large bus that held the German tour group. Once they got word that Svelty had escaped without a trace, Signe, Valerie, and Jack gathered up their camping gear and headed back to Santa Fe. On the long deserted stretch of road from Farmington to Santa Fe conversation turned back to their recent attempt to arrest Svelty.

"She is very single minded in her efforts to control any situation she is in," Valerie remarked.

"You sound like Dr. Goldiamond, Val," Signe mused. "Not bad for a girl that grew up in rural Oklahoma and started out as a stewardess. I'm very discouraged. This was our best chance to nail her. We had warning of the

time and place of her get together and she still outsmarted us and got away!"

"Don't be so hard on yourself, Signe," Jack replied. "The bad guys—Dirk, Richard, Jaramillo, and Janphen will make a mistake and you will get them."

When they got back to Santa Fe, Signe told Chief Hartford about her discouraging trip to Mesa Verde.

"I believe the man Svelty was going to meet, Chief, was a pale, overweight, man in an out of style overcoat," Signe remarked. "Perhaps Svelty is working for the Poles who I think killed Larry."

"At this point, I think that's a stretch, Signe," Chief Hartford replied. "But your hunches often turn out to be right."

Soon Signe was back on Svelty's trail. The red Mustang Svelty was driving was rented in Albuquerque. Signe called Mateo and told him what had happened at Mesa Verde and then she asked him to head back to Albuquerque and see if he could pick up Svelty's trail.

"She is very smart, Mateo, and absolutely treacherous so you must be very careful. I don't want you getting hurt."

"I had a little taste when she kidnapped me," Mateo replied. "I will keep my guard up."

Signe hadn't heard from Pushpa Chatterjee in a few days so she put in a call.

"I've put some more time in analyzing the things we found in Dr. Abramowitz's lab and I'm convinced he was working on the various things that I have previously discussed with you. I'm wondering if some nuclear wannabe didn't have him working on all four ideas. They might need compact nuclear power stations for energy needs, hard to trace isotope poisons to eliminate foes, plutonium triggers and small hydrogen bombs to be members of the exclusive nuclear club. It would be one stop shopping and much easier for a foreign power."

"That is a very clever suggestion," Signe replied. "I want you to make up a list of what countries you believe would be willing to pay for such a nuclear package and I will ask Dr. Obermeyer to do the same."

Once Signe was off the phone with Pushpa, she called the Santa Fe Institute and told Klaus what she would like from him. Then she invited her friend, Jefferson Barclay, to The Shed for some comfort food. Signe had the blue corn enchiladas with red chile sauce and extra cheese. With the first bite, strings of soft yellow cheese ran from the tortilla to the plate. Signe bit them off as the first bite of warm and hot chile entered her mouth. She felt better instantly. Then Signe told Jefferson in detail about the debacle at Mesa Verde.

Back at the station house, she telephoned everyone she knew who was acquainted with Svelty. No one had any good ideas about locating her except Sven Torvaldson the insurance agent who had paid Svelty's husband's life insurance policy. He had overheard her say that she might buy some property in Edgewood twenty-three miles to the east of the Sandia Mountains. Signe sent two officers with pictures of Svelty to show to residents of the small houses scattered in the sparse vegetation there.

Signe spent a quiet evening at home finishing Phillipa Gregory's *The Other Boleyn Girl*. She was again impressed by the plotting and scheming that filled the English court in the 1600s. After she got in bed she talked to Brian for a long time on the phone. He was still worried about Signe's kidnapping in Las Vegas. His only brother, Phillip, the scion of family, had been kidnapped in New Jersey and was never found. Signe described all the measures that were being taken to insure her protection, however, Brian wasn't reassured. She slept well and got to the station early with a list of things to do.

The next day at the office, Signe called Father Edward at the Archdiocesan office and he gave her the names of four Soviet-era Polish Generals that were still operating in Southwest Poland. She called Pushpa for her list of countries that might need Larry's expertise. She came up with North Korea,

Afghanistan, Lebanon, Iran and Poland. As a caveat she also said that geopolitics wasn't her area of expertise. When she called Klaus he rattled off his list which was Rumania, Bulgaria, Poland, North Korea and Chechnya. Signe noted that the two lists had only two countries in common. Signe called her former mentor, Thor Nielsen, in Denmark. He listened to both lists carefully. He thought that most of the rogue countries with the financial means to support a nuclear program were mentioned. His only additions were Al Qaeda, and the Basque separatists in northern Spain.

Signe had her men collect the Kevlar rope Svelty used to escape from Mesa Verde. She also had her men dust her rented mustang for prints and look for other telltale clues. Signe went to the lab to see what Valerie had found.

"No surprises," Valerie said. "All the prints on the car were Svelty's and she didn't leave any personal items except this."

Valerie handed Signe a fifteen inch tall action doll, dressed in black leather, with a pistol holstered on one hip and a coiled black leather whip on the other.

CHAPTER 24

Signe had a message on her desk to call Dr. Pieter van der Waals. She hadn't learned much from him during a long dinner, even though he said he was Larry's closest friend. However, she hadn't been pushy either. She didn't want to spook a potentially invaluable source. Pieter suggested lunch at a misnamed Italian restaurant called O. Henry's in White Rock. Signe said she would be there in an hour. When she arrived Dr. Van der Waals was nervously sipping a Peroni beer. He rose as Signe approached his table covered with a red and white checked vinyl table cloth.

"Detective Sorensen, Thank you for coming so quickly," Pieter said.

"You are an important resource in this investigation, Dr. Van der Waals," Signe replied.

"Was my dear friend murdered?" Pieter answered.

"The FBI avers that he was not, but I can assure you he was," Signe replied in an authoritative voice.

"How terrible," Van der Waals replied with terror in his voice. "Do you think I could be next?"

"I don't honestly know," Signe replied after a pause. "Were you both working on the same projects?"

"Yes and no. I never worked on the small hydrogen bomb that Larry was so fascinated by, but we had other projects in common."

"Just to make this easier, let me tell you what I have discovered about your friend's projects. In addition to the small H bomb, he was working on a small computer controlled nuclear reactor to power small cities, he was working on exotic isotopes that could be used as poisons and he was buildings PITs."

"To my everlasting shame I did some of that work with him," Pieter replied dejectedly. "Now I may die for it."

"You must tell me everything and I will try and protect you," Signe replied.

"Larry and I went on weekend trysts together for years," Pieter began. "We would go to Palm Springs, Las Vegas or Los Angeles and spend the weekend with call girls. At first, it was expensive but bearable, but then as our families grew the cost became prohibitive. We started going less often, but we both missed the trips. We felt we did intellectually challenging work and needed the soothing recreational sex to decompress. After about a year, Larry came up with a plan to generate extra money. At first we did little jobs we weren't assigned to do at the lab. In exchange Larry got wads of used fifty dollar bills."

"How did you know what to fabricate?" Signe asked.

"Larry gave me verbal instructions if it was a simple project. If it was more complicated he drew plans for me. We have worked together for decades. Then when the projects got more complicated Larry built a clandestine lab where we could build the components. It started out as a small facility but as the time went on it grew into a large, very sophisticated laboratory. I was afraid to tell you about it, but I will show it to you this afternoon."

"We found it when we searched Larry's house," Signe replied. "It is one of the reasons I feel my friend was murdered. Clearly, from the size of the lab he was doing a lot of covert work."

Dr. Van der Waals looked surprised and then said, "I wish I had told you about that glorious lab when we first talked."

"It's too late for that now. Are there any other secrets you need to tell me?"

"I don't think so. Larry negotiated all the projects and collected all the moneys. I simply helped with the work."

"For which you were richly rewarded."

"Yes last year I made $900,000 tax free dollars which was eight times my regular salary."

"Who was paying you?"

"I really don't know."

"You must have had suspicions."

"I did and do. But Larry encouraged me not to ask too many questions."

"You must have known that you were using your expertise to aid a country or terrorist group that was inimical to America."

"What you say is true and it is to my everlasting shame. I will never forgive myself for that."

"You must give me all of your records so that I can track down Larry's killers."

"I will start assembling the information as soon as we finish lunch," Pieter said.

Signe drove back down to Santa Fe and went to the stationhouse. A drug rep that Signe had met when she visited The Big Easy had let it slip that Katarzyna, Larry's youngest daughter, had a secret. Jennifer said that Katarzyna was deeply involved with an Arab terrorist group at Tulane. Arthur Bienville, a FBI agent in New Orleans, had been asked to look into Larry's youngest daughter's secret.

"Thanks for helping me with this murder investigation, Art," Signe said once she had identified herself.

"We've been surveilling this group for the past two year anyway," Bienville answered. "I'm glad to help."

"My murder victim, Katarzyna's father, was a theoretical physicist at the Los Alamos National Laboratory," Signe began. "For the last several years he was making clandestine nuclear devices that could be used for assassination or detonation. Some foreign entity was bankrolling this effort. When she was growing up, his daughter carried messages to his handlers. Perhaps she is still involved."

"The local group calls itself the Palestine Islamic Jihad and they have been active among foreign students at Tulane for the past nine years or so. They predate 9/11. They were pretty quiet through the late nineties with fifteen to twenty-five or members. They held rallies and raised money that they sent back to Palestine. After 9/11 their membership quadrupled. They got very aggressive about fund raising from local companies. They asked for money very politely, but the underlying message was that if the corporations didn't contribute their trucks and ships might be sabotaged. The PIJ's coffers swelled to several million dollars."

"So they did have the funds to support some sophisticated research," Signe remarked.

"Yes. And they are still raising a lot of money."

"Can you follow the disbursement of the funds?"

"That is the hard part. They send the money by wire transfer to a parent organization in New York. We know it is converted into cash there. The first part of the transfer is out in the open and legitimate. Then bundles of small unmarked bills are distributed from the city. We have trouble following the cash from there because it travels by private courier."

"If I can establish when Dr. Abramowitz got paid, perhaps we can match a similar amount going to New York a few days before that."

"That might work," Bienville replied.

"I'll call you back when I have something," Signe said before hanging up the phone.

When she finished her call it was six-thirty in the evening and Signe invited Jack to supper. First she suggested a walk around the north side of Santa Fe. Signe had inherited a love of plants from her mother and she wanted to check the local gardens for signs of blooms. At seventy-two hundred feet Santa Fe had a late spring. She had hoped to see roses and hollyhocks in bloom but as she peered into back yards she realized it was too early. She had read that the average last frost at that altitude was May 1st just nineteen days ago. She did see lots of blooming crocuses, daffodils and few early roses. Their bright, solid colors lifted her spirits.

Jack and Signe ended their walk at the Coyote Café, Signe's favorite restaurant. After drinks they shared a calamari appetizer and both had large walnut and blue cheese salads followed by pecan crusted New York steak with a fig-green chile mole sauce. While they were eating Signe asked Jack about his girlfriend.

"How's Rhonda?"

"She is a lot of fun, especially in the sack."

"You've been dating her for months now. That isn't like you."

"Yeah. I think she's the longest relationship I've ever had."

"You'd better watch out. You could propose during a weak moment of post coital bliss."

"She's been hinting around, but I'm always careful to run a hand up the inside of her thigh or change the subject."

"I get the feeling she really cares about you. You could do worse."

"I know," Jack replied as the liquor started to talk. "It's just that I'm looking for someone more like you who is intelligent, elegant and sexy."

"You know that I love you, Jack."

"Yes, I do. But you don't love me quite the way that I love you."

Signe leaned over and kissed Jack's neck just below the angle of his jaw.

They walked arm in arm to the Eldorado Hotel and had a nightcap in the lobby bar. Signe knew that Jack loved her. They had even talked about getting together several months ago, but Signe had tried having a relationship once with a coworker and it had turned out badly. She had reluctantly said she would try dating him but only if he quit his job and went to work for the State Police or some other entity. She also pointed out that she was a workaholic and that they would see less of each other than they currently did as partners. Her previous lover had gotten shot in a drug bust trying to protect her. He was married and left four small children without a father. Signe still thought about Hans regularly and didn't want to repeat her thoughtless mistake.

Jack drove Signe home to her apartment. She spent an hour in front of her Matisse studying it before she went to bed. She still liked the Monet that Svelty had stolen better, but she now appreciated the woman with the apple green nose in the painting.

CHAPTER 25

In the morning Signe was still irate about her stolen Monet. When she first got to the station, she started by calling all of her contacts and asking each one if they had any leads on the whereabouts of Svelty Patterson. No one had seen her since her well-planned escape at Mesa Verde. Dr. Goldiamond was convinced that Svelty's personality would drive her back to the places she already knew. Santa Fe, and especially Albuquerque, were two of them. Mateo Romero had been operating on his own for several days. Signe decided to call him in so they could talk. She reached him by phone and he agreed to be in Santa Fe in an hour.

While she waited, Signe visited Valerie in the lab. She explained to the CSI the money raised by Palestine Islamic Jihad in New Orleans and how it was getting lost in New York.

"Our chances of catching one of these couriers and then getting him to tell us where they are actually taking the money are small," Signe began. "But Agent Bienville and I are hoping we can match an amount of money coming into New York with a payment to Larry. Have you found any record of the money he was receiving? Dr. Van der Waals finally came clean with me and he says that he got $800,000 dollars last year through Larry for his covert work."

"Unfortunately, not," Valerie replied. "But I have a box of journals that I haven't even started looking at."

Valerie went to the corner of the lab and found a dusty brown box and wrestled it up onto the lab table. Both women unfolded the flaps and pulled out a volume. Most of Signe's book contained equations. Valerie's book seemed more like a journal although no dollar amounts were obvious on a quick perusal.

"I start looking at these systematically and put an outline on the computer," Valerie said.

Signe went to look for her sidekick, Mateo Romero. Her assistant was just coming through the door. Despite his short stature and broad girth he always moved with energy. His long gray hair was pulled back and braided. Signe recalled that when he was found in the back of the Tyuonyi ruins at two in the morning his hair was still in perfect place.

"Mateo," Signe called out as she walked toward her sidekick.

"Yah-te-hey," Mateo replied.

"Quit messing with me, pard. That's a Navajo greeting," Signe replied. "You've been teaching me Keresan and there is no such word."

"You're a good student."

"Thanks. I haven't been spending much time with you."

"I'm like a young elk. I learn from the bull elk and then go off and practice it. However, stalking Svelty Patterson in Albuquerque has been a frustrating trial. I've been to all her usual haunts: the Rio Grande House, the Albuquerque Shootists meeting, where she learned marksmanship and her favorite spa at Tamaya. She's not appearing at any of the usual places. I wonder if she has moved on."

"Well, we know she was in southwestern Colorado two days ago. I doubt she flew out of that under populated area. Perhaps you should check the flights out of Albuquerque, Phoenix and Denver. I suspect she is somewhere nearby. For one thing she can only hector me if she stays nearby."

"I can check the airlines. Perhaps you need to check with that Sicilian Inspector again. He sure gave you a solid clue about Mesa Verde."

"Didn't he though? And we still didn't capitalize on it!" Signe said vehemently.

"They always fall into your clutches, Detective," Mateo replied.

"In the meantime, let's she if we can track her electronically," Signe said as she walked toward the laboratory. "Valerie has the quickest computer in the department."

Once in the lab, Signe sat down in front of the computer console and entered Svelty's name. A blue page appeared full of data on the suspect. In addition to her social security number, every bank account, loan and credit card number she had ever held appeared.

"Let's look at any credit card or ATM activity on her active accounts occurring during her past week," Signe suggested.

Both saw a $1000 cash withdrawal from an ATM in Durango on May 19th and a credit card charge for gas in Cuba, New Mexico for $53.46.

"I believe those transactions tell us that she is back in Santa Fe or Albuquerque," Signe replied. "I'll have the Albuquerque Police put out an APB on her."

"I respect your methods, Detective," Mateo remarked. "But Indian ways are often superior when looking for a lost person. Ernesto Chavez is a tracker from our Pueblo. When Cochiti children or livestock disappear from the Pueblo he can always find them. I would like him to help me find Svelty."

"That would be great," Signe answered.

"I will need a personal item of hers."

"Svelty was found in a coma from an overdose last November and I'm sure we still have her clothing."

"I thought that crime occurred in Albuquerque and you and Jack were just helping Lieutenant Archuleta out."

"True. But at first everyone thought that Dirk Patterson committed the crime so they transferred the case to our jurisdiction.

I'm sure we still have the items from the crime scene," Signe said as she walked toward evidence room.

The evidence room of the Santa Fe Police Department occupied a dark, musty smelling area in the basement. Signe walked up to the barred window and filled out a form. She handed it to the clerk who took it with a lazy hand and a yawn. He shuffled to the back of the room, but reappeared after three minutes.

"Sorry. I can't find the evidence. It must be misplaced, destroyed or lost," the clerk said handing the form back to Signe.

Signe knew that clerks in the evidence rooms of police departments were often very incompetent. Often the job went to a policeman that was disabled in the line of duty, but was too young to retire. With no place to go and nothing to accomplish, the clerk did the very least work possible and did it badly.

"Mind if I take a look?" Signe asked smiling.

The clerk opened the door slowly. Signe went to the section marked 2007 and quickly found the month of November. A brown cardboard box labeled Patterson, Svelty was in plain sight on the shelf. Signe pulled it down and spread the contents on a nearby table. Some fancy La Perla underwear fell out along with some black pumps, a white silk blouse, and a stylish black cashmere sweater. Mateo picked up the sweater.

"This will do," Mateo remarked.

Signe refilled the box and handed it back to the clerk. Mateo took the sweater and went to find his tracker. Signe took two cups of coffee into Chief Hartford's office and sat down.

"You've had a frustrating week, Signe," Hartford said looking up from a stack of papers.

"Yes. I was only fifteen feet from cuffing Svelty when she slithered up a Kevlar rope," Signe replied dejectedly. "That was my best chance to capture her and she outsmarted me, Chief."

"She still has a bone to pick with you, so she will be back and you will have another shot at her."

"I need to figure out exactly what she is after. Some of the time it just seems that she is toying with me."

"Like the abduction with the rattlesnakes and beer."

"Or the fancy dress box with live bats and maggots in it."

"The attacks are quirky and whimsical rather than sinister or deadly," Hartford replied. "I don't think she is hooked up with the international terrorists that murdered Abramowitz."

"Let's not forget that Dr. Goldiamond says that Svelty is a female sociopath."

"Is that anything like being really crazy?"

"Oh, yes. However, she is a little hard to understand because almost all sociopaths are men. Those men lack a conscience so they are unable to empathize with what other people are feeling. They go through life trampling on others. Svelty's husband, Dirk Patterson was a good example of a typical sociopath. He did evil things to everyone around him."

"Then Svelty's playfulness is out of character."

"I suppose I need to ask Vivian about that."

"I'm more worried about the fact that you lied to the FBI," Hartford replied.

"I know. It's a federal offense to withhold evidence from them," Signe began. "I never actually lied to Liam Farrell. He is so laid back and uninquisitive."

"That's not an English word, Signe," Hartford replied.

"Well you know what I mean, Chief. The one that I'm worried about is that district director, Blanche Baca C de Baca. She is much more focused. She asked me if there was anything I wasn't telling her and I said that there probably was, but I couldn't recall exactly what it was at that time."

"That is skating on pretty thin ice. I hope you don't fall in."

"I'm pretty sure I will. I just hate having the feds muck around my case in their *knoldesparkers*.

"What the hell are *knoldesparkers*?

"Um. Heavy, ill-fitting, clumsy Danish boots."

"You mean clodhoppers."

"I'm just hoping that Blanche doesn't come back. I can continue to outsmart Agent Farrell and his lackeys. I don't think the FBI realizes what an important case this is. If I get in a jam I think I could go right to the NSA or even better to the CIA. Do you have any contacts?"

"Yes. But let's hope we don't have to use them. They are a great deal scarier and more formidable."

CHAPTER 26

"I need to interview Larry's other two daughters, Chief," Signe said, changing the subject abruptly.

"How did your interview with the youngest one go?"

"She's a professor of microbiology at Tulane. She looks all studious, collegiate, and scrubbed clean on the outside, but she's up to her eyeballs in a Muslim terrorist organization called the Palestinian Islamic Jihad. She sleeps with the boys in the organization and helps them raise money for terrorist activities." Signe said as she tapped her foot nervously. "Larry and his friend may have received up to two million dollars a year for their secret work in Los Alamos. I'm not sure Katarzyna's group has that kind of economic power. Right now I'm trying to determine that with the help of an FBI agent in New Orleans named Arthur Bienville. She also hid secret documents for her father in a culvert when she was growing up. She is quite forthcoming about these matters, and she certainly isn't an innocent."

"Do you think the other daughters are equally culpable?" Hartford remarked.

"Too early to tell, Chief. I paid for the trip to New Orleans to talk to young Dr. Katarzyna Abramowitz out of my own pocket, but the middle sister, Albina lives in Amsterdam. I'll need some financial help to visit her."

"You have been very generous with your own time and money, Signe, and I have a block of federal money that I have to spend in the next sixty days on fighting terrorism. I think your trip fits the bill."

"Thanks, Chief. I'll go make some travel plans," Signe said as she rose to leave.

She found the flights to Europe were quite expensive as the summer high season approached. Thinking of a romantic interlude combined with her interview, she called Brian on a whim. He called her right back.

After an affectionate opening, Signe said, "I have to interview one of my victim's daughters in Amsterdam, and I wondered if we could go together."

"Actually, I have a few light days, and there is no one I would rather spend them with than you, my darling," Brian replied. "Give me the rest of today and tomorrow to complete some nagging issues, and I'll pick you up tomorrow evening at six p.m. Be sure and bring that new La Perla lingerie that we picked out in Las Vegas."

"I can do that," Signe replied. "I want you to bring that woodsy-smelling Burberry cologne that you wore the last time we were together."

"You like that scent?"

"Yes. Just smelling it makes me wet."

Signe hung up the phone and went to her messy desk in the bullpen. As usual it was stacked with reports, pieces of evidence, dozens of pink slips with messages on them, and stale cups of coffee. Piles of paper teetered precariously on three corners. She pulled a large gray waste container on wheels over to her desk and began chucking stuff. Most of the material was no longer useful, but she did find two reports she had been looking for earlier in the day. One was a report of Larry's daily whereabouts for the past three months compiled by the University of California, the entity that oversaw the national labs. Signe noticed several large blocks of time where he was out of New Mexico supposedly visiting test facilities in places like Australia and Chile. Were these visits legitimate or a cover for actual trips to less savory locations and opportunities for clandestine meetings? She jotted the times on a yellow tablet and decided she needed to talk to one of the administrators of the lab about these records. By the end of the work day her desk looked considerably better. However, she noticed that she didn't have a particularly strong feeling of accomplishment. Her murder case was still a mess and that's what she truly cared about.

Uncharacteristically, she invited Chief Hartford to dinner and added Jack, Liam Farrell, her friend Terecita Armijo and Jefferson Barclay to the mix. They went to the Bobcat Bite on the far west edge of Santa Fe for steaks. The restaurant was up the hill from a rutted dirt parking lot. The slightly rundown wooden building was just eighteen by forty some feet in size with room for only five cramped tables. A chalkboard next to the door listed the names, in order, of the waiting diners and number of hungry patrons in each group. Jefferson had thoughtfully brought a twelve pack of Corona and some lime wedges. The six sat on the hoods of their cars enjoying the warmth from the late spring evening and sipping cold beer from the clear glass bottles. Before the drive out, Signe established the rule that no one was allowed to talk about work.

When their name was called they went inside and sat at a small Formica table. Everyone ordered the rib eye steak except for Jefferson who had a cheeseburger. He had just seen an article in *GQ* that rated the Bobcat Bite's burger as one of the twenty best in the entire country. The steaks were perfectly cooked and tender enough to cut with a fork. The buttery grilled flavor filled Signe's mouth. For some reason, most of the dinner conversation was trash talk about Jack's girlfriend, Rhonda. Terecita knew her since she worked at the courthouse. Jefferson knew her from her visits to La Fonda, and even Chief Hartford knew her in some way that wasn't entirely clear. A lot of the comments were about her great 'rack.'

Jefferson told a long funny story about Rhonda and one of friends getting drunk during the holidays in the hotel bar and wandering into the crowded men's room and then insisting that all the men were in the wrong place.

The group headed partway back to town along the old highway and stopped at Harry's Roadhouse and Bar for drinks. It was a rambling old building of brown wood that hunkered on the hillside, many times the size of the Bobcat Bite. Most of the patrons seemed to be regulars dressed in country western gear. They danced, mostly Texas two steps, on the worn wooden floor to George Straight and Dolly Parton songs played loud on the jukebox. Liam got the rest of the night off to a bad start by ordering shots of tequila for everyone. Signe was downing margaritas and had a bit too much to drink. The four men took turns dancing with the two women. Signe and Terecita both voted Jefferson the best dancer. Liam tried to pin Signe against the wall during one of their dances and kiss her. She pushed him away roughly.

"Come on Signe. You're very sensual." Liam said plaintively.

"You have beautiful eyes, Liam, but we have to work together. I know what a bad idea a romance between us would be."

Signe refused to dance with him the rest of the night. By the time Harry's closed, no one was sober enough to drive safely. Terecita thought the six acquaintances were all laughing inappropriately as they climbed into two taxicabs back to Santa Fe.

In the morning Signe had a pounding headache that was only slightly better after two strong cups of coffee. She spent the morning with Valerie looking for financial information in Larry's papers. Neither woman found much.

"Perhaps we haven't found all his papers," Valerie suggested.

"I suppose he could have another lair where he stored sensitive papers," Signe offered. "But it wouldn't be very efficient or convenient for him. He already had a library containing tens of thousands of pages of writing that seemed disorganized, at least to us. I think it's more likely that he used a code."

"I haven't found any spread sheets or journals using numbers," Valerie remarked as she picked up a journal.

"What if he substituted letters for numbers?"

"I never thought he would do that because it is very cumbersome but there is no reason he couldn't have done so. It would require using the same ten letters that represented the Arabic numerals to appear over and over again. I can create an algorithm that looks for a pattern like that."

Signe went back to her newly cleaned and reorganized desk. She set up a white erasable board on the wall to try and collect her thoughts. It had helped her organize her thinking with past cases, especially Manny Ramirez's murder when there had been seven suspects at one time. Her list this time was only slightly shorter:

1.   Polish dissidents.
2.   Polish government.
3.   Palestinian jihad.
4.   A jilted lover.
5.   Svelty Patterson.
6.   The U.S. government.

She had just thought of the last possibility. What if the American authorities had discovered that Larry was selling secrets and building equipment for its enemies? It would be easier for them to rubout Larry and try and maintain contact with the buyers. They could infiltrate the spies and give them faulty equipment at the same time. If CIA publicly accused Larry of treason, his contacts would quickly vanish and a huge public trial would result. That would put egg on the faces of the CIA and FBI because clearly Larry had been selling secrets to foreign powers for years.

Perhaps Liam Farrell, with his pretty eyes, wasn't as slothful and dumb as Signe thought. He might just be marking time and pretending to investigate when the very last thing the feds wanted to do was to uncover the truth. If that was correct, then confronting

Signe with his gun while she was walking was just a little bit of clever stage business. Blanche Baca C de Baca's visit to Santa Fe would then be just a ruse to throw the local authorities off the scent of the government's real killers.

CHAPTER 27

Perhaps she was just getting paranoid. In general, Signe didn't see the world as full of plots. When she was a beginning officer in her home town of Odensee, Denmark, several of the senior officers decided that most of the violence occurring in their little town was due to a gang of drug dealer called the Fredrickson gang. The senior detectives spent a lot of time staking out their leader Hermann Fredrickson. Signe looked at the evidence herself and didn't find it compelling. She was a young officer on probation so she didn't offer her opinion. A few weeks later, Frederickson and three of his lieutenant were arrested and the crime pattern didn't change perceptible. When she transferred to Copenhagen, many of the detectives were working on a Sicilian style gang in Nyhaun that seemed to control drugs, gambling and prostitution. The older detectives made constant reference to the Mafia in New York; however, further investigation showed that there were actually four little gangs that seldom helped each other.

Signe decided to do some more leg work before she decided that her victim's murder was due to a widespread conspiracy in the United States government.

Signe spent the rest of the afternoon packing excitedly for her trip to the Netherlands with Brian. His snow white Gulfstream pulled to a stop at the Santa Fe Airport at six sharp. The copilot took Signe's luggage and she went up the stairs quickly to give Brian a hug and a warn kiss.

"I have been thinking of nothing but you since we planned this," Brian said softly into Signe's neck.

They sat down on a small sofa along the starboard wall of the aircraft and continued to kiss and caress each other ardently. They were quickly airborne and the flight attendant served each a glass of champagne.

"I have a surprise for you," Brian said as he took Signe's hand and led her aft.

When he opened to door, she saw that he had converted two small single beds in the curving rear compartment into one large forward facing bed that occupied the whole compartment.

"That looks much more *hyggelig*," Signe remarked.

"I just had it installed and I'm anxious to try it out," Brian replied.

Signe reached across and loosened Brian's tie before unbuttoning his shirt. Brian set to work on Signe's clothes and with in a couple of minutes both were naked. They faced each other in the middle of the bed on their sides and with Signe's help Brian slipped inside of her. It wasn't Signe's favorite position because of the lack of depth, but it was a good place to start, she thought because it promised more to come. Signe kissed Brian ardently while she stroked his back and neck. Brain gently tried to push his lover into a new position, but she pushed him gently onto his back and lowered her face to his groin. She gently stroked his erection and then ran her pointed tongue slowly up the underside from his balls to the tip of cock. All of Brian's muscles seemed to relax as he let out a small involuntary moan. Signe spent the next thirty minutes pleasuring her lover with her mouth and hands. It was something she hadn't done in a long time certainly never with Vincent or Sven the last two men she had been with.

When she was in the upper form in school in Denmark her friend Ingrid had offered to teacher her everything she knew. Ingrid needed money for art classes so she hooked on the side. She took Signe to the sex shop that was present on one of the main streets of every Danish village and town. The two bought a thick twelve inch dark, long brown phallus with two balls the size of plums attached. Ingrid unwrapped the package on her bed and began to show Signe what she had learned. Ingrid deftly applied her finger and thumbs using then to stroke and tickle. She reported while instructing, that Danish wives abhorred giving blow jobs. It was Ingrid's biggest seller for one hundred and fifty *Kroner*.

"And they are so horny I'm usually done in two minutes," Ingrid reported gleefully. "The most sensitive part of the phallus is this spot on the underside just below the head," Ingrid continued touching the area gently with her index finger after wetting it. "But the next most sensitive area is below his balls. If you place the flat of your fingers there and press firmly I guarantee a response."

Signe tried what Ingrid suggested. Then Ingrid showed her some other little tricks with finger and tongue. Ingrid also gave Signe a book by an American author Susan Minot called *Rapture*. The entire slender volume recorded one woman's thoughts during a single blow job. When Signe left Ingrid gave her the big brown thing to practice on.

Signe applied all her affection and knowledge to Brian's groin. She soon had her lover moaning and lifting his pelvis toward Signe's mouth. When she sensed he was very close to coming she stopped and pressed her thumb and forefinger just below the head of his cock until his arousal decreased. Finally, she engulfed him once again and didn't stop licking and kissing him until he exploded in her mouth.

Signe stretched out beside her lover and kissed his mouth softly. The release of oxytocin following her partner's orgasm caused him to drift off to sleep almost immediately. Signe curled up next to him and was soon fast asleep. She awoke in daylight as the plane descended over the North Sea. The copilot knocked gently on the door and brought them fresh squeezed orange juice and coffee.

They dressed in casual clothes before landing at Schipol the modern airport south of Amsterdam. A limousine drove them to a small canal side hotel. Signe had explained the rings of canals radiating out from the central train station that led to Amsterdam's early amazing prosperity. They checked into the Hotel Rembrandt on the elegant Prinzengracht canal. Signe admired the old, black colored beams in the ceiling and the cheerful blue and white Delft tiles that served as a baseboard in all the rooms. After a quick washing of hands and faces they descended to ground level and walked along the canals hand in hand. Signe had been to the city investigating a murder not many years before, so she took the lead. She wove expertly along the twisting streets to the Dam, or city hall in the center of the metropolis. She found a small ristaffel restaurant and invited Brian inside. Signe thought the staid cuisine of the Netherlands had benefited greatly from the Dutch colonies. The ristaffel from Indonesia was a prime example for her. She quickly ordered two Amstel beers and a twenty-one boy ristaffel. Soon a large bowl of fluffy white rice arrived followed by tray after tray of small dishes contain the prosaic such as peanuts and coconuts, the exotic such as marinated pork and roasted eggplant and the fiercely hot such as shrimp and tiny peppers and beef with a cognac hot sauce. The flight over had been easy in the spacious Gulfstream, but both were a little too tired to talk much. Signe steered Brian away from the really hot 'boys' and corralled them for herself. She was ravenously hungry and called for refills on several of the dishes.

After dinner, Signe found a long slender canal boat that took them on a long ride through the various canals and locks. She told Brian about the very valuable canal side properties with their immaculate brick facades and contrasted Keizergracht (the King's canal) with Herensgracht (the Gentleman's canal) with the Prinzengracht in between. Small lights adorned many of the bridges giving the city a holiday spirit. A cold breeze was blowing off the

North Sea. Signe was already wearing Brian's sports jacket and he had his arm tightly around her shoulder. The last few tourists got off at the stop by the central train station. Signe whispered in Brian's ear and he went off to speak to the canal boat captain. The captain drove the boat to the lively Liedseplein where the lights from all the restaurants, bars and cafe lit the water and live music poured from the outdoor cafes. The captain tied the boat to one of the landing stages and shut all his lights off as he had been instructed to do.

Signe took Brian by the hand and walked him to a cushioned seat in the back of the boat. Once he was seated comfortably, she pulled up her dress and straddled him. After he kissed her mouth and neck and fondled her breast, she released his erection and very slowly engulfed him. She moved up and down very slowly and deliberately, squeezing him at the top of every stroke. She felt his tension building and slowed her motion to prolong his pleasure. Then she moved quickly finally pushing down on him while he moaned several times with gratification. The music was loud enough to drown out his orgasm. Without moving Signe kissed him lovingly as she explored his mouth with her tongue.

"This is the man I told my partner I would date, but never sleep with," Signe said.

"Who me?"

"I am talking about you and your very gentle romantic ways."

"I'm the luckiest man in the world, Signe," Brian replied as he kissed her once again.

After they rearranged their clothing, they stepped onto the dock and walked into Liedseplein. Brian gave the boat captain a generous tip. Signe picked a noisy bar with a jazz trio and ordered two tankards of Grolsch on tap.

CHAPTER 28

After several more drinks Signe's thoughts edged toward the topic that was always on her mind when she was with Brian. She knew a lot about his brother and his father. His father had been a ruthless business man with a great eye for art. Brian's brother, the scion of the family, had been kidnapped and then murdered in New Jersey. She wondered constantly, about Brian's immediate family, but never asked a direct question.

Signe had been in love once, she thought, with an older married detective named, Hans Jorgensen in Copenhagen. Their affair had ended with her lover's death during a drug bust they were working together. His death left four beautiful Danish children fatherless. She vowed at that time not to get involved with another married man.

Signe suspected that Brian had a wife, because when she called him he always had to call her back, and he never volunteered the fact that he was single. Signe never asked about his entanglements, because if she asked a direct question and got an answer she didn't like she knew she might have to leave Brian right then. She decided there, on the Liedseplein, to approach the subject from an entirely different angle.

"Dr. Goldiamond says that I have a fear of intimacy and can't get close to anyone," Signe volunteered after taking a large swallow of Dutch ale.

"That surprises me, Signe," Brian replied thoughtfully. "You are always very open with me. I know you told me that we wouldn't be doing a whole list of things when we met on February 6th but we are doing most of them now."

"I'm flattered that you remember the day we met. However, even though we talk almost every day we have only been together three or four times and each of those episodes has been quite brief."

"Actually we've been together seven times already. Perhaps you're forgetting the car trip to Crownpoint for the rug auction."

"No. I remember sleeping in the Hogan and visiting the seer Barboncito on that trip. The first night we slept together was in Paris and the first time we made love was in Phuket. It just doesn't seem like we've been together seven times."

"We've only known each other for four months," Brian replied. "I'm older than you and I've never known anyone that I was as eager to see again as you. You are like some kind of drug. The more I see you and touch you the more I want to see you and touch you."

"That's an interesting analogy for a maker of pharmaceuticals," Signe replied as she leaned across the table and kissed Brian softly on the lips.

Brian paid the tab and they took one of the long narrow electric streetcars that crisscrossed Amsterdam back to the Hotel Rembrandt. They made soft love before falling asleep. In the morning they ate a traditional breakfast of rusk, tea, cold meat, sliced cheese and herring in an airy basement dining room. Signe decided to take Brian to her interview with Albina Abramowitz as he had nothing better to do. They walked from the hotel to her home at Keizersgracht 29. The cobbled streets along the canal were narrow and congested with cars and black metal posts designed to keep the vehicles from inadvertently running into the murky water. Signe and Brain walked hand in hand talking about nothing in particular. The large doorway was painted a shiny black with a large brass knocker in the center. Ominously the door stood half open in a country known for its regimented security and a bloody footprint was apparent in the entryway. Signe drew her Smith and Wesson and motioned Brian behind her as she crouched down and enter the hallway. Nothing was out of place. The tables were covered with lamps and pieces of porcelain. Signe motioned for Brian to be quiet and follow her. They crept up a curving carpeted stairway to an elegant library on the next floor, which the Dutch would call the first floor. A wall of polished windows faced the canal. The other three sides of the room were lined with floor to ceiling book shelves. A large Persian rug covered the floor. Signe checked all the alcoves to be sure no one was hiding there, before motioning Brian up to the next floor. At the top of the next flight of stairs a pair of white double doors opened onto a large sunlit bedroom. Bloody handprints marked the edge of pure white paint. Signe pushed the door open with her toe and saw blood everywhere. She scanned to room quickly for an intruder and then turned to Brian.

"I want you to leave the building and go back to our hotel. I will contact you as soon as I am done here but it may be several hours."

"Will you be all right?" Brian asked.

"Yes. This is what I do and I'm certain that the criminal has left the premises."

Brian left reluctantly. Signe walked back to the bloody bedroom and crossed the threshold. Lamps and pictures lay scattered and broken on the floor. On the large king-sized bed was the form of a small, naked, female. Signe recognized the pretty, bloodless face of Albina from her father's funeral. The front of her body was covered with a series of long, deep, curved gashes that covered her arms, neck, chest, abdomen and thighs. The bed was soaked with a large pool of blood and blood smeared the white carpeting as well. Signe doubted that that much blood could have come from one small person.

Squeamishness at crime scenes and autopsies was a new attribute that Signe had developed since the Manny Ramirez murder. She walked to the window and looked out at the canal through the leaves of sycamore trees and took several deep breaths. When the nausea subsided she turned back to the body of her victim. This was not her crime scene or her jurisdiction, by any stretch, but she wanted to know more about Albina's death before she called the authorities. She realized that, technically, they should have been called the minute she walked through the front door. She went back to the body, wishing that she had just one sterile glove and checked for *rigor mortis*. She found none. Then Signe rolled the body on its side to make sure nothing was underneath. She found a bloody piece of fancy monogrammed stationery which she put in her pocket after wiping the gore on the sheets. She forced herself to exam the wounds closely. Each wound began shallowly on the right side of victim's corpus and got deeper as it went across her body. One stroke had nearly amputated poor Albina's right breast. Signe was sure the wounds had been inflicted by a left handed person. Also to make such long deep cuts, the weapon was too large for a person to hide it in a pocket or even inside a coat. Unable to think of any other simple tests to perform on her own, Signe called the Amsterdam Metropolitan Politie. She asked for Detective Theo Tiebout and was pleased to hear that he was in headquarters, but tied up on the phone. Signe had worked with him on the murder investigation of a Dutch national named Beatrice Knopp. Ms. Knopp was a prima ballerina that was found dead in a dressing room of the Royal Ballet in Copenhagen when Signe was working there. Signe gained notoriety by discovering that the young ballet star was poisoned by strychnine placed in her ballet shoes. After a few minutes Theo came on the line.

"Signe. How wonderful to hear your voice," Tiebout said. "How are things in the states?"

"Just great, Theo," Signe replied. "But actually I'm here in Amsterdam and I'm afraid I've just discovered a murder."

"You know the Dutch are such a mellow people that we only had fifty-one murders in the whole country last year. But I won't be able to convincing you of that. Where are you?"

"I'm at Keizersgracht 29."

"Nice neighborhood. I'll be right there."

While she waited Signe called Albina's sisters, Katarzyna and Magdalena and told them as gently as she could of their sister's death. She woke both of them from a sound sleep; because she thought they might also be in danger. Katarzyna broke into uncontrollable sobs. It took Signe fifteen minutes to calm her down. Katarzyna thanked Signe profusely for calling. Magdalena, the other sister seemed mostly irritated to have been awakened. Signe detected no sadness from her. She also called Arthur Bienville the FBI agent in New Orleans who was working on Katarzyna Abramowitz's case, to give him a heads up. Theo arrived quickly by police boat with dozens of blue lights flashing and a whooping siren. Two uniformed officers tied the boat to the chocks, and Detective Tiebout bounded ashore in a well-tailored gray suit. He swept Signe into a warm hug.

"You look great!" he shouted as he held her at arms length. "Show me what you found."

Signe led the way to the bloody bedroom and the corpse of the poor victim.

"Her name is Albina Abramowitz, and she is an investment banker here in Amsterdam," Signe began. "Her father was a theoretical physicist in the US. He was murdered twenty-six days ago. I was supposed to interview Albina this morning."

"So you suspect both victims were murdered by the same person."

"Perhaps, but more likely by the same agency. The father was selling high level government secrets to some foreign power or group of dissidents."

"Do we know which one?"

"It's early in the investigation, as you can imagine, so I cannot pinpoint that entity yet. Actually, I was hoping that Albina could give me some much needed clues."

Signe walked out the front door to the canal side for a breath of damp North Sea air.

CHAPTER 29

Signe wasn't done meddling with the murder scene quite yet. She called Brian and asked him to come back to the crime scene. While she waited she went to a nearby *apotheek* and bought two pairs of sterile gloves. When Brian arrived she explained what she wanted to do.

"From the wounds, I believe the murder weapon was a curved blade about thirty to forty centimeters long. Like those hand held scythes you see in old European harvest pictures," Signe reported to Brian. "It is almost certainly made of soft steel or hardened iron. I think it is too large for the murderer to carry inconspicuously on his person, so he or she got rid of it here along the Keizersgracht."

"If I were the criminal," Brian said. "I would make sure no one was looking, and then pitch the bloody thing in the canal after walking a ways. No one would ever find it."

"I'm glad you didn't commit this murder because Detective Tiebout would have the scythe within the hour," Signe replied. "He has a gadget with an electromagnet ring that he can sweep along the canal from back of his police patrol boat which will attract anything made of iron or steel. We have some canals in Copenhagen so we had a similar device. Recovering metal things is easy."

"What would you do with the evidence?"

"I would hide it nearby in a container that is emptied by the *prullenboel verzamelaar* or garbage man or where I could come back and retrieve it tonight. I called you back because I want you to help me search for it."

Signe directed Brian down the street to the south and she headed to the north. A blunt nosed, black, barge entered the canal just then and two men in overalls and wooden shoes began emptying the trash containers along the canal side. Signe walked over, showing her badge and asked them in Dutch to come back later. For the next two hours, Signe and Brian peered into trash and garbage containers. The smells and sights made Brian gag at first, but gradually he toughened. Signe had been involved in enough dumpster searches that she was an expert at breathing only through her mouth. The canal was lined with four-story houses each with a wall of large glass panes directed toward the canal to let in as much of the weak northern sun as possible. Signe thought that her murderer was likely to be spotted by someone if he walked more than one hundred yards with a bloody blade in his hand. She was redoubling her effort when Brian called out.

"Come over here Signe," he shouted down the canal with his voice echoing back along the walls of the houses.

She walked quickly along the cobble stones and found him peering into an old copper trash container full of cuttings from flowers and plants. Along the side both could see something red. They took turns removing bundles of brown flower stalks and faded blossoms and setting them on the street. A rusty iron scythe with a worn wooden handle remained. The blade was covered with dark clotted blood. Signe picked it up by the tip of the blade using her gloved hand and walked back toward Albina's house.

Detective Tiebout was still in Albina's bedroom and the body had not been removed. Signe kept her eyes averted from the unfortunate young woman. Three technicians from the police lab, on their hands and knees, were laboriously labeling and collecting evidence. Signe handed the bloody scythe to Detective Tiebout.

"Where the hell did you find that?" Tiebout asked in a jolly, surprised voice. "You are a truly amazingly intuitive detective, Signe."

"Brian and I searched the canal side, north and south. I didn't think the perpetrator would carry the scythe very far. It wasn't that easy to conceal."

"How did you know the weapon was a rusty old scythe?"

"I didn't. It just seemed likely from the shape of those vicious wounds."

"Anything else you want to tell me that you have deduced?"

"It seems likely that the killer was left-handed because the wounds got deeper as they went across her body from right to left."

"And the murderer's eye color was?"

"Blue, of course," Signe replied sarcastically.

"At that is based on?"

"This is the Netherlands and over ninety percent of your citizens have blue eyes."

"Could I deputize you to help me with this investigation, Signe?"

"Perhaps."

Signe took Brian's arm and guided him down the stairs and out of the house. They took a water taxi to the Rijksmuseum. Signe thought the red brick building looked like an old overgrown school house. The two spent the next three hours lost in the art treasures of Rembrandt, Vermeer, Hobbema and Ruisdael. They admired the quality of the four hundred year old painting. They walked across the canal for a traditional Dutch lunch of croquettes at an outdoor café. Then they walked across the park to the Van Gogh Museum. Brian and Signe admired the hundreds of complex paintings dashed off by the one eared painter, until the guard asked them to leave at closing. They went to the *D'Vijff Vlienghen*, The Five Flies, for a leisurely four course dinner of modern Dutch cuisine served in rooms with dark low beams, a low fire in the fireplace, and original Rembrandt lithos on the walls.

Over dessert, Brian said, "I have to fly home tomorrow, dear. You are doing so well with the murder investigation, I think you should stay. You could be a real help to the local authorities."

"Thank you, I think I will."

They lingered over coffee and brandy at The Five Flies and then went to a series of jazz clubs in Amsterdam and its suburbs. Back at the hotel at 4 a.m. both fell into bed. Signe barely heard Brian leave the next morning. She showered and dressed and after a large breakfast walked to police headquarters at Beursstraat 33. Uniformed policemen were going in and out of the front door. It was an old, gray, stone building and Detective Theo Tiebout's desk was on the second floor. Signe found Theo talking on the phone. He motioned her to a seat. First she found a cup of strong coffee and poured Theo one also. When he finished on the phone he put down his pencil and turned to her.

"The murder of Albina Abramowitz is very unusual for our placid city," Theo began. "When drugs were a problem here, this kind of violence spilled over every so often. Now that marijuana is available in legal head shops and all of our heroin addicts are on methadone, drug crimes have essentially disappeared. The French say the reason we have no crime is we have legalized everything. They miss the point."

"Are you saying you think this is a drug crime?" Signe asked incredulously.

"Not at all. However, it represents a level of viciousness that we don't see anymore."

"Did the neighbors hear or see anything?"

"I'm afraid not. They had seen Albina's husband, Waander Alkmaar come home from work that night, carrying his briefcase, as he always did."

"So what is the couple's story?"

"They are both investment bankers. Albina worked for Lodh Holding NV. She had been employed there for five years, but had been promoted several times. Her supervisor said that she didn't appear to have any enemies. Waander was also an investment banker who worked for the much older Amsterdamsche Wisselbank. He had moved to Amsterdam from 's Gravenhage, the places Americans call The Hague for some reason. You can see from their canal side mansion that they were both very financially successful. They had no children. They were both members of the People's Party for Freedom and Democracy, known as the VVD. Despite the noble name their only goal is to promote private enterprise."

"Clearly, the wife should not have been murdered and the husband shouldn't be missing."

"But that isn't the case is it? Who would have committed this crime in the US?"

"Well had sixteen thousands homicides last year compared to your paltry fifty, but the majority of them were committed by people that knew their victims. So I would have to say that at this time the husband would be the chief suspect in America. But you have so few murders it may be impossible to say here in the Netherlands."

"We are a small country with a long coastline to the west and north and we have monitored people leaving the country by car, train and plane for the past four hours, and we haven't turned up any sign of Mr. Alkmaar."

"So you think he is still in the Netherlands?"

"It's likely. He has a large circle of family and friends in Holland and we are systematically checking them right now."

"How can I be of the most assistance?" Signe asked.

"I think you could probably help us the most by attending the autopsy and seeing if anything suspicious shows up. I'll have an officer take you to the necropsy lab."

Signe was taken in a police Porsche to the VU Medisch Centrum. For some reason, the young Dutch police officer decided to turn on his siren and flashing blue lights and speed through central Amsterdam and onto the A-10 freeway. By the time he got to the Amstelveen exit, he was going 220 kilometers per hour. Signe thought the Porsche handled the excessive speed better than her

BMW would have. He dropped Signe at the ambulance entrance with a big smile, and she was directed to the autopsy room in the basement of the hospital. Signe wondered if the racing had been the shy young man's way of flirting with her.

CHAPTER 30

A cheerful young pathologist named Dr. Ellen Thieme showed her to the changing room and handed her a set of scrubs. Signe changed quickly and when she entered the green tiled room Dr. Thieme was examining the exterior of the young victim's body with an assistants help. All of the slashes were on the anterior side of the woman's body. Dr. Thieme examined each one carefully and described it while her assistant took pictures with a large black Nikon. A wave of sadness swept over Signe as she looked at Albina's perfect young back and the devastation someone had visited on her neck, breasts, belly and thighs. Over the years, Signe had gotten more and more squeamish about violent crime scenes, but now she didn't feel any of the nausea. Perhaps it was just the fresh red blood that upset her stomach.

Turning to Signe Dr. Thieme said, "I find no external clues other than the nineteen brutal slashes to this young woman's ventral surface. The cause of death was a cut that went between her ribs and lacerated her heart. She bled to death from a cut in her right ventricle. There are bruises on all of her knuckles and skin under her fingernails indicating that she fought back courageously, but finally to no avail.

The assistant placed the body neatly on the table with a block under the head and Dr. Thieme made a large Y shaped incision from just inside each shoulder to the top of the sternum and then straight down to the pubic bone. She quickly extracted the lungs, remarking on their normal color and weighed them followed by a detailed inspection of the heart.

"The valves, arteries and chambers of the heart appear perfectly normal," Dr. Thieme said into the microphone while looking at Signe.

She examined the liver, spleen, small and large intestines quickly and then isolated the stomach, cutting along the greater curvature and dumping the contents onto a wooden board. She picked through the contents with a long pair of forceps placing small pieces into sample bottles.

"Looks like normal stomach contents from breakfast," Dr. Thieme said nonchalantly. "Pieces of bread and cheese except for several pieces of partially dissolved white and blue tablets. We will have enough to determine their composition."

Dr. Thieme turned away from the autopsy table peeling off her mask and gloves.

"Aside from the brutal gashes, Ms. Sorensen," Dr. Thieme said. "This was a routine necropsy."

As the two women were leaving the autopsy room, the assistant called out to both of them in Dutch. When they turned back he was holding a small square of metal in a pair of forceps.

"He says he found it imbedded in the soft tissue under the victim's tongue," Dr. Thieme said as she wiped it off and handed it to Signe.

Signe tucked the titanium square in her pocket. She thought that it resembled the metal chip that Bernadette had slipped her when she did Dr. Abramowitz's autopsy. Signe changed and walked out the emergency room door where the young policeman in the Porsche was waiting with his engine running. He popped the door and watched Signe slide her long shapely legs into the sedan. He sped out of the parking lot and was soon speeding along on the freeway at over 200 kilometers per hour. Once traffic had lightened he placed his right hand just above Signe's left knee.

She made eye contact with the handsome officer and said, "Geen, Dank, u."

Then she let him remove his own hand to show that she harbored no bad feelings about his pass. When she got back to the central police station, Detective Tiebout seemed excited.

"We found Waander at his parent's home in the countryside. He should be here any minute," Detective Tiebout remarked.

Just then officers hustled a young handcuffed man dresses in a well-cut European suit and with a shock of brown hair into the department. When their eyes met, Signe thought he looked very frightened.

"We found the husband," Detective Tiebout said. "What did you find out at the autopsy?"

"No surprises. The toxicologies are pending, of course, but the pathologist will sign it out as healthy young woman, COD—multiple slash wounds."

"We found Waander Alkmaar hiding under a bed at his girlfriend's house on the Herrengracht."

"Do we have a motive then?"

"Conveniently, he says that his wife was broad minded and knew about his exotic mistress from the Congo."

"What does the mistress say?"

"She wasn't at home. But we have lots of pictures. She works one of the canal side houses of prostitution, you know the ones with the big picture windows, and is also an exotic dancer at the Casablanca Club. It's an upscale strip club with an entrance fee of one hundred Euros. She calls herself Kitten Kitten Keeme."

"Does she have a rap sheet?"

"Yes and its long," Detective Tiebout said as he handed Signe a sheet of paper.

Signe studied it for several minutes.

"Aside from this one battery, all the charges are for prostitution and drug offenses. I thought both were legal in your commonwealth."

"Prostitution is as long as the act is carried out in the right venue with an appropriate license. A lot of the trollops work on the side because they can pocket more money if they aren't paying a license fee. Our dour mayor wants the tax on every sin so he can use it for the support of orphans and widows."

"What about drugs?"

"Marijuana is legal in Amsterdam and sold openly as you know. Heroin isn't legal but as soon as a resident gets addicted we slap them on methadone. The problem is those that want to use cocaine and ecstasy. Johns tend to ask prostitutes where to get them to intensify their pleasure. The girls can make more off the drugs than from the tricks, but it's against the law in the Netherlands."

"If Kitten is Waander mistress, why does she need to deal drugs?"

"Look at her rap sheet. The drug charges stopped about three years ago. I suspect we will find that Waander or some other well-healed man took over her bills at that point. I'm going to interrogate him. Do you want to wag along?"

"In the states we say tag along," Signe replied. "Yes, I would like that very much."

Detective Tiebout led the way to a small gray interrogation room that was stuffy and much too warm. As he entered the room he threw onto the table a series of garish, eight by ten photos of Albina Abramowitz lying in a pool of blood in her bed.

"We like you for this heinous murder, Mr. Alkmaar," Tiebout said as he entered the room, slamming the door behind him.

"I loved my wife," Waander said in a shaky voice. "I could never do anything like that," as he turned the photos face down on the table.

"You have a very expensive mistress," Tiebout continued. "If your wife didn't object to the cheating, she certainly didn't like the vast amount of Euros it took to keep her. How long have you been running around on your poor wife?"

"I have been with Kitten Kitten for twenty-seven months and Albina knew about it from the beginning because I told her."

"Why would your wife have ever accepted such a relationship?" Detective Tiebout asked skeptically.

"She didn't like it at all, but she loved me. She thought I was going through a phase and that I would get over it."

"But obviously you didn't," Signe said sarcastically. "Until now." As she turned the pictures glossy side up again.

"If you had such a perfect relationship, why did you kill her?" Tiebout asked.

"I didn't kill her! We argued yesterday, but when I left the house she was fine. Well, I mean she was upset, but she wasn't hurt in anyway. I'm not a violent man. I could never do anything like that!"

"What was the argument about?"

"It was about a car that Kitten Kitten wanted. She said she was going to leave me if I didn't get her a new black BMW 760L. It cost 98,000 Euros and I could finance it at three percent interest at the bank. We would hardly notice the payment. Albina didn't see it that way. She was hoping my infatuation with this woman was over, and she saw the car as a several year commitment."

"You are either the dumbest man or the most selfish man I've ever met," Tiebout remarked as he got up and left the room.

"Did Albina have any Polish or other eastern block friends?" Signe asked once Tiebout was gone.

"Only one, an émigré named Urszula Stephanie, who has been a very bad influence on Albina."

"In what way?"

"Albina was never interested in politics and now that is all she can talk about."

"How did she meet Urszula?"

"She came to Albina's bank, Lodh Holding NV, and invested some very old gold bars that came from somewhere in the Polish Republic. No one in the Netherlands asks a lot of questions about old currency or old art. Almost all of it turns out to be connected to the persecution of the Jews during World War two and the confiscation of their assets."

"Isn't it unfair to just ignore what happened?" Signe asked.

PART 4

CHAPTER 31

Signe asked Detective Theo Tiebout to take her to Kitten's place of employment

"You can refer to her as Kitten, but you have to address her as Kitten Kitten, or she won't answer," Tiebout remarked.

"So you know her?"

"One of her clients turned up dead in her bed, at her establishment on the canal, about three years ago. The man was an older Brazilian and Kitten Kitten claimed that just after he came he went. She called the authorities right away, didn't disturb the crime scene, and didn't rob him after he died. He still had 18,000 Reals in his pocket."

"She must be quite a woman."

"You will see," Tiebout said as he helped Signe down into a police boat.

Surface traffic at that time of the day was clogged in central Amsterdam. The black and white police boat sped through the congested canal, the large wake striking the stone walls. They went to the Singel Canal where many of the prostitutes displayed themselves in large picture windows fringed with red velvet. The driver pulled the boat up to one of the more prosperous looking buildings and tied up. A very tall, young, black woman sat in the window in high heels, silk stockings, no panties and a red camisole.

"I thought Kitten Kitten was from the Congo, which is mostly Bantu and I expected her to be quite short," Signe remarked.

"You would be right except that Kitten Kitten's family migrated to the Congo from Kenya, to the east. Both of her parents are Maasai," Tiebout said.

They knocked on the door and were shown in by a very slender woman who was at least six feet six inches tall. She had large, almost certainly artificial breasts and she was as black as a piece of coal and just as shiny. Signe guessed that she weighed only about one hundred and thirty pounds. After Tiebout made introductions Kitten Kitten offered them both tea and a seat.

We are here about the murder of Albina Abramowitz," Tiebout began without preamble.

"I didn't know the beetch," Kitten Kitten said with a heavy British accent.

"Why do you call her a bitch?" Signe asked.

"She stood between Waander's and my happiness."

"In what way?"

"She begrudged me jewelry, fur coats and a new BMW."

"That's patently ridiculous!" Tiebout blurted out. "Waander was married to Albina."

"Yes, but I'm the one he loved."

"If that was the case, why didn't he get a divorce?"

"He didn't get a pre-nuptial. She threatened to take everything he had."

"So you did have motive for killing her," Signe suggested.

"Perhaps, but I didn't do it. I didn't even know what she looked like."

"Where were you last night?"

"I was home alone."

"Not a very good alibi. We need to search the premises."

Tiebout and Signe began systematically searching the small business. Signe has never seen so much elegant underwear. Tiebout found some marijuana and a pipe in a drawer, but no other drugs or paraphernalia. Stacks of euros were stashed in a bottom drawer. Underneath, Signe found a handkerchief with dried blood on it. She showed it to Kitten Kitten.

"It is from my recent menstruation."

"I need to take it for analysis," Tiebout said, placing it in a plastic bag.

"Anything else you want to tell us?" The detective remarked receiving no answer, as he moved toward the door.

Once outside, Tiebout walked Signe toward the police boat. Just as they reached the steps onto the boat, Kitten Kitten came running out of her little establishment wearing only a pair of bright blue tap panties. Men from the sidewalk along the canal who had been ogling the sights, walked quickly in her direction.

"I know who committed the murder!" Kitten Kitten yelled. "It was that belligerent harridan, Urszula."

"What makes you say that?" Tiebout asked.

"She had Albina under a spell, but recently Albina's been breaking free. They were having violent arguments."

"About what?" Signe asked.

"Albina would never say very much, but she was trying to get her involved in some dissident Polish cabal. I only heard a little bit about it."

"We will check it out," Detective Tiebout remarked. "Thanks for the tip."

Once they were on the boat, Signe and Tiebout sat outside.

"Kitten is certainly an exotic and uninhibited creature. Do you think she committed the murder?" the detective asked Signe.

"She had motive and opportunity," Signe relied. "I was leaning toward a male perpetrator, but I hadn't considered a woman with arms that are probably at least forty inches long. She could swing that rusty scythe with devastating effect. I think she's a possibility. I think we should bring her in and interrogate her. "

Tiebout gave the driver an instruction in Dutch.

"I'll bet you're hungry. I told the driver to take us to the Luxembourg Café. It's nearby. A lot of people think it is the best café in Europe."

They sat at a rickety table in the back near the canal. Signe ordered erdesuppe, a Dutch speciality. When the pea soup arrived a rich aroma surrounded it. The soup was so thick that Signe's spoon stood up in the bowl. She ate large spoonfuls with gusto mixed between bites of warm dark bread.

Once her hunger abated, Signe said, "I'll go interview Urszula Stephanie at her workplace."

"I can have her brought in," Tiebout volunteered.

"Thanks, but I usually learn a lot more from talking to them on their own turf."

"In that case, she works for the PVDR, in English it is the Front for Polish Worker Liberation. I'll have the pilot take you there after I get out at the station."

After Detective Tiebout was dropped off, Signe enjoyed a long canal ride into the ancient eastern part of the city where *De Oude Kerk* or old church was located. The PVDR was located in a rundown brick building with weeds and trash in the entry way. Signe thought it very uncharacteristic of the overly tidy Dutch. Urszula Stephanie was still at her cluttered desk even though it was six p.m. She greeted Signe warmly, standing up and shaking her hand. Signe noted that she had deep blue eyes and fine blond almost white hair. However, most notable was her delicate porcelain white skin. Signe took an immediate liking to her. Signe had a brief regret that she had given up having relationships with women. Urszula offered Signe a seat, and Signe showed her her credentials.

"I'm here about the brutal murder of Albina Abramowitz," Signe began.

"I was devastated by the news," Urszula replied wiping an eye. "It's already seven. Would you have dinner with me so we can talk?"

They hopped onto one of the long narrow streetcars that crisscross Amsterdam and got off at the Central Station. Urszula led the way to Dorrius, a traditional Dutch restaurant nearby. After selecting a bottle of French Bordeaux, Urszula ordered for both of them starting with a zesty Zealand bouillabaisse garnished with garlic croutons followed by a large green salad. Between courses, Urszula spoke of meeting Albina and their fondness for each other. For the main course they had a hodgepodge of endive with meatballs.

"As I got to know Albina, I realized that she had a very unhappy marriage to Waander," Urszula continued. "He had this dreadful mistress who was in the sex trade, and he wouldn't give her up. Albina loved him too much to leave him. She just kept hoping that he would come to his senses. They had dreadful fights over her that lasted several days."

"Was Waander ever physical with Albina?"

"Oh, yes. She had black eyes and bruises on her neck that she tried to hide with makeup. Once she went to the hospital. I think it was for a broken rib."

Urszula ordered hangop a traditional Dutch dessert for them both to eat with their coffee. She explained that it was buttermilk, Dutch rusk, cinnamon, brown sugar and cream.

"How did you two get to be such good friends?"

"I brought some old gold jewelry, ingot, and coins from southwestern Poland to her bank for deposit," Urszula answered.

"How did you come to have it?"

"Oh, it wasn't my gold. It belonged to a prewar council in the town of Stanislawów. Members were in their eighties and dying off each year. They wished to convert the gold into currency. I was just their intermediary."

"Where did the gold come from?"

"I wasn't told and felt that if I asked too many questions I wouldn't be given the job as intermediary. However, there were twenty-four thousand Jewish people in Stanislawów in 1939 at the beginning of the war, and at the end, as if by magic, there were none."

"So you suspect the gold was taken from the residents of the Jewish ghetto in Stanislawów."

"I don't suspect. I <u>know</u> that is where it came from."

"Isn't there a possibility of returning the gold to the heirs of the rightful owners?"

"The Nazis killed six million Jews in their horrifyingly efficient concentration camps before the end of the war. Additionally, there are no records of the Jews that lived in Stanislawów before the war. I looked in the city hall, and the Schutzstaffel or SS burned all the records of the Jews who lived there in the city square. I could spend years looking for the rightful heirs and find none."

"How very sad."

"At least the old revolutionaries who will get the money didn't kill their fellow citizens and almost all of them fought against the Nazis and then the Soviets."

"Who murdered Albina?" Signe asked abruptly. "Waander's girlfriend said that you did it."

Urszula blushed all the way to the roots of her hair.

"I did not!" Urszula said vehemently. "We were the best of friends. We had loud arguments because I was trying to get her to be more liberal. I would never harm her."

Signe paid for dinner. Urszula called for a cab. Signe's hotel, the Rembrandt, came first. Urszula leaned over and gave Signe a warm, wet, lingering kiss. It reminded Signe of some of Bernadette's first soulful caresses. Signe kissed her back just as ardently and then slipped out of the cab.

CHAPTER 32

When Signe returned to her hotel, there was an urgent fax from Liam Farrell.

Detective Sorensen-

Lawrence Abramowitz had a secret laboratory doing work for an enemy of America. What do you know about it?

Call me urgently.

Liam.

Signe went to a transatlantic phone and dialed Liam's cell phone.

"Talk to me," Liam said without preamble.

"I stumbled on the lab, by accident, during my search of Larry's house," Signe began. "I wanted to tell you about it, but I knew that would bring the whole clumsy US law enforcement *apparatchik* down on my ass. I hired my own scientist to investigate what Larry was doing in that lab. I will share that information with you, when I get back to the states, but I won't share it with that bitch, Blanche Baca C de Baca or the rest of your inept organization. Deal?"

"You are asking an awful lot, but I'll consider it." Liam said. "Call me the minute you get back in the states."

In the morning, Signe told Theo Tiebout about her dinner with Urszula Stephanie.

"So who committed the murder?" Theo asked.

"I don't know, but my intuition tells me it wasn't Urszula Stephanie. Waander is my prime suspect. Sorry, I wish I could help some more, but I need to get back to New Mexico," Signe said thoughtfully.

"Thanks for your assistance. I'll have you taken to the airport."

Signe got on the next flight to Dallas. Unable to sleep on the west bound flight, with sunlight streaming in through the jet's oval windows. Signe took out a yellow legal pad and tried to organize her thoughts about the murder. When she tired of thinking and her eyes felt sandy, she looked down on Iceland: Denmark's icy possession in the north Atlantic. In Dallas, she caught a flight to Albuquerque and was met in the baggage area by her partner, Jack. After a big hug, Jack snagged Signe's suitcase. On the ride back to Santa Fe the two made small talk about George Bush's recent visit to the Land of Enchantment before turning to their case.

"What's been happening in the investigation, partner?" Signe asked.

"Very little. Agent Farrell called about Abramowitz's secret lab, and I just referred him to you."

"I'm going to try and talk with him about keeping that sophisticated lab just between us girls."

"Good luck with that. Just between us girls? You know more American idioms than I do partner."

"When I was a teenager in Odense my girlfriends and I thought it was cool to speak in English and especially slang. We never spoke Danish to each other. I was fifteen when MTV aired. After my parents went to bed I got to watch "the Monkees" and "REO Speedwagon." Do you remember how exciting that was?"

"I was only twelve at the time," Jack replied.

"Fair enough. How did Farrell find out about the clandestine lab?"

"You, Valerie, and I discovered it, and I don't think any of us leaked the news. You showed it to Pushpa. She seems discreet. And anyway, who would she tell? What about Abramowitz' best friend, the Dutch guy?"

"Dr. van der Waals? That's a very good idea. I think we should go visit him."

"It's seven thirty. I think we should go to the Coyote Café for drinks and supper and visit van der Waals in the morning."

They sat outside at the restaurant not because it was really warm enough but on the hope that in future weeks it would really be cozy under the New Mexico sky. After a quick Margarita, Signe started with avocado tomatillo dip and fire roasted salsa with mounds of warm tortilla chips. She followed that with Eduardo's mole chicken tacos served with borracho beans. After eating, Jack and Signe lingered over another drink before Jack drove Signe to her apartment.

In the morning, Jack picked Signe up for the ride to the national lab in Los Alamos. After showing their badges, they were directed to a small building on the thirty-six square mile campus. Jack got lost twice and had to ask for directions. They finally arrived at a World War II quonset hut. The sign out front read: Adv. Isotopic Cogeneration and Rehomogenation. Signe found it completely abstruse. Inside the building, Dr. Pieter van der Waals was sitting nervously at his deck flipping a pencil.

After reintroducing themselves, Signe said, "We need to talk some more about the murder of your friend, Larry Abramowitz."

Van der Waals quickly took a piece of paper and scrawled 'not here' on it. He pointed toward the door and walked out of the building in that direction. Jack and Signe followed. They got in a car and Dr. van der Waals directed Jack west until they came to Valle Grande. Jack pulled over to the side of the highway and all three sat on the car and looked out over the vast field of grass.

"Did you tell the FBI about Larry's underground laboratory?" Signe asked without preamble.

"They brought me into their offices and made me sit in a dim, hot, room for what seemed like three or four hours, then two agents came in and sat very close and shouted questions at me," Pieter said in anguished voice.

"What did you tell them?" Jack asked.

"I told them everything I knew. I'm not a brave man."

"So, you told them about the rogue lab?"

"I'm sure I did."

"Larry must have known you would do that," Signe replied thoughtfully. "That's why he didn't ever tell you who you were working for. Isn't that correct?"

"I asked Larry repeatedly who we were working for, but he always changed the subject or said it would be better if I didn't know."

"How did he pay you?"

"I got stacks of worn US greenbacks."

"Do you still have some of the payments?"

"Yes. I've saved most of them."

"I want you to let me borrow them so I can study the bills in our laboratory for clues. I'll have Jack pick them up this afternoon."

Jack drove a shaky Dr. van der Waals back to his office.

"If the FBI wants to talk to you again, tell them you want a lawyer and then call me."

"I'm sorry?" Pieter asked.

"It's all right. They were going to find out about the lab sooner or later."

On the drive back to Santa Fe, Signe got a call from Brian.

"I've got some good news for you, darling," he said. "Your Monet has been found in Dresden."

"You mean your Monet. How did it get to Dresden?"

"A man pretending to be a private collector sold it to their big museum the *Staatliche Kunstsammlungen*. In fact, he sold it to them for one million three hundred thousand Euros! I just had it appraised, and it is worth only half that. They must have really wanted it to complete their collection."

"We have data bases full of stolen treasure from gold doubloons to Aston Martins. Isn't there one for paintings?" Signe asked.

"Of course, and I filed a report on your *Nymphaea* painting with the lost arts and antiquities data base the day it disappeared. Unfortunately, there are twenty missing Monet's someplace in the world."

"Shouldn't the curators of the Dresden Museum have known that that oil was hot?"

"I think they knew and thought they were far enough off the beaten track.

"They're not the Metropolitan Museum or the Louvre after all and thought that they would get away with it at least for a few years."

"If the painting was fronted by one of Svelty's associates, then she is two million dollars richer," Signe replied.

Signe went to the fax machine and waited for the transmission. When it came in, the quality was poor. Signe moved it to a spotlight to study it closely, particularly the man's eyes.

She called Brian back, "That is the man that assisted Svelty with my abduction in Las Vegas."

"Are you sure?"

"Yes. I'll call Interpol and send them the fax. When was he in Dresden last?"

"Two weeks ago."

Signe got two large cups of coffee and went into Chief Hartford's office.

"I haven't seen you since we had steaks at the Bobcat Bite," Chief Hartford said as he took a long sip of coffee.

"A lot has happened since then, Chief. I went to Amsterdam to interview Albina Abramowitz, but she was murdered with a rusty scythe the day I arrived. We don't know who murdered her."

"What else has happened?"

"Brian's Monet, the one that was stolen from my apartment, was offered to a museum in Germany recently. The man who sold it is an accomplice of Sveltys. Unfortunately, that means that Svelty's pockets are well lined, and I can expect some extravagant tricks from her soon."

"Do you think it's possible that Svelty is in the employ of the henchmen that killed Dr. Abramowitz?"

"Perhaps. You know I've puzzled a lot about her. I don't understand her motivation. She's spent a lot of time making me uncomfortable and unbalanced when she could just as easily maim or kill me."

"I think you need a new approach to that truly lovely sociopath," Chief Hartford replied.

"Mateo sent a tracker after her; believe it or not Ernesto Chavez sniffed one of her cashmere sweaters before he set out. I'll check with Mateo."

"Perhaps you should get some tips from Dr. Vivian Goldiamond, too. Svelty Patterson is capable of making a lot more trouble."

"They have a drawing of the man who fronted the Monet. I'll send it to you. I believe it is the same tanned, heavy set man that abducted me in Las Vegas."

After she left the Chief's office she called Brian to update him on his Monet.

Brian said. "I'm sending the Gulfstream to get the painting in the morning."

CHAPTER 33

Jack drove Signe to Mateo Romero's house south of Santa Fe. Signe always enjoyed driving up to Mateo's chocolate brown house near the plaza. No trees or plants clustered around the houses just loose brown dirt. Jack parked by Mateo's bright blue door. As she knocked she recalled that the blue color was intended to ward off evil spirits. Mateo answered the door as he wiped his floury hands on an apron.

"Welcome," he shouted out in Keresan.

He showed Jack and Signe into his cluttered office and offered them a seat.

"I missed you," Mateo said to Signe.

"I missed you, too," Signe replied promptly. "I went to Amsterdam to interview one of Larry's daughters, Albina, but the day I arrived she was brutally murdered. You could have helped me with the investigation."

"Who did it?" Mateo asked.

"I like the husband."

"However, the murder occurred the day you arrived," Mateo began. "Perhaps her death is related to your friend's murder."

"I like the way your mind works," Signe replied.

"Have you heard anything from your tracker?"

"Ernesto is doing well. He got very close to her twice. Dr. Goldiamond is right. She goes to the same places over and over. Her poles are Taormina, Lvov, Poland, Oklahoma, Albuquerque and Portland, Oregon."

"Lvov is right next to Stanislawów in southwest Poland. Albina's friend, Urszula is from there," Signe replied thoughtfully. "Does Ernesto know where Svelty is right now?"

"No. She moves around very quickly."

"How does Ernesto get around without having a lot of shekels?" Jack inquired.

"He boards the long dog—Greyhound and the rest of the time he rides his thumb," Mateo replied.

"That doesn't explain Sicily," Signe piped up.

"He has a friend who's in a pottery school in Catania which is near Taormino. He does the leg work for Ernesto."

"I want his advice about which of those places that she visits would give us the best chance of catching her," Signe remarked.

Mateo invited them into the dining room for an earthenware bowl of steaming hot lamb stew flavored with rosemary and thyme. They ate silently, dipping warm, homemade flour tortillas into the rich stew. When everyone was full, Signe pushed her chair back.

"I think we should put our heads together and decide who offed my friend Larry right now," Signe said.

"Don't forget about his poor daughter Albina," Mateo offered.

"You don't think she was murdered by her philandering husband?" Jack asked.

"I think it was the Polish dissidents," Mateo offered. "And if not them, them the Polish government."

"What about the crazy North Koreans?" Jack volunteered.

"I think the whole crime looks a little subtle for them," Signe remarked. "The other suspects on my list, in addition to the Poles, are a jilted lover, the New Orleans' Jihad, Svelty and the US government."

"I think the jilted lover idea is ridiculous," Jack remarked. "How old was Larry?"

"He was born in 1934. So he was only sixty-nine. When I dated him he seemed quite preoccupied with sex. Plus van der Waals reports that a few years ago the two of them were going all over the Southwest for assignations with call girls."

"That's my point. Those 'ladies' were compensated for their services," Jack replied.

"Good point," Mateo remarked.

"I like the Palestinian Jihad group in New Orleans for this crime," Jack offered.

"The one that Katarzyna Abramowitz is mixed up with?"

"Yes. If by 'mixed up with' you mean she gave all the young Muslim militants blow jobs," Signe replied.

"I need to check with Arthur Bienville, the FBI agent there, and see how his investigation is going," Signe replied, ignoring Jack's remark. "At first we didn't think they had the cash for it, but they had an elegant money laundering scheme. What about a secret, underground operation or 'black op' by a legitimate government?"

"That is a very cynical idea," Jack replied. "You actually think that Poland and the United States are capable of that?"

"I need to ask Dr. Klaus Obermeyer, my Eastern European expert, if he thinks the Poles are proficient enough to do that. As to the United States, they have performed black ops in Nicaragua, Pakistan, Saudi Arabia and East Germany. Last year the NSA tried to stage an Al Qaeda plot in the Philippines. They were discovered because their bomb builder, Michael Meiring, accidentally ignited the device he was building thereby blowing both of his legs off. The FBI was definitely involved."

"But all of those incidents were overseas," Mateo remarked.

"Yes, but I already said that by murdering Larry the FBI gets rid of a serious security breech and keeps the egg off their faces for not catching him sooner." Signe continued, "He had been a serious threat to US security for decades."

"The problem with black ops is that they always come out in the end," Jack observed. "And then there is all hell to pay."

"Also I believe Larry was worth more to the CIA alive so that we could feed misinformation to the Soviets and finger all of his contacts," Mateo remarked.

"I hope I'm wrong," Signe concluded.

Signe and Jack thanked Mateo for the savory stew and good company and then excused themselves. Jack drove them back to Santa Fe. Signe checked her desk for important messages and found that Liam Farrell had called three times and Blanche Baca C de Baca had called once. Signe hoped if she could finesse Liam, Blanche would keep her big nose out of the case. Signe called Liam and set up an intimate lunch at The Compound on Canyon Road. She arrived early and asked for a small private room in the back of the restaurant. When Liam arrived Signe gave him a warm kiss on the lips and then took his hand and led him to their small dining room. Signe had ordered two dirty vodka martinis with three olives each.

"Thanks for the invitation," Liam said as he pulled Signe's chair out for her.

The martinis arrived promptly. The angular glasses were sweating on the outside.

"You're welcome, but I needed to apologize to you," Signe said as she rested a hand on top of Liam's hand. "I was wrong not to tell you about Larry's lab the minute I found it. However, I was worried that if I did, the government would take over in their heavy handed way and slow down my getting the answers I needed."

"You're forgiven," Liam said as he leaned over and kissed Signe on the neck.

Signe felt a shiver of pleasure go through her body.

"I hired a theoretical physicist from Sandia to analyze the purpose of the lab," Signe remarked. "This is what she told me. Larry's lab was capable of building prototypes of compact nuclear power stations, isolating hard-to-trace isotopes for poisoning foes, constructing plutonium triggers and designing small hydrogen bombs. I haven't decided yet what foreign entity would benefit most from these four capabilities. Perhaps you can help me."

"I've gotten to know Larry's good friend, Dr. Pieter van der Waals. He might be of some assistance."

"He certainly is bright. I just worry that after all his years working for the lab he may be too close or that he might unintentionally tell someone what we are up to."

"You are probably right. Who do you suggest?"

"Dr. Pushpa Chatterjee, the physicist I mentioned, seems bright and willing to help us. I can arrange a meeting, if you like."

"That would be great."

"I told you about the murder of Larry's daughter in Amsterdam. She has a close Polish friend named Urszula Stephanie who is from Stanislawów in southwestern Poland. Can your contacts check her out?"

"Of course."

Signe and Liam had eaten a cream of asparagus soup, Caesar salad and were now working on a rare New York strip steak with Béarnaise sauce as they talked. Signe had ordered a bottle of 1993 St.-Emilion. When they finished eating, Liam slid over and kissed Signe. Detective Sorensen was actively seducing Agent Farrell to advance her case. Signe let him proceed while she secretly prayed for Brian's forgiveness. When they left the restaurant Signe promised that she would go to dinner with Liam in a few days.

When she got back to the station Signe's head was clearing from the wine. She put a call into Arthur Bienville in New Orleans, since it was only an hour later there.

"I wanted to follow up with you on Katarzyna Abramowitz following her sister's murder," Signe began.

"She went to St. Louis for the funeral and then came right back here," Arthur began. "She met with the leaders of the Palestine Islamic Jihad. My sources say they talked about stepping up their demonstrations and vowed to shake the community down for more money. As you know, we have followed their mules to New York with their clandestine funds. I'm working with a task force there that has been tracking laundered money since 9/11. They have promised results within a month. Katarzyna has been more demure since her sister's murder. She goes out clubbing less and doesn't stay 'til four a.m. anymore, which I appreciate."

Signe ended the call, found Jack and took him to the Coyote Café for drinks and an early dinner. As usual, they agreed not to talk about work. Jack spoke about his girlfriend, Rhonda and his plans to go on a diving vacation in three weeks. Signe feeling a little guilty talked about how much she cared for Brian and how guilty she felt for petting and fondling Liam at lunch that day.

"You are just trying to advance this very complicated double murder case," Jack replied. "I would have done the same thing."

"Yes but you're a man, Jack."

"One of the reasons I love you so much is you sometimes act impulsively just like a man."

The two walked arm in arm to the rooftop bar of the La Fonda Hotel for a few more drinks. Signe took a taxi home and slept fitfully because she had had too much to drink. In the morning she had a headache, and skipped breakfast.

CHAPTER 34

Signe was just enjoying her third cup of coffee when she got an emergency call from her assistant, Mateo Romero. His usual calm, soft voice was shaky and panicky.

"Ernesto Chavez is dead," Mateo said.

"What happened?"

"He was decapitated."

"Oh my God! Where did it happen?"

"On New Mexico Highway 22, just outside the pueblo."

"Are you at home?"

"Jack and I will be right there."

Signe found Jack and they drove out of town at a high rate of speed in their armored squad car that Signe called C Vicky. She and Jack had been shot at so many times in the past eight months that Jack had a standard black and white patrol car modified to protect them. Signe called that first vehicle the Crown Vic. Unfortunately, it was blown up by a homemade bomb right in front of the station house by the three crazy Livingston brothers from Austin. Jack had a second black and white car armored, christening C Vicky, and it was in this heavy vehicle with steel in the doors and bullet proof glass in which they were riding. Jack had turbocharged the engine so C Vicky would still go one hundred and ten miles per hour and right now he was doing one hundred and thirteen miles in light traffic. The patrol car screeched to a halt in front of Mateo's blue door in Cochiti Pueblo. Signe sprang from her seat before the car was fully stopped and barged into Mateo's home without knocking.

"Mateo?" Signe yelled as she walked toward his office.

"Here," He replied in a sad voice from a back room.

As she entered the room a heavy scent of burning herbs struck her nose. She suspected Mateo had been chanting and praying.

"I'm so sorry about Ernesto," Signe said as she wrapped the short man in a bear hug. "I want to know everything. Our chances of catching these monsters are improved if we go after them quickly."

"He was hitchhiking to Portland, Oregon where Svelty has a small apartment. It is packed with electronic surveillance equipment and an employee of hers, Bob Miller, tracks people she is interested in from that location. He sends locations to a GPS that Svelty carries. You should have C Vicky checked for a tracking device, Jack."

"I *will* do it today," Jack replied.

"As Ernesto walked along the side of the highway, a dark sedan slowed as if getting ready to stop and pick him up. Witnesses say the darkly tinted passenger window went down and a long silver blade came out and lashed toward Ernesto, severing his head from his body. His trunk spurted streams of blood before toppling toward the shoulder of the road. Ernesto's head bounced once and then rolled rapidly along the road like a gory soccer ball before coming to rest on the tarmac."

"How horrible!" Signe exclaimed as she reached for Mateo again. "Who saw this happen?"

"A young couple from the pueblo was walking to their fields at the time," Mateo replied. "They were deeply shocked by what they saw."

"We need to interview them as soon as we can," Jack remarked.

"We can walk to their house," Mateo said as he gestured toward the door. "Josephine and Gabriel Arquero are two of the young people who have stayed in the pueblo. They are very simple people who didn't finish high school, but they are good hearted."

The sun was just beginning to warm the bare earth as the three walked across the deserted plaza and toward the edge of the pueblo. The Arquero's home was small and the finish stucco coat on the building was missing in several places. The adobe bricks could be seen underneath and were wearing away. Mateo knocked twice on the rickety door and then went in. The couple was huddled together in their dark living room on an old green sofa that was losing its stuffing. Mateo introduced everyone and then turned a wooden chair around and straddled it.

"We wish to catch the people who committed this heinous crime," Signe began.

Mateo translated Signe's remarks and then said, "They don't speak English well, so I will translate into Keresan."

An exchange ensued between Mateo and the Arqueros.

"The car was a large black sedan with heavily tinted windows. They aren't very knowledgeable about cars. I'll show them pictures of big BMWs, Chryslers and Mercedes later. However, the sedan had a white license plate with blue letters."

"So, Texas plates. Did they get any of the letters or numbers?"

"Only the last two—UF."

"I'll put out an all points bulletin for Santa Fe, Bernalillo, Cibola, Torrance and Valencia County and give them what we've got," Jack remarked. "The car can't be more than eighty miles away."

"This smells like Svelty Patterson to me," Signe said in an exasperated voice. "Arrest her electronics guy in Portland and sweat him. Perhaps he knows where Svelty is right now. If I am getting to know her ways, I suspect she didn't drive the black murder sedan more than forty miles. If I were her, I would ditch the car in the biggest city, Albuquerque. I'll call in some favors. I'd ditch the car someplace with a big parking lot and lots of cars like the airport or the malls since it is Friday."

Signe went outside to call the APD on her cell phone. Jack and Mateo asked the Arqueros more questions, but neither of them had seen the people in the car, and the sedan sped away. After thanking the farmers, the three headed back to Mateo's home. They assembled around Mateo's dining room table.

"Did Ernesto have any enemies?" Jack enquired.

"No. He lived with his parents. He was quiet and kept to himself but well liked in the pueblo," Mateo replied.

"Does this execution remind either of you of anything?" Signe asked.

"It has a Muslim jihad quality to it, like the beheading last year of the journalist Daniel Pearl, who was working for *The Wall Street Journal* in Pakistan," Jack offered.

"Can we link this murder to Katarzyna's Palestine Islamic Jihad group in New Orleans?"

"I'll call Arthur Bienville right now and see if any of the group is traveling," Signe remarked as she started dialing her cell phone.

"I must spend some time with Ernesto's poor mother and father and start making funeral arrangements," Mateo said as he rose from his chair.

Jack and Signe drove back to Santa Fe in C Vicky. First, however Jack looked under the car and found a tracking device attached inside the right rear bumper.

"Damn, Svelty," Jack remarked as he took the battery out of the device, he noted that the red light on it stopped flashing, and threw it in the back seat so he could give it to Valerie for analysis in the lab.

When Signe stopped at her desk she had a message from a detective at the Albuquerque Police Department. A black 780 il BMW with heavily tinted windows had just been found in a deserted corner of the parking garage at the Sunport. Its Texas license plate was 807 RUF. There were no clues where the occupant or occupants had gone next, either by air or land. Signe felt that Svelty had again made a clean getaway, but she had a clerk check all the flights out of Albuquerque for any suspicious names. Signe decided to place all of

Svelty's five hiding places under surveillance. She had already established contacts for four of the locations, but not for Lvov, Poland. Signe called Urszula Stephanie to see if she could help.

"Urszula. This is Signe Sorensen calling. How are you?"

"I'm still broken up about Albina's death. I burst out crying every day.

She was my best friend, but I had no idea I would miss her so much. Have you found her murderer?"

"I'm afraid we haven't made much progress," Signe replied. "The problem is the motive. So far there just doesn't seem to be one. I can't imagine who she would have made that angry. After all she was a bland, sweet, married, investment banker without a secret life that I know of. But I need your help on something that may be related."

"Anything."

"A sociopath named Svelty Patterson seems to be mixed up in this crime and she has an apartment in Lvov, Poland. I need a contact there to shadow her."

"Do you want someone official like the *Policja* or a citizen who does surreptitious work, what you would call a private detective?"

"Who would you recommend?"

"I have a friend, Zbigniew Poplavok, who is an excellent investigator."

"Can you put him in touch with me?"

"Yes. I'll have him call you in the morning."

"Thank you," Signe replied. "I'll have Detective Tiebout, from Amsterdam call you about his investigation of Albina Abramowitz's murder. I want you to call me if I can help you in any way." Signe said before she snapped her phone shut.

Signe called her friend and consultant, Dr. Pushpa Chatterjee.

"Hello, Pushpa," Signe began. "How are you?"

"Busy, but good. They put me on a new project at Sandia Labs and there is an impending deadline."

"I will just need a little of your time," Signe commented. "Your analysis of Larry's lab was most helpful. However, all four of the projects you deduced he was working on would have been useful to a variety of foreign powers or revolutionary groups. What I need from you is a timeline on these projects so you can tell me what year a rogue agency would have initiated these enterprises. Then I want you to tell Dr. Klaus Obermeyer, my eastern European expert about your timeline. I'll set up the meeting."

CHAPTER 35

Signe spent a quiet evening at home cooking Frikadeller for dinner. She had been homesick for the past two weeks, which surprised her. The pork meat balls made with bread crumbs, onion and milk reminded her of her mom and dad in Odense. She ate two platefuls with white potatoes and red cabbage. The warm brown gravy she scooped over the flattened meatballs and potatoes made her taste buds explode. When her son Axel was living with her in Santa Fe they had nothing but problems. He was doing badly in school and had impregnated his barely sixteen year old girlfriend. Back in Denmark Axel was apprenticed in a woodworking program and had graduated to working on small sailing ships. He seemed content and fulfilled. Signe picked up the phone and started to dial before she remembered that it was 3 a.m. in Denmark. Instead, she called Brian. He called her right back.

"Hello, stranger," Brian began. "I had a wonderful time with you in Amsterdam, except for the murder. Any breaks in the case?"

"I'm afraid not and I'm frustrated by how little I can do from here."

"I've been buried since I got back trying to get the FDA to approve of a new drug."

"We lost one of Mateo's friends in a horrible way. He was helping in a very generous way and ended up paying the ultimate price. I'm not even going to tell you how because we are all having bad dreams about it. I'm suspicious that the diabolical Svelty Patterson was involved."

"I'm sorry. I wish I could hold you."

"Me too. Thanks for getting the Monet back. I didn't realize how much I missed it and you. Now I'd better get some sleep."

"Good night. I'll call you soon."

Signe was awakened once during a nightmare in it a disembodied head spurting blood rolled down a deserted New Mexico highway toward a very colorful red and purple sunset. Fortunately, she was able to go back to sleep.

In the morning, Signe met with Chief Hartford briefly and then headed to a ten o'clock meeting at the Santa Fe Institute. She wanted Dr. Chatterjee and Dr. Obermeyer to talk face to face. Signe had Jack drive up into the hills of Santa Fe to the undistinguished faux adobe buildings of the Institute. Signe knew that these unpresupposing buildings housed many of the smartest people in the country, if not the world. Jack let her off in front of the political science building. Signe bounded up the stairs to Dr. Obermeyer's office. When he invited her in he was playing with a large multicolored model of a molecule.

"I'm trying to discover the cause of autism," Klaus remarked.

As always, Signe stared at his never combed hair before remarking, "Isn't that a little bit out of your field?"

"We're encouraged to look at unique new projects. Last week I was working on the disappearance of amphibians from Panama."

Dr. Chatterjee knocked shyly on the door, and Signe made the introductions.

"I'm trying to bracket the beginning of Dr. Larry Abramowitz's treason," Signe began without preamble. "He was developing a suitcase sized H bomb, exotic isotopes to use as poisons, plutonium triggers and a small sealed nuclear reactor. Can you tell from his work when he started and about how long he worked on each of these projects, Pushpa?"

"Some are easier than others, Signe," Dr. Chatterjee began. "There are signs in the lab that Abramowitz kept animals, such as rats at one time. He probably tested small doses of isotopes on the animals. I suspect he scrounged the isotopes from other scientists in the lab and lied about what he was doing. There are only a few really poisonous isotopes with long enough half lives to damage a human organism. I suspect he could have completed that work on effective agents and the LD50 in four years."

"Is the time line similar for the other projects?" Dr. Obermeyer asked.

"No. The PIT"s or plutonium induced triggers would only take a few weeks for him to fabricate. Remember that Abramowitz helped fabricate the triggers for the first hydrogen bomb when he was still a precocious kid barely out of his teens. The sealed thorium nuclear reactor for generating power required some ingenious hardware but mostly demanded a sophisticated computer that could run without any human intervention. I think the program would have taken three or four years to write."

"The self-contained reactor would have the broadest appeal particularly to third and fourth world countries," Signe offered. "Almost any government would pay big money for it."

"We've pushed the time line back to 1999 so far," Klaus remarked.

"I believe that the trunk sized hydrogen bomb took the longest to develop," Dr. Chatterjee continued. "The necessary components have been written about on the web for thirty or forty years. The computer and triggers aren't big, but miniaturizing the fuel for the bomb would be a major feat. Larry solved the problem by mixing a variety of proton sources, deuterium, tritium and other exotics. The ratio had to be exactly correct, and he would have had to sneak time on Los Alamos's biggest computer to model the explosion. I have no idea how he got away with that. Overall though, I think it would have taken eight or nine years to get as far as he got. I think his design was completed about four months ago."

"Maybe that is the reason his was murdered at this time. He'd have finished his work for them, and they might have wanted to shut him up for good,"

All of the Eastern satellites were restless and interested in pulling away from the Soviets. I could see groups in Czechoslovakia, Rumania, Hungary, Poland, and Estonia being interested in Abramowitz's work. It would give their governments bargaining chips they could use against the reeling Russians."

"Can you narrow that group down at all?" Signe asked.

"Yes. I suspect that the Poles and the Hungarians would have the wherewithal and the nerve to fund such complicated espionage."

"We already have contact with a dissident group in southwest Poland," Signe. "What do I need to learn about Hungary?"

"They had a very aggressive revolutionary council and started a lot of initiatives against the Soviets. They even organized some ill advised incursions into Soviet territory. The Hungarians were tried and summarily executed by the Soviets."

"Is there anybody left there to visit?" Signe asked.

"Few are left, but I'm sure I can get the names of a couple of them."

"This meeting has been very useful for me," Signe remarked. "It will help me focus on where to look for Larry's murderer."

Signe walked Pushpa out. Jack was waiting at the curb and the three of them went to the India Palace for some spicy Indian food. Signe had her favorite—baingan bhartha an eggplant dish baked in tandoor with herbs. Jack talked about his girlfriend, Rhonda and Signe told both of them about her lover, Brian. Pushpa launched into a hilarious discussion of her very traditional parents attempt to arrange a marriage for her.

"My family is from Bhopal in the very conservative northern part of India. I am an only child and my parents started arranging a marriage for me when I was thirteen. They picked a man from a rich neighboring family who was twenty-nine and weighed over five hundred pounds. When I was around him I felt like a tiny bird, an oxpecker near a large smelly water buffalo. He slept all the time and I cried for hours after every visit. I soaked my pillow until it made me cold, and I ended up throwing it on the floor. I was feeling more and more despair and even considered running away to a cousin in Kerala. My friends knew my betrothed who was named Priyanka and made fun of him all the time. We were all Hindus and my girlfriend and I talked about sex all the time. They called him 'prick-yank' and laughed every time they saw him in the neighborhood."

"Weren't you kind of young to be talking about sex all the time at thirteen?" Jack asked.

"Are you familiar with the *Kama Sutra*, the Hindu book of love? My friends and I started reading our parent's copies when we were eight. It describes sixty-four types of sex acts. Have you ever seen the illustrations?"

"What happened next?" Signe asked ignoring the question.

"My parents hooked me up with a rich rice merchant who had one son. He had very long fingers and was quite pretty, but when I met him he was so shy he couldn't speak a word to me. All he wanted to do was read. He always brought two books to every one of our meetings. I began planning to run away again, but my favorite aunt, Anupama, could see how distressed I was and spoke convincingly to my parents. By then I had passed my exams and was accepted at university. My parents, who were in an arranged marriage and very happy after twenty-three years, threw up their hands and told me very solemnly that I could pick my own mate. And now I'm thirty-five and no one has come along."

"That isn't very old in America," Signe offered in a consoling voice.

"In India where arranged marriages occur when the girl is fourteen, I'm an unmarriageable spinster many times over," Pushpa remarked with a sigh.

Jack filled everyone's cup with fresh tea and Signe proposed a toast.

"Here's to the chic, beautiful, intelligent and sexy Pushpa Chatterjee. She straddles two cultures successfully and can puzzle out the machinations of one of America's cleverest traitors!"

Jack drove Signe back to the station after she hugged Pushpa goodbye. Signe put in a call to her son, Axel.

After they had talked for awhile, Signe said, "You sound good."

"I am."

"I miss you every day. How about coming here for a visit?"

"I'd like that. I have a holiday from my apprenticeship in two weeks. How about then?"

"That would be great. I love you, Axel."

CHAPTER 36

Signe walked into the laboratory at the station house to visit with Valerie. They hadn't talked for two weeks, and Valerie seemed delighted to see her. She pulled Signe into a warm hug.

"What can I do you for?" Valerie asked.

"You have read all the journals and papers from Larry's house," Signe began. "What have you found from your analysis?"

"I found some of Svelty's hiding places, but Ernesto, may he rest in peace, did a better job of following her to her funky hiding places."

"We have shadows now on all her peripatetic locations."

"The titanium chip that Dr. Gilchrist found in Larry's shoulder was a locator device. It must have been put in several years ago because the battery was dead. I charged it back up, and identified three receiving stations—one in Finland, one in Tripoli and one in Argentina. It's quite likely that these stations are used by a variety of organizations to follow their clients both legally and illegally."

"See if you can learn more about the owners and their customers."

"Okay. I also told you about the list of assignations that Larry engaged in that I found in a hollowed out book. I followed up on all the names and addresses. Unfortunately, most of them were quite dated. Here are the names of three call girls that are still in business."

"I'll have Jack interview all three of them," Signe replied. "Do you have any ideas about Albina's murderer?"

"It's very hard to analyze the raw data from a continent away. I think the crime scene investigators in the Netherlands are well trained, but they don't get much experience because there are too few murders in Holland. I suspect that at some point the two of us should go over there and look at what they have."

"I don't know how we would arrange that, but let me think about it."

"In the meantime could we spend sometime together?" Valerie asked in a husky voice. "You know how I feel about you. My feelings have just gotten stronger over the past several months."

"You have been very honest about your feelings toward me, Valerie," Signe replied. "But I'm just not gay."

"So, that report from Art Johnson that you were petting at Geronimo's with a woman was false?"

"No that was an accurate report," Signe replied without embarrassment. "I was with Dr. Gilchrist, but I was just experimenting. What I found is that I love foreplay with a woman. Their touch is softer than the inside of a rose petal and it makes me tingle. Women know how to start at the edges and move to my white hot center. Men are usually too brusque and firm with their touches. But then once I'm excited, I have a yearning to be filled up. For me a woman simply can't do that. I need a phallus. It's nothing personal."

"That night I slept with you was the happiest of my life," Valerie said wistfully.

"That wasn't exactly consensual, Valerie. I didn't invite you to sleep with me. You snuck into my bed after I was sound asleep."

Signe stood and walked toward the door of the lab.

"You are an exceptional CSI, Valerie," Signe said. "Don't let your feelings destroy the good work we do together."

Signe left the lab and was walking toward her desk when she thought about her boss. She felt like she hadn't apprised Chief Hartford of her recent thoughts about the murder of Larry Abramowitz. She got two large cups of fresh, strong coffee and walked into the Chief's office.

"I seems like we haven't talked forever, Chief," Signe remarked as she slumped into a chair.

"I thought you had thrown me over and had discovered a new advisor, maybe someone from the FBI."

"Absolutely not true. You are my mentor and I always rely on your wisdom and experience to guide me. Currently, I'm totally perplexed in my investigation of Larry Abramowitz's murder. Also, as you know, his daughter, Albina, was brutally murdered in Amsterdam. I have a list of perpetrators but I'm not totally confident that it covers all the possibilities."

"Let me see your list."

Signe pulled a list out of her pocket and placed it on Hartford's desk. He studied it for several minutes without saying a word.

"The Hungarians were also active at that time, and Dr. Obermeyer thinks they should be on the list."

"You certainly have taken a global approach," Chief Hartford remarked.

"So, you think it is wrong?"

"Not necessarily, but I would look at something simpler and closer to home."

"Give me your thoughts."

"What if Larry committed suicide? He had to be worried every day of his life about getting caught for selling government secrets. He was quite a ladies man when he was younger. Maybe he wasn't as successful in getting women to fall for him or he couldn't perform like he used to and that pushed him into a depression that he couldn't handle."

"I can have Valerie check his log of tricks, but he had plenty of money to pay for call girls."

"You dated him for a while. Tell me what he was like."

"We barely dated. We just went out to dinner a couple of times. We certainly didn't have sex. He talked about it a lot though. He didn't come across like someone who was impotent. I didn't ever sense that he was depressed. In fact I was always impressed and commented on his *joie de vivre*. Besides, why would he bother to stage a suicide in Valle Grande?"

"Perhaps he was afraid that if he was exposed as a spy, it would embarrass his three daughters. He was smart enough to stage a very believable suicide that the FBI would never be smart enough to unravel."

"If it was a suicide, how did he do it? Nothing was found at his autopsy other than an old heart attack," Signe replied. "And his toxicology showed very little."

"Signe, you and I both know that Dr. Larry Abramowitz was clever enough to kill himself in a variety of ways without the CIA, the FBI, and the NSA ever finding out what killed him. I'm not so sure he could outsmart you, though. Dr. Chatterjee found a bunch of poisons that Larry was investigating for use by a foreign power, but perhaps he did that research to find an undiscoverable way to end his own life."

"What you are saying is correct. Pushpa said Plutonium 238 and Neptunium 237 are both highly radioactive and deadly. One of the isotopes Polonium 210 is a real killer, but she also said there are thirty-three isotopes of that one element and some have half lives of only one second. He also was investigating several other toxic isotopes. Perhaps you are right."

"I may not be, but it is a simple explanation of the physicist's death."

"As to his three daughters, I'm not sure yet, but I think they may have known exactly what he did and may have even helped him commit treason."

"So you don't buy the suicide angle?"

"No I don't. I don't think it fits with his personality, but I will reinvestigate the possibility."

"Another possibility is that some local killed him. I suspect there are many people in Los Alamos that were jealous of his success. He began working at the lab as a young man and had a lot of triumphs from the beginning with the triggers he designed for the first hydrogen bombs. You said he got an award for that and he was only in his twenties. Then he went on to work in this highly demanding area of science for the next several decades. He had success after success over time. Certainly other scientists at the lab and at other nuclear labs who didn't do as well had to be envious. I wonder if someone didn't get sick of his triumphs and do him in."

"Do you having anyone specific in mind?"

"I'd start with a list of researchers or technicians that the national lab fired in the last three years."

"That would be a reasonable place to start," Signe replied as she rose from her seat.

She went to the desk and called one of the administrators in the human resources department at the Los Alamos National Laboratory. Soon, a list of scientists and technicians that had been let go from their positions since the year 2000 arrived on her computer as a multipage email. She scanned the list briefly and no names jumped out at her. She was already late for a dinner with Liam Farrell. She drove to Santacafe where Liam was drinking bourbon on the rocks at the bar. Signe grabbed the seat next to him and ordered a vodka martini with three olives. They talked about world events and the local Santa Fe gossip.

Once they were seated, Signe ordered a baby arugula salad with figs followed by pan seared diver scallops with fresh parsley linguini. Liam ordered a porterhouse steak and a 2001 Far Niente chardonnay which went well with the scallops. Farrell changed the subject of their discussion gradually to Larry Abramowitz's laboratory.

Over coffee, Signe took Liam's hand in hers and confessed. "I had no business flirting with you over our lunch at The Compound," she began. "I find you very attractive, but I'm in a very satisfying relationship already. I was just trying to keep the FBI from shutting down my investigation of the clandestine lab. I have no problem working with you and I will share everything I have discovered with you. I simply have a deep aversion to your boss, Blanche Baca C de Baca. I find her intrusive style insufferable and I will do anything in my power to avoid working closely with her."

"I understand what you are saying, Signe," Liam replied sympathetically. "The more I can keep that woman out of my investigations the better I like it."

"Great. Come to the station tomorrow and I will have Valerie, our CSI, give you copies of everything we have."

They shared a chocolate-hazelnut mousse torte with brandied whipped cream and coffee. Then Liam walked Signe to her car. They agreed to talk at least weekly about the murder.

That night Signe read a book about Marc Chagall that Brian had sent her before going to bed.

CHAPTER 37

Signe had barely settled at her desk the next morning when she got a call from Arthur Bienville.

"Our moles have been busy tracing the money collected by the Palestinian Islamic Jihad," Arthur began. "The first thing is that even though they are a small group, probably less than thirty active members, they have collected on the order of thirteen million dollars over the last fourteen months."

"How did they manage to do that?"

"Basically they extorted the money from businesses in New Orleans by threatening the CEOs with terrorist acts like 9/11 if they didn't give the PIJ regular infusions of cash. They even staged a violent robbery of a suburban savings and loans. They all wore black and white checkered keffiyehs on their heads ala Yasser Arafat. They only got fifty thousand dollars from the robbery but they killed the assistant manager and wounded three of the clerks so there was a lot of blood. The band of robbers included two cameramen whose sole job was to film the burglary from every possible angle."

"So the robbery was theatre to help the PIJ raise funds," Signe remarked.

"Exactly. And it worked exceptionally well."

"Have you been able to trace the disbursement of any of these millions?"

"Yes. I told you we already knew that first the money goes to New York by courier. Then we found it went to Pakistan, Palestine and Amsterdam. Surprisingly, none of the money seems to have gone to New Mexico."

"Perhaps the money goes some other place first before coming to the traitors in New Mexico. I'm surprised that none of the money is going to Eastern Europe."

"Thirteen million dollars will buy a lot of influence and terrorist episodes."

"How much of the money went to Amsterdam?" Signe asked.

"Almost seven million dollars."

"That's more than half of the total funds. Where did it go in the Netherlands?"

"To the Amsterdamsche Wisselbank."

"Isn't that where Albina's husband, Waander Alkmaar, worked?"

"Yes. However, it isn't clear if it was Alkmaar's account or not. The bank claims that Dutch law protects them from having to reveal the details of any client's account. We even threatened them with a Homeland Security agreement that was just signed with the Netherlands, the Wisselbank claims they know nothing about the law and their rules for protecting their clients go back five hundred years."

"I'm getting nowhere here on solving Dr. Abramowitz's murder. I may just go to Amsterdam and try to solve his daughter Albina's murder. I strongly feel that her death is related to her fathers. The homicide detectives there are very bright, but they have too few murders to solve each year. They are like fighter pilots that never actually fly a jet. They spend all their time in training. Hopefully there is some more homeland security money I can use to go over there. Fax me pictures and profiles on all of the PIJ mules so I can show them around Amsterdam if I go."

Signe sent an email to Chief Hartford asking for financial support for her trip. Then she called Dr. Vivian Goldiamond, the department psychologist. Dr. Goldiamond had a break in her schedule and invited Signe to come right over. Signe walked across the station house to the psychologist's welcoming office. The heavy drapes, books and statues with soft lighting always felt soothing to Signe. Dr. Goldiamond showed Signe to a seat.

"I think I need a lot more advice about Svelty Patterson and how to handle her," Signe began.

"What has she been up to?"

"She kidnapped my helper, Mateo Romero. Then she kidnapped me while I was in Las Vegas. We got information that she would be at Mesa Verde. We laid a trap for her and I got within fifteen feet from her before she escaped. Next she beheaded a young Cochiti Indian who was tailing her."

"When you first told me about Svelty, I told you I thought she was a rare female sociopath, and as such she would get worse over time. It seems to be happening and now she has reached a stage where she has committed murder and is very dangerous."

"You need to teach me more about the psychology of this disease and how it progresses."

"I can give you some reading from books and journals but the writing is arcane."

"I'm sure I can plow through it and then come back to you with questions."

"I have another idea," Dr. Goldiamond said, glancing at her appointment book. "I'm interviewing a probable sociopath, Sam Pinkerton, next hour. I've never done this before, but I can hide you in the next room and you can listen to our interview."

Vivian showed Signe to a storage room next to her consultation suite. There was a pass-through from the room to the interview room. Signe pulled up a chair and waited. Soon a curly headed young man came in and sat on the sofa. After some pleasantries, Dr. Goldiamond asked about his recent activities.

"What has been going on in your life recently?" she asked.

"I've been very lonely as I told you, but then two weeks ago I met a cute woman at a bar."

"Tell me about it."

"After working late, I went to Garduño's for a drink. While I was drinking some bourbon, I noticed a petite woman in a short skirt at the bar. I watched for a while and she seemed alone, so I sent a drink over which she accepted somewhat reluctantly at first. She drank it slowly over the next forty minutes or so and then when I sent her another she picked it up and walked a little unsteadily over to my booth. She said her name was Holly. We talked easily for an hour or so and then I suggested dinner. I took her to a French place in the northeast heights. After dinner I asked her if she wanted to come to my apartment and I was surprised that she said yes."

"You can be very charming when you wish to be," Dr. Goldiamond remarked. "We've talked about that before."

"I started caressing her thighs and shoulders on the way to the apartment and she leaned over and kissed my neck and ran her tongue up to my ear. It made me crazy. I could barely drive. I sped up to eighty so we would get there quicker. The minute we got through the door we grabbed each other in an embrace and I pushed her against the wall and fondled her through her clothing. We were both panting. I lifted her up and carried her into the bedroom, threw her down, and started tearing at her clothing. Once she was naked I kissed and rubbed her everywhere. I unzipped my pants and climbed between her legs. Just as I started to enter her she pushed me back and said, 'Stop! I can't do this.'"

So you stopped, of course."

"No I didn't. She was wet and I knew she wanted me. I drove my erection into her and moved until I came while she beat on my chest with her fist and begged me and begged me to stop. I watched my face in the mirror over the bed while I was in her. I thought I looked handsome and very detached. When I rolled off of her she jumped up and threw a stone bookend at me. I grabbed the other one as she ran out of the bedroom and threw it as hard as I could. It struck her upper arm. I think I broke it. She grabbed her slip and shoes and ran out of the apartment."

"And you went after her to make sure that she was all right, and to see if she needed to be driven to the hospital to have her arm x-rayed."

"No. I didn't. I was done with her. She had just teased me and teased me and then tried to get me to stop but I didn't."

"So you let a nearly naked woman you had just sexually assaulted and then injured leave without offering any aid?"

"Yeah. She got what she deserved."

"How did you feel about this whole episode?"

"Nothing, I guess I liked the rough sex, but my penis was numb after I screwed her. I went into the bedroom and fell asleep."

"Did you try and find her the next day to give her back her things or check to see if she was okay?"

"No. I didn't have anyway to contact her."

"Our session is over. What you have just told me is appalling. You raped a woman and seem to feel, even now, that you had every right to do it. Don't bother to make another appointment with me."

Dr. Goldiamond got up and walked into the room where Signe was observing.

"That was a lot more than I bargained for!" Dr. Goldiamond exclaimed. "I was unsure until now about his diagnosis, but now I'm sure that he is a severe and dangerous sociopath. He exhibited his inability to delay gratification, narcissism, superficial charm, callousness, glibness and especially his lack of empathy."

"And you can't do anything to help Holly," Signe observed in a discouraged voice. "Because of patient client privilege."

"You want to bet?" Dr. Goldiamond replied. "He committed a felony so he isn't protected by the client protection law. Even before they changed the practice act, I went after any lawbreaker who confessed to a crime during therapy. I got reprimanded once by

Hartford for doing that but it didn't stop me. I will find Holly and help her file charges against Mr. Pinkerton."

Signe left Dr. Goldiamond's office shaking her head over Sam's unfeeling behavior.

CHAPTER 38

Signe inquired from the payroll department about the availability of Homeland Securities funds and found that there was money coming in every month that had to be spent quickly, or it was lost. She told Chief Hartford that she wanted to use some of the money to investigate Albina Abramowitz's death in Amsterdam. She described a possible Al Qaeda connection with the Palestinian Islam Jihad in New Orleans.

"There is so much government guilt money right now, Signe," Chief Hartford said shaking his head. "I'm tempted to send you first class just to use up some of the funds."

"I'm not comfortable with that Chief. When it came out it would just look bad, but I would like to take Valerie Sanderson along. She is a very bright CSI and the Dutch investigators are weak in that area. I will need some strong science if I am to have a chance at solving this crime."

"What makes you think that the father—daughter murders are linked?"

"For one thing, murder is very rare in the Netherlands, so there must have been a compelling reason to end her life. Even more persuasive is the fact that she was murdered just minutes before I was scheduled to interview her about her father's death. Besides, I'm really stumped on Larry's murder right now."

"Go ahead and take Valerie with you," Chief Hartford said as Signe stood up to go. "And good luck. You probably don't need luck because you always get your man in the end."

Signe went to her desk and booked two coach seats from Albuquerque to Amsterdam leaving the next day. On such short notice the seats were expensive, but the department appeared to have anti-terrorist money to burn.

Valerie was excited to hear that she was going along and was chirping in glee on the phone. She took the rest of the day off to get her hair and nails done.

In the morning Jack drove both women to the Sunport. They flew to Dallas and then to Amsterdam. Valerie was so excited that she jabbered constantly. Signe finally asked her to be quiet so she could read and catch a nap. When they arrived at Schipol, Ted Tiebout had two *politie* officers help the women through customs and drove them to their hotel. Valerie lay down on one of the feather filled dunnas covering one of the beds.

"No you don't," Signe said in a loud voice. "We are going to the police station to look at evidence. It's only 10 a.m. here."

"But I'm so tired! I'll just take a thirty minute nap."

"No you won't. We need to get you out in the daylight and reset your clock," Signe said as she guided her toward the door.

The two officers drove Signe and Valerie to a restaurant near the central *politie* where Detective Tiebout was waiting for them. All three ate hearty breakfasts of cheese, cold meats and rusk with chocolates sprinkles called *hagelslag*.

"Tell Valerie and me what has broken open on the Albina Abramowitz murder," Signe began.

"I'm afraid very little. Her husband, Waander Alkmaar and his mistress Kitten Kitten are still suspects but neither have cracked as you say in the states."

"What about that beautiful Polish girl, Urszula Stephanie?"

"She suddenly decamped back to her home country right after you left."

"I would like Valerie to spend a couple of days in the residence where the murder was committed."

"My technicians have been over that canal house very carefully, but of course Valerie can spend as much time as she needs there."

"Perhaps one of your CSIs would like to join her."

"Of course, I'll have an officer take her there right now," Detective Tiebout said reaching for his cell phone. "What are you planning to do Signe?"

"I want to go over the evidence with you, if I may."

"We can walk to the police station right now."

Signe and Detective Tiebout walked out of the restaurant onto a crowded sidewalk and a soft mist. The two hurried a few doors to the police station. The box of evidence was found quickly and Detective Tiebout carried the box to his desk. He opened the box. Both put on latex gloves. Signe picked up the scythe that she and Brian had found in a trash bin near the murder site.

"Is this an unusual tool in the Netherlands?" Signe asked.

"Unfortunately, not. Thousands of gardeners, farmers and landscapers use tools like this to trim around trees, fences and posts."

"Do we know where it was made?"

"That one was made in Groningen and it's about fifteen years old. The company is still in business and they make about twenty-five thousand per year."

"And there were no finger prints?"

"There were a few fingerprint ridges, but you can see that the handle is badly worn wood with no smooth surfaces. We couldn't get enough to get a match."

"What about the metal cap?"

"What metal cap?" Tiebout asked in a questioning voice.

"This piece which connects the blade to the metal handle. There might be something underneath it."

"I'm sure we didn't look there. I'll take it to the lab."

"If you don't mind I'll have Valerie do it when she gets done at the scene today."

"Sure."

"What about the pieces of the dress she was wearing?"

"You can see it was cut to ribbons. There is nothing special about the fabric. It is a knit fabric that came from an exclusive dress shop on Singel Canal."

"The scythe was so sharp that it didn't bunch the fabric up. The fabric clung to her skin as the blade sliced the tissue underneath. Let's look at the blade and see if we can figure how it got so sharp."

Detective Tiebout picked up the scythe and took it to the lab. They both looked at the blade under a low powered microscope for several minutes.

"There are perpendicular lines from the thick part of the blade to the sharp inside curve of the scythe," Signe remarked. It looks like someone went back and forth with a Carborundum wheel."

"That may be an important clue. I would sharpen a curved tool like that with a wand sharpener and I think most Dutch people would do the same. I'll have a detective check our suspects and see if any of them own an electric grinder with a Carborundum wheel."

Signe and Tiebout spent the next several hours, with a short break for lunch, looking at other evidence without making any important findings. Valerie arrived tired and dirty from the crime scene.

"I never saw so much blood," Valerie began. "You told me she only weighed ninety-five pounds. She must have lost every single drop of her blood in the attack. The pattern of the blood spatter leads me to conclude that the killer was left handed just as you surmised, Detective Sorensen. The victim's bed faced the canal so the droplets sprayed from left to right. However, after mapping the blood I found a small percent of droplets, perhaps only two percent, which clearly splattered from right to left."

"So what is your hypothesis?"

"I think the killer cut himself on that very sharp blade and as he wound up to cut her again, he sprayed his own blood in the opposite direction. I meticulously collected sixty of those drops of the thousands of drops on the carpeting. I dropped them off in the lab for blood type analysis and DNA sequencing."

"Good work, Ms. Sanderson," Detective Tiebout said enthusiastically.

"Thanks," Valerie said as she blushed.

"I want you to look carefully at the murder weapon, Valerie," Signe interjected. "I have it laid out in the in the lab."

Detective Tiebout led the way to the lab and Signe handed Valerie the scythe. After putting on gloves, Valerie examined the worn weapon first with a hand held lens and then with a low power microscope.

"Was this metal cap removed?" Valerie asked as she pried off the piece of metal that connected the wooden handle to the old blade.

"No it wasn't," Detective Tiebout said.

"There is a lot of dried blood here," Valerie said as she pointed to the knurl of the wood handle.

Valerie divided the knurl into six segments and scraped each separately
into a clean test tube.

"If there is more than one persons DNA on that handle, how can you possibly separate one from another?" Detective Tiebout asked.

"I can't but the FBI lab in Washington can. They can not only sequence DNA, but quantitate amounts also. That is the reason for sending six samples. If one sample shows six percent of allele seventeen and another sample shows fourteen percent than it is a mixture of DNA from two or more people. I would like to have this sample in the FBI lab by early tomorrow morning."

One of the Dutch CSI nodded yes and took the samples from Valerie as soon as they were correctly labeled. Ted Tiebout suggested taking Signe and Valerie to dinner while they awaited preliminary results on Valerie's DNA samples from the crime scene.

Ted walked them to a nearby Indonesian restaurant. On the way he explained how imported recipes from the Dutch colonies had enlivened cooking in Netherlands. They turned into the crowded, noisy little restaurant, Aneka Rasa, redolent with the smells of spices and cooking meat. They crowded into a small Formica table with three Dutch sailors. Ted ordered Heinekens for everyone and a ristaffel with forty boys or side dishes to put on mounds of fluffy white rice. Signe talked excitedly about Amsterdam while they waited for their food. Small dishes of bland and spicy topping began arriving every few minutes on large trays carried by sweating Indonesian waiters. Signe hadn't realized how hungry she was. She sought out the hottest curry and hot pepper toppings.

CHAPTER 39

After eating they went back to the police lab.

"The American CSI was right," Greta the Amsterdam lab technician said. "There were two kinds of blood at the crime scene. We completely missed the competing blood spatter patterns."

"Did you find any matches for the second DNA?" Tiebout asked.

"We don't have any hits so far, but we just started the comparison with the data bases."

The girls caught a trolley car to their canal side hotel, The Golden Tulip. Signe had reserved two rooms since Chief Hartford had a lot of money and she didn't feel like battling with Valerie's attraction for her. Both of them were beyond tired and slept soundly. In the morning Detective Tiebout took both women back to the crime scene. They spent two hours looking in nooks and crannies of the house and found little except for a few fibers which they collected and labeled. Then Signe noticed there would be a good view of the murder scene from a third floor room, on the opposite side of the canal with windows and no curtains.

"Think of the view of this room from that room," she said pointing out the window. "Have you talked with the residents of that domicile?"

"No, but I will have someone do that today," Detective Tiebout said as he reached for his phone.

The three walked back to the police station stopping at a canal side herring stand for a snack. Each had *Hollandse Nieuwe* or a fresh raw herring cut into sections and served with chopped onion. It was brought in daily from the North Sea by fishing boats. Signe was surprised at how sweet the fish tasted. The sun was just beginning to warm the northern city. After they ate, they strolled leisurely to the police station. Signe had asked that interviews with several suspects be scheduled for the afternoon. They started with Kitten Kitten. She was shown into a cramped interrogation room. Signe noted her inappropriate outfit of blue silk tap shorts, tight black halter top and platform shoes that laced nearly up to her knees. Signe reintroduced herself as she came into the room and then sat opposite the prostitute.

"You are a person of interest in the tragic murder of Albina Abramowitz," Signe began.

"It is impossible that you would still think that I committed that crime!" Kitten Kitten said in a loud voice with a British accent.

"You had been the victim's husband's mistress for four years and you hated his wife, therefore you had a strong motive to murder her."

Kitten Kitten took out a cigarette and asked for a light. Signe tossed a lighter in her direction which she caught adroitly in her left hand.

"Also, the murderer was left landed, just like you," Signe remarked.

"That does not establish anything," Kitten Kitten replied haughtily.

"Where were you the afternoon of the murder?"

"I already told the politie I was shopping for lingerie in the *Oude Kerk* area."

"So you don't have an alibi."

"No, but I didn't kill that pathetic, frigid woman!"

"You look good to me for the murder and I will ask Detective Tiebout to file charges against you. You are not a citizen of the Netherlands. Even if you get off you'll be deported back to the Congo as an undesirable. You and I both know that you can't have the kind of lifestyle in Kinshasa that you have here."

"I don't care for your threats, Detective Sorensen. I have clients beside Waander Alkmaar and two of them are senators in the upper house at The Hague. They find me quite exotic and I believe they can protect me from deportation."

Signe glanced involuntarily at Kitten Kitten's coal black legs which she guessed were at least forty-two inches long.

"The senators may not be too excited to get involved with a prostitute who is having an affair with a prominent married banker."

"Those two chubby pink men will do anything I want, all I have to do is crook my little finger," Kitten Kitten said as she extended a little finger which was nearly as long as Signe's entire hand.

"You've been singularly unhelpful during this interrogation."

"I'm sorry you find me so. It's just that I didn't have anything to do with the murder."

"Before we stop, let me just show you a picture," Signe said as she slid a faded black and white photo across the desk top.

"Oh my God! *Faddens!* Where did you get this?" Kitten Kitten cried out.

"Detective Tiebout just gave it to me. I believe it is a picture of your niece Dakaria Sekenani whom you smuggled into the Netherlands eight months ago."

"You wouldn't deport her!" Kitten Kitten shrieked. "Please, tell me you wouldn't deport her!"

"That would seem to depend on your cooperation," Signe replied.

"She is fourteen and if she goes back to her family she will be subjected to female genital mutilation. That would cause her horrible pain and change the rest of her life."

"I agree. That would be barbaric and unforgiveable in this day and age. You have the power to prevent that if you start talking."

"I'll tell you anything you want if you will guarantee that my niece can stay in the Netherlands. I'll even confess to the murder."

"Kitten Kitten you know that I am from America and I can't speak for the Dutch authorities. But if you cooperate fully, I will do everything I can to save Dakaria."

"Albina and I used to have a very cordial relationship. I gave Alkmaar some things, mostly sexual, that Albina wasn't willing to give him and she gave him lots of things, like listening to banking stories that I wouldn't do. We made a pretty good *ménage à trois*."

"You don't mean that the three of you cavorted in the same bed?"

"Of course not, Albina was much too uptight for that!"

"What happened?"

"Albina expected Waan would tire of me after a time just like he did with his other women, but he and I developed this deep attachment. As we explored our sexuality, despite our dissimilar appearances, we were like twins in our desires and pleasures. Sometimes we would spend an hour touching the inside of each others upper arm in as many different ways as we could possibly imagine. It would stoke our mutual desire."

"If Waander told Albina about the things that you and he were exploring together, I suspect it would have made her insanely jealous," Signe remarked.

"That probably was the reason that things changed between us about a year ago."

"Tell me about your recent involvement with both Waander and Albina."

"I went to their house nine days ago."

"Wasn't that the day of the murder?"

"Yes."

"What was your reason for going there?"

"I was still trying to get her to agree to let Waander buy that BMW for me. I was going to turn around and take a loan out on it so Dakaria would have some security."

"How did the visit go?"

"Quite well at first. Albina offered me tea in the library and initially we visited about noncontroversial topics. We talked about the recent elections to the city council and the huge raise in taxes to pay for the new tram lines. Then things changed suddenly. She started berating me about her husband and the fact that we were spending two nights together every week and usually one weekend each month, but we had been doing that for at least eighteen months. She said that she hated the way he behaved after a visit with me. He was smiling, attentive and joyful. I didn't know what to say. I suggested that he was like that when we first got together, but it wasn't actually true. When he first came to our apartment he was usually fidgety, distracted and irritable. It took me a couple of hours to get him relaxed."

"Did she begin to calm down?"

"No. She got more and more hysterical and ran up to her bedroom. I thought about leaving, but I was very anxious about Dakarai so I followed her. When I entered her bedroom she was crying loudly. She was pulling at her clothing and scratching her face. She came at me and scratched my neck and face. Her nails were very sharp. I grabbed both of her wrists and held her hands away from me while I tried to calm her. Gradually over thirty minutes I talked her down. Finally, she was just sobbing softly. I put her in bed with her clothes on and left."

"So, when you left you are saying she was distraught but calm and physically okay."

"Exactly."

"When did you learn she had been murdered?"

"Someone called me the next afternoon. I tried to call Waander immediately, but I couldn't reach him."

"Is there anything else you want to tell me?"

"Yes. Waander's institution, The Amsterdamsche Wisselbank, is one of the most conservative banks in Europe. But recently they have been involved in laundering questionable money. It made Waander very nervous. He considered resigning over it."

Remembering Arthur Bienville's conversation, Signe asked, "Did he tell you where the money was coming from or where it was going?"

"He didn't know or he would have told me. I'm sure of that," Kitten Kitten replied. "Recently, some middle eastern countries have bought large blocks of Wisselbank stock, so they got to appoint several bankers to the board of directors. Waander and several of the other junior investment bankers were alarmed the minute they heard this was happening."

"Thank you for your candor," Signe said as she stood up. "If you remember anything else please call me or Detective Tiebout and I will put in a good word for Dakaria Sekenani."

CHAPTER 40

Signe needed some alone time and went back to the *D'Vijff Vlieghen*, the Five Flies, where she had eaten with Brian for a leisurely canal side dinner. She requested a table in the low ceilinged first floor. The ceiling was supported by large black beams and she sat across from a Rembrandt drawing that she could admire during dinner. The drawing was entitled <u>Noah's Ark.</u> As the ark loomed in the back in sepia, supplies and animals marched up the gangplank in orderly pairs. A turbaned leader, probably Noah gestures from the left foreground. She had warm asparagus with oak smoked Norwegian salmon and drank a couple of glasses of white wine followed by a salad of bitter greens with a Bosc pear and gorgonzola cheese. She talked to a Danish family at the next table for the better part of an hour before ordering a veal cutlet with butternut squash, crispy potato salad and a grappa sauce. After finishing her bottle of wine she ordered coffee and warm chocolate gateaux with chocolate mousse and hazelnut ice cream. When she was done with her dessert she sat quietly at her table feeling fully satisfied. She walked to her hotel along deserted streets. Despite the warm night and light sky, only a few Amsterdamers were out walking. Couples walked with their arms around each other stopping every few minutes for a firm hug and a deep kiss. It made Signe feel horny and lonely. When she got to her room, she kicked off her shoes, lay back on the down covered bed and had a long transatlantic talk with Brian before she went to sleep.

In the morning she rubbed the sleep out of her eyes and went to the station house for an early interrogation. When she arrived Waander Alkmaar, dressed in a conservative black banker's suit with narrow lapels, was already sweating it out in a small room. Detective Tiebout handed Signe a large cup of strong coffee as she entered the room.

"Your long standing mistress, Kitten Kitten, was very forthcoming yesterday, Waander," Signe began. "I thought she was my best suspect yesterday, but now I'm not so sure. I'm beginning to think that you committed this crime."

"I loved Albina and I still do!" Waander whined loudly.

"I think Albina was mighty tired of Kitten Kitten and her greedy ways. You told your loving wife you wouldn't give up your mistress. Albina also knew that your bank was laundering terrorist money for the first time. You and I both know that that is a very slippery slope. Suddenly, you weren't such a solid cash cow. I believe she was heartily sick of you. You were tired of her harping and you didn't see anyway out of it other than to kill her!"

"I didn't kill her!"

"I don't think you meant to when the argument started, but she brought up all the old sore points. You lost your temper. Then you hit her, and it did shut her up temporarily, and it must have felt very good. Then you lost control didn't you?"

"I lost my temper but that isn't how it went. She brought up all the sore points—Kitten Kitten, the BMW, the laundered money and our sexual problems. Suddenly we were fighting a couple of times a week. I think it was because our sex life had vanished. We both used it in the past as a way to relieve tension."

"What happened?"

"I'm a Dutch person, and it isn't easy for me to talk about this, Detective, especially with a woman I don't know."

"However, it may be important."

"Well then, about a year ago I started having trouble when I was with Albina and then I became totally impotent. We tried a bunch of different costumes and remedies, but it didn't help."

"Perhaps you have a medical condition."

"Possibly, but I was never, ever impotent with Kitten Kitten or any of the other prostitutes. Albina never asked about that, but I believe she suspected and that is what made her furious. She talked with me about divorcing perhaps three months ago."

"That would have been devastating for you financially," Signe suggested as she fished for more information.

"Albina didn't come from a rich family," Waander said. "But she made more money at her bank than I did and she saved everything she got. I'm sure I shouldn't tell you that I'm a spendrift. My money is gone before I even earn it."

"It's 'spendthrift'. So far, you aren't doing a very good job of convincing me you didn't commit the murder. You had motive and opportunity. What about your alibi?"

"The afternoon of her tragic death I was evaluating an abandoned factory in Eindhoven that the bank is trying to sell."

"How many people did you see that day?"

"I'm afraid I didn't make contact with anyone. The factory was abandoned, as I said. I spent my time making measurements and taking photographs. It's a dusty empty place."

"So you don't have an alibi either. I'll have to ask Detective Tiebout if he wants to formally charge you with first degree murder and make you post bond. You disappeared right after the crime."

"I was simply distraught and went to my parent's house in the country for some solace. I wasn't exactly fleeing from the politie or you."

"Excuse me, if it didn't exactly look that way to us. I'll be right back."

Signe left the room and went in search of Detective Tiebout. She found Ted sitting at his desk typing forms. She explained to him what she had learned from Kitten Kitten the afternoon before and then what Waander Alkmaar had just said.

"Even though he looks like the perpetrator, if we arrest him and book him, his bank will have bailed him out in an hour. Maybe he wouldn't be so cautious if we just let him go and tailed him. Perhaps he will contact someone or do something that will help us convict him."

"All right I'll have him released."

"Is there anyone else for me to talk with?" Signe asked.

"Actually, yes. They just brought in that neighbor across the canal that had the great view of Albina's bedroom."

After stretching her stiff legs and taking two quick swallows of old coffee that made her grimace, Signe walked into another interrogation room. She was confronted by a neatly coiffed and carefully made up elderly Dutch woman in an old fashioned, dark blue suit.

As she sat down, Signe said, "Good morning. I'm Detective Signe Sorensen from America, and I would like to ask you some questions."

"*Goedendag*," the woman said as she drew herself up to her full height of perhaps five feet.

Even though Danish and Dutch often sounded similar, Signe recognized she would need a translator to catch the nuances of what her witness said. She stepped out to ask for help and used the pause to find a fresher cup of steaming coffee. Once reassembled, Signe began her questioning. She learned that Beatrix Hendrikson was in her apartment the afternoon of the murder.

"Did you see anything unusual as you looked across the canal that gray afternoon?"

"A shiny black sedan pulled up to the curb," Mrs. Hendrikson reported in guttural Dutch. "They left the motor running. Regrettably, I didn't see the passengers exit the motorcar."

"Did you see any movement in the bedroom after the car arrived?"

"You should know that I don't snoop on my neighbors, but I saw some sudden movements in the apartment. I didn't think much of it at the time. The Alkmaar's were always fighting and often they were very physical, striking each other and throwing books and even lamps. However, this seemed different somehow. I walked over to my windows to get a better view. It seemed to me that three people were involved."

"Men or women?"

"The light was bad. There was a reflection on the window glass that made it hard to see even with my opera glasses, but I believe two women and one man."

"Allowing that the murder victim was a woman then the perpetrators were a man and a woman working in concert. What more can you tell of them?"

"Little I'm afraid. They were covered with long dark cloaks, hoods and boots. I can provide you with no details other than that the woman was of medium height and the man somewhat taller."

"Surely you watched them reenter the car."

"Yes, of course, but they did so very quickly and the vehicle obscured a clear view. The car sped down the canal side for a half a block and then stopped abruptly for a few seconds before turning right and speeding off."

"You got the license plate?"

"I did and then I couldn't find a pen and paper. I kept saying the letters and numbers over and over in my head while I rummaged through drawers. When I finally got a scratchy pen I could only remember the first letter which was a 'C'."

Signe's shoulders slumped with disappointment.

"Is there anything else you remember seeing?" Signe asked through her translator.

"No, but I sent my butler down to the Alkmaar's doorway after the car left," Mrs. Hendrikson replied in Dutch. "I though I saw something flash on the steps and he found this."

Mrs.Hendrikson handed Signe a small dull metallic wafer. Signe recognized it immediately as being identical to the one that was found in Dr. Abramowitz's body. Suddenly and finally the two murders are tied together, Signe thought.

PART 5

CHAPTER 41

Signe took the metal wafer to Valerie.

"I left that metal lozenge in Santa Fe," Valerie said. "How did it get here?"

Its not the one they found in Larry's body," Signe said. "Mrs. Hendrikson's butler found it on the street when the murderers left the house. In their haste they must have dropped it. I believe it is the first solid evidence we have that the two murders are linked. What have you found in the lab?"

"The other blood found on the carpeting at the crime scene was a different blood type than Albina's," Valerie remarked. "It seems likely that it belongs to the perpetrator. It was type B positive. I was just checking it with electrophoresis for other characteristic genetic markers found in the blood. Walk over to this analyzer with me."

Valerie walked across the lab to a gleaming white and chrome machine and tore off the printout.

"The other person has sickle cell trait, so she is almost certainly black."

"That must mean that Kitten Kitten is the murderer!"

"Perhaps, but probably not. She already confessed to being there the day of the killing and they had a fight. Did anything else turn up?"

"We have some partial prints that don't match any in the data bases and some random fibers."

"I don't think anything is going to break until we get some information about the mysterious black car and the two people that Albina's busybody neighbor saw. I'll let the local police work on finding the vehicle they have all the resources. In the meantime I'm going to go and visit Axel for a few days."

Signe had a quick lunch of a traditional Dutch croquette and hurried to the central station. She caught an express train south and sped through Leiden and The Hague before crossing into Belgium. In Antwerp she caught a local train full of noisy raucous school children to the east and got off in Bruges. She had heard several people rave about the beauty of the medieval city. Axel was waiting impatiently for her at the train station. They took a taxi to the Relais Oude Hous de Reelleart where they had a room overlooking a canal. They went to a local restaurant where they had Carbonnades a la Flamande, a Belgian specialty of beef and onions cooked in beer and served with potatoes. They talked for a while and then retired.

In the morning they explored the old city walking to The Church of Our Lady, one of the tallest brick buildings in the world. They spent a long time looking at Michelangelo's Madonna and Child in the narthex.

"How are things with Birgit?" Signe asked.

"We had a lot of fun at first. We liked the same activities and really enjoyed each others company. We had some great weekends sailing, sometimes with Dad and sometimes by our selves. She even developed an interest in basketball which isn't common for a girl. We were really compatible sexually. I thought we might really last. Then all of a sudden everything changed. It seemed like Birgit had to be in charge of everything. At first I just went along with it, but then it started to annoy me. I pushed back, but she wouldn't give in on anything. Then it just started making me sullen. I didn't call her as often."

"Is she an only child like you?"

"No, but she is the oldest of five."

"She's probably used to being in charge. Your father Raz and I were both first borns and I think that was the main reason we didn't stay together. Perhaps you two can work it out."

"I really do like her. I will give it another chance, *Moder*."

They walked to the center of town and climbed to the top of the belfry on the west side of the square. It was a long hike up the wide, worn, slate stairs. When they got to the top they were both gasping for breath. It was several minutes before they could even appreciate the view of the ancient town and the North Sea. After a lunch of fried eels they sought out some paintings and found ones by Hans Memling and Jan Van Eyck. They found *The Virgin with Canon van der paele* by Van Eyck at the Groeninge Museum. At the St. John's Hospital Museum they found an exquisite miniature shrine to St. Ursula with a variety of costumes and diverse landscapes.

Signe was an expert at combining work and pleasure. A banker in Bruges had recently transferred there from Amsterdam, where he had been a banker at Lohd Holding NV. He had been Albina's boss for several years. Signe had put in a call and they were scheduled to have supper with the banker Gerhardt Neuhausen.

Axel and Signe took the train to the nearby village of Zeebrugge nearby on the North Sea. They settled into the lush lounge of the De Duc Bourgogne Hotel. Axel had a local draft beer, and Signe had a vodka martini with her traditional three olives.

"I wish you lived closer, son," Signe said.

"I'm done with my apprenticeship in four months, and I may work as a shipwright for a while but then I think I'll look for another line of work. Carpentry keeps my hands occupied but not my mind."

"What do you think you'd like to do?"

"Perhaps I will go into law enforcement like you and dad."

"What does your father think of that?"

"He likes what you do, and he thinks you are very good at it."

"If you decide to do that I hope you get your training in America and work in the US. There is just a lot more crime to fight there. You didn't think much of the states the last time you were there."

"Yes, but I was less mature then and I didn't like what I was studying. The case that you are working on now is truly complicated and interesting from what you have told me. It seems to involve rogue organizations and governments, from all over the world."

"You know, Axel that most cases aren't like this one."

"I understand that, *Moder*."

Gerhardt Neuhausen arrived just then in an impeccable pinstripe suit, white shirt and dark red bowtie. He introduced himself and acted very nervous. They were shown to a window side table that looked out on the Come canal. Neuhausen constantly fiddled with his bow tie and impeccably trimmed moustache. Signe decided he had obsessive compulsive disorder. It was confirmed when the banker asked the waiter almost a dozen trivial questions about the items on the menu. While they were all eating seafood appetizers, Signe asked Neuhausen about Albina.

"How well did you know Ms. Abramowitz?"

"We worked together every day for almost six years. I was her boss and more importantly her mentor. I believe I taught her banking. She was a dear friend. I was devastated by her murder."

"Who do you think could have committed such an awful crime?"

"I can't think of anyone in the banking world who would do this. She was universally respected and liked in the investment banking profession," Neuhausen said as he fussed with his bow tie.

"You must have known about her personal life as well."

"Unfortunately, I knew her husband Waander. He saw marrying Albina as a positive career move. I don't know what she saw in him. She could never explain it to me in terms I could understand. He must have taken his first mistress within a month of their marriage. The first one wasn't a bad sort. Her name was Trijntje and she was a fresh banking apprentice. She didn't have a calculating bone in her body. The next one was a very sexy young secretary without a brain in her head but with a very seductive body that she flounced around in low-cut tops and tight skirts. Her name was Ingmar. Waander was crazy about her and lavished her with jewelry and furs. She soon tired of him. That's when he caught sight of that flashy African prostitute walking along the Singel Canal one day. She had a power over him from their very first meeting that never dissipated. Albina hated her enough to have her killed or kill her herself."

"Those are strong words."

"Yes, but that is exactly how she felt."

"I'm afraid Albina approached her lover about killing Kitten Kitten."

"I didn't know she had a lover and that doesn't sound very Dutch."

"As you know she wasn't Dutch, but American and, yes, she took a lover mostly to get back at Waander but then apparently she began to like it."

"Tell me about him."

"He has a very Dutch name Arend van Oosterwijk, but he is actually Sicilian. Albina was quite sure he was a black marketer dealing in art, jewelry and gold. Despite that, he was always very courtly with Albina. He treated her like she was a delicate little princess."

"Where might I contact him?"

"I have no idea. He seemed to just materialize out of the fog every few weeks."

"Did you ever meet him, or did Albina ever show you a picture of van Oosterwijk?"

"Yes. I ran into them walking near the Concertgebouw Hall one rainy night. She introduced me, and I got a good look at his face. He was swarthy with a large moustache. If Albina had a picture of him she probably kept it in her secret safe deposit box at the bank."

"Do you know how to access it?"

"Yes, she told me once. It is registered under her mother's maiden name which was Kaatje Rosinyenko."

The main course of fresh fish in a cream sauce arrived and everyone stopped talking. When they finished, they had strawberries in cream and strong aromatic coffee. Signe and Axel said goodnight to Gerhardt Neuhausen and thanked him for all his information. They walked to the train station in the fog.

"That is exactly why I think I might want to be a detective," Axel said as he walked along.

"Why?"

"Look at the great leads you got from a man that most investigators wouldn't have even bothered to interview."

CHAPTER 42

In the morning Signe and Axel had a hearty breakfast of herring, cheese and pumpernickel bread.

"I have an idea," Axel said. "I still have a couple of days off. Instead of going back to Odense, let me come with you and find Arend, that Sicilian guy."

"That could be fun and I get to spend more time with you. When you are done eating have the concierge change your train ticket."

They walked leisurely to the train station and caught a local train from Bruges to Antwerp and then an express back to Amsterdam. Signe called ahead and had the Amsterdam police send a car to the train station. She had them driven directly to the Lohd NV Holding Bank. Detective Tiebout had called ahead so that Signe could inspect the safe deposit box registered in Albina's mother's name. The bank was in a large limestone building in a prosperous part of town. The safe deposit boxes were two floors below ground in a musty area that Signe suspected was below the water level of the canal. Once the clerk was gone Signe and Axel opened the box and spilled its contents on the marble table. Several large slightly yellow unset diamonds spilled onto the table. Next came piles of old Russian gold coins. Several black and white photos with torn corners were stuck to the bottom of the metal box.

"Wow! Some of those diamonds are five or six carets," Axel exclaimed.

"I suspect the stones alone maybe worth almost half a million dollars."

"Most of these photos are decades old but this one is quite recent," Axel said as he handed one picture to his mother.

"This swarthy man is probably Arend, Albina's lover," Signe said. "His dark eyes and black moustache don't look very Dutch."

"What should we do with the other things in the safe deposit box?"

"It's a question of where they would be most secure so we can examine them further. I always come up with questions later that I haven't thought of and that call for a reexamination. It was pretty easy for two foreigners to gain access to this box, so I believe the evidence would be safer in the police station."

Axel placed the items in a small canvas bag that they had brought along. They exited the bank and took a trolley car to the police station.

"Aren't you afraid to get on a trolley with that many valuables in your possession?" Axel said softly after looking around.

"Not as long as you and I stay calm and look as matter-of-fact as possible. No one will suspect that we have millions on us." Signe responded.

When they got to politie central Signe led Axel to the crime lab. Axel handed the canvas sack to Valerie for cataloguing and analysis. Signe kept the photo she suspected was of Arend and then went in search of Ted Tiebout.

Once she found him she placed the picture in front of him and said, "I believe this to be a picture of Arend van Oosterwijk, Albina's mistress."

"I didn't know she had a lover," Tiebout said in a surprised tone. "How did you ever find that out?"

"I met her mentor when I was in Bruges."

"You Americans are never off duty."

"I'm Danish, remember."

"You know what I mean."

"Yes. They are a driven people who work long hours and seldom take vacations. My chief went fishing in Florida recently. It was the first vacation he'd had in twelve years. But they really do accomplish an enormous lot."

"This photo is of a young very middle eastern looking man. His visage doesn't fit with a name like van Oosterwijk."

"Albina's mentor thinks he is a black marketer dealing in art and jewelry."

"I'll talk with all the detectives that work bunko in Amsterdam and send out a bulletin with his picture on it to all of the politie stations in the Netherlands."

"Tell me some of the places where black marketeers congregate in Holland.

"There is a bar called Cap Horn in the recently gentrified Nyhaun area where they gather some times to trade hot merchandise," Tiebout said after some thought. "If you go there you need to have a tight roll of worn Euros to place on the bar so they will know you are a trader."

"Is there anyplace else we should check?" Signe asked.

"There is a suburb full of warehouses called Nieuwendam to the north of Amsterdam across the ship canal. It's a rough, run down area with a workingman's bar called Sluyswacht.

"We'll try the Cap Horn tonight," Signe said.

After a traditional Dutch dinner, Signe and Axel boarded a screeching street car which took them to the complex of tracks in front of the Central Station and then boarded a number nine trolley that went past the bar. The door of the Cap Horn was of heavy, worn wood. Inside it was smoky and dark with only a handful of patrons. Both ordered large glasses of Amstel after sitting on two rickety bar stools. Signe placed her roll of money on the worn damp surface of the bar. She watched the rest of the bar in reverse by looking in the cracked mirror behind the bar which was partially plastered with business cards and notices. All eyes turned her way when she put the wad of bills on the table. After ten minutes a man from a back table approached and asked Signe if she was buying or selling in Dutch. She showed him a picture of Arend.

"I'll pay for information about this man. Do you know him?"

"I saw him in here once about a year ago, but not since," the man replied.

Signe gave him fifteen Euros. Over the next forty-five minutes, three other patrons sauntered up but none of them recognized Arend.

Signe and Axel decided to try the bar in Nieuwendam and took a local train there. As they approached the dilapidated building the partially lit neon sign hissed and thick fog like giant bales of hay rolled in. Signe checked both of her guns before going through the street side door. Sluyswacht, unlike the first bar, was packed with workers in worn dirty clothing. The noise from all the conversation and a jukebox made it hard to be heard. Signe gave Axel a copy of the suspect's picture and they split up moving in opposite directions around the room. An hour later they met up again at the bar and Axel ordered two beers.

"Most of the seamen I talked with were cooperative," Axel began in a loud voice. "They just didn't know the suspect."

"It was the same for me," Signe replied. "I suppose we should call it a night."

Signe was paying for the beers when a short dirty workman touched Axel's sleeve.

"Ich knows the bloke in the peecture," he said in guttural English.

"And your name is?" Signe enquired.

"Hans. I can take you to him," Hans said as he jerked his head toward the door of the bar.

Signe paid for the drinks and slid off her stool. Despite his short stature the man walked quickly. The two followed him for several twisty blocks through the now impenetrable fog. Finally, he turned into a door with a very dirty, glass pane on top and a single, bare, light bulb illuminating it. The hallway smelled of stale urine and heavy food odors. Hans led them up two flights of creaky stairs to a door with the number thirty-seven on it. Hans wrapped sharply twice on the worn gray-brown door. A small caliber bullet tore through the center of the door. Hans fled down the hall quickly. Signe slipped her Smith and Wesson from her shoulder harness flipping the safety off. She pulled her .32 caliber backup pistol from her right ankle and flipped it to Axel. She fired three shots in rapid succession through the door.

"I don't want you to fire that weapon, Axel unless I am down or I tell you to," Signe said in a soft calm voice.

Signe signaled for Axel to give the door a kick. The edge splintered and then the door swung wide on its two remaining hinges

"Now stay completely behind me," Signe barked as she entered the dark apartment.

She moved quickly through the first cluttered room with her pistol held level in front of her in both hands. She kicked at spaces that weren't well illuminated. She found nothing in the kitchen or bedroom. A dirty shower curtain was pulled across a tub in the bathroom. As Axel pulled the curtain aside the suspect's boots were just sliding out a small window. Axel sprang across the room stepped on the edge of the tub and pushed his shoulders through the open window. Signe followed right behind him. The roofs outside were peaked and shrouded in darkness but Axel was much quicker than the escapee and wrestled him down on the next roof. While Axel held the suspect down on the shingles, Signe handcuffed him. She was about to Mirandize the prostrate man when she remembered that she wasn't in the US.

Signe turned to Axel, "You didn't exactly follow my instructions, Son."

"You are right. I'm sorry *Moder*," Axel replied. "I just got caught up in the heat of the moment."

Signe called Detective Tiebout on her cell phone and requested assistance with the suspect. Help was at least forty minutes away so

Signe and Axel moved the suspect down off the roof slowly using a nearby fire escape after first freeing one of the suspect's hands from the cuffs. Once on the pavement they searched the suspect's pockets and found identification documents with four different names.

Tiebout's men arrived in just under twenty five minutes in four Porsches with blue lights flashing and sirens wailing. Axel loved every minute of it.

CHAPTER 43

The shooter was pushed roughly toward the smallest interrogation room his fingers still inky from fingerprinting. The heat was turned up and he was left to sweat. Signe and Detective Tiebout went through the things found in the suspect's pockets. Among them they found several crumpled Euros, two keys and four separate ID cards each bearing a different name. Tiebout handed copies of the identification documents to a clerk so the names could be run through the identification systems in the Netherlands. He also sent a tech into the interrogation room to take a Polaroid picture of the dejected man.

After pulling Axel aside, Signe closed a door to a small unoccupied office and sat down.

"I can't believe I got you involved in the middle of a shootout," Signe began. "I was gambling on how few firearms are accessible in this country, but clearly I was wrong, and I inadvertently put your life in danger. I apologize for that. If you ever get into this line of work, I will be sure you are well-trained before you face another mortal threat."

"It wasn't your fault, *Moder*," Axel replied. "And it was very exciting."

"Detective Tiebout said I could interrogate the shooter. You can sit on the other side of the one-way mirror and listen in if you want."

"Sure."

After getting up from her chair, Signe picked up a pad of paper and pencil and went into the interrogation room.

Before sitting down she said, "I'm Detective Signe Sorensen, and I wish to ask you some questions. You need to tell me the whole truth. Right now you are facing eight to twelve years in prison for having an unregistered firearm. Luckily for both of us, you missed. Otherwise, I would be in the hospital or morgue, and you would spend the rest of your natural life in jail. What were you thinking when you fired?"

"I was afraid," the man said. "I had been robbed and assaulted twice in the last two weeks in that room. The first time I lost twenty thousand Euros worth of jewels."

"The only good news for you," Signe replied. "Is that the loot didn't belong to you anyway. You had stolen them."

"We have all of your fake IDs, but I don't think we know your real name."

"I'm not sure it's all that important."

"You are going to jail for a long time in any case, but things can be easy or hard for you," Signe remarked offhandedly.

"My name in Arend von Oosterwijk, and I was born in Delft of parents that emigrated from Syria."

Signe stared into the swarthy man's eyes intently before saying, "If you are telling me the truth, tell me something that no one but a lover would know about Dr. Albina Abramowitz."

"She had a brown mole beneath her left breast," Arend replied thoughtfully after a pause.

"What a clever lie!" Signe shouted back remembering the destruction of the front of Albina's thorax by the murderer.

Flipping a pen toward Arend's face she noticed that he caught it easily with his left hand. She was positive that the murderer was left-handed, but then so was one out of every ten adults she recollected.

"Tell me about her family, specifically her younger sister," Signe retorted.

"I don't know anything about her family. Our times together were very brief, and we talked almost entirely about sex and arranging our next meeting."

"How long were you lovers?"

"Six, seven months."

"I think you are lying and that your real name isn't Arend von Oosterwijk."

Pushing her chair back, Signe left the overheated interrogation room and went to check on the shooter's fingerprint search. As she rounded a corner she bumped into Ted Tiebout.

"How's the interview going?" Ted asked.

"I think he is a very clever liar who is just stringing us along. I'm going to check on his fingerprints."

Valerie had helped collect a clean set of prints and run them through the Dutch and the European Interpol data basis. Eventually they got a hit from the southern region of the Netherlands. The prints matched a petty criminal with a long rap sheet named Vito Catania. After printing out the sheet with Vito's picture on the top, Signe threw it down in front of her suspect.

"Okay. You got me," Vito said resignedly. "I never screwed your victim, but I didn't murder her either."

Without even sitting down Signe stomped out of the room and slammed the door. She reviewed the interview with Axel who had been watching from outside. She focused on her mistakes and missteps. Then after a big hug she sent her son to the *Centraal Station* to catch a train back to Odense.

Then Signe set up a conference with Detective Tiebout and two other homicide detectives. She poured each a large cup of coffee before she began.

"I think our murder investigation of Albina Alkmaar is stalled," she began. "I want some ideas for getting it back on track."

"We've tried to locate the BMW that was seen outside the crime scene," one of the detectives said. "The first letter on the plate was C, but almost forty percent of the car plates in the Netherlands begin with that letter. More useful is the fact that we have relatively few large BMW's. When we crossed the two bits of evidence we came up with only sixty-eight vehicles. We have already investigated and cleared about half of them."

Signe realized that she and Valerie had spent quite a bit of time trying to unravel this case, and that currently they were at an impasse. She had Valerie copy all of the files and booked a flight home. Before departing they had a traditional Dutch lunch at Dorrius. Valerie had veal croquettes with dark bread and mustard sauce. Signe had a rich pea soup with smoked sausage and rye bread. Jack picked the two women up in Albuquerque and drove them to Santa Fe. The hot New Mexico sun warmed Signe as she stepped out of the Sunport. She realized she had been bone chilly every minute of her visit to the Netherlands.

Seated comfortably next to Jack in C Vicky, Signe turned to her partner and asked, "Anything exciting happen while we were gone?"

"Another district judge was found dead. Same circuit as Judge Manny Ramirez, the guy whose murder you solved in the spring."

"Was it murder or suicide?"

"It isn't clear yet. The State Police are investigating Judge Barry Avalos's demise. That officer that tricked you about April fool's day is the lead on it."

"What were the circumstances?" Signe queried.

"His body was found at the bottom of the Rio Grande gorge below that six hundred and fifty foot tall bridge, and his car was nearby."

"Sounds like suicide to me." Valerie piped up.

"Yes, but his car was wiped clean of all fingerprints or any other clues. There was no suicide note. Supposedly, his wife said he wasn't depressed. In fact, he was getting ready to leave on a month long fishing trip to Alaska in a week."

"What kind of cases had he been working on?"

"No idea, partner. But you are wondering if this death is related to Abramowitz's murder, aren't you?"

"It would be a stretch, but it's easily settled by asking Judge Terecita Armijo what she knows."

Signe dialed her friend on her cell phone.

"Good afternoon, friend. This is Signe. What do you know about the death of Judge Avalos?"

"It was so unexpected, Signe," Terecita replied. "He was the senior barrister in the district. He had his pick of cases. He was still trying to find a replacement for Judge Ramirez, but everything else seemed good on the bench."

"Had he been involved in deciding any controversial cases that inspired a lot of dissent?"

"Not any more than usual just the run of the mill murder, mayhem and abuse."

"How about in his personal life?"

"Pretty ordinary stuff, Signe. He was divorced once years ago, which is about average for a lawyer. He remarried, has a three year old son and seemed to be very happy."

"I'm trying to relate Avalos's death to the murder of Dr. Larry Abramowitz, Terecita, but I guess I'm drawing a ..."

"Wait a minute," Terecita interrupted. "I'm forgetting all about the Han case."

"What can you tell me?"

"Dr. Xian Han was a theoretical mathematician at Los Alamos for a dozen years, and then he was accused of stealing a powerful computer from of the lab and selling the hard drive to a foreign power. Just when he was getting ready to testify the Los Alamos police got a 911 call to his house. They found his wife standing over him with a butcher knife in her hand. He had been stabbed in the heart. She was incoherent but claimed he had threatened her. They had been married for thirty years and there was no history of discord. Barry tried the lady. The DA presented it as an open and shut case with overwhelming evidence, and the jury convicted her of second degree murder after deliberating for only two hours. Barry told me he didn't believe she did it. He thought the evidence was too perfect."

"What could he do about it?" Signe asked. "The jury had spoken."

"Yes, but he just couldn't let it drop. It seemed over time as though it upset him more and more. He spoke about the case with increasing vehemence."

"Now I'm definitely interested," Signe remarked.

Signe said goodbye to Judge Armijo and the three rode the rest of the way to Santa Fe in silence.

CHAPTER 44

After a long talk with Brian, Signe settled down in front of her Monet and just looked at the soft, soothing image of the lily pond and the pink globular flowers floating placidly on the glassy surface. She told Brian that her time in Holland and Belgium had been unproductive, just a lot of red herrings except for the time she spent with Axel. She downplayed the shot fired by Vito Catania to keep from frightening her boyfriend. Still jet lagged she slipped between the covers, sure she would awake at three a.m. as the sun got high in the sky in Amsterdam.

Once she was awake, with no possibility of further sleep, she drove to the police station and made herself a strong cup of coffee. She set up a white erasable board next to her desk and wrote the names of the two murder victims—Larry Abramowitz and Albina Abramowitz Alkmaar across the top. Next to their names she placed Barry Avalos's name hoping she might find a link. It was only four a.m. and her mind wasn't completely clear. However, she knew that sometimes in such fuzzy states she made startlingly accurate inferences. What if both Larry Abramowitz and Xian Han had known too much about the pedaling of secrets at Los Alamos and had to be silenced? Two premature deaths in such a small community would generate a lot of suspicious talk. So perhaps the murder of Dr. Han by his wife was staged and Judge Avalos wasn't fooled by the murder. She wondered if her friend, Judge Terecita Armijo could get a clandestine copy of the trial record for her to read.

Driving home yesterday Jack said that regional FBI director Blanche Baca C de Baca had visited from San Francisco while Signe was out of the country. Apparently the visit had been as unpleasant as her first visit with waves of sarcasm and implied incompetence on everyone's part. Perhaps the FBI was as suspicious as Signe was quickly becoming of the deaths in Los Alamos. After ringing Liam Farrell's cell phone she remembered how early it was but decided to let the call go through. He answered on the fifth ring.

"Haallooo," Liam said in a groggy hoarse voice.

"Hey," this is Signe. "How the hell are you?"

"Actually I was sound asleep and having an erotic dream about a beautiful woman that just might have been you. Throw a robe on your luscious body, come over and I'll tell you all about it in detail."

"You are quick on your feet. I just forgot how early it is. Maybe some other time. What can you tell me about Director Baca C de Bacas visit?"

"That it was just routine? 'Cause that is what she said at first."

"And then she went on to say?"

"Let me put my robe on."

"You are just teasing me, Liam. Are you telling me you can't think naked?"

"I think fine, it's just about other things. She asked a lot of questions about the murder of this theoretical mathematician from the lab named Dr. Xian Chang Han."

Much as Signe disliked Blanche, both of them seemed to be thinking in the same direction.

"I just heard about it yesterday," Signe continued. "But it just sounds like a domestic quarrel gone badly. Were there any drugs or alcohol involved?"

"Nothing that is recognizable in the West. They had a lot of substances wrapped in folded paper of different colors and small brown bottles, but all the writing was in Chinese."

"What did the tox screens show?"

"I'm not sure any were done. The initial investigation was by the bozo Los Alamos Police whose big crimes are bicycle theft and jaywalking. By the time we knew about it Han was buried in a Chinese cemetery in San Francisco," Liam replied.

"How big was Mrs. Han?"

"Why do you ask?"

"I'm wondering if she was big enough to kill her husband with one knife thrust."

"That's a good question. She was about four eleven and weighed about one oh'five dripping wet."

"How big was he?"

"No idea. Like I said, never saw him."

"Did she show any defensive wounds from the fight?"

"Not a one. She had perfect brown skin without a blemish and immaculately done nails."

"So after thirty years of blissful marriage, she delivers one thrust that pierces his ventricle and he dies. Is that as fucking unbelievable as it sounds?"

"Yeah, I suppose. But why do you care, anyway?"

"I am surprised that there were two strange deaths in the little burg of Los Alamos in two months," Signe mused. "I guess I wonder if they are related."

"I think that is a stretch, Signe."

"Both were scientists with the highest security clearance. Both died unexpectedly. Both had diverted secrets or info from the lab.

What if they were working for the same controller and both of them had outlived their usefulness?"

"That's a lot of 'what ifs'."

"Come on Liam. Use your imagination. None of them are that big a stretch."

"Meet me for breakfast and we can talk about it some more."

"I can't today, Liam, but perhaps sometime soon."

After saying goodbye Signe got very excited about the possible connection between the two murders. She wondered whom she might call to confirm her hypothesis. She thought of Dr. Klaus Obermeyer, but then remembered that he didn't know anything about the scientists at the national lab. Her next thought was about Dr. Pieter van der Waals. Signe put in a quick call.

When the phone clicked on Signe said, "Sorry to call so early Pieter, but I have an important question for you."

"Ya!"

"Did you know Dr. Xian Han?"

"He came to the laboratory in nineteen eighty three, the same year I did."

"Did you work together?"

"We worked together on a project to estimate energy yields of underground hydrogen bombs the first three years we were here."

"Did you get to know his wife?"

"Yes. Our families did things together. We were handicapped at first by the Han's poor English, but they were quick to pick up English."

"Did they know Larry's family?"

"Yes. Larry worked on the physics of a nuclear power plant with Han and then later they worked together on the mathematics of plutonium triggers. Also, the Han's had two daughters that were the same age as two of the Abramowitz girls. Now there is a private academy on the hill, but then there was only public school. Only a few kids went to classes in Santa Fe. They would have had Brownies, school sports and field trips together."

"How about other social events?"

"I remember seeing the Hans at barbeques and picnics that the Abramowitz's gave."

"Anything else you are forgetting?"

Pieter thought for several minutes and then spoke, "Of course! Larry and Chiacochito, that is Mrs. Han, had a fairly public affair just after the Han's arrived here."

"Wow! Tell me more about that."

"Mrs. Han was very lonely when she first came to Los Alamos. She was isolated by her inability to speak English, and Larry was always on the lookout for women. He especially liked small women like Chiacochito. It's an old story. He preyed on her vulnerability, but then it went on longer than most affairs which only last six months."

"What fueled it?"

"They seemed to develop a fairly deep affection for each other beyond the 'limerance' or fun of sex with a new partner. Both seemed to feel like outsiders in America. They ended up being good sounding boards for each other. Then they got careless about their meetings and Xian caught them having sex in his house. He went to Larry's wife, Kaatje and told her everything."

"What did Larry do?"

"First he denied it. Then he begged his wife's forgiveness. She wasn't sympathetic because Larry had had so many previous affairs. Then he moved out and said that he would marry Chiacochito . He stayed in a grubby little apartment for six months, but he missed his daughters and they missed him so he went back home."

"Did he continue to see Mrs. Han?" Signe asked.

"I don't have any solid evidence, but I believe he did. Until very recently."

"What is your evidence?"

"Just before Larry was murdered, he and I were working in the lab in the basement of his house and he left an encrypted email up on his computer. It was from Chiacochito. I printed a quick copy. She was writing about a passionate afternoon of very prolonged and passionate sex they had had recently and she wanted to thank him for it. She said he had held her right on the brink of an orgasm for nearly fifteen minutes so that when she finally spilled over it was very powerful."

"Did she know about Larry's private lab?"

"Not that I'm aware of, but they must have had assignations at his house. It was the logical place for them to meet. After sex I'd bet he wrapped her in a fluffy robe and showed off his fancy equipment. I know I would have. Then he probably got aroused again and bent her over one of those large vibrating machines and took her again."

Signe was surprised by Dr. van der Waals openness with her, but she didn't want him to stop talking.

"I'm wondering if randy old Larry had affairs with any of the other women in Los Alamos," Signe queried.

"I know he had flings with a couple of secretaries a long time ago, but neither of them work at the lab anymore. Besides, once Larry and I started getting money from the secrets we sold we could hire, how shall I put it, more experienced and, therefore, more exciting women."

"I want you to write down everything you remember about the affair," Signe said. "Seal it in an envelope and I'll send an officer to pick it up later today."

CHAPTER 45

Getting up from her desk, Signe put Chiacochito's name on her board with a heavy line to both Larry and Xian Han. She wanted to pick her friend, Jefferson Barclay's brain about the Han's. Like most of the scientists at Los Alamos since the Second World War she suspected the Chinese couple came to Santa Fe to misbehave. These episodes included excessive drinking, drugs, kinky sex trysts and even the peddling of America's secrets. If the Han's did, she was sure Jefferson would know the details. Signe also knew it was far too early to call her late sleeping friend who caroused nearly every night until two a.m. at all the local night spots. Instead she put in a call to her colleague, Ted Tiebout in Amsterdam where it was a respectable two in the afternoon.

After a greeting Signe said, "How are things in Amsterdam?"

"The weather has been beautiful both sunny and warm. I miss having you around to test my hypotheses and to try out the new restaurants."

"Any breaks on Albina's murderer?"

"I would have to say yes. We finished our investigation of the black BMWs that Albina's neighbor saw the day of the murder and we found it abandoned in downtown s-Gravenhage, the place you call The Hague, right across the street from the Maritshuis. It had obviously been abandoned in a hurry. They hadn't removed any incriminating evidence at all. We found maps that had the Alkmaar canal house marked on it. There was black clothing in the trunk that may have blood spatter on it, and there were dozens of fingerprints that we are analyzing now."

"Try to match the prints you found to the partials that I found on the scythe they dumped at canal side."

"That's a good idea. I'll have the CSIs working on that. They learned a lot of new techniques from your assistant, Valerie. We also found some lead-colored paint on the bottom of a discarded pair of shoes. We will search the local shipyards for a match. Perhaps we can find the murderer's hiding place. I should have some answers for you in a couple of days."

"Did Urszula Stephanie resurface in the Netherlands?"

"She came through customs from Germany at a small rural border crossing in the farming village of Nijegen last Saturday. It's our smallest sleepiest little customs shack. It seemed like she was trying to sneak back into the country. Usually she flies into Schipol and plops her tattered Polish passport flamboyantly on the customs counter just begging someone to challenge her."

"Was she questioned about entering the country from this rural crossing?"

"Yes. Reportedly she was unruffled and said she had business in northwest Germany before returning to Amsterdam."

"Where did she go after that?"

"She went straight to her office all the while trying to shake the tail I had on her. She doubled back; then waited at one of our few lights through the green; and then sped off on the red. She even went the wrong way on two one way streets."

"So her actions were those of a law abiding citizen except for the reckless driving?"

"Yes, but we know from Interpol that she has been mixed up with illegal currency transfer, smuggling bearer bonds and mostly slipping Polish Nationals to the West and to America. She never comes into the Netherlands clean."

"Except this time, Ted."

"I think I'll drag her in and question her just to let her know we are watching."

"Okay. Call me when you get the results on the fingerprints."

Signe walked over to the laboratory to talk with Valerie Sanderson who had just arrived at work.

"How are our tails on Svelty Patterson going?"

"She closed her electronic surveillance operation in Portland after we found all the bugs," Valerie remarked. "The technician who was running her office was found beaten nearly to death two blocks from her little lair. I'm sure Svelty did it herself. Then she spent a few days with her parents in Oklahoma. Their age has made them both pretty feeble. After that, she appeared in Taormina, Sicily with a darkly handsome younger man. They ate out every night always late and at conspicuous outdoor tables, holding hands and kissing between courses. They got completely naked and made love on the beach one sunny afternoon, not very discreetly I might add," as Valerie spilled some eight by ten glossies on the desk. Once they went to the ancient Greek theatre near town and made love by the full moon. Here are the pictures."

Another series of glossy black and white eight by tens were spilled on the counter by Valerie.

"Look at this one," Valerie commented.

As she pointed at a picture of Svelty supporting herself with her elbows on an ancient stone with her legs extended up and backward. Her lover was nestled between the tops of her thighs and he held one thigh easily in each hand. It made Signe think of a human wheelbarrow.

"That young man is very athletic as well as very passionate," Signe remarked.

"One of the many advantages of a younger lover," Valerie remarked as she placed her hand on Signe's forearm.

Having been over this ground before with Valerie, she simply moved her arm and asked, "Where did she go next?"

"She disappeared completely. We have failed to detect her at any of her other haunts."

"What do we know about the handsome young man?"

"He is a very bad former KGB hit man from Minsk named Arkady Shilkloper," Valerie replied. "He was very hard to find, but finally turned up on a database that was smuggled out of Belarus recently."

"What is he doing in Sicily acting like a new groom?" Signe queried.

"I have no idea. It is totally bizarre. Perhaps he has been hired to take her out."

"Is this his *modus operandi*?"

"Absolutely not. He doesn't go through this elaborate, prolonged, stylize courtship like an Australian lyrebird. He shoots his victims without a word of warning, on a rainy night with poor visibility from across the street when they walk under a streetlight."

"How many times has he killed?"

"I only have a bad translation of the database, but their estimate is sixty times. Admittedly, most of the people he killed were thieves, murderers or enemies of the state in their own right. The world is probably a better place without those sixty some men and three women. Until now all of his hits have been predominantly in Moscow with some in Minsk, or St. Petersburg"

"What is he doing in the west? Vacationing?"

"I don't know. Interpol is trying to help me with that."

"How could he possibly have hooked up with our darling Svelty?"

Valerie thought a while before replying, "I don't know. They seem to run in completely different spheres. Of all the entities that you have considered in this complicated investigation, only the Polish government and the Polish underground could vaguely connect Svelty and Arkady."

"Try crossing their names in all the Eastern European data bases and see what comes up," Signe said as she walked toward the door.

Finally, it was barely late enough to call Jefferson Barclay and Signe reached for her phone.

"Good morning, stranger!" Signe yelled into the receiver. "Get out of bed and get some clothes on. I'm dying to see you. Meet me at Tante Maria's in thirty minutes."

Signe knew that Jefferson simply had to throw some clothes on and walk across the plaza to the restaurant. Signe slid into a vinyl lined booth near the door and sipped her coffee until Jefferson arrived still looking sleepy.

Signe ordered huevos rancheros with two eggs over easy.

"Red or green?" the waitress asked with her pencil poised.

"Christmas, please," Signe answered.

"I haven't seen you in weeks Jefferson," Signe chortled. "What's been happening?"

"I have a new friend. His name is Jason and he runs a modern art gallery on the south side of Taos," Jefferson said in a contented voice. We've been taking road trips when the gallery is closed on Mondays and Tuesday."

"Anything else?"

"One of my best friends, Lobsang Lhalungpa, a Tibetan monk was killed by a hit and run driver on St. Michael's Drive. He was named one of Santa Fe's living treasures in 1998 and he was teaching me Buddhism."

"I don't know a lot about Buddhism old friend," Signe rebutted. "But I do know that the faithful are not allowed to gamble, smoke, drink, swear or engage in homosexual acts. Which of these were you planning to give up?"

"Actually, Lobsang and I were just starting to discuss that. But it is a gentle religion and I'm sure that the all exalted Buddha wouldn't even want me to give up all of them at once."

"I suppose you are right."

"The man that killed him was drunk at the time. His name is Roque something and it is reported that he had been stopped for driving drunk. He also had three DWIs in the eighties and nineties. Then, four times between 2000 and 2003 the police just put him in protective custody at the Santa Fe County Jail until he sobered up."

"Shame on us, Jefferson. That is an abysmal failure of the system. Does the drunk live here in Santa Fe?"

"No," Jefferson said dejectedly. "He is from one of the pueblos and the land owned by them is so large and desolate that there are a lot of places to hide. Plus the Anglo police force doesn't have near the presence or freedom of movement on the reservation to track down a felon. How much does a Pueblo Indian really care about a Tibetan Monk?"

"I will have Mateo Romero help us with this, Jefferson. He is well connected with all the Pueblos."

CHAPTER 46

"I'm really struggling with this murder case, friend," Signe said as she took a large swallow of coffee.

"You're always fraught with doubt in the middle of one of your murder investigations," Jefferson replied. "Why don't you ever pick an easy case where a jealous wife murders a philandering husband that you can solve in thirty minutes?"

"It almost seems the cases pick me rather than the other way around," Signe mused.

"It stretches your ability each time."

"I suppose you're right about that. At least I don't ever get bored."

Signe and Jefferson walked back to the hotel, and Signe drove to the station house while thinking about what her next move should be. She went to the lab first to see if Valerie had turned up anything new.

"I found some scratch paper tucked in an old book that seems to be a rough draft of an ad," Valerie said as she handed Signe a yellow tablet with faded writing in pencil on it.

The cursive was hard to decipher but seemed to say—'Nuclear physicist, age 51, seeks summer position in NATO country 1999.

Has highest government clearance. Available 6/1/1999 until 10/2/1999. Reply to LA at box 1636.'

"I believe he sent it to *The Bulletin of the Atomic Scientists.*"

"Perhaps it's a coded message to Larry's handler," Signe suggested. "It seems too brief to be a real job request to me. It doesn't even specify an area of nuclear physics that he is adept in. Plus it has a lot of numbers in it that could be code. Also his age is wrong. He was fifty-five in 1999."

"I just found it yesterday," Valerie replied. "I haven't really had a chance to work on breaking it down. I got a new automated code breaking algorithm from Interpol. I'll feed it the message."

"Print me a copy also so I can work on it," Signe suggested.

With a problem like this, she would usually pin a copy to her bathroom mirror. In that way, she looked at it every morning as she was getting ready for work so the numerals would be constantly spinning around in her mind like a slot machine that never stopped.

When she got back to her desk the desk sergeant reported that a woman had been waiting to speak with her. Signe asked that the visitor be sent back. A tall blond woman in blue suit approached Signe's desk.

"Are you Detective Sorensen?" the woman shouted loudly.

"Yes, I am," Signe replied startled.

The woman swept her arm across Signe's desk dumping all off the accumulated files and papers onto the floor.

"I want you to leave my bloody family alone!" the woman yelled.

Signe jumped up from her chair. The woman was cuffed by the time Signe leveled her Smith and Wesson at the woman's sternum. The two detectives pushed her roughly down into an armless wooden chair.

"Who the hell are you?" Signe barked.

But as she said it, she recognized the woman as Larry Abramowitz's oldest daughter, Magdalena.

"I'm Magdalena Dershowitz, oldest daughter of Dr. Lawrence Abramowitz and you are destroying my family!" Magdalena shouted as she struggled to free her hands. "First my father dies, and then my sister is brutally murdered while you are within sight of her home in the Netherlands. I hold you responsible. Now there are only two of us left."

"How can you possibly blame me for either of those tragedies?" Signe replied incredulously. "Are you crazy? I've devoted every waking hour to solving those two crimes for the past month. Your father was my good friend. I visited your younger sister in New Orleans at my own expense to learn more about your father's murder. It may have just been bad luck that your other sister was brutally murdered while I was in Amsterdam to question her."

"Our family was fine until you began sticking your big nose into our affairs," Magdalena said petulantly.

Signe motioned for the cuffs to be taken off. Another officer handed Magdalena a cup of tea.

"I hope to be part of the solution, not part of the problem," Signe replied sympathetically.

Then she said nothing for several minutes.

"What do you do?" Signe asked quietly just to make conversation.

"I'm a technical computer specialist in the US embassy in Cracow, Poland," Magdalena said in a reasonable voice for the first time.

"How long have you held that position?"

"I have been worked in the embassy there for ten years in a variety of different jobs. At first my mother was alive, and I could visit her on weekends. Then I married a Polish Jew."

"When did you and your father become estranged?"

"About twelve years ago. I loved him a great deal. He was a workaholic but it was the constant affairs that finally drove me away from him. It hurt my mother so. The other two girls always sided more with him. Even though we disagreed about our parents we

273

always remained close. I can't bear the loss of my sister Albina. Her murder makes me cry every day."

"My role in this case, Magdalena, is to solve both the murder of your dad and your sister. Can you accept that?"

"Yes. I just have a lot of anger and I don't know where to direct it. I'm sorry."

"There are a lot of connections between these murders and Poland. Perhaps we can work together to solve these awful crimes. But first, I need some lunch would you like to join me?"

"Yes. Our family always ate at The Ore House on the plaza. Would that be okay?"

"Of course."

Signe drove to the plaza and parked in an emergency vehicle spot. They had to wait a few minutes for a table. Signe never ate there, so she let Magdalena order blackened prime rib with garlic sauce for both of them. Signe enjoyed the contrast of the black, hot, and chary outside to the pink soft flavorful middle. During lunch Signe told her guest about the ancient Polish helicopter part she found near her father's body in the Valle Grande and the titanium chip that had been implanted in his body. Magdalena had met Albina's Polish friend, Urszula Stephanie once, but Signe filled her in on Urszula's connection to the old generals, the contraband money and jewels from Statislow that she smuggled into Holland.

"It surprises me that Albina would have a dear friend who did that," Magdalena remarked. "She was always the most righteous one of the three of us. I never knew her to do anything wrong."

"You did know that she had taken a lover before her death?" Signe remarked.

"Yes, but it was a desperate measure that she only took him because her husband, Waander was so awful. It was really out of character for her and she agonized over it."

"Did you ever meet Arend van Oosterwijk?"

"No. I was supposed to visit last May, but at the last minute the Soviets held surprise maneuvers near Poland's eastern border and all leave was cancelled. I did see a picture though, and he was tall and quite handsome"

"He had a very Dutch name. Did you think he looked Dutch?"

"Oh, no. He had black hair and brown eyes. Albina said that he treated her very well, in an almost courtly manner."

"If you have the time I want to show you something that is important in your father's investigation," Signe said as they both finished their coffee after passing on dessert. "I could just tell you about it, but, I believe, seeing it will have more impact."

"My flight back is open."

They walked out into a warm quiet summer afternoon. Signe drove north out of Santa Fe past the rows of white gravestones in the National Cemetery. The rest of the ride to Los Alamos went quickly. Signe opened the back door of Larry's house with her key, and instead of going into the kitchen turned down the stairs to the basement. She hit the button at the bottom of the stairs that opened the big door into the secret lab. Signe let Magdalena wander around the shiny equipment without comment for fifteen minutes.

"According to my consultant, all this equipment is state of the art. No one in Los Alamos, including your father's good friend Pieter van der Waals, knew of its existence," Signe said.

"Why did Dad need such an extensive and expensive clandestine lab?"

"That's what I was hoping you could tell me. Did he ever mention it to you?"

"He must have been doing work for other countries and selling the results to pay for the equipment. And you think the sales were to an enemy?" Magdalena said.

"I don't honestly know, but I'm trying very hard to figure out where the information is being funneled. I know you father paid Doctor van der Waals over nine hundred thousand dollars for surreptitious work your father had him do. Also, your Dad would never tell Pieter where the money came from. I believe your father was protecting him and probably at the same time protecting himself."

"I would like to help you, Signe in any way that I can," Magdalena said.

"Then before you go I will give you all the information I have about the Polish helicopter, the underground generals, Urszula Stephanie and a private detective I have used in Poland. We have also accumulated some info about Statislow."

"If you give me the titanium chip that was found in my father's body, I can use the embassy resources to track its date and location."

"That would be very helpful," Signe replied as they started the drive back to Santa Fe.

"I never heard of a technician in an eastern bloc country that wasn't a spy," Signe mused to herself.

CHAPTER 47

Before going home Signe went to the office and added some more information to the white board that stood next to her desk. As she wrote on the board Signe wondered if she had been played by the three Abramowitz sisters. At the funeral they had all expressed their anger at their father for his affairs and the resulting lack of contact with them. But Signe was a stranger to them and perhaps they were just being secret about their complicity. Katarzyna had carried espionage messages as a child and was an intimate member of a Palestinian Jihad organization. Magdalena had worked in the American Polish embassy for years as a technical expert. Signe knew that American embassy technical experts were good at communications, but their main occupation was to work as a spy. Albina seemed the farthest removed from subversive activities in her staid role as an international investment banker. However, she had been brutally murdered just minutes before an interview with the woman who was investigating her father's murder.

Katarzyna seemed the most open of the sister's and it wasn't late in New Orleans. Signe decided to call to see if she could trick the young sister into revealing something.

After a few minutes of small talk, Signe said, "I just left your sister. She blamed me for all the Abramowitz family problems so she started out very angry. I tried to explain my position and after a time she settled down. We visited your dad's house and ended up having a very frank visit. I showed your sister your father's state-of-the art laboratory."

"She told me about the work you and your sisters were doing with your father over the past six years," Signe lied.

There was a pause on the other end of the line. Then Katarzyna said, "My sister called me from the airport before her flight. She didn't mention anything about the past six years, though," she replied cagily.

Signe ended the conversation suspecting that her hunch was correct. Larry was probably the smartest human she had ever known. Why should the daughters be any less remarkable? Quite probably they were wily as well.

Signe went to *The Coyote Cafe* for a glass of chardonnay and lamb chops so rare she would have been embarrassed to eat them in front of others. She watched a very handsome Hispanic man with a homely woman. Her face looked as though God had grabbed her nose just as she was being born and pulled it, so that the whole center of her face had shifted forward dragging her upper lip and part of her forehead. She imagined the man stayed with her because she was very athletic and talented in bed. She imagined the woman over the man in the posture of Russian bareback rider with a stiff spine. On further reflection Signe thought her imagining had more to do with her own state of horniness than the libidinous state of her neighbors. After all, it had been eighteen days since Signe had practiced an extended and varied fellatio on her lover, Brian. She went home and wrote him an erotic email that featured sex in a famous museum at night, before drifting off to sleep.

In the morning she decided to call all her investigators together to see if they could develop some new leads. Signe had Valerie bring all the clues they had to the station conference room. She had assembled them in a pile by chronology in the center of the table.

Mateo, Jack, Liam and Valerie arrived before Signe. She reviewed the facts of the case before opening the meeting to discussion.

"It has been forty-two days since Dr. Abramowitz's body was found in Valles Caldera," Signe began. "We have several suspects, in fact, almost too many but after six weeks, no clear path of investigation that will lead us to the perpetrators. Often an important clue that will lead to a resolution is right in front of us but just hasn't been evaluated properly. That is the reason for having Valerie assembles all of our clues this morning. I'd like everyone to spend the next forty-five minutes just looking at these items without trying at first to form any hypotheses."

Signe picked up the piece of helicopter landing gear that she had found in Valles Grande. Jack worked on the photos and clues from Albina Alkmaar's murder scene in Amsterdam as he hadn't seen them before. Mateo worked on all the material that related to Svelty. He was still upset about the beheading of Ernesto Chavez the young Cochiti tracker that had been murdered just outside the pueblo. Mateo was sure that Svelty had not only planned the beheading but swung the thin steel blade herself. Liam worked on the factors that suggested that both Albina and Larry were murdered by the same group. Everyone worked quietly on their materials until baskets of red chile meat burritos arrived from *The Shed*.

After eating, the participants took turns describing what they had been working on. Liam Farrell went first.

"I tried to relate the murders of Albina and her father, Larry," Liam began. "I concluded that their two murders were unrelated. They were killed on different sides of earth, succumbed to two totally different *modus operandi* and most importantly there was no common motivation for their murder. I believe the temporal relationship of the two events was just a cruel coincidence."

"I agree with Liam," Valerie volunteered. "I broke the murder of Dr. Abramowitz and Albina Alkmaar down into fifty elements proposed as important factors in linking murders by the American Forensics Institute and there were only three matches which suggest it is very unlikely that the murders were committed by the same person."

"However, if you add in the recent murders of Judge Barry Avalos and Dr. Xian Han perhaps you have more compelling evidence of a cover up," Signe suggested. "Then you have death by isotope, scythe, bridge and carving knife. It begins to sound like a game of Clue. Santa Fe has a murder rate of about eighteen per hundred thousand, but murders in Los Alamos are almost as rare as those in Holland which are fifty times less common than in the US. Then these four events look quite anomalous."

"I focused solely on the murder of Albina," Jack began. "But I need to inform you that I wasn't in Holland to examine the clues from her case first hand. The other three murders could be a contract murders meant to silence a witness, but Albina's murder was a crime of passion. I can't look at the photos of her slight naked white body sprawled across her bed without getting sick. Those vicious cuts from the scimitar were delivered slowly over thirty or forty minutes with infliction of maximum pain and blood loss. Therefore I think the murderer knew her well and was very angry. I don't sense such anger in any of the other cases."

"I worked on an ad for employment that Larry published in 1999," Valerie began. "It contained a bunch of numbers, some of which we knew were wrong, and Signe and I wondered if the ad might be a coded message to Larry's handler. I fed it to a new code breaker computer program, and it was indeed a coded message but unfortunately it was from one of Larry's girlfriends about a weekend meeting in Palm Springs."

"I wouldn't be at all discouraged by what you found," Signe replied. "What you learned is that Larry used secret codes and you know the general method he used for encoding. Now let's find some more messages and we might find out who was paying him to spy."

Mateo was the last person to talk about his findings.

"I have been pursuing Svelty Patterson since she kidnapped both me and Signe on separate occasions. Then when Ernesto was beheaded I saw traces of Svelty's cruelty in the act and I redouble my efforts. Dr. Goldiamond predicted that Svelty would return to the same places over and over again. Therefore, I staked out Albuquerque for several days. However, the only one of her haunts she has visited recently is Taormina with a new lover named Arkady. Currently both of them have dropped out of sight again. I suspect they are busy planning a new operation focused on Signe."

"I have two problems with Svelty," Mateo said. "First, I object to her thoughtlessly violent behavior which probably includes a murder. Secondly, I fail to grasp her motive for pursuing and threatening Signe. Svelty has received nothing but assistance and succor from Signe. After her overdose, when she was in a coma for weeks Signe was the only one who visited her."

"She may not even have known I was there," Signe replied.

"She was certainly told about it by the nurses, techs, and doctors," Valerie replied.

"Perhaps in her twisted mind she associates Signe with everything that has gone bad in her life-Chloe's death, Dirk's downfall, some economic distress and loss of status in the community. If Signe is destroyed she may think then everything will go back to being good."

"The other possibility is that she is working with the murderers," Jack suggested. "She could offer a lot of inside info on Signe's habits."

"I think we need to track down her new boyfriend, Arkady Shilkloper," Signe remarked. "Perhaps he can enlighten us about Svelty's motivation."

"And how would you go about locating him?"Jack asked.

"First I would contact Urszula Stephanie. She has a lot of contacts in Eastern Europe," Signe replied. "But my ace in the hole is a private investigator in Lvov, Poland named Zbigniew Popalov."

CHAPTER 48

Signe went to her desk to process what she had learned from her team. Everyone agreed that Svelty Patterson was a violent and unpredictable person who operated for unknown reasons but always with impunity. Signe planned to ask Chief Hartford for additional manpower to track the sociopath down. The longer she worked on the case, the more ties she found to Poland either official or unofficial. She put in a call to Detective Ted Tiebout in Amsterdam and asked him to double up his surveillance on Urszula Stephanie. Ted reported that she usually stayed in Amsterdam and its suburbs when she visited the Netherlands. However, this time she had already made two trips to Groningen and one to Delft to meet minor underworld characters and fences.

After dialing the phone to talk with Zbigniew, Signe was handed an urgent message on a pink slip by the desk sergeant.

'Meet me at Camel Rock in thirty minutes. I have info that will solve your murders. J. Destroy this note.'

Sometimes Signe felt Americans read too much Robert Ludlum and Tom Clancy for their own good. The simple transfer of low grade information that could easily be accomplished in the security of the station house was obfuscated by amateur cloak and dagger effects. Doubting anything useful would result, she had Jack drive her to Camel Rock. Signe thought the pile of rock looked so much like a camel that it was certainly manmade; however no New Mexican ever admitted it. Standing alone on the back side of the rock a young man looked anxiously at each tourist that approached in the fading sunlight.

"Are you 'J'?" Signe asked in a conspiratorial voice.

Motioning Signe closer, the man said, "Yes."

A tall, very slender, young man in an ill-fitting gray sweatshirt with a hood grabbed at Signe's arm.

Pulling her arm back, Signe asked, "Who are you?"

"You may call me Jeffrey," the young man replied in a whisper. "And I work as a janitor in division X at the National Lab."

"I never heard of that. What the hell is division X?" Signe asked derisively.

"It's all the projects that are too secret for even the people who work at the lab to know about."

"So how long have you worked there?"

"Nine years this fall."

"What kind of stuff are they working on?"

"I can't tell you that, and even if I could you wouldn't believe it. It's way beyond your wildest imagination."

"Okay. Then what did you want to tell me?"

"Can I trust you?"

"You didn't contact me by accident. You checked me out thoroughly before you contacted me and you know that I am discreet and careful. Now what do you have to say?"

"I went camping in the Valle Grande with Larry in April," Jeffrey replied.

"Were you there when Larry was murdered?" Signe asked urgently.

"Not exactly. I had been tracking an indigo bunting and had climbed nearly to the top of a large hill near the camp called Cerro de Trasquilar. I heard the 'thucka, thucka' of a helicopter coming in very low and landed. I crept halfway down the hill to glass the campground with my binoculars. There were only three people in the chopper and they moved around the camp quickly."

"Were they men or women?"

"The undergrowth was thick and I couldn't tell. Two of the individuals appeared to be carrying rifles so I was afraid to approach any closer."

"How long were they there?"

"Perhaps forty minutes. Then the chopper took off to the north. I checked carefully to make sure they hadn't left anyone behind, and then I hurried down to the campsite. I found poor Larry's body and I tried to give him CPR like I had been taught at the lab, but there was no sign of life."

"I examined that campsite very carefully and I found no evidence that another camper had been there," Signe remarked dubiously.

"I'm an amateur forensic scientist and I'm also very compulsive. I made sure that all evidence of my having been there was removed. I checked carefully for hair and fibers on my knees before I left."

"One of the details that neither I nor the FBI pursued was how Larry got to the Valles Caldera."

"I have a 1969 International Travelall and Larry knows all the back roads in the area. We took some washed out narrow forest service roads. We parked about three miles away from our campsite," Jeffrey replied smugly.

"How did you know Dr. Abramowitz?"

"We met when he did a project in division X about five years ago. We had a mutual interest in camping and bird watching so we took car trips around the northern part of the state."

"Did you two do that frequently?"

"No. He preferred to take a woman if he could find one or pay one to tag along. That way he could satisfy two of his passions at once."

"So you were his second choice?"

"That's correct. But over the years we got to be pretty good friends."

"From watching and talking with you, Jeffrey, I was wondering if you might be a homosexual."

"What fucking difference does that make?" Jeffrey yelled shaking his fist at Signe. "You people are all alike trying to pigeon hole everyone so you can feel superior! It's a fucking shame!"

Unsnapping her holster, Signe said, "Put your fist down right now!"

She pressed a button on her walkie-talkie summoning Jack from Vickie C. Jack was by Signe's side in two minutes.

"Cuff him. We're taking him in as a hostile witness," Signe remarked as she pulled Jeffrey's hands behind his back.

Jeffrey mumbled a string of expletives under his breath that Signe couldn't understand. Neither Jack nor Signe spoke to Jeffrey until he was placed in an interrogation room in the station house. Signe uncuffed the witness and motioned for him to sit down.

"Great way to treat someone who is only trying to help the police solve a case," Jeffrey muttered almost incoherently.

"This murder occurred on April 30th and you contacted me today, approximately six weeks later. You sir, have known about this murder for a very long time, and you knew you had important information about the case that no one else could provide. You told me that you are a student of forensics. Therefore, you knew exactly how vital your timely information was. Were you sleeping with Larry?"

"I want a lawyer," Jeffrey answered.

"No you don't," Signe snapped. "You know I'm not going to charge you today. Mostly I'm just frustrated with your push and pull. You offer to help me, and then when I question you, instead of being open and honest and helpful, you threatened me."

"I'm gay. I wanted to sleep with Larry, but I never did," Jeffrey replied. "I'm sure Larry was a homosexual, but the idea frightened him so much that he retreated into raging heterosexuality."

"What's your evidence?"

"He let me give him massages all the time. It made him moan with pleasure. When we went camping he let me crawl into his sleeping bag with him in the morning when it was cold."

"I think you may be reading something into his warm and friendly nature, Jeffrey," Signe said looking at him sadly.

"I don't agree. I have a card from him at my place that expresses his true feelings."

"Let's go get it right now," Signe suggested. "I'll have Jack take you there."

Once Jack had corralled Jeffrey and left, Signe put in a call to Zbigniew, her PI in Poland.

"Most of my clues suggest that the murderer I am tracking came from Poland. It could be the legitimate Polish government, but it's more likely to be some dissident generals or a breakaway group of radicals in Statislow," Signe began. "I need some thorough investigation of all these possibilities. The loose cannon in all of this is Urszula Stephanie, as we have discussed before. I'll send you twenty thousand Zlotys as a down payment on your expenses. We have a lot of anti-terrorism money right now and you may need to hire assistants or pay off government officials."

"I need to start by bribing some people in the US Embassy," Zbigniew said. "They have their ear on what's going on in the country."

"Contact Magdalena Dershowitz, she's a computer technician in the Embassy in Cracow and mention my name. She'll help you. Larry Abramowitz was her father."

"What are you looking for, specifically?"

"Larry was doing research in a wide range of subjects related to nuclear physics and he was selling those secrets to the highest bidder. I'd like to know who was buying and why they stopped if they did. I'd like to know if they murdered him and if so why. Also, why did they spend so much effort making the murder look like death by natural causes? They did such a good job that they fooled the FBI."

Signe and Zbigniew discussed a few other issues before hanging up and agreeing to talk in a week. Jack had just come back from driving Jeffrey to his place.

"The kid lives in a cave," Jack said in disgust.

"You mean his apartment is a dark mess?" Signe replied.

"No I mean he lives in a damn cave!" Jack ejaculated. "He took me up canyon to the north and west and then we walked across this dry field. He has a door that he only added two years ago. He's very proud of it. He's lived there for almost ten years. It's damp and it's cramped. He can't even stand up!"

"What does he do for light, for heaven's sakes?"

"He's stolen electricity from somewhere. I didn't want to get into it."

"Did you examine Larry's so called 'gay' card?"

"Yeah. It's very ambiguous like the other stuff Jeff told us about. I'm not convinced that Larry was even latently homosexual."

"Jeffrey is the only eye witness to the murder and I think he knows more about the murder of Larry Abramowitz than he is letting on," Signe replied. "Let's get a search warrant and see what we can sweat out of him."

CHAPTER 49

Signe invited her friend Terecita Armijo to go to dinner with her. Signe suggested La Casa Sena. She hadn't been there to hear the singing waiters for months. Terecita came straight from her work at the courthouse. Signe was already working on a pitcher of icy margaritas made with El Tesoro tequila. It was an unseasonable eighty-five degrees in Santa Fe and the cold drink tasted wonderful. Signe poured and handed Terecita a brimming glass. After a quick swallow, an appetizer of mussels, shrimp and clams in a Chimayo red chile sauce arrived. They both had a salad of multicolored sliced beets with slivers of Vidalia onions in a wine vinegar sauce. While they waited for their main courses, Terecita spoke about how she was controlling her work addiction.

"I joined the Newman League at the Cathedral. They have a group for young single professionals and it's fun, even though it is mostly women. I was hoping for more eligible males, but I've gotten a couple of dates out of the group. My parents were staunch Catholics when we were kids. I sort of drifted away from the church in college and then even more in law school. I really like the companionship and I get to confess my sins every week!"

"Wow. That sounds great for you. I was pretty worried about you the last time we talked. I'm sure you were making good judicial decisions but I know they were rattling around in your head after you had rendered your decision. Now you can be absolved of all guilt every week. I wish I could be Catholic like you. It seems like a simple way to live."

Both had ordered salmon with a pomegranate glaze surrounded by Brussels sprouts and new potatoes. The waiter presented both plates with a flourish. Terecita was in a good mood and drank nearly a bottle of chardonnay while she ate. By the end of the meal her speech was slurred and she had become very talkative.

"I miss Manny Ramirez," Terecita said in a plaintive voice. "And I miss very much Barry Avalos. He had come to fill a similar role in my life once Manny was murdered. I had come to rely on him."

"Have you heard anymore about the investigation?" Signe asked.

"Yes. The de, de detective told me all about it but I'm not supposed to say anything," Terecita said in a voice that was still slurry from drink.

"I'm sure he would have told me if I had been around, since I'm in law enforcement," Signe replied hopefully.

"I suppose you're right," Terecita said in a slurry voice. "Detective Don Montgomery said this death wasn't a suicide. There wasn't a note, the car was wiped free of any evidence including prints, and Avalos fingernails showed bruising."

"Why would the department cover up a murder?"

"I'm not sure. I know it came from higher up. Perhaps someone in the department was involved. I could feel that Montgomery was afraid to pursue it."

Signe decided not to push for any more information. She helped Terecita up and drove her home.

In the morning Signe talked with Jack about what Terecita had told her. Jack had always had better relationships with the State Police than she had.

"I'll just drive over there now and see what I can find out," Jack said as he headed toward the door.

Signe had gotten a search warrant for Jeffrey's cave. She rounded up four officers in uniform and headed up into the hills behind Los Alamos. On the drive the banter in the car was about a new blues bar in Tesuque. It had opened six weeks before and all the officers had been there at least once.

"They had a twelve string guitarist last weekend," Connie a new recruit volunteered. "Her playing was better than her voice. They had a good crowd."

"I went opening night and the place was just jammed," Sergio exclaimed. "It was better a couple of weeks later, although there was a fight over a girl at the end of the evening. That friend of yours, Detective Sorensen, from the FBI, Farrell, had had way too much to drink. He hit on this blond who was clearly the property of this tall lanky cowboy. They had been rubbing each other at the bar for over an hour. Farrell went over a little unsteadily and started talking to her. The cowboy let him talk to her for about a minute before he chimed in belligerently. As their voices rose I moved closer. Then the shoving started as the blond ducked out of the middle. Farrell got in the first punch but the cowboy staggered back and delivered a crushing blow to Farrell's jaw that sent him to the floor. He got up quickly and sent two rapid fists to the cowboy's gut.

"I can't believe a club like that didn't have some security," Signe interjected.

"They had two skinny kids on duty. They took one look at the size of the two fighters and decided to work crowd control, just keeping the other patrons back and safe. Another cowboy tried to enter the fray but the first one motioned him back. Farrell got in another couple of blows that drove him against the bar. I thought the cowboy looked finished. Then he surprised me by pulling a knife out of the back of his belt. I couldn't believe security hadn't relieved him of that at the door. The cowboy thrust the blade up toward Farrell in a flash. Your friend got his crossed hands inside the knife and sent it clattering to the floor. Then the strangest thing happened the two assailants hugged each other."

"What did you make of that?" Signe asked incredulously.

"It turned out that the whole thing was staged by Farrell. He's starting an ultimate fighting club in Albuquerque, and they were drumming up business. They walked through the club handing out business cards. The blond helped. Farrell told me he was pretty bored with the FBI because Santa Fe is so peaceful."

"Why doesn't he transfer to Philadelphia or Washington?"

"Apparently he's tried without any success."

As they approached the fields near Jeffrey's cave, Signe made a mental note to learn more about FBI agent Liam Farrell. She had written him off as just lazy, but perhaps there was more to him than met the eye. The four officers spread out and crossed the field toward the door that led into Jefferies' cave. Some litter was scattered in the brownish prairie grasses, but nothing that seemed incriminating.

Signe knocked politely on the small white door which reminded her of a door in the Shire where the fictional Hobbits live. No answer. She knocked again harder. Just as she called an officer forward to force the door, she heard a faint rustling. Jeffrey opened the door slowly, eyes blinking as he adjusted to the light.

Holding up a legal sized blue paper, Signe said, "Jeffery Huntsinger, I have a warrant here to search your premises. Please step outside."

Signe had been warned about the dim light. Every officer had brought two powerful flashlights. The cave consisted of three small rooms, a kitchen sitting room, a bedroom and a bathroom without a bathtub or shower. All the rooms had low ceilings and piles of magazines and news papers everywhere. Most of it seemed old but carefully catalogued and organized. There were complete collections of *Out, Freshmen, Genre* and other gay men's magazines that reminded her unhappily of searching Vincent Jaramillo's storage area during a previous case. Filling one oak bookcase was a boxed set of *Forensic Magazine*. One officer found a small black book that must have listed gay contacts since ninety percent of the names were male. Larry's name and phone numbers as well as his shoe size and shirt size was listed there.

Jeffrey got more and more agitated as the officers went through his things often leaving them in some disarray. He would follow one officer for thirty or forty minutes and then follow another. Signe watched Jeffrey slip a kitchen knife in a large magazine he pretended to be reading. Before he got himself into more trouble, Signe invited him to come outside.

"You've read about searches of premises before Jeffrey when you studied forensics," Signe said. "You know it can be upsetting for the occupants. Of course most of them are guilty and you probably aren't, but no one wants their things gone through. I know it would make me nervous to have someone go through my things."

"I can't fucking believe you are treating me like this," Jeffery whined. "Larry was my dear friend. I saw him murdered and I was only trying to help you!"

"As I already told you, you didn't come forward for six weeks and despite your interest in forensics you haven't given me one single clue even though you witnessed the murder. I'm more than a little frustrated with you!"

"I should have tried to stop those three people. I didn't know they were murderers, but I knew they were up to no good. I should have helped my friend, but I was so afraid."

"Let's sit down out here," Signe said gesturing toward an old wooden case. "Despite your interest in forensics you don't have any training in law enforcement. I certainly don't think anyone would expect you to confront three terrorists with a bird book."

Once they were seated Signe said, "Hand me that knife that you slipped into that rolled up magazine you are carrying."

Jeffrey looked surprised but then sheepishly passed the knife over to Signe handle first.

CHAPTER 50

In another forty-five minutes the officers had completed their search. They packed up their cameras and took two boxes full of materials. Signe escorted Jeffery back to his front door.

"You should be able to pick these things up in about three weeks," Signe said gently.

Jeffrey went through the crooked hobbit door to his cave without saying a word. On the way back to Santa Fe the officers talked about new clubs and restaurants in town. The consensus was that the usual crop of new restaurants had started up in the spring but none really stood out. They were a little too expensive for a working bloke and tried a little too hard with their décor. One officer had been to *A la Mesa* for a fresh combination of Mexican and European food. He liked the service, but found it a little expensive. Others mentioned old favorites like *Tomasita's Santa Fe Station.*

"I here there are over three hundred restaurants in Santa Fe," Signe remarked. "And some of the old standards like *The Pink Adobe, Santacafe, The Compound,* and *Coyote Café* are still among the best."

Two officers carried the evidence from Jeffrey's cave into the lab for cataloguing. Signe sat down at her desk and looked at her pink phone messages. Then she started leafing through the piles of unopened mail. Absentmindedly she put in a call to Jefferson Barclay.

"I collected all the nights that Larry Abramowitz and Chaicochito Han spent together at the La Fonda hotel," Jefferson remarked. "They stayed here quite regularly from '97 to '02. Larry was a showoff and stayed in the bridal suite if it was available. I remember being on a first name bases with them both. Her Chinese first name was impossible to pronounce and Larry called her Chaco for short. They snuck away for weekends camping there and I remember both of them saying how magical they thought the Anasazi ruins were. Chaco told me they usually hiked from the camp ground to one of the smaller less visited ruins like Pinetop House or Wijiji. Then they took off their clothing and spent the weekend naked except for their hiking boots."

"Why did they stop coming in 2002?" Signe asked.

"I'm not sure. Perhaps they just found another venue. I certainly never heard them have any kind of disagreement in all those years."

"Could you call your friends at the other fine hotels and see if Larry's name appears in the register for the last of 2002 and first part of 2003?"

While waiting for an answer, She absent mindedly tore open a thick manila envelope. When she pulled out the contents, a popsicle stick wound tightly on a rubber band spun around rapidly disbursing a fine white powder into a cloud over her desk. She had attended all of the classes on terrorist attacks using infectious vectors such as brucellosis, plague, or anthrax. She stopped breathing immediately and fell to the floor before crawling out of the room. At the doorway she stood up, took a lung full of air, hitting the emergency alarm as she rose. The double door to the room slammed shut.

Within in minutes three officers arrived pulling on white hazmat suits. The sergeant asked Signe what had happened.

"I opened a large manila envelope on my desk and a white powder filled the air," Signe replied.

"Who was it from and was it sent regular mail?" the sergeant asked.

"I have no idea. I didn't look."

"How many times did you breathe after the dispersal?"

"I didn't."

"Excellent. Then you are dismissed. We need to check on the two that are still trapped inside," the sergeant said brushing past Signe.

The building was evacuated and Signe spent the afternoon at home working on papers she had brought home the week before. She cooked Danish red cabbage with bratwurst for dinner and had a long talk with Brian before going to bed.

In the morning the police station was still locked down. Signe talked to the sergeant in charge of the decontamination. The powder wasn't risin or anthrax and probably not another poison but simply finely ground up powdered milk. Further tests were being done in Albuquerque. The two detectives trapped in the room with the powder had been kept overnight at St. Francis Hospital.

"What did you learn from the envelope?" Signe asked.

"Very little. It was a standard envelope with no return address, no finger prints. The postmark was from Denver. However, the flap was sealed with human saliva so we can do a DNA analysis."

What a major breech of secrecy, Signe thought.

"I haven't kept up on bioterrorism since our class several months ago," Signe remarked. "Are there a lot of incidences world wide right now?"

"Actually, no," the sergeant replied. "A dissident in Uzbekistan took out his local headman and his tribal council with some aerosolized hanta virus. He managed to kill eight out of eleven but it took the better part of three weeks. By then even the primitive rural health officials had a pretty good idea what the agent was and who was the vector. Also, there was a small scale risin outbreak in a Japanese subway. Some fanatic group fighting development released the poison, but they only managed to kill three."

"What do you think of this attack?" Signe asked.

"In the end it will probably turn out to be a hoax meant to scare you. The thing is you seem a lot more curious than frightened."

"I've been being stalked by a clever and diabolical woman for the past several months. This is just the kind of thing she is capable of doing."

"What can you tell me about her?"

"Valerie has a rather fat set of files on her. Why don't you take a look?"

"What is her name?"

"Svelty Patterson."

As the sergeant headed for the lab, he said, "Thanks."

Signe went to the front desk cleaned the big department coffee pot throwing away the morning's tarry residue and grinding a pound of fresh beans from Starbucks. After grinding all the beans carefully, Signe buried her face deep into the grinder and inhaled deeply. Signe heard that men loved the smell of bacon. For her it was it the aroma of freshly ground French roasted coffee. She stood by the coffee maker guarding it jealously and took the first two cups before heading to the Chief's office.

Signe boss was sitting at his desk reading an article about bone fishing in the Florida Keys. Signe hadn't talked with her boss and mentor in weeks and she certainly needed some help with her floundering murder investigation. Signe handed over a large steaming cup of coffee and sat down.

"What's this white powder scare all about?" Hartford asked as he put his magazine down.

"My gut feeling is that this is Svelty making trouble again, Chief," Signe replied. "She seems to rear her ugly head every few weeks just to let me know she's out there. None of her stunts are very deadly or dangerous. They just seem to serve as a reminder that she isn't happy."

"Any new ideas about her motivation?"

"I'm afraid not Chief. I'll go over it again with Dr. Goldiamond."

"How is the solution of your murders going?"

"Not very well. There are several suspects that I'm considering but none stand out as a clear leader. I'm still surprised at the number of connections with the Polish entity both official and unofficial. I have a private detective, Zbigniew Poplavok in Poland who is uncovering leads for me right now. If the leads heat up I may go to Poland on some of our antiterrorist money."

"I'm also investigating Judge Barry Avalos's demise. I don't think his death was a suicide. He may have learned something about Larry Abramowitz's murder. Unfortunately, that murder is being investigated by the State Police, and you know how well I get along with them. Xian Han's possible murder by his wife may be involved somehow in the mess. You will have to help me discover the results by the officers across town."

"How did relations with you and the State Police get so bad?" Hartford asked.

"It began as a jurisdictional battle over who would investigate the murder of Chloe Patterson, I believe. You remember the body was found in the horse barns at the State Fair and the State Police by tradition had always investigated crimes at the fair. I told them at the time that I would lead the investigation and demanded that they leave and I don't think they ever quite got over it."

"I'm sure they were angry that an inexperienced young foreign woman officer was telling them what to do. The State Police are a lot more chauvinistic than we are."

"I was hopeful that your connection with Dr. Claus Obermeyer arranged by your Danish mentor would be of more help," Chief Hartford remarked.

"He clearly is very smart and Eastern Europe, especially Poland, is his field of concentration. However, despite his brains and connections he hasn't given me a solid lead or even a concrete suggestion so far. He may simply be busy with other things that he feels are more important than the murder of a washed up scientist."

"I think you should give up on him, Signe. Perhaps you do need to go to Poland to solve this murder."

"I have solved the Chloe Patterson murder and the Manny Ramirez murder so I could leave the Larry Abramowitz murder unsolved. I would still have a sixty-six percent success rate. That equals the solve rate for murder in America in the last decade.'

"You aren't going to quit and you are going to solve this crime especially since there may actually be three crimes-Larry Abramowitz's murder, that of his daughter, Albina, and perhaps even Judge Barry Avalos."

PART 6

CHAPTER 51

When Signe had been gone on a trip to Argentina once, Jefferson had sleuthed out a suspect and shaken him down. She hoped he would be able to help her again. She called him at work.

"I want you to follow up on Chaco Xian and see what you can learn about her activities since her husband's death," Signe told the concierge.

"The last time I did that with that fairy Stephen Samuels you weren't very happy," Jefferson said. "I got the feeling you didn't think I knew what I was doing."

"Actually, I was impressed by the job you did on pure instinct. We both know you don't have training in law enforcement, just good instincts. I was just a little afraid that when you pushed your suspect hard, which you almost always have to do, that you might get hurt."

"Thank you. I'll get right on it."

Then Signe went to the laboratory to check on the white powder found in her office.

"Tell me what you found on my desk, Valerie," Signe said as she breezed through the lab door.

"Just as you suspected, it was ninety percent powdered milk that had been ground to a very fine powder. Some benign lyophilized lactobacillus, serratia and peptococcus had also been thrown in," Valerie replied.

"Any other clues?"

The perp was very careful not to leave any marks on the envelope but then carelessly licked the envelope. There was just enough saliva residue to sample DNA and I got a match with Svelty Patterson. You don't seem very surprised, Detective."

"This little caper had Svelty written all over it," Signe replied. "Sometimes she is like a large swarm of gnats buzzing around my face. I was hoping her new boyfriend, Arkady Shilkloper would keep her in the sack all day and that she would forget about me."

"I think your personalities locked together when she was in a coma in Albuquerque," Valerie replied without hesitation. "You know that you were the only one who visited her."

"But I had nothing but positive feelings for her during that time; even though I didn't think she was going to survive."

"Somehow she got her wires switched. You need to visit a witch and have the feelings removed or reversed."

"Mateo is friends with a bruja. He could refer me to her."

"That is exactly what you don't need. A bruja is a black witch and responsible for all manner of curses and incantations that hurt people. They are the ones that put human skin, teeth and bones on your roof when they lay a hex. You want a white witch, a curandera. They aren't as easy to find as the black witches, but they seem to be just as powerful. Mateo will be able to give you a couple of names. In the meantime check your roof for bones and hair. But if you find them, let Mateo dispose of them. It has to be done in a certain way so that you don't bear any of the long term consequences of the curse."

"I just wish it was that easy to shake Svelty," Signe replied in a dejected voice.

She walked out of the lab. The only positive result from the anthrax scare was that the large room where all the detectives had their desks had been emptied and cleaned for the first time in years.

Signe had been forced to go through teetering piles of paper on both of her desks and file the small percentage of items she didn't throw away. She put in a call to Mateo but he was away at a sing for a sick pueblo member. Signe ordered some food from Casa Sena and carried it home to eat with a bottle of Pinot Noir. After dinner she put in a call to Brian. He complained about how long it had been since he had seen her and suggested a weekend interlude in northern New Mexico.

"One of the oil companies owned seven hundred thousand acres of pristine wilderness in the corner of the state," Brian remarked. "Ted Turner bought the whole kit and caboodle for a boxcar full of bills and it has some of the best trout fishing in the southwest, not to mention bison, elk and cougar. Let's go."

"I'm a European girl, Brian," Signe replied. "I'm not too sure about camping."

"It isn't camping, darling, the oil men built a two-story log lodge that is three hundred feet long and full of every amenity and there are small houses all over the property with tidy white walls and pressed bed clothes. It's actually very European looking—perhaps rural French."

"In that case, when do you wish to pick me up?"

"Friday afternoon so we can land at Vermejo Park Ranch well before dark. The landing strip is wide and flat but it doesn't have lights."

"I don't have any fishing clothes," Signe remarked.

"My personal assistant has all your sizes. I'll bring everything you need with me including waders and a fly fishing vest."

Whatever that is, Signe thought to herself. Signe climbed into bed with her new book, *All the Pretty Horses*, but soon she was fast asleep. She set herself two tasks for the next day—to have Mateo hook her up with a curandera and to spend some time with Liam Farrell. She thought he had been playing dumb with her and she was embarrassed to admit that she seemed to have fallen for it. As soon as she awoke, still in her nightgown, she called Mateo. She explained Svelty's latest trick and told of Valerie's idea to set her karma straight by exorcising the spell.

"I believe those are valid suggestions," Mateo replied. "Call Beverly Manyspirits at 867-1636 and you can make an appointment to see her."

Signe wrote the numbers carefully, fighting her tendency to invert numbers. Then she stared at the numerals for several minutes without saying a word.

"I believe I recognize the numerals in that phone number, Mateo. They are the box number used by Larry in his ad several summers ago. Valerie and I both felt that the advertisement was a coded message that so far we have been unable to crack. Perhaps Larry used Beverly as an advisor or a conduit to transmit information to his handlers. Does any of this make any sense?"

"A connection between a Cochiti curandera and a theoretical physicist from Los Alamos?" Mateo queried. "I believe Sherlock Holmes would find it quite preposterous, Detective Sorensen."

"Yet the chances of those seven numbers occurring randomly in the same order is only one in ten million," Signe replied after doing a quick calculation in her head.

"Dr. Watson would find it's hard to argue to with your logic, Detective," Mateo replied pensively.

"Hook me up with her as soon as you can," Signe said excitedly.

Mateo dialed the number himself and Beverly Manyspirits answered and said they could come over to her house in the pueblo. Signe had Jack drive her to Mateo's house near the plaza, and then Mateo and Signe walked the three short blocks to Beverly's home. The roads between Cochiti adobes were dusty and devoid of any vegetation. If they ever elected a Dane governor she knew his first official act would be to plant hollyhocks, Shasta daisies and zinnia beside every door. It was early in the day but the temperature had already soared. Signe felt a rivulet of sweat running slowly down her spine. Beverly's door was the traditional bright blue color. Mateo knocked and then walked in. The front room was cluttered with stacks of old newspapers and empty aluminum beverage cans. Beverly, in a tattered housedress, sat at a table cluttered with dirty dishes. If she was a witch she certainly didn't know the spell that cleaned her rooms and washed her dishes, Signe thought.

"This is the woman I told you about, Beverly," Mateo said as he gestured toward Signe. "She ha been haunted and pestered by a woman to whom she extended every good thought and hope."

"Tell me about this woman," Beverly said as she fixed her soft brown eyes intently on Signe.

"Her name is Svelty Patterson and she is the stepmother of a young murder victim I was investigating. She went into a prolonged coma following an overdose of barbiturates. It was either a murder attempt or a suicide attempt. She was deeply unresponsive for weeks and during that time I was the only one who visited her. Surprisingly she came out of it, and after weeks of rehab returned to her normal self."

"During the period when you visited her you were communicating with her through a nontalking channel. Were your thoughts of her of the universal peace and goodness type like Buddha or did you stand to gain something personally if she managed to awake?"

"Mostly the former. However, my murder case was at a standstill and Svelty potentially held the key to unlocking the case if she were to survive."

"With mixed motives like that the victim's subconscious may have decided that you were an enemy not a friend and the feeling may now be so deep in her brain that she can't verbalize her antipathy toward you."

"Can this error in perception be fixed?" Mateo asked.

"Yes," Beverly replied. "Let me gather a few things from the clutter and I believe we can straighten this out right now."

Beverly lifted her thick body from the table and went into another room. She returned in a few minutes with a stone mortar and pestle and several stalks of herbs in her other hand. She plucked leaves from the stalks carefully and added them to the mortar before grinding them. Then she placed the powder in a chipped tea cup and added hot water from the stove. She bowed her head and chanted softly under her breath for several minutes then handed the cup to Signe. The mixture had a bitter aroma and an even more bitter taste like aspirin mixed with powder found in pecan shells. Signe felt a strong urge to gag, but forced the hot liquid down her throat. Beverly spoke several more incantations, now in a loud sing-songy voice before placing both of her hands on the top of Signe's head. Signe slipped a fifty dollar bill under one of the saucers before Mateo walked her home. He showed her to the old overstuffed sofa in his office and helped her lie down. She had never felt that tired in her life and was instantly asleep.

CHAPTER 52

When she awoke Mateo led her to the dining room and offered her a small bowl of delicious soup—chicken and dumplings with carrots, parsley and marjoram.

"Perhaps I'll never hear from Svelty again," Signe said hopefully.

"Beverly isn't very imposing to look at, and her house is a mess but she has broken a lot of curses over the years," Mateo offered.

Jack came by a few minutes later after picking up some evidence in Albuquerque and drove Signe back to Santa Fe. She checked her messages and found an urgent one from Jefferson. She rang the direct line to the concierge's desk at the La Fonda Hotel.

"Apparently Larry and Chaco were quite an item around town for almost three years," Jefferson began. "They didn't try and keep anything secret. They were seen walking around the plaza holding hands and kissing on street corners. They frequented Casa Sena where they kissed and fondled each other in a corner booth.

One of my gay friends saw Chaco sitting across Larry's lap at Harry's Roadhouse.

They were in the darkest corner dry humping each other."

"What did her husband Dr. Han think of that?"

"Apparently affairs are common in Chinese marriages, but it is the husband that cheats. A wife that strays brings embarrassment to her husband and shame to her family. Apparently after he discovered the affair he started beating her."

"Why didn't they just divorce?" Signe asked.

"Their entrance visas were tangled together somehow, and if they dissolved their marriage both of them would be forced to go back to the mainland within six months. Neither of them wanted to do that. They wanted their two children to be able to stay in America and eventually become citizens."

"Are the children in danger of being deported now that their father is dead?" Signe asked.

"They have a lot more to be worried about now that their mother has been charged with murder, I would think," Jefferson said.

"How did you happen to know so much about the Hans and their problems?" Signe queried.

"I've always been interested in the machinations involved in heterosexual relationships. Straights always frown on gays for having transient, superficial relationships, but my observation is that heteros are just as fickle and act on nearly every itch they feel in their groins."

"That's not a very flattering picture, friend. I suppose I should talk with Mrs. Han. I'll call back after I talk with her," Signe said hanging up the phone.

She had the desk sergeant locate Mrs. Han, who was currently being held for evaluation at the Central Prison in Los Lunas. All prisoners in New Mexico, whether men or women, first went to Central for an assessment before doing their time there or at another facility. Signe knew that all female prisoners in the state eventually served their time at the prison in Grants, New Mexico. Signe called Jack and told him bring C Vicky to the front door so they could take a trip south. Jack talked nonstop for the ninety minute drive.

"I had to break up with Rhonda," Jack began.

"You've been together for three and a half months, which is a long time for you," Signe remarked.

"Yah, I know. She's been a lot of fun and she's just great in bed. Rhonda is the first woman I ever met who wants sex more often than I do. I just don't trust her anymore."

"What do you mean?"

"We moved in together after we had been seeing each other for two months. When we first started going out, she seemed just as honest as she was hot. I'm scrupulously honest with you but tend to be a little shifty in my relationships."

"Don't you know by now Jack that dishonesty indelibly poisons any relationship?"

"Yes, but I'm always trying to make myself look a little bit better than I really am to impress the chick I'm with. I pretend to be a little brighter or a little kinder or a little suaver than I really am, and of course it never works out in the end. I just end up looking foolish."

"Well, what exactly is the problem with you and Rhonda?" Signe queried.

"Things keep disappearing around my place. First it was my cell phone, then a favorite old watch that wasn't worth much and then my check book. Now I can't find my check book."

"Are you sure you didn't misplace them?"

"I don't lose a lot of stuff, Signe. I'm fairly compulsive, and, besides, I tend to put things in the same place."

"What happens when you ask Rhonda about these things?"

"Well, I'm not very cool about it. There isn't anyone else in my apartment, Signe. We don't even have a cleaning lady. So my thinking is that if it's missing, Rhonda did something with it and I am pissed off. Right away, I start shouting and swearing and accusing her of lying. She's Irish and hotheaded, so she starts yelling back. Right away we're in an uproar that generates a lot more heat than light. Once, I almost hit her I was so furious. Twice we both got so angry that we pushed each other".

"It doesn't sound good to me, partner. Did any of the stuff ever turn up?"

"Yes. The watch turned up inside the case of a wooden mantle clock, and the checkbook was inside a large financial envelope from last February."

Signe asked, although she was sure she already knew the answer, "Any chance you put those things there accidentally, Jack?"

"No possible way. Sometimes you stop in the garage on the way into the house to put a new tool away, and while you are unwrapping it, you set your keys on a top shelf so both hands are free. If I don't go anywhere 'til the next day, I can spend a good forty minutes then looking for my keys getting angrier and angrier as the minutes go by. This isn't like that because when I find my keys in the garage, I remember putting them there the day before and think, how stupid. When I find these things, I have no recollection of how they got there."

"I just don't see what Rhonda gets out of these games, Jack," Signe replied after a few minutes thought. "If Rhonda is sick of you, why doesn't she just move out? I like it when things make sense. This doesn't."

"In any case, I'm going to ask her to move out. I'm tired of the aggravation."

Jack had just stopped C Vicky at the reception center of Central—the New Mexico State Prison in Los Lunas. He parked the car in a spot marked, 'Visiting Officials Only.' Signe jumped out to stretch her legs. Jack and Signe entered the facility and presented their IDs. After passing through several hallways painted a dull gray-green, Signe inquired about the location of Chaicochito Han. After waiting for many minutes the clerk confessed she was unable to find the prisoner. Jack threw up his hands in frustration. Signe demanded to see the warden immediately. At least that got the clerks in the processing area scurrying around a lot faster. Now they were all speaking Spanish rapidly in high pitched voices blaming each other for an inability to find inmate Han. A door to the administrative wing swung open, and Warden Jose Romero and two aids walked toward Signe and Jack.

After introducing himself, the Warden asked, "What seems to be the problem here?"

"We drove down from Santa Fe to see one of your prisoners, Warden, and now it seems she can't be found," Signe replied.

Warden Romero turned to one of the gray-headed clerks and said, "*Cual es el problema pentacampeon?*" In a very angry voice.

The gray-headed clerk looked away in exasperation and then mumbled something back in Spanish.

"We will have this problem solved in three minutes," the Warden said turning to Jack. "In the meantime stop into my office for a cup of coffee."

The Warden led the way into his office with his two assistants following at a respectful distance. The assistants handed Jack and Signe cups of hot coffee that tasted old. Signe looked for a plant to surreptitiously pour it on. The warden asked a couple of questions about law enforcement in Santa Fe before they were interrupted by the gray headed clerk. Mrs. Han had been discovered. Apparently she had been registered under her first name Chaicochito rather than Han. Signe wasn't surprised. The woman's first name sounded more indigenous to the Southwest than Han. The two were led to a nearby conference room in the women's wing where Mrs. Han sat quietly with her arms folded. Signe thought she looked very small and very discouraged. Signe motioned for Jack to wait outside.

"I'm Detective Sorensen of the Santa Fe Police," Signe said in a warm, soft voice as she placed her palms over the woman's tiny hands.

The prisoner immediately broke into a loud combination of both crying and moaning in a high pitched voice while she rocked back and forth. Signe sat quietly holding the slight woman's hands for fifteen minutes. Gradually the sobbing subsided.

"I need to ask you some questions about your husband's death," Signe began softly.

"I never loved my husband," Chaicochito said in a barely audible voice. "Our marriage was arranged by our parents who said we would come to love each other.

It never happened. We didn't even <u>like</u> each other. Xian consummated our marriage violently after four months of my resistance. I was left with bruised ribs, a broken finger and I became pregnant for the first time."

CHAPTER 53

"We both did very well at school," Chaco continued, "And got sent to Jiao Tong University in Shanghai. We studied mathematics and the more we fought the better both of our grades got. Then we got sent to Cambridge for two year post doctorals and I gave birth to my daughter there. Neither of us wanted our children to grow up in China, so we scoured the Commonwealth and European countries for jobs. We got positions at the Lawrence Livermore Labs in California and after five years transferred to Los Alamos National labs."

"What about the fighting?"

"It only got worse. Initially we used our hands and feet but soon we needed sticks, batons, numchucks and shurikens or throwing stars. We were very careful not to leave scars where nosey colleague could see marks and query us at work. I sent Xian to the hospital twice once with a broken arm and once with a broken toe. But none of the doctors or nurses pictured me, the diminutive, soft spoke wife as an abuser. I knocked Xian out during one vicious fight with numchucks. He was out for three hours and I started to panic. I was just about to call an ambulance when he woke up."

"What about you and Larry?" Signe asked.

"We met at a lab Christmas party. Xian and I are Shinto but it seemed politically smart to go to Jesus' birthday party even though we didn't believe. Also, once the children got older they enjoyed the decorations, the singing and especially the presents. Larry and I simply bumped each other while we were getting a refill of punch and I felt a deep shiver spread through my body. In all my years with Xian I never felt anything like that. I let Xian have intercourse with me every fortnight. I would get in bed naked, but wrap a thin scarf around my neck, face and head. I would solve mathematical equations in my head while he did his business. Then I would get up and wash every trace of him off of my body. I scrubbed my body with a coarse brush until my thighs and breasts bled. After a few times I think he became aroused by the ritual of the scarf. When he came to bed he already had an erection. Also it made it easier for him to image he was with someone else. Besides the scarf wasn't a problem because Chinese don't kiss."

"I asked you about Larry and you are telling me about Xian, again," Signe observed.

"So sorry," Chaco replied. "After the shiver I set down my cup of punch and pulled him behind a temporary curtain next to the table. I pressed my body firmly against his and he kissed me on the mouth. I had never experienced that before and I felt a deep wave of ardor. Between passionate kisses we agreed to meet the next day at the county park which is usually deserted. My heart raced all day and I couldn't sleep that night. I felt like school girl when I saw him sitting at a picnic table at the back of the park. Los Alamos is high in the mountains, but it was a warm June day with no wind. Larry laid out a blanket behind some bushes. He took off all my clothes and was on top of me in minutes. He kissed me and licked me everywhere. He found the healing scratches on the inside of my thighs. I was embarrassed, but I told him where they came from. I got so wet between my legs. That had never happened with my husband. Then he made love to me very slowly. After that we met at least twice a week. At first we were very careful, but later I wanted him so badly that we started taking chances."

"Did Xian every catch you?" Signe asked.

"No but he came very close. We were doing it on Larry's desk when my husband dropped by unexpectedly. I barely had time to grab my panty hose and panties and crawled under his desk. It was a long meeting and I had terrible cramps in my thighs by the time he left. We were more careful for a while but then went back to our old ways."

"I want to hear about the day you killed your husband," Signe interjected.

"It was at the end of a long fight. We were both tired. He had started it by hitting from behind with a numchuck. It hurt badly. I caught him with a shuriken in the flank. He left it in so he could feel the pain as he came toward me. He ripped my clothing and grabbed both of my breasts and twisted. I shrieked in pain. He slid his hands up around my neck and squeezed hard. We were in the kitchen and I reached for something and ended up with a carving knife in my hand. I leveled the blade and pushed it toward his chest. I pushed it forward and felt his shirt part and the resistance of his skin. Once past that the blade was very sharp and advanced easily. I felt his heart beating against the tip of the knife. He was still choking me and I knew I would lose consciousness in seconds. I pushed the knife forward it went so effortlessly, like soft butter. All those decades of abuse came down to less than a second. Xian's fierce grip on my neck suddenly loosened."

Chaco bowed her head and seemed to be crying softly. Signe waited.

"Do you wish Xian was still alive?" Signe asked.

"Yes. There was some real affection buried in our hatred and we had been together for almost thirty years."

"Were you ever offered money by a foreign power for information you had been given at the lab?" Signe asked shifting subjects when she hoped Chaco was still vulnerable.

"Yes, several times," Chaco replied. "Several spies from Russia, Rumania, Poland and especially China approached me. They offered me lots of money and gifts, but I swear I didn't ever cooperate with any of them."

"I believe what you are saying is true, but you must have been tempted. Raising two children on government salaries in an expensive town like Los Alamos must have been very difficult."

"It was a constant struggle mostly because Xian was a wastrel when it came to money. If he saw something he wanted he just bought it not matter what the cost. He didn't even haggle over price like every self-respecting Chinese knows to do. I looked into every possible way of making more money and selling information from the lab was definitely the most lucrative. Russia paid the best. But I even talked to that lab tech that lived in a cave. He wanted to be the middle man between me and a group of Polish spies."

"Do you mean Jeffrey Huntsinger, that weirdo that works in X Division?" Signe said in a surprised voice.

"He offered me $40,000 for six months worth of the yellow pads I scratched ideas and doodled on."

"Did Larry ever talk with him?"

"You mean about selling secrets? Not that I know of. I know they bird watched and camped together."

"Did Larry ever mentioning selling government secrets, perhaps during pillow talk?"

"What means pillow talk?"

"You know. After sex when you are both relaxed and lying open in each others arms."

"No. Larry was such a good lover I was usually exhausted and fell right to sleep."

"Did you notice that Larry seemed to have lots of money? More then he would get as a senior scientist at the lab?"

"Yes. He had lots of money and he was very generous with me. I suspected a secret source of funds, but he never told me where it came from."

"Think of all the times you were together," Signe probed. "He must have let something slip."

After a long pause, Chaco said, "One night when we were out for a rare dinner alone he got a call on his cell phone and before he got out of hearing range I heard him say 'Stephanie' but I didn't hear anything else."

"Any other instances?"

"No."

"Were you surprised when Judge Avalos committed suicide?" Signe asked.

"Yes. As you know he was the judge at my trial. Did you know him?"

"No."

"He sat on an elevated chair above all of us in court. However, he seemed animated, cheerful, and involved in the case. I sat in court for ten mostly boring days and I never detected any despondence or depression. Besides, I heard he was the youngest judge on the bench. He had his whole life ahead of him."

"Thanks for talking with me," Signe said, getting up abruptly.

Signe felt she had gotten a lot from Chaco and wanted to review her answers before she asked the murderer anymore questions. She found Jack in the waiting area reading a recent issue of "Law and Order Today." He jumped up and escorted Signe to C Vicky opening the passenger door for her with a flourish. They headed north.

"Learn anything?" Jack asked.

"Not very much," Signe reflected. "But the lady has had a pretty twisted life. I suspect she is very good at lying. It would probably be worth talking with her again. Did anything come of your nosing around the State Police about the judge's suicide?"

"No one over there believes Avalos killed himself, but they haven't found any clues as to who might have done it and they have no motive."

"I think Xian knew a lot about Larry including the people he worked for and that Avalos uncovered something during the trial that made him suspicious."

"It sounds like we have a big investigation in front of us partner," Jack replied.

CHAPTER 54

Signe sat quietly for a few minutes watching the open fields roll by on both sides of the road south of Albuquerque. It was the middle of June, the hottest month in New Mexico, and Signe thought the plains around Los Lunas looked like it. The vegetation was brown, short, and covered in dust with a lot of whirling dust devils. The temperature felt at least one hundred. In two weeks the monsoon would start and New Mexico would receive seven inches of rain, not much but enough to green up the plains. The afternoons would be filled with thunder and lightning as thunderheads rolled across the valleys followed by torrential rain. In addition, Signe remembered, that fortunately temperatures would be cooler then.

Jack was busy driving and lost in his own thoughts. Signe's mind wandered to her home in Denmark with its one hundred and seventy rainy days each year. She thought about her son, Axel, whose woodworking apprenticeship would conclude in three weeks. Signe was almost always focused on the present. She usually had plenty going on in her life and particularly in her work to fully occupy her mind. However, as Jack negotiated the long slow right turn from the mesa top down to the Rio Grande River, she wondered where she would be in ten years. She would be forty-seven years old and she was sure she would still be working hard as a detective. She felt she would be offered some department head and administrative jobs over that time frame if her success in solving the most challenging cases continued. However, she also knew she would resist with all of her being getting stuck with a desk job or simply managing the work of a group of detectives no matter how great the financial rewards.

Signe was much less certain about the future direction of her personal life. She had had a child, albeit by accident, and didn't feel a need to repeat that experience despite loving Axel fiercely. When Axel fathered a baby, in Santa Fe, by his trashy girlfriend, Irma Perez, Signe noted she had no parental feelings for the baby, who looked more Danish with blond hair and blue eyes than native to New Mexico.

She was more concerned about what sort of primary relationship she would be in at age forty-seven. She had had a number of partners since she left high school. One of her partners had been a woman and she was approached frequently for some reasons she didn't understand by gay women. She loved the softness of the intimacy between two women, but she also realized that for her a sense of being filled and completed was missing unless the sex she was having was with a man. She had had relationships with several men and she looked back on them all with a distinct sense of pleasure. She had learned a lot from her partners and most importantly almost every assignation had been a lot of fun. Some Danish women of independent spirit never married but had a series of long and short relationships with remarkable and attention-grabbing male partners who often turned out to be not much. These strong women seemed able to slough the shallow ones easily. Karen Blixen, Asta Nielsen, Anna Archer, and Thit Jensen came to mind. For some ill-defined reason Signe thought she was a one-man woman, she just had to find the right male. Perhaps it was Brian she mused.

Signe suggested that Jack get of the freeway and head west down Central Avenue to The Artichoke Café for an early supper. Jack found a parking place right across the street which made him chuckle since such a spot was so unusual. Signe took a large pad of paper and a heavy black marker into the restaurant with her.

"It's time we settled this murder," Signe announced, as she took a large swallow of water with lemon in it.

"Not one of your famous lists of prospects," Jack said in a mocking voice. "I figured you to have this one wrapped up by now, my beautiful partner."

"Well why don't you just tell me who did it?" Signe snapped back. "You are as smart as I am and as well steeped in this case."

"I think the spectacularly beautiful Urszula Stephanie did it in cold blood."

"Urszula has motive, opportunity, and means," Signe replied thoughtfully. "Plus I sense that she is hard as diamonds beneath her stunning exterior. I wouldn't be surprised if she was the one who funneled money to Larry for the stolen secrets."

"Who do you think did it, partner?" Jack replied.

"How about Gerhardt Neuhausen?"

"You can't be serious! I never even heard of him! I cry foul. That sounds like *Dues ex machina.* I'm sure I'm mispronouncing it, but it's that thing in literature where an intractable problem in a story is suddenly resolved when the author introduced a brand new character."

"My mistake. I thought you met him, but of course you weren't in Amsterdam when Albina was murdered. He was Albina's supercilious mentor and boss," Signe replied. "He was very jealous of her easy success and now she had taken a lover to boot."

"But you told me about him, he was just an investment banker, not an international killer."

"Yes, but he was older and claimed to be in the Wehrmacht, however there was some evidence that he was really Waffen Schutz Staffel or SS. Neuhausen may have been assigned to the Auschwitz concentration camp where Larry Abramowitz was held captive in 1945."

"Okay. I agree. He should be on the list."

Signe quickly wrote out the rest of her list:

Jeffrey Huntsinger.

Stephanie Urszula.

Gerhardt Neuhausen.

Waander Alkmaar.

Liam Farrell.

Michelangelo Bachechi.

Dr. Pieter van der Waals.

A Polish national.

Julia Roberts.

Jack studied the list. He burst out laughing and then said, "Julia Roberts. How do you figure?"

"Just a little joke, Jack," Signe replied and she drew a line through number nine just as their fried calamari appetizer arrived.

"Tell me about the others," Jack remarked.

"I already told you what I know about number two and three. I think number one, Jeffrey Huntsinger, is a strong suspect. He admitted he was camping in the woods with the victim. While quite smart, Jeffrey was easily influenced, and he lives in a cave so he obviously needed the money. Waander Alkmaar, number four, had a mistress he wouldn't give up and he had just found out his wife Albina had a lover. If he killed Larry he would receive a large enough sum of money to disappear forever. Michelangelo, number six, is a very long shot I admit, but he has lots of criminal experience and will do almost anything for enough money."

"You skipped Liam Farrell," Jack remarked.

"I've gotten to know Liam fairly well while investigating this case," Signe replied. "On the surface he looks like a not very bright, quite lazy FBI agent with no future, stuck in a small station that has little crime. Not all towns with a population of eighty thousand are so crime free. Camden New Jersey has seventy-nine thousand people but is one of the least safe cities in America. I was looking at national crime statistics yesterday and our neighbor Los Lunas is the fifty-seventh least safe in the entire country and Belen is much worse at thirty-three."

"But I took another look at Farrell," Signe continued. "After you told me how well he handled himself in that fight in Santa Fe. It seems it was all a ploy for this fight club he's starting in Albuquerque. That is certainly an activity that the FBI would frown on. So I think Liam is more than he seems and is very ambitious. He is willing to jump over his traces to get ahead. He would certainly know how to cover up a crime."

"Dr. Pieter van der Waals is a much more complicated suspect. Van der Waals and Abramowitz were best friends for decades and Larry had given Pieter large amounts of money derived from their clandestine spying and experimenting. At some point Pieter must have gotten jealous. After all Larry controlled all the contacts, set the prices and distributed the money. Ostensibly, the arrangement protected van der Waals as the weaker of the two, so if he every got caught and questioned he wouldn't be able to reveal anything."

"I like van der Waals for this crime," Jack replied. "Whenever I'm around him he gives me an uneasy feeling."

With perfect timing their entrées arrived. Jack had ordered a grass-fed veal scaloppini with spinach spaetzle. He had a big spinach salad with bacon on the side. Signe had a five-spice pan-roasted duck breast with curried vegetables and Basmati rice. Both were hungry and ate without talking. They split the bill and hurried to the car. Once they were heading north, Jack got back to the list.

"What about the Polish national on the list?" Jack asked.

"It's very amorphous I'm afraid. I don't know who the person is, but there are so many Polish clues—the Polish helicopter, the scientific papers, the experiments that Larry did and the Polish hangers-on."

As Jack climbed over La Bajada hill a huge, nearly full moon rose as large as a garbage can lid over the Sangre de Cristo Mountains. Below the bright reflected white light the mountains appeared black. At the base of the mountains the city was a thick multicolored necklace of lights stretched from west to east. Signe was sure it was one of the prettiest views in the world and she remembered why she had left Denmark.

CHAPTER 55

"That is something you won't see in Denmark," Jack said as he nodded toward the scene in front of them.

"Tomorrow, Jack, I think you and Mateo and I should divide up our list of suspects," Signe suggested. "And try and eliminate several of them quickly. Then we can concentrate our fire on the one or two that remain."

"Sounds good to me partner," Jack said as he stopped at Signe's apartment gate and opened the car door for her. "You know I love you."

Signe skipped up the front walk and entered the apartment as she turned on all the lights. Signe sat across from her beautiful Monet kicked her high heels off and wiggled her toes with pleasure. She picked up a book she was reading called *Passionate Minds* a story of the great love affair of the Enlightenment between mathematician Emilie du Châtelet and the poet Voltaire. Just now the two were trying to survive court intrigues at Versailles and escape agents of the king. Signe fell asleep on the sofa. She hated waking up at 3 a.m. with aches in her legs and binding from her clothing and underwear. This particular night she was awakened by the ringing of her phone.

Signe fumbled for the receiver and answered in a husky voice, "Hello."

"Detective Sorensen, this is Rhonda Richards, your partner's girlfriend," she said in a tearful and panicky voice.

"What's wrong?" Signe replied in a clearer voice.

"We have only met once, but I didn't know who else to call," Rhonda replied.

"Jack was abducted an hour ago by three people."

"Did you notify the police?"

"No. They said they would kill him if I called the police."

"Don't make anymore calls. I will be right there."

Signe put in a call to Mateo Romero and asked them to meet her at Jack Gallegos's apartment. She drove her BMW at high speed through the dark deserted streets of Santa Fe. She had an emergency flashing light under her front seat that attached to her roof with a magnet, but there was so little traffic, she decided not to use it. Signe wondered if the abduction had something to do with their murder investigation. Jack went out of his way sometimes to taunt criminals that he caught and as a result many of them ended up hating him. So the abductor could be anyone. Unfortunately, many of Jack's collars were petty, repeat criminals with a penchant for violence. As she screeched to a stop in front of Jack's rental everything appeared quiet. He lived in a rural six unit apartment on a dirt road in far northern Santa Fe.

As she hurried up the walk something glinted in the grass. She pulled a sterile glove from her coat pocket, bent down and picked up a worn two Euro coin. The front door was ajar and Signe slipped inside. Rhonda was sitting, bent over on an old dark green sofa. She was sobbing so loudly she didn't hear Signe enter. Signe sat down beside her. Rhonda's side was covered with thick dark red blood.

"Are you hurt Ms. Richards?" Signe said as she began involuntarily checking

Rhonda's limbs for wounds.

Signe noted a large bloody area on the back of Rhonda's left calf but her skin seemed intact and she didn't wince as Signe probed the area.

"No I slipped on this large puddle of blood in the bedroom."

Signe jumped up and went into the bedroom. A thick, large, dark pond of blood was located at the foot of the bed. If this is Jack's blood Signe thought, his chances of surviving this vicious attack are small. If the body contains nine pints of blood there are at least seven pints here on the floor and he will go into shock and die without aggressive emergency medical treatment. The arrival of two uniformed officers and Valerie, the CSI, interrupted her thoughts.

Signe rose and as she did, spoke to all three, "My partner, Jack Gallegos, was abducted from this apartment this evening. I want you to analyze the clues in this bedroom, Valerie. I would like you two officers to check the perimeter for any signs as to what happened here."

"I saw tire tracks on the way in," Valerie remarked. "We need to make a cast of them."

Valerie placed a large case on the bed, took out her Nikon and took a rapid succession of long range and medium range photos of the room. She dropped to her knees and took a small sample of the blood from the large puddle on the floor. She placed the blood in a test tube and added four drops of a reagent before sealing the tube and shaking it vigorously.

"This isn't human blood, Signe," Valerie remarked. "I think it is probably porcine. I can tell you positively once I get a slide under a microscope. I'm telling you that right off because if this large puddle is all Jack's blood his chance of surviving is less than ten percent."

"You are reading my mind, Val," Signe replied. "Thanks for the reassurance."

Valerie began processing all of the surfaces in the room, looking for fingerprints, fibers and smudges. Signe needed to find Jack before the trail got cold. She put in a call to her assistant, Mateo Romero and got permission from her Chief to assign two more uniformed officers to the case. The first two officers had cast the recent tire treads in front of the apartment and found a torn black, nylon duffle bag in the yard. Signe interviewed tenants in all the other apartments with little result. Only the couple next door had heard anything unusual. About two hours ago they had heard loud voices from Jack's apartment and then the sound of a heavy chain being pulled across the floor. The voices didn't alarm them because the neighbors said Jack and Rhonda had noisy sex at least everyday.

Valerie was ready to make a preliminary report.

"This is a very clean, very professional job," Valerie began. "There are no fingerprints. Not even smudged ones or partials. However, I did find one partial footprint in the blood. I also found a torn finger from a latex glove. It may have enough skin cells and oil to do a partial DNA analysis. I'm sure I can at least get the sex of the perp."

The last two uniformed officers canvassed the neighbors. Shortly, one came running to see Signe.

"I spoke to the older couple that lives upstairs," Officer Guadarama said. "They have a lot of spare time to be nosy about their neighbors. They saw a large, black, late model sedan pull up to the apartment this evening. Three people got out of the car and went in. The neighbors heard some loud talking. Then four people left. One had something over his head like a hooded sweatshirt."

"Thanks for that officer. That's enough of a description to put out an APD. Please call the station and initiate one. Come to think of it, Jack's new phone has a new fangled GPS feature on it. See if the dispatcher can get a signal back and locate the phone."

Signe went back to re-interview Rhonda, hoping that she had remembered an important new detail.

"Jack told me he wasn't very happy with you about his personal things that kept turning up missing," Signe began.

"I know how much those incidents disturbed Jack, but I swear, Detective; I had nothing to do with the objects disappearance and strange reappearance."

"Perhaps the same persons that abducted Jack broke in from time to time and relocated his articles just to rattle his chain and disturb your relationship," Signe remarked.

Signe's cell phone rang startling her.

After she recovered, she punched the send button and said, "Sorensen."

"This is Agnes Spelling in dispatch from Santa Fe, Detective. Officer Gallegos's phone is on and he is heading north at a high rate of speed."

"What a valuable bit of news, Agnes. Can you pinpoint his location?"

"You may not know that the cell towers in the northern part of the state are pretty sparse. At first I thought he was going to Española but just a few minutes ago it shifted to the east toward Nambe."

"I'll get my map out but it sounds to me like they might be taking the high road to Taos," Signe observed. "There is very little traffic on that road at night and it would be a good way to avoid detection. They don't know that Jack has a phone on him that is capable of giving us his precise location."

As soon as Mateo arrived Signe filled him in quickly as she directed him back to his car.

"We are not that far behind them and should have a good chance of catching them on such a slow road," Signe suggested. "If we could get a second car to head south on the same road our chances of apprehension would at least double. The problem is I don't know a modern enough or well manned enough force to mobilize in that area. Perhaps Liam Farrell could help if he isn't at his fight club in Albuquerque. Signe dialed his private cell number. He answered on the third ring.

"Farrell," Liam said in a deep loud voice.

There was a lot of shouting and whistling in the background.

"This is Detective Sorensen," Signe replied in a loud voice. "And I was hoping you could help me if you aren't to busy."

"I'm recruiting fighters for my club in Albuquerque," Liam replied. "I'm actually at a clandestine amateur club in a barn north of Española. The talent is terrible. Just a bunch of clumsy putzs looking to get hurt. There is no one here I can possible use. The only thing I'm jealous of is the crowd. I'll bet they have two hundred and fifty spectators at fifty bucks a head. Any excuse to get out of here will work for me. What can I do?"

"My partner Jack was abducted this evening from his apartment and is being taken north probably on the high road to Taos. I need someone to speed to Rancho de Taos and drive south on New Mexico 518. My assistant Mateo and I are north of Santa Fe on US 285 we are just passing camel rock."

"I'm leaving right now," Liam concluded.

CHAPTER 56

"I will call you in forty minutes," Signe replied as she hung up her phone. Signe had given Mateo a flashing red light for his last birthday. She pulled it out from under the seat slapped the magnetic bottom on the roof and activated it. Mateo took the Pojoaque exit with skill and accelerated through the stop sign. From now on the road would be dark, narrow, and curvy Signe knew. But she had observed moonrise the night before and knew it would help light the way once it got up over the mountains. Signe was trying to think like the abductors. They had eschewed blasting down I-25 to reach Albuquerque with all of its hiding places. She thought they were worried they might be snared by a quickly set road block along the way. The same applied to I-25 north except there wasn't a big city until Colorado Springs more than three-hundred and forty some miles away. Roads in her home country of Denmark and in the eastern United States resembled a net that had been laid on the map. In the west the roads were fewer and much less branched. She knew the abductors were in a large late model sedan, not as SUV. Therefore all the rutted, steep side trails off the high road to Taos were out of play.

Her only worry was a good blacktop road that went southwest out of Peñasco that went through Tres Ritos and then turned south eventually terminating in Las Vegas and the freeway. She voiced her concern to Mateo.

"You could use the State Police for some help if your rapport with them wasn't so damn tragic," Mateo replied.

"It's one a.m. and I won't be able to play all nicey, nicey with the chief of State Police right now, Mateo," Signe replied in an exasperated tone revealing her fatigue.

"One of my oldest friends is a sheepherder near Mora," Mateo began. "I'm sure 518 runs right through the village. Let me call him."

No one answered until the eighth ring.

"Yell-llo," a sleepy voice said.

"Miguel? This is your friend Mateo. I need your help."

"Si mi amigo. Anything. Just call me back in the morning," a still sleepy Miguel replied.

"No. I need your help now friend. I need you to check the road outside your window for a large, black, sedan. If you see one drive by, call me at this number. This would be most likely to occur in the next ninety minutes but I'm sorry to say it could occur anytime during the rest of the night. At least the moon is up."

"No problema amigo," Miguel replied. "I have two mucho sick ewes that I need to attend anyway."

"I'll call you in the morning either way," Mateo said closing the phone.

Turning to Signe, Mateo said, "Even with this moonlight those criminals could pull off anywhere cover the car with a few branches and we would drive right past them."

"You're correct," Signe replied. "I suspect they think they have the jump on us now though and by tomorrow we will have roadblocks set up all over the northern part of the state. The roads are so sparse they know we could monitor the upper third of the state with only five or six black and whites. I think they want to get Jack out of our reach for good."

"Have you figured out why they abducted Jack?" Mateo queried.

"You know I haven't," Signe mused. "If I can figure out the reason for the abduction it often helps me deduce who the perpetrators are. Jack is smart, strong, and resourceful. They must have wanted him badly because he will be a handful to control. I'd rather try to manage a herd of chimps than keep Jack for any period of time. I have to believe that his kidnapping has to do with our case. I think the perpetrators want to slow us down. Perhaps we are getting a little too close."

"Do you think they will kill him?"

"They might. They have already killed Larry Abramowitz, Albina Alkmaar, Ernesto Chavez, and probably Judge Barry Avalos. Killing is clearly in their domain. However, I suspect they are just throwing us off the trail by forcing us to stop investigating and start looking for Jack."

They turned off the main road into the village of Chimayo and explored the few side streets for vehicles that didn't look like they belonged. They paid particular attention to the area around El Santuario de Chimayo the small hillside church which was swarmed with true believers each Easter. A cluster of parking lots, and back alleys clustered around the squat little chapel to accommodate worshippers. All seemed quiet. Signe called Agnes in dispatch.

"I'm losing signal as he goes into the hills around Mesa de la Ceja," Agnes began. "Also, as I told you, the transmitting cells are farther apart in mountains because there aren't many customers to pay for them. I'll also call the State Police. I believe they recently installed a stronger receiver than we have."

"Thanks for your help, Agnes. Keep us posted," Signe replied.

Signe called Liam Farrell.

"How is it going?" Signe asked in a loud voice.

"I was in the gorge along the Rio Grande River where I'm sure there wasn't any service most of the time," Liam replied over some static. "There is no traffic and I made the forty-three miles from

Espanola to Rancho de Taos in thirty-seven minutes. I turned south on 518 and just passed through Talpa. No sign of the black sedan. Where are you?"

"We just passed Rio Chiquito. We checked all the side streets in Chimayo around the Santuario and that took some time. If I'm right you might make contact pretty soon. If you do, you'll have the element of surprise but unfortunately there are three culprits in the car with Jack and I suspect they are heavily armed. Perhaps you should follow them and wait for us to back you up. I'd hate you see you get killed."

"True. If you were there you could at least hold my head in your lap and stroke my brow while I breathed my last," Liam replied sarcastically.

"All kidding aside, I really appreciate your help on such short notice."

"You'll owe me big time after this, Signe," Liam replied.

"If we have them trapped in a pincer we should contact them quite soon," Signe replied ignoring Liam's last remark.

Mateo drove through Truchas, and then Trampas where the road was hilly but at least straighter. Both were such small villages that all the parking places for a foreign vehicle could be seen easily from the road in the moonlight. The next village, Chamisal, was a little larger and it took ten minutes to drive up and down the side streets looking for the kidnapper's car. Luckily the felons had picked a vehicle that stood out in northern New Mexico, Signe thought. An old Ford F-150 pickup would have been much harder to find.

Mateo slowed as the hills and turns tightened. He drove through Vadito and then into Peñasco the last small village on the high road to Taos.

Signe decided to wait for Liam in Peñasco. They pulled off the road in front of the darkened front of the Peñasco Valley Food Store. Both put their seats back and closed their eyes. It was two thirty. Twenty five minutes later Liam pulled up beside them.

Signe got out of the car and said in a quizzical tone, "How did they elude us?"

"I bet they holed up some place along the way," Liam said.

"Let me call dispatch in Santa Fe and see if Agnes is getting any signal," Signe said as she stepped away from the buildings to get a better signal.

When she came back Signe said, "Agnes has had no signal for the last eighty minutes. Even using the State Police receiver, which is five times more powerful they can't get any sign from Jack's phone either. The last positive signal showed Jack was just east of Chimayo. I'm positive that we are close."

"Let's spend the night here and start searching again at dawn," Mateo suggested. "I know the owner of the Martinez y Ewens Anasazi Ranch. It is a bed and breakfast which is just down the road."

"Would you mind having the State Police put a perimeter on the four roads that lead out of this area?" Signe asked Liam.

"Not at all," Liam replied as he reached for his phone.

Mateo got in his car and Liam and Signe followed. When they reached the ranch, Mateo rapped loudly on the ranch house door. A sleepy gray-haired woman in a quilted robe and slippers opened the door. After a short discussion Mateo motioned for Signe and Liam to come in.

"Fortunately, Millie has three rooms left," Mateo began. "She asked if I was hungry and I said I was ravenous. She's making us huevos rancheros right now."

Signe hadn't even realized how hungry she was, but one look at Liam told her that he was famished also. After decades of making breakfast for eight to fifteen ranch guests, Millie was very fast. She had three plates of fresh fried eggs on tortillas with heaps of beans and rice all smothered in a thick red chile sauce on their plates in minutes. Signe savored each mouthful, dipping her warm buttered flour tortilla in egg yolk. Once they finished eating, Millie gave them three keys and they walked to three adjacent cabins. Signe slipped her clothes off quickly and realized she was just as horny as she was sleepy. If Liam were to knock on her door she knew she would go to the door naked and invite him to come in. She slid between the cool slightly rough sheets and felt them rub pleasantly against her thighs and nipples. She was asleep in seconds.

CHAPTER 57

At dawn there was a gentle knock on Signe's door.

She sat up still groggy and then called out, "Come in!" before remembering she was naked.

Liam came into the sitting room fully clothed.

"I hope you slept well," he said stumbling around in dark room.

"Yes. Just not long enough. And you?"

"You know I was so hyped up from the high speed drive it took me about ninety minutes to unwind," Liam said. "I even came over and rapped on your bedroom window, but you were fast asleep."

Emboldened by his revelation, Signe grabbed the top sheet and wrapped it loosely around her body, under her arms, revealing the curve of her breasts and her long slender thighs. She walked over and grabbed her clothing and went into the bathroom. Leaving the door ajar so she could talk, she dropped the sheet, peed as quietly as she could because she had to go badly. Then she pulled her clothes on and walked into the front room.

"What is our best next move, Liam?" Signe queried.

"I have an idea," Liam said softly taking Signe's hands in his and kissing her gently on the mouth.

Signe kissed him back for at least two minutes and then pulled away.

"Wow. That feels wonderful, but I'm too worried about Jack to give you my full attention. Can we put this off until later?"

"Okay. Then lets got some breakfast," Liam replied.

They walked hand in hand. When they got to the dining room, Mateo was already eating. Signe was ravenous even though she had just eaten five hours before. She ordered a sourdough waffle with real maple syrup, sausage and a grilled tomato. Mateo had already laid all the maps out on the breakfast table. Liam checked on the roadblock he had set. The State Police hadn't encountered any suspicious cars during the night. Mateo checked with his shepherd friend. His ewes were better but no large sedans had blasted through Mora during the night. Signe was becoming more confident that she had the abductors surrounded. She called Agnes just as she was getting off shift.

"I'm not getting a signal right now from Officer Gallegos's GPS," Agnes said, stifling a yawn. However, I did get a faint signal for about five minutes at four twenty-five. I didn't call because I wasn't sure it was anything real, but the more I think about it the more I think it was real."

"Perhaps he is trying to save his battery, and when his captors were distracted or asleep he turned it on for a few minutes," Signe proposed. "Where did the signal come from?"

"About two miles southwest of Peñasco," Agnes replied.

"We must be right on top of them, Agnes," Signe remarked. "We are at a bed and breakfast in Peñasco."

Mateo and Liam, overhearing the conversation, were wolfing down a couple last bites of food and clearing the dishes into the kitchen sink.

"Unbelievable," Signe said to no one in particular. "Agnes says that the criminals spent the night about two miles southwest of here!"

"Let's go find them," Liam said as they all moved toward the door.

After thanking Millie for her hospitality, the three got into their vehicles and drove east on Highway 518. They explored every driveway and side track as they went. They fell into a natural pattern of one car waiting on the main road while the second car examined the offshoots for signs of the abductor's car. After two hours they had gone a little more than two miles. A sign on their right announced the Institute for Buddhist Studies. Several small adobe buildings were clustered around a larger two story building down a dusty unpaved road. Next to the largest building sat a dirty black four door BMW 745. Liam and Mateo checked out the car while Signe knocked on the door of the central building. An elderly man in a saffron colored robe and a gray beard that extended down to his waist greeted Signe with a deep bow.

"I'm with the Santa Fe Police and I'm interested in the people that were in that big black sedan," Signe began.

"They are disciples from the Shin Buddhist temple in Berkeley and they were joining a group from here that is going to tour sacred sites in Mongolia," the old Buddhist said.

"How were they dressed?"

"All four men wore saffron robes and seemed very well kept despite the lateness of the hour."

"How are they traveling and where are they going?"

"They are in an old yellow school bus. They have to catch an early chartered flight out of Santa Fe. They are going from Santa Fe to Cincinnati, Cincinnati to Rome, Rome to New Delhi, and then Delhi to Ulan Bator."

Signe ran to the car and grabbed her phone but the battery was nearly dead. She ran back into the main building and asked the head monk if she could use the phone. She called the Santa Fe Airport and asked for the tower after identifying herself to the operator.

"This is Detective Sorensen. I fly out of your airport frequently on a Gulfstream 600 with Brian Hagen. A charter flight to Cincinnati may have a kidnap victim on it," Signe said quickly. "Has it taken off yet?"

"Yes ma'am, it left about twelve minutes ago," the air traffic controller said.

"Please call the pilot and have him return to the airfield."

"What do you want me to use as an excuse?"

"Say that the guy who drives the fuel truck found a discrepancy in his figures and he doesn't think the planes wing tank has enough one ten fuel to get them to Cincinnati."

"That ought to do the trick," the airport worker replied.

Signe requested that two black and whites race to the airport and hold everyone on the charter until she got there. In ten minutes the air traffic controller called back to say that he couldn't reach the plane. The radio appeared to be broken.

More likely off, Signe thought. I think that proves that Jack and the abductors were aboard. Signe called police in Cincinnati and explained her dilemma. She had the sergeant on duty fax a picture of Jack to the Cincinnati authorities. Signe thanked Liam for all his help and they agreed to have dinner the next week at a place that he picked. Mateo drove Signe back to Santa Fe and helped her update the APB they had put out on Jack.

Signe went to the lab to see what Valerie had found at Jack's apartment.

"What have you got for me?" Signe asked.

"I know what car the tire track came from," Valerie responded pertly.

"I don't need that anymore, Valerie. I have the whole car for you. It's being towed down from the high road right now. What else have you got?"

"The pig's blood that was all over the floor isn't much help. It didn't have any anticoagulants in it so it probably came from a local slaughterhouse. I had an officer check the five abattoirs in Santa Fe and one of the owners said someone came by yesterday for a galloon of fresh blood. I sent the sketch artist out to get a drawing of the man. I found part of a latex glove and did a partial DNA analysis on the few epithelials I got. It was only useful for determination of gender which was female."

"That doesn't mesh with the Lamas description of the group of four that visited his monastery last night," Signe began. "He described them as a group of four men. One was so sleepy that the other three had to hold him up. I suspect that the sleepy one was Jack and that he had been drugged into unconsciousness. But he certainly would be able to tell if one was female."

"Perhaps it was like Dan Brown's interpretation of Leonardo's *The Last Supper*," Valerie commented. "One of the disciples looks quite feminine."

"You mean the reverse," Signe replied. "But I understand what you are saying. I'll call the monk back right now."

The head monk answered on the third ring. Signe described her dilemma to him. He thought for a minute before replying.

"The visiting monks from Berkeley didn't arrive until about two-thirty. I was tired and the light was poor," the monk began. "The generator is shut off at 8 p.m. to save money and I only had a candle to light my way. The two in the back were quite hard to see and one had a saffron hood pulled up over his or her head. That one could have been a female. They were here for only a short time and then they boarded the school bus for Santa Fe."

Valerie had overheard the conversation and chimed in, "You think that female was that cuckoo Svelty Patterson. Don't you?"

"Yes! Damn it!" Signe said. "When I heard the three assailants described as males by Rhonda I was reassured for once that Svelty wasn't involved. Now this caper has all the whimsy and quirkiness of that sociopath, Svelty."

"At least she never really hurts anybody," Valerie replied. "Remember when she kidnapped you in Vegas and put you in a room full of rattlers as thick as your thighs?"

"Yes, but she also probably was the one that turned Ernesto Chavez's head into a soccer ball with a machete," Signe retorted.

"And sometimes these high wire stunts go wrong. I want my partner back and I want him to have all his body parts attached."

"I'll pull out the file that lists all the crazy places Svelty has been seen" Valerie said. "I can call each one and see if she has been spotted."

"Thanks for you help with that. Give me a call."

Signe moved toward the door. Valerie put a hand on Signe's forearm.

"I almost forgot to tell you that I found a scrap of paper inside one of the pillowslips that had a short message on it: 'find: F'. But the capital F was upside down and backwards."

"That's amazing," Signe replied. "I found a similar symbol on some files in Anthony 'The Squid' Squitero's office when I was investigating Chloe Patterson's murder last fall.

CHAPTER 58

Signe had been so busy that she had talked with her boss and mentor in weeks. She found some special coffee beans she had purchased for just such an occasion, ground up a batch and brewed a pot being careful not to clean the pot first. The aroma nearly drove her crazy. She took two large steaming cups into Gerald Hartford's office.

After sitting down opposite him she said, "Hey, Chief. How are you doing?"

"I'm pretty worried about Jack, Signe." Hartford replied. "Who do you think has him, and why?"

"I believe it's related to the Abramowitz murder, Chief, but I don't know exactly how," Signe began. "After talking with Rhonda, I thought Jack was abducted by three males, but we have some limited DNA evidence that one of the kidnappers was a woman. That always brings Svelty to mind."

"She seems to always be lurking around the edges of your cases, Signe, but I don't understand her motive," Hartford replied. "What's her beef?"

"She had a love hate relationship with her husband Dirk Patterson, but before his brutal death he nearly killed her. Dirk held large insurance policies on his daughter Chloe and also on Svelty. As he got in more and more financial difficulty his behavior toward both women deteriorated noticeably. Toward the end, he treated his daughter so badly that I pursued him relentlessly but I can't think how that would lead to Svelty's unending pursuit of me. Svelty never cared for Chloe but she accepted her as a major part of her father's life. You know the two of them were only five years apart in age. Chloe was only twenty-eight when she died!"

"From an age perspective, they should have been sisters," Hartford remarked. "Maybe some of the tension came from that."

"There is something else going on here that I haven't discovered Chief," Signe replied.

"Women are so complicated, Signe. There must be a third player that we haven't considered. Who comes to mind?"

"Svelty had a lawyer named Robert Van Merritt but they seemed to hold each other at arms length. Anthony 'the Squid' Squitero and his girlfriend Wanda De Berneres aka Rosie Bachechi aka Sandra Vitari come to mind. Tony was Dirk Patterson's right hand man throughout the whole case, but they also had a close personal relationship. One of them may have been much closer to Svelty than was apparent."

"I don't know who the third person in this puzzle is, Signe," Hartford mused. "But I don't think we've stumbled on the person yet."

As she got up from her chair Signe said, "I will get Jefferson Barclay to do some sleuthing for the fall of 2002. Perhaps he can link another person with Svelty Patterson."

Signe sat down at her cluttered desk and put in a call to Jefferson, the concierge at the La Fonda Hotel. She explained what she needed and Jefferson said he would get on it right way. First, he had to remind Signe that he had gotten useful information from Stephen Samuels the English pleasure class judge at the Santa Fe state fair. Jefferson had acted on his own while Signe was in Argentina and when she returned she worried that her friend had gotten in over his head. She felt she should warn him again.

"If you stumble onto something, Jefferson, you must contact me right away," Signe remarked. "I know you are very capable but I have a lot of resources that can help you find the correct answer quickly."

Signe grabbed a second large cup of her special coffee and put in a call to her investigator in Poland. On the first two attempts, Signe couldn't get through. Signe always imagined her connections to Eastern Europe finally reached the local wiring which hadn't been maintained in fifty years and sent the signal into a snarl of uninsulated wires. On the third try she heard a husky growl on the other end of the wire.

"Popal, here," Signe's private eye said.

"Are you ready to give me a report on the politics in your neck of the woods?" Signe inquired.

"What is 'neck of woods'?" Zbigniew Poplavok replied.

"I'm sorry, Popal, it's just an American colloquialism," Signe replied. "I have a habit of collecting them. Can you give me a report?"

"Ja," Popal answered jovially. "It's a bit more complicated than I anticipated so pull up a chair and I'll tell you what I learned from poking my nose into things."

"All right. I hope you have some answers for me. Did you get the monies for the investigation?"

"Yes. It's most unusual to get paid in Poland before you do the work!"

"I'm just glad you could work on it with so little notice."

"The story of Poland goes a long way back. It became a unitary country in the tenth century under the Piast dynasty. But from the beginning it suffered from being a large flat country directly between two very pugnacious neighbors—Germany and Russia. During the First World War, when Poland was divided an underground formed that is still extant today and the people you are interested in are still part of that faction. After World War One, your President Wilson reconstituted Poland as a country. The underground became moribund until September first of 1939 when Hitler's blitzkrieg rolled across the border of Poland. The underground was led by Leszek Balcerowicz. They sabotaged the Nazis at every turn while losing more than eighty percent of their partisans."

"I read that long suffering Poland lost the highest percentage of its citizens in the War," Signe interjected.

"After the war Poland became a satellite state of Russia and Leszek now fought the communists. It wasn't until the trade union Solidarnośc gained ground that Poland had some real freedom. And now it would seem that Leszek could rest on his laurels."

"But he had spent his whole life resisting," Signe interjected. "And he didn't know how to do anything else."

"You are exactly right and then he started buying secrets from Russia and the west," Popal said.

"Did any of the payments go to Dr. Van der Waals or Dr. Larry Abramowitz in Los Alamos?" Signe asked excitedly.

"I don't know where they went presently, but I will know shortly."

"What was Leszek Balcerowicz up to?" Signe queried.

"He has an organization in southwest Poland called the Proletariat Revolutionary Council and there goal is to overthrown the legitimate government of Poland and then threaten their ancient enemy to the west—Germany and to the east—Russia. It is a very grand and crazy plan," Popal remarked.

One of the other detectives handed Signe an urgent message while she was waiting to hear Leszek Balcerowicz's grand plan. It was from the Albuquerque office of the FAA. Signe said a quick goodbye and dialed the number. Her friend Art answered on the third ring.

We just got some feedback on the plane to Ulan Bator that you were following. One of the monks on the plane complained of severe chest pain and they diverted to Fort Smith, Arkansas to get emergency medical help. The airport personnel reported that four monks got off the plane and crowded into an ambulance that raced into town with sirens blaring. Signe put in a call to the Fort Smith police and asked them to check all the ERs for the arrival of a saffron robed quartet. She was sure the three abductors and her partner Jack had changed clothes and sped off in another direction.

Signe got her Polish private eye back on the phone so that they could finish their conversation.

"Leszek wants to take control of the area around Lvov by electing partisans that support him to all the local councils," Popal continued. "Then he wants to take over the provisional Polish government either through the buying of votes or by blackmailing the current officials. He goes back so far that he knows everyone's dirty laundry. He could use exotic isotopes to poison uncooperative officials."

"Once he controls the government he wants to threaten both his neighbors with nuclear blackmail. Right now he sees German as the weaker of the two major powers, so he would probably threaten them first. A trunk sized atom bombs could be the devices used to cause the Germans to capitulate. That's why I think Dr. Abramowitz was paid by Balcerowicz to research and build these devices. I just can't say who the middle man was just yet. But I have a series of contacts and leads that will help me determine that."

"Get back to me as soon as you establish that link," Signe remarked before hanging up.

Signe wanted her partner back and she wanted him safe and sound. A call to the Fort Smith Police Department revealed that a check of the city and county ER hadn't revealed a quartet of monks coming to their facility for emergency care. Signe wasn't surprised. She laid out a map of the United States and tried to figure where the kidnappers had taken her partner next.

Signe had a quiet dinner alone at The Coyote Café and then drove home. She hoped for a good nights sleep but instead dreamed all night of mayhem performed on her poor partner.

CHAPTER 59

In the morning, Signe put in a call to her assistant, Mateo Romero. She thought that Svelty Patterson was involved in this abduction. As an obsessive compulsive Svelty tended to go back to the same places over and over again and Mateo knew all of her hiding places. Mateo recalled that Svelty's parents lived in Oklahoma. He looked up their address and sent the State Police to check the site for traces of their daughter and Jack.

Signe put a call in to her friend, Jefferson Barclay.

"Any fresh ideas about who Svelty might have been close with in the fall of 2002?" Signe asked.

"I checked Svelty's New York lawyer, Robert Van Meritt out and as I said, I don't think he had more than a professional relationship with Svelty. I also checked into Roger Clayton, Wanda DeBerneres's guy that she had on the side. He had plenty of time for another dalliance but I viewed the reservation book from The Compound, where he worked, and her name doesn't appear there anytime during the fall. Also, I showed a picture to Roger's landlady and she didn't recognize her. So I believe he is out. Besides he wasn't worldly enough for Svelty."

"Another person I considered was Christopher Malloy, the reporter for *The New Mexican* that savaged you on the front page. He is from Ney York and spent a lot of time at the Tamaya Resort sitting in the bar indulging in drinks he couldn't afford on his reporters salary. You remember that Svelty also spent a lot of time at the Tamaya spa. I know the concierge there. He owes me a favor. I'll check to see if either of them rented rooms during the day under their own names or under an alias."

"That is a great idea, Mateo. That never occurred to me." Signe replied. "I've never been as angry as I was after Malloy did that hatchet job on me and the Santa Fe Police Department and our homicide investigations."

"You were so angry that morning. I was afraid the top of your head was about to blow off."

"Anybody else you've come up with?" Signe queried.

"Yes and I saved my best contender for last and that is Sven Tor

would still have a sixty-six percent success rate. That equals the solve rate for murder in America in the last decade.'

"You aren't going to quit and you are going to solve this crime especially since there may actually be three crimes-Larry Abramowitz's murder, that of his daughter, Albina, and perhaps even Judge Barry Avalos." What about Sven Torvaldson, the guy from American National Assurance Company? His company held the insurance policies that Dirk Patterson took out on his wife and daughter."

"That is a total surprise to me," Signe remarked. "He was so sexy mostly because he was Scandinavian. I ran out on him after some very heavy petting one night at the Eldorado Hotel. Then later we had a weekend tryst at Rancho de San Juan. Partly it was a payback for the night I got him totally aroused and then ran out on him. However, I have to say we were very gentle and loving with each other in a gorgeous venue. We probably made love fifteen times that weekend."

"Straight people like you are so different from gays," Jefferson replied parenthetically. "If I almost had sex with a hunk and then we got together several weeks later the sex wouldn't have been soft and gentle."

"You don't benefit from millions of years of evolution, Jefferson, which has tuned men's and women's psyche to each other and subtly matched their genitals and their responses to each other. If a generation is twenty-two years, straights get 45,000 chances every million years to improve. The most perfectly sexual gay couple in the world has no off spring," Signe concluded.

"That is so arrogant, Detective!" Jefferson ejaculated.

"Prove me wrong," Signe taunted.

Jefferson decided to go back to the business at hand and said, "I'm starting a time line for Svelty and Sven during the fall of 2002. So far I can put them in the same place at the same time six times that fall, and I'll bet I can find a bunch more."

"Get back to me when you've finished your investigation," Signe said, hanging up.

Signe had cramps in her thighs from sitting so long so she walked over to the lab from her office, mostly to stretch her legs. She also wanted to see if there were any new developments in the search for Jack. Valerie reported nothing new. Signe went back to her desk. Just as she sat down the phone rang. It was Signe's friend from Amsterdam, Detective Ted Tiebout.

"Hey, Ted," Signe began in a lilting tone. "What's up?"

"The crown has encouraged the district attorney in Amsterdam to charge Waander Alkmaar with murder of his wife Albina Abramowitz. They took him before a grand jury and they returned a unanimous verdict of first degree murder."

"I'm stunned," Signe replied.

"I couldn't believe it myself," Tiebout replied. "I remember when I heard this I said, *ongelooflijk*, incredible to my assistants."

"How did this happen?"

"Albina's bank, NV Lodh Holding is well connected with the mayor of Amsterdam and they have kept the pressure on to find the murderer. Also, the Alkmaar family is well known in Amsterdam they are very wealthy cheese merchants and have bent a lot of rules in their climb to the top."

"Do you think Waander did it?" Signe asked.

"I think he is very capable of such an act," Tiebout replied without hesitation. "But somehow I don't think he did it."

"Does the DA have a strong case?"

"I would say no. No prints on the murder weapon, no witnesses. His alibi is his mistress, Kitten Kitten which isn't the best. His prints and DNA are all over the crime scene, but then he lived there."

"When does the trial start?"

"*Woensdag* the eighteenth," Ted replied.

"That's in two days," Signe replied resignedly.

"Will you be coming?"

"Of course. But that means I have to leave tonight."

"I'll have you picked up at Schipol."

Signe turned the investigation of Jack's disappearance over to her assistant, Mateo. Jefferson would keep looking for the mystery link to Svelty. Then Signe put in a call to Brian. She felt bad calling him for a favor although they had talked for over an hour two nights ago.

Once he came on the line she said, "Hello lover. I just got surprised by a trial in Denmark and I need to be there tomorrow."

"I have a big meeting to win approval for a new drug for the next two days, but after that I'm available," Brian replied in a loving tone of voice. "But I can have the Gulfstream at the Santa Fe Airport in two hours."

"Are you sure?"

"Of course. I'm just sorry I can't go across the pond with you."

"You're *overtreffen*, my love."

Signe called Hartford on the way to her apartment and told him her plan. Then she packed quickly remembering that even though it was mid June, Amsterdam would still have rainy, cold days with a breeze off the North Sea. She ate a quick meal before going to the airport. The sleek white Gulfstream landed ten minutes later. The friendly copilot helped Signe aboard and they were soon airborne. She had been struggling with reading *Montaigne, The Complete Essays* for the past three weeks but knew she would get half of it read that night. She settled onto a chaise with a blanket over her legs and a glass of chardonnay.

Several hours later she moved into the bed in the back of the jet just after they refueled in Iceland. She slept soundly until the plane landed in the Netherlands.

Detective Tiebout's assistant took Signe to her favorite hotel, The Golden Tulip. Signe resisted the urge to take a nap. She took a water taxi to Prinzengracht, perhaps her favorite canal, and had a leisurely walk along both sides. She spent an hour looking at Delftware before Ted called her.

"What are you up to?" Ted remarked.

"Shopping on the Prinzengracht," Signe replied breezily.

"*Bent u honger lijden?*" Ted queried.

"I'm famished," Signe replied as her stomach rumbled in agreement.

"Take a taxi to Blauw aan de Wal in *Oude Zijde* it means ancient side and it's not far from you. It's down a tiny alley."

"See you soon."

After large schooners of Amstel beer Signe had the langoustine with lemon marmalade and Ted had poached beef with truffle and bacon. Over coffee and *boerenmeisjes* for dessert they picked apart Waander Alkmaar's case. Both concluded that the sybaritic young Dutchman would be found innocent. Signe spent the rest of the day at the Van Gogh Museum and went to bed early.

In the morning, Detective Tiebout escorted Signe to the Osdorp high security courthouse. The gallery was packed an hour before the proceedings began. Tiebout flashed his badge and got two seats in the front row. When Waander was brought in, in shackles he looked pale and haggard. The three judge panel sat along one wall behind a long dark wood elevated dais. Lawyers wore black robes with a broad white collar that extends in the front to the waist. It reminded Signe of American choir boys.

The prosecution went first led by Jan Willem DeGroot. Ted said he had been in the prosecutor's office for fourteen years. He was tired and hoping for a judgeship in a rural province. Ted thought Waander was very lucky to have this DA and that the mayor of Amsterdam probably had a hand in the selection. DeGroot presented his case in a low singsong voice over the next three hours. Despite the large, graphic, color pictures of Albina's corpse the judges were yawning during the first half hour. After DeGroot's presentation it was very clear that a vicious and passionate murder had been committed although it seemed someone unclear who the perpetrator was. After a brief lunch break, the defense took the field.

CHAPTER 60

Remko Roosjen led the defense. Known throughout the country because of a many thousand Euro TV, billboard and magazine advertising campaign even his high-pitched nasal voice was familiar to most Dutch people. He had a huge head with layers of curly grey locks that made him look like an aging lion. Piercing blue eyes completed the picture. Signe wondered if a charismatic lawyer had as profound an effect on the outcome of a case in the Netherlands with three judges edeciding as a jury of twelve citizens did in the United States. Ted thought that Alkmaar's would benefit from the one to two hundred thousand Euros his family paid for their son's defense. Roosjen hammered on the lack of Waander's prints on the putative murder weapon for nearly thirty minutes. Signe was surprised at how many different ways the lawyer could express one very simple fact.

Next Roosjen spoke at length about the defendant's alibi. Supposedly, Waander was with his mistress, Kitten Kitten Keeme the day the murder happened. His alibi was described as a stable citizen of the Netherlands who ran a successful business while failing to mention that it was a canal side house of prostitution with a ten by fourteen foot plate glass window facing the sidewalk and canal. He also failed to mention that KKK often sat in the window in a much abbreviated costume. Roosjen presented six years of tax returns from Inland Revenue showing that Miss Keeme, after deducting a large sum sent to charities in Kenya, had paid a hefty amount of money in taxes to the Inland Revenue department of the Netherlands. Signe decided that prostitution protected and even encouraged by the local government was a very lucrative business.

"Tell me Ms. Keeme about the day of the murder," Remko Roosjen said in a booming voice that filled the courtroom.

"Waander came to my business about eleven in the morning. I finished with a customer, and then we closed the curtain on the canal side and made love for the next hour or hour and a half. When we were finished I moved Waander to a day bed in back. I cleaned up and opened the curtain on the picture window."

"What happened next, Ms. Keeme?" Roosjen asked.

"I entertained three more customers," Kitten Keeme replied.

"What was Mr. Alkmaar doing while you entertained your clients?"

"Sleeping and then working on papers he brought with him. He also liked to watch me through a small peep hole while I worked."

"So, on the day of the murder, Mr. Alkmaar was with you from before eleven in the morning until three-thirty in the afternoon and never left your establishment."

"That is correct," Kitten Kitten said forcefully.

"Therefore, your honors, my client, Waander Alkmaar couldn't have committed this heinous crime," Roosjen concluded.

The DA countered with only one question.

"Who were the three clients, Miss Keeme that you entertained while Waander was hiding in your back room?" DeGroot asked.

"Unfortunately, I don't know any of their names, Sir."

"How strange that you have such detailed and voluminous tax records, but no record of these clients," DeGroot remarked sarcastically. "How do you explain this?"

"Some men are exceptional in their personality or physique or endowment, but others are just unremarkable in every way."

"So you are saying you had three absolutely bland naked men in a row and no log book entries or credit card slips to show for all your exertions," DeGroot remarked with disbelief in his voice.

"Objection!" Roosjen boomed.

"Overruled," The judge on the right replied.

Court was recessed for the day. Ted and Signe agreed to meet later for a light supper and then a concert from Amsterdam's world famous orchestra at the Concertgebouw. It was midafternoon so Signe took a trolley car the *Nieuwe Zijde*, or new side of the Amstel River. She walked quickly to the nearby Anne Frank and found the perpetual line outside shorter than usual. As she went through the dimly lit quiet canal side house, she was reminded of the somber fact that young Anne lived here for two years before being exposed and sent to a concentration camp. Next, Signe explored the orderly streets and canals there before ducking into the delightful and playful Amsterdam Historic Museum.

She had a quick dinner with Ted at an Indonesian restaurant featuring a deliciously fresh *rijsttafel*. They walked arm in arm across the Museumplein to the concert hall with its classic façade. The concert was a Beethoven symphony in the first half that made the celebrated string section of the orchestra sing and gave Signe shivers. The second half consisted of Bartok's Festive Overture followed by a sonorous Mozart concerto. Ted walked Signe back toward her hotel. It was warm and still nearly full light at 11:30 p.m. on June 18th the longest day of the year, save three. The streets were full of people holding hands and laughing and talking. Ted insisted on buying each of them a shot of genever, the local juniper flavored gin, in the glittering Leidseplein. Several drinks later they were still talking and when Signe arrived at The Golden Tulip around 3 a.m. it was nearly dark.

Signe arrived at the Osdorp courthouse before 10 a.m. She had a dry mouth, a slight headache and mild nausea. The morning was spent recalling the pathologist who performed the autopsy and asking additional questions of the CSI's that processed the crime scene. Signe didn't hear anything that changed her mind about the case. It was clearly a single sadistic assassin who snuffed out young Albina's life with no remorse or hesitation. It certainly wasn't clear to Signe Albina's husband, Alkmaar been that premeditated murderer.

The judges ordered a brief lunch break, in hopes of beginning final deliberations Thursday afternoon. Signe was amazed at how quickly justice was rendered in a country where the legal profession was almost entirely on salary. No one except, Remko Roosjen, Waander's hired gun, made a lot more money if they stretched out the number of witnesses, length of depositions and used extra verbose expert witnesses.

When Ted and Signe came back to the Osdorp courthouse all the seats were taken and the aisles jammed with reporters, Waander's friends and colleagues in anticipation of a verdict. Once all three judges were seated Roosjen called Waander Alkmaar to the stand in a booming voice. Waander walked tentatively to the witness chair in an expensive, well-tailored, dark-blue suit. After the witness was sworn in Roosjen approached him with his first question.

"Did you kill your wife?" Roosjen asked very slowly and very deliberately.

"I did not," Waander answered without hesitation. "I loved my wife and I am saddened every day by the loss of her."

"What can you tell the judges in your own defense?" Roosjen asked.

"We were planning to build a summer house in Den Burg on the island of Texel. We also were planning to have a baby."

"What proof do we have of this?"

"Albina discussed both of these things with her friends. You can ask Urszula Stephanie."

"Your honors, my client, Waander Alkmaar did not kill the woman he loved. They had plans for their future—together. I implore you to vote unanimously for acquittal," Remko Roosjen intoned as he took a seat.

"Your witness," the Judge intoned nodding toward the DA.

"Did you, Mr. Waander, have a serious long-term relationship with a prostitute named Kitten Keeme?"

"Yes."

"Did your wife know about this relationship?"

"Yes."

"Did she tell you that this relationship was jeopardizing your relationship and she wanted you to stop seeing this notorious prostitute?" said Jan Willem DeGroot.

"Not exactly."

"Then tell us exactly what your deceased wife said?"

"She was saddened by my other relationship, but she never asked me in so many words to give her up."

"Let me hand you a copy of the deposition given by your wife's best friend after the death of your wife," DeGroot said. "Please read the section I have marked."

Waander took the document in trembling hands and read, "Albina asked her husband repeatedly to give up Ms. Keeme, the mistress that was destroying her marriage. Albina told me that sometimes she asked in a soft, reasonable voice, sometimes in a more forceful voice and sometimes in a rage punctuated by throwing china across the room. She felt that with Kitten out of the picture that her marriage would return to the way it had been when they were first married and very much in love. That they could build the cottage on the North Sea that they had dreamed of, and more importantly start planning for a child."

"Does any of this ring true, Mr. Alkmaar?" DeGroot asked with his face only two inches from Waander's face.

"From the very beginning, Urszula never liked me or anything I stood for," Waander began as he looked at the three judges. "I believe her remarks were colored by her attitude toward me."

"I believe you, Sir, are guilty of the premeditated murder of your most innocent wife Albina Abramowitz Alkmaar and that you should receive the maximum sentence for this monstrous crime. Nothing further."

Jan DeGroot moved quickly back to his chair and sat down, his black robe swishing around him. The crier announced that the judges would retire to decide on a verdict.

PART 7

CHAPTER 61

Signe went to the airport to meet Brian. His new drug had won government approval which should mean between thirty and fifty million dollars in business for his company over the next ten years. He was still jubilant about the decision. A limo was waiting to take them to Signe's hotel. Brian ordered two bottles of champagne and caviar from room service. Then they slowly undressed each other with pauses for caresses and kisses. They had been lovers long enough by now that they knew each others preferences in bed without asking.

Both liked extended foreplay so that the excitement built slowly to the coupling of their bodies. Both liked mouth music, so they usually had a friendly tussle over who got to put their mouth on their partner's genitals first. Then each struggles to be creative and fresh with lips, tongues and fingers. Signe had found that firm pressure using three fingers below Brian's testicles gave him a steady pleasurable sensation. She had won the tussle this afternoon possibly because of Brian's jet lag. As the sun streamed into the room and lit up the pile of white sheets she worked her way up and down her lover's body with energy and affection. After twenty minutes Brian was beginning to squirm more and more. Very slowly she engulfed him with her soft wet mouth and then began moving up and down his shaft.

Brian enjoyed the erotic sensation until he couldn't stand the tension any long and with one swift motion flipped her onto her back and entered her very slowly. Signe focused on that filling sensation that pleased her so much during intercourse. Both were suddenly overcome with desire and passion and began moving quickly and forcefully so that their bodies were soon pounding together. An outsider would have had trouble telling whether they were fighting or making desperate love. Finally, they came together for the first time. Brian gave several low pitched moans and Signe contributed several higher pitched cries. They created a brief a cappella tone poem. Then the lovers fell away from each other panting and lay on their backs holding hands. After three or four minutes Signe heard Brian snoring. The combination of postcoital oxytocin release and jet lag had overwhelmed him. She kissed him gently on the lips and poured herself a cold glass of champagne.

She climbed out of bed naked and checked her emails back at the office. When she was finished she padded back over to the bed and roused her lover with her hands and mouth. When his erection returned, she climbed on top, guided him into her and rode him without pausing to the strongest orgasm of her life.

They polished off the champagne and caviar before showering together, quickly dressing and heading out into the warm Amsterdam night. They headed directly to the Leidseplein a noisy, crowded square they remembered from their last visit. They had several rounds of Oude Genever, the Dutch precursor of gin. Then they headed over to *d'Vijff Vlieghen,* The Five Flies, for a rich dinner based on old Dutch ingredients like chard and Brussels sprouts given a modern twist. They walked leisurely back to the hotel stopping every few feet to embrace and kiss.

In the morning they flew back to Santa Fe. They landed at 2:07 p.m. Signe got in her car and drove to the station house. She left a note on Chief Hartford's desk detailing the results of Waander Alkmaar's trial. Then she addressed the tragedy of her overloaded desk. Stacks of case folders, plastic bags filled with evidence and phone message slips threatened to fall off each corner of the desk. She always felt she had too many important things to do rather than try to resolve her messy desk. Right then however she had to admit that she didn't have a whole lot to do. She sat down resignedly in her chair and started leafing through all the dated material. Four hours later with two coffee breaks her desk was clear. She got a clean rag and dusted it off. Now she was yawning every two minutes from jet lag. She drove home and after calling Brian, slept for fourteen hours straight.

In the morning she woke at 4 a.m. showered, dressed and headed into the office. It was almost noon in Amsterdam so she put in a call to Detective Theo Tiebout.

"Thank you for all your hospitality, Ted. What's your next move on Albina's murder?" Signe asked.

"I am not completely sure what the Amsterdam DA is planning," Theo replied. "I know he is very suspicious of Urszula Stephanie. At one point he thought about using Waander's trial to mine for information he could use against Ms. Stephanie. As you saw from the trial, that didn't pan out. Do you feel that the same person murdered father and daughter?"

Signe thought for several minutes before replying, "For me the two crimes are very different in their MO's and most criminals just aren't that imaginative or even that smart. Therefore, I believe we are dealing with two murderers. However, I also believe the two crimes are linked by a common motive."

"And what <u>was</u> that motive, Signe?" Theo asked provocatively.

"Let me see if I can state it correctly for the very first time," Signe mused. "I believe that someone, who was very high up, got frightened that his or her elaborate plan to steal nuclear secrets from the mountains of New Mexico was about to unravel and bring the whole fragile framework, built over more than a decade down."

"That sounds pretty grandiose," Theo replied.

"Believe me, Ted, these were some very important devices that could, if applied judiciously, upset the power balance in a whole geopolitical region."

"I know enough to realize that Dr. Larry Abramowitz, with the help of his friend, Dr. Pieter van der Waals, built the devices, but how did poor Albina, a successful investment banker in her own right, get sucked into this maelstrom?"

"I wish I knew for sure," Signe said wistfully. "If I did, I believe I could tell you who exactly who murdered her."

"What is your hypothesis?"

"One possibility is that Albina was actively involved in soliciting the agreements with her dad that resulted in the research. In that role, she may well have been involved in the transfer of secret documents and materials to the buyers. Let's say it was the Polish rump government, just as an example.

She would have been in her teens when she started, but she told me that she doing espionage drops at a culvert in Los Alamos when she was only twelve or thirteen."

"Was she really capable of all that?" Theo asked.

"I didn't get to know her before she was murdered, but she was certainly smart enough and I think of the three girls, she loved her dad the most. On the other hand, she may have only gotten involved at the end when Abramowitz's handlers were getting anxious for the final results they had paid so much for. Or alternately, they began to worry about being discovered. As the years went by, more and more people would have known about the project. Everyone who knew had to realize that the secrets which would have rocked the Los Alamos National Lab for years could be sold for a lot of money. And after 9/11 everyone involved had to be nervous about additional snooping by the FBI, CIA, and especially the NSA."

"As soon as the DA decides what he is going to do next I will call," Theo Tiebout replied.

"Thanks for all your help, Theo," Signe replied.

"*Tot ziens!*" Ted replied. Ringing off.

Signe's dear partner, Jack had now been missing for a whole week. Signe was deeply concerned and surprised that his whereabouts hadn't been discovered. She called Rhonda, Jack's girlfriend, who broke down on the phone after saying that she had heard nothing while Signe was away in the Netherlands.

Valerie in the crime lab had gone back over all of the evidence from Jack's apartment, the sight of the abduction and found nothing.

"After my first analysis, I said it was a very professional job," Valerie began. "We got the make and model of the car right away. Their only mistake was the fingertip of the glove they inadvertently left behind. It only had enough DNA on it, as you know, to give us the female sex of an assailant. I'm sorry I can't be of more help, Signe."

"I want you to go back to the apartment and interview Rhonda about Jack's items that were displaced over the last few months. Catalogue each item and detail where it was found and check each one meticulously for fingerprints and DNA. My theory is that the abductors were trying to get into Jack's head before they carried him off and perhaps they slipped up during one of their visits."

Signe called her assistant, Mateo Romero next. He had continued to track Svelty's movements during her absence. Signe strongly suspected the female sociopath was behind the abduction of her partner. Mateo reported that Svelty hadn't been seen in any of her old haunts except for a brief visit to her apartment in Taormina, Sicily. It had occurred during the middle of the night.

"She was only there for twenty minutes in the middle of the night, and we missed her," Mateo said in a frustrated voice. "She always had a predictable circuit of places that she visited. It seems that now that she is hooked up with Arkady Shilkloper he has pushed into a new orbit that includes Minsk, Torcello, an island in the north Venetian lagoon, and Sapporo, Japan."

"I am increasingly worried about Jack. He has been gone for eight days now. Can you track her in any of these new areas?" Signe asked.

"Unfortunately, we don't have stringers in any of these places, but I'm working hard to correct that, boss."

"Jack Gallegos is a New Mexican through and through and trust me he wouldn't like any of those places," Signe opined.

CHAPTER 62

If Jack had been transported to some exotic location by Svelty, he would do anything in his power to tell Signe where he was. He had managed to keep his cell phone during the first few days of his kidnapping, and as a result Signe had almost had a chance at freeing him in Peñasco before the Buddhists spirited him away. Even if Jack still had his phone it wouldn't work overseas. If Jack was left alone he might find some other way to send a message to his partner. He was quite clever electronically.

Signe had just spent four hours going through the messages on her desk and she hadn't discovered anything suspicious. However, she also knew she hadn't looked at every communication with the goal of finding a hidden message from her partner. She went back to her desk and pulled out all the messages she had saved, and was surprised to find that almost 150 remained. She set aside all the messages from local numbers and she was left with twenty-seven pink slips which she studied with care. Most were from names and numbers she didn't recognize. She also realized that Jack had never shown an aptitude or interest in cryptograms or puzzles. Three from overseas had detailed messages, but Signe could find no hidden pattern in two of them. She found the third one intriguing for some reason that she couldn't specify. Signe wrote this one out word for word on a white chalk board by her desk:

To: Detective Signe Sorensen

From: J. Saggello

Date: 6/13/03

Message: I need to speak with you urgently about

the recent establishment of an international ring of

Italian kidnappers. They are targeting a southwest

drug manufacturer.

Commissario Solie Cortello

Telephono 0-7191979

Despite staring at the message for several minutes, nothing came to Signe's mind. She left the message in plain sight so that she could study it every time she walked by her desk. When she thought about Jack now she got a bad feeling. He had been gone for nine days. Svelty's pranks were usually short. She worried that sometime one of her stunts would go astray and her victim would be inadvertently killed or maimed. Signe decided she needed more manpower to find Jack. She wandered over to her boss's office. The Chief invited her in and poured her a cup of aromatic coffee.

"I'm worried about Jack," Signe said as she slumped down in a chair.

"I agree," Hartford replied. "There were only four reports of kidnapped officers in the entire United States last year and one of them turned out to be a wannabe impersonating a state trooper in Missouri."

"I'm just worried that the trail is getting cold and right now I can't follow his trail further than Fort Smith, Arkansas."

"When I got that news," Hartford said. "I widened our search from the southwest to the whole country. Also his picture and name were posted at every airport in the country in case someone tried to spirit him overseas, but so far nothing has turned up."

"If this is Svelty's work, she used to ratiocinate in a circle from Albuquerque to Oklahoma to Portland to Taormina and then circle back around. Now she has a whole new circle that includes Minsk, Torcello and Sapporo. My notion about her change of venues is that it was brought about by her new lover, Arkady Skilkloper. We had cultivated a group of informants that checked all the old haunts. Now we have to develop new stringers in the new places, and I'm afraid we are running out of time."

"There is a Brotherhood of Police national hotline that helps with unusual situations that involve officers in distress. As soon as we are done here I will contact them."

"What else should we be doing that we aren't to find Jack, Chief?" Signe asked in a concerned voice.

"If he is still alive, Signe, he will try to contact us. It may be very brief or deeply disguised so be on the lookout for it."

Signe rose from her seat and with her coffee in hand left Chief Hartford's office. It was after six p.m. and Signe's internal clock was still out of whack from her trip to the Netherlands, but she was astonishingly hungry. She called her friend Jefferson Barclay and agreed to meet at Santacafé for supper in half an hour. When Jefferson arrived Signe was sipping a gin martini with three olives. Jefferson sent the restaurant so much business from the hotel that they were seated at the best table in the first room.

Jefferson started with shiitake and cactus spring rolls and Signe had shrimp and spinach dumplings with Tahini. Jefferson ordered a bottle of Far Niente chardonnay.

As they ate their appetizers, trying to hide their hunger, Jefferson spoke first, "I spent a lot of time while you were in Holland investigating your sex buddy, Sven Torvaldson."

"I find that a little harsh, friend," Signe replied. "I only had one weekend tryst with him. It was his blond hair, blue eyes and hairless chest. What can I say? He matched my image of a Scandinavian god."

"And you think gay men are superficial," Jefferson snorted.

The waiter came to their tableside and made a fresh Caesar salad in a large teak bowl. He rubbed cloves of garlic vigorously on the walls of the bowl as Signe smelled the pungent garlic aroma. He cracked two raw eggs into the bowl and adding a large bunch of romaine lettuce with the juice of a large lemon, olive oil and a dash of Worcestershire sauce as Signe studied every detail. He added crisp croutons before piling both of their plates with the green salad topped with a long, slender anchovy.

"In any case your buddy has mistresses all over northern New Mexico and in several other states. However the important part is his link to Svelty.

I told you before you left, that I could put Sven and Svelty in the same place six times in 2002. With further research, I found seven more times when they were together for a total of thirteen trysts."

Jefferson's entrée, a rare grilled rib eye with red chile Béarnaise sauce arrived along with Signe's pan seared Chilean sea bass with fresh parsley linguini. All conversation stopped for several minutes. Danes have reputation for eating very quickly, but Signe set a record finishing her bass and linguini, even wiping her plate with a piece of bread.

"I'm truly embarrassed by what you have learned about that slime Torvaldson," Signe continued. "But is he involved in Jacks disappearance?"

At that moment two chocolate—almond tortes with strawberries and whipped mascarpone cream arrived, followed by two cups of French roast coffee.

"I'm not sure," Jefferson said in a concerned voice. "I know that the two of them got together and probably had some prolonged steamy sex, but so far I can't link Sven to Jack's disappearance."

"How can I help you get the answer to this question?" Signe queried.

"I have to home in on the night that Jack was kidnapped," Jefferson replied. "Sven was supposed to be at a meeting at the home office of his insurance company in Chicago that night, but he checked out of the Ritz- Carlton early that day, left in taxi and he could have been back in New Mexico in time for the crime but so far I can't prove it. I gave his secretary a phony story about a charge filed on his health insurance for that day. She truly didn't know anything about his whereabouts. She said he kept an early appointment the next day. I thought about calling his wife but I couldn't dream up a good enough story to chance it."

"That's okay," Signe replied. "I'm sure Sven didn't have a GPS on his phone. The police were among the first to get that on their Motorola units. But I do have a friend at the FAA who can search all westbound flights for him as long as Torvaldson didn't use an alias."

Signe and Jefferson finished their desserts down to the last possible speck. Jefferson walked Signe to her car and gave her a warm hug. Signe drove the few blocks to her apartment and fell into bed. She woke at 3:30 a.m. after a nightmare. Jack had been tortured by being wrapped in barbed wire after being confined in a wooden chair. Then he was dragged down a country lane behind a pickup truck. In the dream she was handcuffed to a utility pole and struggle though she might couldn't help her beloved partner. Jack's screams awoke her. When fully awake, she was covered in sweat and her heart was still racing. She took a long warm shower and after twenty minutes felt better. She awoke early the next morning, but procrastinated around the apartment reading and straightening up so she didn't arrive at the station until almost 10:30.

First, Signe called her friend, Art, at the FAA and explained what she wanted.

"We have more flights to monitor in the summer," Art said. "I suppose because of summer vacation, but I'll devote a couple of hours to the search. If I get lucky, I may have an answer tomorrow. Otherwise it might take a week."

"Thanks for your help, Art," Signe replied.

CHAPTER 63

Signe looked at the phone message she had written on her erasable board and suddenly realized that the whole message was an anagram. She must have been overly tired or jetlagged when she wrote message. It was so obvious. 'Saggello' rearranged into Jack's last name 'Gallegos'. The phone number as Jack's birth day. The Commisario's last was 'Cortello' which rearranged easily into 'Torcello.' She had trouble with 'Solie' until she found a tattered Italian to English dictionary. It was obviously an anagram for 'isole' or island in English. Signe grabbed the phone and called Hartford and then Mateo in quick succession.

"We need to get some authorities onto the island of Torcello in the north Venetian lagoon," Signe said with introduction.

"I can have a police boat there in twenty minutes," Hartford said excitedly.

"We need something a little stealthier so they don't move Jack to Burano, Murano or another more populated island."

Mateo said he had the name of a PI in Venice, Lorenzo Vianello, who could look over the dark, tiny island this evening without arousing a lot of suspicion.

Signe picked the latter of the two options. She considered flying to Torcello right then, but she was afraid that the peripatetic Svelty might be half way around the world by the time Signe got there and have dragged poor Jack with her. Signe liked action better than sitting around but she was impulsive and sometimes headed off in directions that turned out to be dead ends. While she waited for news from the Veneto she decided she could shakedown Sven Torvaldson. She sent a black and white from Albuquerque PD to handcuff Sven in his office and bring him to Santa Fe. While she waited she reviewed her list of suspects in the Larry Abramowitz murder investigation. She and Jack had compiled a list of suspects in the case a couple of weeks ago. Signe had spent three days in Amsterdam observing Waander Alkmaar and after watching him she decided he didn't have the willpower or skills to organize a complex well-orchestrated murder in the US. She dropped him from the list.

She had also put Michelangelo Bachechi, a mid level New Jersey Mafioso on the list almost whimsically. A quick call revealed that Bachechi had been in Fort Dix Federal Prison, New Jersey during the entire months of April and May when the murder occurred. He was also dropped.

The local FBI agent that Signe had originally thought was lazy and not very bright was also on the list. She had gained new respect for him when they worked together on the search for Jack in Peñasco. She called him up and set up dinner the next night at the Inn of the Anisazi. Signe got a call from the desk clerk to tell her that her interogee was there and mad at everyone. Signe walked right over to the interrogation room.

"What the hell, Signe!" Sven yelled out as she entered the room. "Drag me up here with no notice and in cuffs."

He stood up.

"What the hell is this about? I need a lawyer!!"

"I'm sorry about the cuffs. That wasn't intended," Signe lied as she slipped the cuffs off. "It's about Svelty Patterson."

"My god! Is she all right?" Sven replied rubbing his sore wrists as he cooled off.

"As far as I know, yes. Lord, she has nine lives," Signe responded cheerfully. "Our sources tell us that you and she have become 'close' and I need to find her quickly on an important matter."

"I won't deny that we have spent some time together, mostly because you know better," Sven replied. "But it wasn't anything more than some recreational sex."

"Were you sleeping with her when we were seeing each other?"

"Is that an official police department question?"

"No. I'm just curious."

"Fair enough. Let's see. We had that great weekend at Rancho San Juan in March of 2003. So, I guess the answer in yes."

"You bastard."

"Oh, you're going to claim you didn't have a good time?"

"No. That would be unfair. It was a very pleasant and erotic weekend. Thank you for it."

"You're welcome."

"So where is Svelty?"

"I don't know for sure. We don't see each other much since she hooked up with Arkady. I haven't gotten an email from her in two weeks, but she seems to be spending more time in Italy."

"Taormina or Torcello?"

"Wow. I'm impressed. You have been doing your homework to know about both of those places. I'm not sure. Why do you ask?"

"My partner, Jack Gallegos, was kidnapped nine days ago and I suspect she was involved."

"I will keep my eyes and ears open, Signe," Sven replied.

"The officers will give you a ride back to Albuquerque."

"Next time let's just talk on the phone," Sven said as he walked out the door.

Signe knew Torvaldson pretty well and decided that he wasn't involved in Larry's murder. He was a lover not a murderer. She decided to drop his name from the possible murderers list. Signe's list was now reduced from nine to six:

1. Jeffrey Huntsinger.
2. Stephanie Urszula.
3. Gerhardt Neuhausen.
4. Liam Farrell.
5. Dr. Pieter van der Waals.
6. or a Polish national.

Signe plotted ways to foil each of the half dozen people on her list. She was tired of this investigation and wanted to know that the person, who murdered her friend, even if her acquaintance was a Polish spy, was behind bars. She spent the rest of the afternoon calling locals about Dr. van der Waals and Jeffrey Huntsinger.

She learned that van der Waals was deeply in debt to just about everyone, and that he was away from Los Alamos for long periods, but nothing else. No one knew where he was going. If Larry Abramowitz had been close to being discovered for selling secrets to a foreign power, then Pieter van der Waals was in real danger. Larry had been very careful to build a firewall between himself and his friend and co-worker, but Signe had pierced that firewall easily and Larry was smart enough to know that, in the end, he really couldn't protect his friend.

When she turned her attention to Jeffrey Huntsinger she reviewed his wobbly career at the lab. He had flunked out of Harvey Mudd College in Claremont, California and then had been at Stanford for six months. He had an IQ of 184. He lived in a cave for some unknown reason. So he was smart enough to carry out the murder and hide his tracks well. She would have Valerie check out his childhood for the triad of terror: late bedwetting, fire starting and cruelty to animals. In her interview with Jeff he had admitted to being a homosexual after she had badgered him for a long period. She would have Mateo check out Jeff's lovers. Perhaps one of them would be able shed some light on the murder.

She was tired mostly of thinking. She left the office and drove to her favorite restaurant, The Coyote Café. She had two quick margaritas and then ordered a barbequed duck quesadilla appetizer. While she munched she mulled over her complicated case. Her friend Larry was very smart. If he was about to get exposed wouldn't he have sensed it coming? Perhaps there was some clue in his voluminous papers that would reveal who he was afraid of and why. Signe called Valerie's answering machine and explained what she wanted and offered to pay for a translator of documents that were written in Polish or German.

Signe ordered a mesquite grilled rare New York strip steak with poblano peppers and shallot roasted fingerling potatoes on the side. She had a glass of Susana Balro malbec with her steak. When she was finished she talked with her favorite waiter about the new hot spots for eating in Santa Fe. Nothing sounded remarkable. She drove home slowly, glad that she didn't hit a DWI checkpoint on the way. Once home she fell asleep quickly. However, soon she started dreaming about her partner Jack. In the worst nightmare Jack was dangling down a shaft into a cave by a rope that ended fifty feet above the rocky bottom. She had just gotten back to a deep dreamless sleep when her cell phone rang.

"*Senora Sorensen?*" A strange voice said. "Commissario Lorenzo Vianello."

"Yes?" Signe said in a sleepy voice. "*Parla inglese?*"

"Yes, detective. Apologies for calling at such an hour, but I was told you were anxiouses to know the results of my outcome tonight."

"You are correct," Signe replied. "I'm trying to find my partner who was abducted from America. *Che cosa hai trovato?*"

"Do you know Torcello?" the Commissario asked.

"Unfortunately, inspector, I have never been to Venice."

"It is a small low-lying island in the north lagoon. It is where Venice started, but it eesn't, how shall I say, crowded like its neighbors Burano and Murano. It ees a perfect place to hide."

"Did you find anything?"

"There ees a house by the old campanile that has been vacant for months. But now it ees *occupado*. It ees raining hard here but there are three *uomo* in it. One of the *uomo* looks like the picture you faxed us."

"Can you interrogate them?"

"No. Right now I am just a private citizen. I can come back earlyin the morning and interrogate them about their business here."

"That should be fine. They don't act like they are going anywhere," Signe replied. '*Buona notte.*"

CHAPTER 64

Signe couldn't go back to sleep she was sure that her partner, Jack, had been found. She got dressed early and went to work. She knew it was seven hours later in Italy, so she called Commissario Vianello the minute she got to her desk. His secretary explained in broken Italian that the Commissario was in the field and couldn't be reached for approximately two hours. Signe thanked her and said she would call back.

Just to kill time, Signe decided to look into the file on Judge Barry Avalos that Jack had been working on. After Manny Ramirez, Avalos was the youngest judge on the Santa Fe District Court. His badly crushed body had been found at the bottom of the Taos Gorge Bridge. His car was parked at the middle of the span. Neither Jack nor Terecita Armijo thought that Avalos had reason to take his life. Both were very suspicious that he had been murdered.

Signe found Jack's file on the case easily. It wasn't very thick and contained mostly hastily written notes in pencil. A memo did state that officer Don Montgomery was the lead investigator working on the case at the state police. Signe called across town to speak with the officer. She found out that Montgomery had transferred to the California Highway Patrol in San Diego less than two months ago.

She put in a call. After identifying herself she asked to speak with officer Don Montgomery. Surprisingly, after a pause a warm male voice came on the line.

"Montgomery."

"My name is Signe Sorensen, officer," Signe began. "And I am a member of the Santa Fe Police Department."

"I remember you aren't you from Denmark? Didn't we pull an April Fools joke on you sending you and another rookie cop out to Cabezon Peak looking for a fictitious body?"

"Yes. You are correct," Signe recalled with embarrassment. "You had a lot of years with the New Mexico State Police if I remember correctly. What made you suddenly decamp?"

"Are you on a secure phone?"

"Yes. I'm at the station and we sweep all our lines every fortnight."

"Good. And what I tell you stays between us?"

"Yes," Signe replied after a brief pause.

"Then, the reason I left is because of the Barry Avalos case. Do you know about it?"

"Yes. My partner, Jack Gallegos, before his was abducted was working on it and we had talked about it. He didn't think it was a suicide."

"He was right on," Montgomery replied with real feeling. "The Judge had no reason to kill himself. The car they left on the bridge, his car, was ultra clean, no discarded wrappers or cups, no papers, no suicide note, no DNA and especially no fingerprints!"

"It sounds rigged," Signe responded.

"It was murder. Yet I was ordered to stop investigating it and to sign it out as a suicide. I couldn't do it. That is why I quit the job I loved."

"Who do you suspect killed the Judge?" Signe queried.

"I don't know, but whoever it was is particularly well connected. Someone high up in the state or federal government told the State Police Chief how the investigation would go."

"Was the Judge involved in any high profile cases where discovery could have put him at risk?" Signe enquired.

"I may be wrong, but I don't think this crime had anything to do with Avalos's legal work."

"What other things was involved in?"

"He was a lifelong resident of Santa Fe. He was raised in that poor neighborhood southwest of the Plaza. He got in some trouble with the law over drugs and burglaries when he was in high school," Montgomery said. "Some caring teacher got a hold of him and got him into the local Boy's Club. Once they found out how smart he was, that got him into classes that challenged really him and he never looked back. He has always hiked here, around Los Alamos and in the Jemez Mountains. Recently he had gotten involved in orienteering."

"What's that?"

"A competitive form of land navigation," Montgomery replied. "Two or more guys attempt to go from point A to point B as accurately as possible using a map and compass. It's usually done in wilderness areas."

"Do you think that the Judge may have accidentally stumbled across something during on of these orienteering exercises that got him killed?"

"I thought of that. I got info from his wife about these trips, and believe me there were a lot of them, and I was checking them out when I was forced to close the case by the Chief."

"If I were to reopen this case surreptitiously, Don, who else could help me?" Signe asked.

"Mrs. Avalos was just great and would help you in any way that she could. She never bought the idea of a suicide. She knew him best and was certain he hadn't killed himself. He also had several orienteering buddies. The leader of the group is Herb Upton, a high school algebra teacher."

"I will try and match some of Avalos's trips and locations with the important dates and times of my murder investigation," Signe replied thinking ahead.

"You need to be very discrete about your inquires, Signe, or the State Police Chief will come down on you like a ton of bricks. He'll accuse you of meddling in a case where you have no jurisdiction. I was a decorated fourteen year veteran of his department and he brushed me off like a fly."

"I'll be cautious. Is there anything else you can tell me?"

"Yeah. His dog disappeared the same weekend his body was found."

"What does that mean?"

"I have no idea."

"Thanks for all the info. When I get stumped I'll give you another call."

"I hope to God you find the killer," Officer Montgomery said.

They traded cell numbers before Signe hung up. She felt like she had just stumbled onto something that might be very important. Perhaps Jack had found some of this same information and it was the reason he was kidnapped. She put in a call to Venice, Italy.

"*Buona sera*," Signe said to the secretary. "Is Commissario Vianello in?"

"*Si. Un minuto.*" The secretary replied.

"Detective Sorensen?" Vianello said in an excited voice. "Ees not goood. *Le persone* ees *svanito*. Vee got to the *pensione* before dawn. It was a mess but no one was there. I believe they left by speedboat. There are *mille* places to hide in the lagoon, and the wild part of Croatia ees only one hundred and sixty kilometers away."

"Please bag all the personal items in the pension and check for fingerprints and DNA," Signe replied in a disappointed voice.

Signe hung up the phone and called Mateo mostly so she could verbalize her disappointment. Now she wasn't even sure that it was Jack who was being held on the island of Torcello.

In thirty minutes Commissario Vianello called back. One of his men found a message written in charcoal on the hearth of an obscure upstairs fireplace. The Commissario faxed it to Signe:

SS—WITH SV AND ARK TO RUSS. L, JCG

Signe no longer needed fingerprints or DNA. Her partner had been kept in the house by Svelty and her lover and now the three were headed to Russia. Perhaps to Minsk, Arkady's old stomping ground, Signe thought or somewhere else in that vast country where Signe had no connections, but at least her partner was still alive!

Signe called the Chief and told him the news which was both good and bad. Then she called Mateo and set him to work setting up a network in Russia to snare Svelty. Her mind was whirling with ideas about how to catch up with her partner Jack. Her reverie was interrupted by her cell phone. It was Detective Theo Tiebout from the Amsterdam Municipal Police.

"We apprehended Urszula Stephanie last night she crossed first into Germany from Poland and then went to the little border station at Nijegen. The DA has already announced that he will try her for the murder of Albina Alkmaar."

Signe remembered that Larry's lover had overheard him say Stephanie on his cell phone during a rare dinner date.

"When will the trial start?" Signe asked.

"I would expect that it won't be for two or three weeks. I will keep you informed," Theo replied as he rang off.

Signe wanted to get some other people off her short list of suspects so she put a call into Liam Farrell. Her excuse for calling was to fill him in on the latest developments in Larry's murder investigation.

He thanked her and then said, "Last time we talked you expressed some interest in the afterhours fight clubs. I'm organizing good dockets four nights a week now. The female boxers and the bare knuckle last man standing fights are the most popular. I have a good card of events tonight. Would you like to go?"

"Very much."

"We have to go to the south valley in Albuquerque. I'll pick you up about nine. If we stay for the whole card you won't be home until five."

"I'm game," Signe replied seductively.

"I seldom take dates to the fights so wear something low cut, so I can show you off," Liam said softly.

Signe reminded herself that she was working before she said, "I'll see what I can do."

Liam pulled up at her door promptly at nine in a stretch black Hummer limousine. He wore an expensive black tailored suit with a white silk tee shirt underneath and a long white silk scarf around his neck. Signe wore a bright red low cut dress with a short tight skirt and five inch black heels. She had tried to coax her modest sized breasts into a tortuous bra that made her look bigger on top, but decided it was too uncomfortable to wear for a long evening. She put her hair up and managed to look both sexy and elegant at the same time. She slid into the air-conditioned back seat feeling on top of the world.

CHAPTER 65

A starched linen cloth covered a small table in the back of the limousine. On it were a pot of caviar, jumbo shrimp and cracked crab claws and heavy Sterling silver silverware. Liam poured a flute of Dom Perignon champagne for Signe and then one for himself.

"Where are you taking me?" Signe asked in mock distress. "This looks more like the Santa Fe Opera than a fight club."

"We have had a couple of moments together, Signe, but I thought it was time we had a really memorable evening," Liam said as he bend over and kissed her gently on the mouth.

They both relaxed and ate the crab and shrimp with scoops of black salty Beluga caviar washed down with the champagne, as the Hummer sped down I-25. They stopped at a rundown wooden barn in Albuquerque's south valley that was surrounded by a dusty parking lot full of pickup trucks, vintage sedans and several low riders resting three quarters of an inch off the ground. It looked like a rough area and Signe noted that the limo driver had a Hispanic assistant that without being fat weighed about three hundred and fifty pounds. Liam was greeted at the door by three bouncers with wads of bills folded lengthwise between each finger so that hundred, fifty and twenty dollar bills were readily available. Most patrons were paying one hundred and fifty dollars to get in, Signe noted. Three obviously armed men stood nonchalantly arms folded in front of them near the gate keepers. There was a sudden crush of thirty or forty mostly men in suits and work clothes that was calmed quickly by the armed guards.

The tent was crowded right up to the top bleachers. The noisy crowd was almost entirely male. Signe observed every kind of dress from designer suits to worn sports coats to farm work clothes covered with dirt.

Liam whispered his ideas about the fine points of fighting in Signe's ear. Next was a five round boxing match between to welterweight women that ended in a split decision. So far, that was Signe's favorite match except for blood since one of the fighters had a profuse bloody nose starting in the second round. Next was a four man wrestling tag team that just confused Signe. During the fourth round one of the tag team was hurled out of the ring after a helicopter and nearly landed in Signe's lap. Tito and Liam warded off the large mass of flying sweaty flesh.

A forty minute intermission followed. Seven or eight men came up to Liam during the break to pay their respects. The first fight of the second half of the program was a ten round straight boxing match which had Signe on the edge of her seat. The last item on the card was a bare knuckled fight without rounds until one man was standing. The taller fighter had a left hook the other fighter couldn't defend. However, the blond had a vicious quick kick. After forty minutes the ref called a time out to swab the ring of blood and gore. They fought for an additional hour until the blond, lying on his back, gasping for breath, gave the surrender sign.

Signe was excited by what she had seen. Once she was in the limo she climbed onto a surprised Liam's lap and started kissing him. They kissed and fondled each other all the way back to Santa Fe. Signe wanted to make love but she was also thinking of Brian her perfect boyfriend.

When they got to Signe's apartment she slid away from Liam and said, "Thank you for a very exciting evening. I badly want to have you in and ravish you; however there is an honest man in my life right now whom I don't want to deceive. Will you forgive me if I take a rain check?"

Liam sat up and straightened his rumpled tuxedo shirt before he said, "Yes, darling, you would be worth waiting for."

Tito opened the LIMO door and Signe stumbled up the steps unsteadily with her high heels in her hands. She slept as if she had been drugged.

When she got to the station house in the morning she was headachy and a little nauseous. Perhaps she had had more beer the night before than she remembered and then there was the two bottles of champagne. The desk sergeant came back to the detective's offices to tell Signe that there was an irate caller demanding to speak with her. Signe sat down and picked up the receiver.

"I demand that this ridiculous investigation into Larry Abramowitz death be stopped. He died of a heart attack! What is wrong with you people? I talked with Larry's dear friend, Pieter van der Waals yesterday, and he is sinking fast. He can't sleep or eat or work. He has lost forty pounds. I can't believe you think he is a murder suspect."

As the enraged man stopped to take a breath Signe butted in," Who is this?"

"Why it's Dr. Obermeyer, of course. Are you losing your mind young lady?"

Out of the blue, Signe remembered that Obermeyer was a fellow Dane who was a scholar at the local think tank, The Santa Fe Institute.

"I'm very sorry to hear about Pieter," Signe replied. "I will have one of my associates speak with him and reassure him, however he has been engaged in clandestine activities. Obviously, I can't go into the details with you, but if you knew what was involved you would want me to proceed."

"*Vaeldig!*" Obermeyer replied. "I want a written report when this is all over!"

Before she could reply he had slammed the phone down. Signe was shocked. Dr. Klaus Obermeyer was a jolly, ancient Kris Kringle like talking head who lived at the Santa Fe Institute and just pontificated. She started to call him back but decided against it. Instead she put in a call to her friend and colleague, Mateo Romero.

"Good morning, friend," Signe began in a cheery voice. "I need your help.

"Anything. You know that."

"I just got an irate call from Dr. Obermeyer about Larry's friend Dr. Pieter van der Waals. Klaus thinks Pieter is just about to crack because he is a major suspect in his friend's death—which he still is. Could you meet with him and reassure him?"

"Of course. I'll visit him at the lab later this afternoon, partner and blow some smoke from the peace pipe."

Before it got any later, Signe put in a call to Commissario Vianello, in Venice, to see if there were any new clues as to where her partner had gone.

Luckily, Lorenzo Vianello was in.

"*Buona sera,* Detective," Lorenzo Vianello replied in a sonorous voice.

"Any more information about my partner?" Signe queried.

"Zee DNA ees back and you were right about who was in the house on Torcello—Jack Gallegos, Svelty Patterson and Arkady Shilkloper. However, they didn't go to the closest port in Slovenia but all the way down the Adriatic to Split, *unfortunatamente.*"

"I suppose it will be easier to get transportation from there into the underbelly of Russia or Belarus."

"*Vero,*" Vianello replied.

Signe kicked herself for not insisting the Venetians capture the kidnappers when they were first discovered. It would be days before she could establish a network of stringers in Belarus that could help her find her partner.

Signe grabbed a cup of coffee and walked over to the laboratory to talk to Valerie. She had asked Valerie to go back and review all of Abramowitz's papers and look for evidence that someone was after him. She had also asked Valerie to locate items Jack felt had been moved by Rhonda and analyze them.

"Jack reported that his fishing box, his humidor, his cassette recorder and his barbeque lighter were hidden by Rhonda, just to irritate him," Valerie began, "But you thought Jack's abductors might have done it to encourage Jack and Rhonda to fight with each other."

"Did you find anything?"

"I could only find three of the items, but I went over them with a fine toothed comb. There was no DNA on any of the items, but I did find a fingerprint on the inside of his humidor. It was a perfect match with Svelty's right middle finger. You were right that she was part of this caper, Signe."

"What about your review of Larry's papers?" Signe enquired.

"I hired both a German and Polish translator that had no connection to Los Alamos," Valerie began. "They spent a hundred hours looking through his voluminous papers and journals. We started at the time of his death and worked backwards."

"The documents were badly disorganized," Signe interjected.

"That is an understatement. We did the best we could to catalogue them as we went."

"Did you find anything?"

"Yes and no. In his last issue of the <u>Bulletin of the Atomic Scientists</u> we found a copy of a note he sent to his daughter Albina. It said, *sa juz blisko*, which is Polish for, 'they are getting close'. He sent that cryptic message one week before his body was found."

"But who are 'they'?" Signe asked in an exasperated tone.

"The three of us searched everywhere for that answer, but we found nothing," Valerie replied. "I'm sorry."

"This is the most frustrating case I have ever worked on!" Signe replied in frustration. "There are so many dead ends. Whoever bought those nuclear secrets from Abramowitz and van der Waals was very clever. I know I must catch them, but I don't know how I am going to do it."

CHAPTER 66

Signe seldom stayed discouraged about one of her cases for long. However, she felt all of her usual holes had been fished out. When she was investigating Manny Ramirez's murder she broke the investigation open by visiting Anthony 'the squid' Squitero. Perhaps she could head off in a very different direction and get some important info about Larry's death. She decided to work on the death of another judge, Barry Avalos. Don Montgomery had told her that the State Police were conducting the investigation and that it was going nowhere. She also had had an adversarial relationship with the NMSP. It began when there was a turf war at the State Fair over the Chloe Patterson's murder scene.

Signe decided to call Brenda Lee Avalos, Barry's widow. She was surprised to find her number listed in the phone book. She dialed. It was answered on the third ring.

"Hallo, y'all," Brenda answered with a southern drawl.

"Mrs. Avalos, this is Signe Sorensen of the Santa Fe PD and I am investigating your husband's murder."

"Thank gawd. Someone believes my beloved husband was murdered," Brenda Lee said in a drawl.

"I need to interview you before I can begin my investigation," Signe continued.

"Please come right over. I have three small children. I hope you don't mind the mess. I live at 232 Camino del Monte Sol. It is just off Canyon Road."

"I can find it. I'll be there in twenty minutes. May I bring you a coffee from the Green Mountain Roasters?"

"Yes. With lots of cream and sugar."

Signe drove her BMW and was there in fifteen minutes. The house was an old but well maintained chocolate brown adobe with a huge cottonwood in the front yard. Brenda Lee held the front screen door open. They settled in the living room. A child on a tricycle or scooter rode noisily through the living room every couple of minutes.

"I need to tell you about my current investigation, so you will understand how I stumbled on your husband's murder," Signe began. "On April 30th the body of Dr. Larry Abramowitz was found at a campsite in Valle Grande. Originally, it looked as if he died of natural cases, perhaps a heart attack. However, further investigation showed he was deeply involved in selling nuclear secrets to a still unidentified foreign power. Tell me about your husband's death."

"His body was found at the bottom of the Rio Grande Gorge on Friday, June 6th," Brenda Lee began. "He was the senior judge in District Court and loved his work. We had a happy marriage and he doted on our three children. We weren't in debt and he was looking forward to a month long fishing trip that was to begin a week after his murder. Barry did not kill himself, Detective."

"Did he know Dr. Abramowitz?"

"My husband was a Santa Fe provincial. He didn't have a lot of ties to Los Alamos and I never heard him mention that name."

"Could he have been mixed up in spying or some type of espionage?"

"Absolutely not. He was born in Sandoval County. He never traveled overseas in his life. He was a Democrat and he loved America."

"Could he have bumped into something that he wasn't supposed to know or see?" Signe queried. "I know he was into orienteering."

"That is a possibility."

"In that case, I need to study everything you have that pertains to his orienteering."

"He has a very cluttered office here in the house. I meant to start clearing it out but every time I go in there I burst into tears."

"We can give you help with that," Signe replied.

She called the station and had Valerie and two uniformed policemen sent to the house. They brought banker's boxes, labelers and two laptops for recording everything they found. Signe helped with two drawers of the file cabinet. She found several files about orienteering but none that gave Barry's individual trips. Signe thought about having them work through the night, but this was a peripheral aspect of her case and so far they had turned up nothing. They quit at five, and Signe took them all to the Second Street Brewpub. She ordered beer steamed mussels and baked Brie with roasted garlic and sour dough bread for everyone. Several beers later they headed home. Signe spent the evening reading Steve Berry's The Amber Room and had a long talk with Brian before going to sleep.

In the morning, they met as agreed at the Avalos house. All three had red eyes and runny noses from all the dust they had stirred up in the office. The Judge was disorganized, but also a hoarder who never threw anything away. Valerie and one of the officers wore masks over their noses and mouths. Signe found boxes of papers from high school and college. Valerie found four files that related to the Judge's orienteering. Each took one and sat down in the nearest chair. Notes and papers with scribbling fell out of each one. Signe tried to sort her folder by date, but gave up after about ten minutes. Next she tried to enter each paper on the computer by date and location. It looked like Judge Avalos went land navigating about every two weeks in every piece of wilderness throughout New Mexico and western Arizona. Finally, Valerie sent one of the officers for a large piece of paper that she taped to the wall and divided sections into years. Each searcher entered the date of the trip he had found in his folder. After three hours they had entered one hundred and thirteen orienteering trips and not one seemed related to Dr. Abramowitz or Dr. Van der Waals.

They broke for lunch and went to ToCa a micro-hood at the top of Canyon Road. They headed to the Teahouse for the best BLT in town which they ate in the shaded Zen gravel garden. The trees along Canyon Road changed gradually from Cottonwoods at the bottom to Ponderosa Pines at the top. Signe thought the pines were cooler. They lingered over their ice teas not wanting to go back into the stuffy, dusty adobe that was cooled by a noisy swamp cooler. When they got back to the house they had all decided separately that they weren't going to find anything. After another hour and a half when everyone was dusty and sweaty one of the officers suddenly spoke out.

"I've got something!" Officer Cervantes called out.

He showed the others an orienteering trip that began on Sunday, April 27th and went along the western and northern part of the Valle Grande. His location was precisely recorded several times each day. Signe realized she needed a large topographic map to plot where Larry's body was found in relationship to where Barry had land navigated.

Reading Signe's mind, Valerie said, "I have a detailed set of topo maps in my lab."

They gathered up their things, thanked Mrs. Avalos, and headed to the station. They cleared everything off of the large conference table and laid out a series of maps. Valerie and Officer Cervantes plotted Judge Avalos's orienteering trip, while Signe located the spot where Abramowitz's body was found. When both were plotted on the map Valerie spoke first.

"Bingo! When he rounded the north side of Cerro San Luis, Avalos was about forty yards from where Abramowitz's body was found. If he hiked by at the right time he would have seen everything."

"I'll bet he saw the murder," Signe offered. "And that is why he in turn was murdered. He must have told someone about it or at least written down what he saw."

After a long pause Signe continued, "I told Brenda Lee all about Larry's murder and from her reaction, I don't think her husband told her a thing. Perhaps he told Terecita Armijo, his Judge friend. More likely, he probably told the State Police exactly what he saw and they did absolutely nothing about it."

"The Judge may have information hidden someplace in his house," Valerie volunteered.

"Or in a safe deposit box," Officer Cervantes chimed in.

"Very good," Signe replied. "Can the three of you search the house and I'll get permission to open the safe deposit box.

Signe called Brenda Lee back to bring her up to date on what they had discovered.

"We believe that your husband saw the murder in Valle Grande and we believe that is why he was killed," Signe began. "Are you sure that your husband didn't mention anything about seeing something, anything, unusual during his orienteering trip in late April?"

"I have thought hard about all my conversations with him up until the time of his death and he said nothing about Dr. Abramowitz or observing anything suspicious on his trip to the Jemez."

"Is there anyplace where either of you hid things around the house that you wished to keep secret?"

"I never did. I don't believe Barry did either. We were completely open with each other."

"May we look through the house?"

"Tear it apart if you need to, hopefully you will find out who killed my husband and why."

Signe had Brenda Lee and the kids leave for the day and then sent a team of detectives and patrolmen to dismember the house. They spent two days looking everywhere including in the sink traps (were they found a diamond ring Brenda Lee had lost), beneath the insulation in the attic, inside the linings of all the Judge's clothing, outside and underneath each drawer in the house (where they found some pictures of topless women that apparently the Judge didn't want his wife to know about). Finally, one of the detectives searching in the crawl space under the house and battling numerous black widows in their nests came across a dusty manila envelope inside one of the furnace vents.

CHAPTER 67

Inside were some glossy eight by ten black and white photos of an ancient helicopter that the detective thought looked like a pregnant guppy and three men in overalls. The detective whooped with joy and crawled out from under the house, knees aching. He took the envelope and raced across town with his siren blaring to the lab in the station house.

Valerie heard him arrive and couldn't resist commenting, "I'll bet that's the fastest ride a stack of papers ever got across the capitol."

"Do you have any idea how damn hot and spidery it was under that old house?" The detective replied.

"Are you arachnooophobic?" Valerie said in a drawn out sarcastic voice.

"Not until now," the detective replied involuntarily wiping his hands on his sleeves and pants.

Valerie set right to work on the photos and soon had an incomplete set of prints. She copied them and ran them through CODUS. She got a hit, but unfortunately the prints were Judge

Avalos's. She called Signe right away. Next she analyzed the photos of the three men in each photograph. By enlarging and then increasing and decreasing contrast, she got sharper features. She applied a new program that allowed her to rotate the faces for a sharper view. One man wore a cap making recognition difficult. It wasn't the cap so much, Valerie decided, as the shadow the cap cast across the upper part of the man's face. Once she had the best likeness she could possibly get of all three men she called Signe.

"The only prints on the picture were from the victim and I have three faces for you to study," Valerie said into the phone.

"I'll be right over," Signe replied. "And call the Chief. He's been around the block and may recognize one of them."

Signe and Chief Hartford arrived at the same time. Both took large magnifying glasses and put the blowups under bright lights and studied them quietly for thirty minutes.

"I don't believe I've ever seen any of them," Chief Hartford began.

"I think they have an indistinctly foreign look," Signe offered. "Their sideburns are a bit to long for Americans. The guy in the baseball cap looks vaguely familiar. Show it around the station house, please."

"These photos are the surest evidence we have that Judge Avalos was murdered," Chief Hartford said.

"Compare this face to all the facial recognition data bases, even though they aren't very good, but they are all that you have," Signe began. "And send copies to Special Agent Bienville in New Orleans, Special Agent Farrell here in Santa Fe and Detective Tiebout in Amsterdam. Also alert Interpol. I'm just sorry the trail is so cold.

Have one of the patrolmen run the pictures over to Mrs. Avalos on the off, off chance that she saw one of them."

Signe's lateral move had paid off handsomely she thought. Of course, she wished now she had played this card earlier, but hindsight was always so much better. She spent most of her time following leads that turned out to be red herrings. Her compulsive mind tolerated the mess and confusion of an unsolved homicide as long as she got to tie up all the loose ends once it was solved.

She decided to check with her contacts after sending pictures of the three men that had murdered her friend, Larry. Liam Farrell was in LA recruiting fighters for his very lucrative fight club. He had never seen any of the three men. Art Bienville, her FBI contact in New Orleans, hadn't seen any of the three either. He reported that Katarzyna, Larry's youngest daughter wasn't teaching during the oppressively hot summer session in New Orleans.

"She's working fulltime for her little subversive Islamic group the PIF," Art told Signe. "They are still laundering money in New York and sending it here and then sending it by courier to the southwest. The guy that mules the money for them is very smart. I've had him followed several times, but he always gives us the slip in Amarillo or El Paso. The surprising thing is that they are moving more money now than when your mole, Abramowitz was alive. Have they recruited a new scientist to spy for them?"

"That suggests that someone in that little nest of spies is still active," Signe remarked. "Redouble your efforts and see if you can follow that money to the last pair of dirty hands here in New Mexico."

"I'll see what I can do," Art replied before hanging up.

Finally, Signe called Theo Tiebout.

"What's new, Ted?"

"Stephanie's trial will be starting in two days. The DA is telling the *Dagblat* that he has an open and shut case and that she will be convicted."

"I suppose she is her usual haughty, beautiful self."

"Even more so. On another matter, I didn't recognize any of the three men whose faces you faxed. Although the man with the ball cap on looked vaguely familiar. There is something about their haircuts that looks Eastern European to me. Maybe, Rumanian or Polish."

"I had exactly the same feeling about the guy in the hat," Signe replied. "But so far it hasn't come to me who it might be."

"Will you be coming for Urszula Stephanie's trial?"

"Most likely, unless I get a very solid lead on my kidnapped partner," Signe replied. "Last time I had the abductors in my sights, I hesitated and they slipped away across the Adriatic."

"Let me know your travel plans if you come to the trial, so I can pick you up when you arrive," Theo replied before hanging up.

Signe called her friend, Terecita Armijo and invited her to dinner. They agreed to meet at the Cowgirl Hall of Fame. When Signe arrived every seat was taken and Terecita was drinking a second mojito. Signe ordered her standard gin martini with three olives. Signe brought her friend up to date on her friend, Barry Avalos, but omitted telling her about the photos that they had found.

"I knew he wasn't a suicide!" Terecita exclaimed. "Thank God. I couldn't have misread him that badly. Ever since his death, I've been searching for the clues that I missed the week before his demise. I was convinced that he had given me a clear sign about what he was going to do to himself, and that I had failed to intervene."

"Now you can be at peace about that," Signe replied. "However, I do need your help to discover who did murder him and why."

"Well, first of all, you can eliminate everyone at the courthouse where he worked. He was universally liked and admired," Terecita observed. "The rest of the time he doted on his family. He didn't smoke, drink or use drugs. When he wasn't working his pastime was orienteering, just about the nerdiest hobby that exists."

Signe and Terecita picked up their glasses and walked across Guadalupe Street to the Zia Diner. Signe ordered a meatloaf with green chile in it that was covered with smooth brown gravy. Terecita had a bacon and Gruyere cheese quiche.

Signe continued, "Then who did murder your friend and why?"

"As a judge one always deals with criminals who feel they were unjustly convicted even though deep down they know they did even worse things that no one ever discovered. They often talk of revenge but very few of them have the means or the energy to carry it out. I remember a family named Livingstone that decided their father wasn't guilty of murder. They were the exception. After Manny Ramirez convicted the old man, the three sons came after the Judge."

"I remember them," Signe commented. "One of them ended up shooting my friend, Lisa Gonzalez."

"Barry didn't have any cases like that in recent memory. So I don't think it was a disgruntled defendant that killed him."

"Plus it looked like a very professional job. The sort of thing that a hit man or team of hit men would do."

"Then I am at a loss," Terecita said in a soft sad voice.

For some reason, Signe decided not to tell her friend about the pictures that were found. The restaurant wasn't crowded so they ordered a bottle of prosecco and sat back to talk. Terecita had joined a church and had met two single men that she was dating. Around the courthouse she had

only dated cops and lawyers and had trouble distinguishing which group made the worst partners. She found them all to be prevaricators with inflated views of their own importance.

Signe told Terecita about her son, Axel, who had finished his apprenticeship as a carpenter and was planning to go into law enforcement. He had a girlfriend named Brigit who made him laugh and he reported they had great sex. However, he didn't seem to want to get married. Signe was thankful for that. She told Terecita all about Brian—the gifts he gave her, his shyness about being naked around her unless they were in bed and how he spent thirty minutes pleasing her in bed before they had intercourse.

"You are lucky to have him," Terecita remarked.

"Believe me. I know that."

"But you still don't know his situation."

"I'm afraid to ask. I know he has a wife and children I suppose. Knowing might change my feelings for him and I'm just crazy about him. I only had one lover who was married and he died in my arms. My heart was broken and I didn't think it would ever mend. I felt so sorry for his wife and four children."

"You shouldn't feel so guilty about his death. You weren't responsible."

"I was and I wasn't. He was perfectly safe where he was when the drug bust fell apart, and he came over to protect me. That is when he was totally exposed and got shot."

CHAPTER 68

Terecita and Signe had both had enough drink that their speech a little thick especially their r's and s's and their walking was wooden. They left their cars and shared a taxi home. Signe read only two pages in her book before she was sound asleep.

In the morning Signe arranged a flight to Amsterdam, as Brian's Gulfstream was spoken for. When she arrived in Schipol, Ted Tiebout was waiting at the gate with a rumpled sports coat on and a big smile on his face. He took her to a canal restaurant, *In de Oude Heden*, for a traditional breakfast of sliced cheese, cold cuts and rusk. It was the same breakfast that Signe was raised on in nearby Denmark.

"I just heard yesterday that Albina's mentor, Gerhardt Neuhausen, committed suicide," Theo said while they were eating. "Apparently he dressed up in his Waffen SS uniform and shot himself in the temple after ingesting some potassium cyanide. He wasn't taking any chances."

"Was Albina mentioned in a suicide note?"

"Yes. He wrote how much he cared for her and missed her."

"So you think it is unlikely that he killed her."

"Very unlikely."

"I'll take his name off of my suspects list."

Theo drove her to the Osdorp Courtroom in the southern part of Amsterdam. It is a light stone building set off by itself, and is the same place where Albina's husband, Waander Alkmaar, was acquitted of murder. The security measures and the packed gallery seemed just the same, to Signe. Three judges sat at an elevated dais along one wall just as during Waander's trial. Urszula Stephanie was brought in in shackles that clinked as she walked. She stood very tall and seemed self assured if not arrogant. After the court was convened, the murder charges were read in a loud voice. She looked beautiful in a grey silk dress with wavy long blond hair and bright blue eyes. Signe always thought that Urszula had the most perfect unblemished skin she had ever seen.

Signe leaned toward Theo and said, "Have you ever seen anyone so beautiful?"

"She is fine-looking all right," Theo replied. "She is only part Polish, you know. Her mother is from around Lvov, but her father's people came from the southern part of Denmark right on the border with Germany."

"How did she get to be such a Polish patriot then?"

"You know how the partially entitled are often the most vocal," Theo replied thoughtfully. "She has been deeply involved in the Polish underground since she was a teenager. She joined youth organizations in her early teens and rose through the ranks quickly. She was particularly adept at moving money, jewels, and documents across the border. Urszula has probably acted as a mule several hundred times. The value of the goods she has transported could easily exceed four hundred million Euros."

The middle Judge stood and intoned the charges which were a violation of Albina Abramowitz Alkmaar's civil rights, battery, robbery, infliction of great bodily harm, and murder in the first degree. Urszula and her attorney stood during the reading of charges. She seemed defiant. Her attorney, Inge Ruysdael, a young public defender seemed overwhelmed.

"If Urszula Stephanie knew she was a suspect for murder in the Netherlands why did she take the chance of coming back to Amsterdam?"

"I believe the answer is that she is so self-confident that she didn't think she would be caught. She also thinks that little border crossing she uses in Nijegen is too small and sleepy to do a competent job. She probably noticed that the little customs house doesn't have a computer," Theo whispered.

Jan Willem DeGroot, the prosecutor, started the proceedings.

"Members of the judiciary, I will demonstrate beyond a shadow of a doubt that the accused, Urszula Stephanie, viciously murdered the victim, Albina Alkmaar in a brutally and inhumane manner. This murder was made more heinous by the fact that Ms. Stephanie and Ms. Alkmaar were best friends. Ms. Stephanie killed her best friend because Albina threatened to expose her. For a number of years, Stephanie had bought government secrets from a large US nuclear laboratory and sold them to the Polish underground. Albina found out about this and told her friend she needed to stop immediately or risk trial and possible execution."

"Despite only trying to help her friend, Your Worship, Albina was rewarded by being filleted by her 'friend' in one of the most vicious murders in the city in the last decade. We will prove that Ms. Urszula Stephanie committed this crime."

"DeGroot sounds like he has the goods," Signe whispered to Theo.

"He always starts out like this," Theo replied. "He sounds bullet proof at first. I've watched him enough over the years to know that as the trial progresses there will be holes in his case."

"The first witness, Gerhardt Neuhausen, committed suicide," DeGroot continued. "But he was Albina's mentor and wrote things that are pertinent to this trial."

DeGroot pulled a sheaf of documents from a worn brown briefcase.

"I wish to enter these papers as exhibit number one and to read an excerpt to the court."

He handed a copy to the Judges and to the opposing counsel.

DeGroot began to read from the document, "Ms. Alkmaar and Ms. Stephanie had been very close friends for the past two years until Ms. Stephanie had too much to drink one night and got very talkative about her espionage work. She told about some nuclear secrets she was buying in the US and selling to the Polish underground. I happened to be there and a sudden change came over Albina. She had been drinking also and began to upbraid Urszula and call her crazy. She warned Urszula that she could be tried for espionage and executed. Two nights later, I was at dinner at *The Five Flies* and they were in the next room. They had a frightfully loud fight that lasted for forty-five minutes. It began in the restaurant and then continued outside. The next day, she told me that their friendship had ended. Albina didn't realize that I had been in the restaurant that night."

"How unfortunate that your witness is dead and therefore cannot be cross examined," Inge Ruysdael remarked sarcastically.

"This is the last testament of a man who is now dead," DeGroot replied. "He has no reason to lie to us. Now let me call a witness who can deepen our understanding of the motive for this crime. Gina Salieri please come forward."

The clerk called for a lunch break. Ted and Signe walked to a nearby canal and ate *broodje croket* a deep fried meat ragout with a hard boiled egg and a bottle of Amstel.

Ted raised his bottle and clinked it with Signe's bottle and said, "*Eet smakelijk,* which means enjoy your meal."

Back in the courtroom, a slender, young Italian woman arose from the gallery and walked forward. Once seated DeGroot began to question her.

"Tell me about your relationship with Ms. Alkmaar."

"I came to Amsterdam to learn about the international banking business and Albina was my mentor and my desk was next to her. One afternoon, about a week before she was murdered a call came in from Ms. Stephanie. I transferred it to Albina. They talked in a normal tone for twenty or so minutes and then her voice began to rise. Soon Albina was arguing in a loud voice. She shouted that she was planning to call the authorities unless Ms. Stephanie stopped immediately."

"Thank you, Ms. Salieri. Your witness Jan DeGroot said.

"Did she say what she wanted Urszula Stephanie to stop?" Ms. Ruysdael asked.

"No she did not."

"Your Highnesses, these two women who had been best friends could have been talking about anything," Ruysdael said.

Next DeGroot called a neighbor of Albina and Waander named Niels Jacobsen. He was an accountant who had lived in the neighbor for thirteen years. DeGroot asked him about the afternoon of the murder.

"I was coming home for lunch," Jacobsen affirmed. "I saw a woman walking toward me on the sidewalk with a small, rusty scythe that she attempted to hide under her coat. I found it most unusual."

"Do you see that woman in the courtroom today?" DeGroot asked pointedly.

"Yes. I had seen her before in our neighborhood and today she is sitting right their," Jacobsen said raising his right index finger toward Urszula Stephanie.

DeGroot presents three other witnesses that had heard parts of

angry conversations between the two women and then he rested his case. Signe felt that only the written testimony of Gerhardt Neuhausen and oral testimony of Niels Jacobsen had been compelling. However, Signe felt the prosecutor had established motive, method and opportunity. Inge Ruysdael called her first witness, Nat van Hals in a tentative voice.

"Tell us how you knew Urszula Stephanie," Inge began.

"She worked for the Amsterdam Free Housing Advertiser when she was in Holland," Nat said in a tentative voice. "We got to be friends about three years ago."

"Where were you on the afternoon of May 23rd?" Inge asked.

"Working at the Advertiser." van Hals replied.

"And what happened that afternoon?"

"I had a forty minute talk with Urszula."

"And where was she?"

"She was in Lvov, Poland."

"So the afternoon that Albina Alkmaar was murdered the accused was seven hundred miles away in southwest Poland. Your witness."

"Tell us a little more about yourself Mr. van Hals," DeGroot.

"What would you like to know?"

"How about your heroin addiction, your restraining orders, and your time in prison?" DeGroot retorted.

"I haven't used heroin in almost a year."

"Is that because you take methadone everyday?"

"Perhaps."

"You served three years in prison for beating your wife and breaking her arm and leg. It required sixty stitches to close the wounds you gave her.

"Her arm was only sprained," van Hals replied.

"Are you testifying here of your own free will today, or did they offer you something?"

"They said if I told my story I would get two years off my probation."

"One last question. How did you know Urszula was in Poland?"

"Because she told me she was there."

"So all your testimony is worthless," DeGroot concluded. "Urszula called you. She could have been at the corner drugstore."

Ruysdael called two more weak character witnesses and then rested her case. Theo knew that the defense had decided not to call Urszula to speak in her own defense because they found her too volatile. Each lawyer gave a summary of the case. The three judges left the courtroom to deliberate, and the courtroom cleared. Many reporters and lawyers stepped out of the courtroom to smoke.

CHAPTER 69

Signe and Theo knew it would take the judges at least a couple of hours to reach a verdict. They went to a crowded nearby coffee shop. Both got large cups of very strong Java. When they were finished they ambled back to the courtroom just as the bailiff signaled that a verdict had been reached. Signe and Theo filed back in and took a scat. The bailiff ordered Urszula to stand.

The middle judge stood and began to read in a magisterial voice.

"The Eighth District Court of the Prefecture of Amsterdam finds the defendant Urszula O. Stephanie guilty of violation of the deceased's civil rights, and of assault and murder in the first degree. You are hereby sentenced to the maximum sentence of twenty-one years in prison. In one month you will be tried in this courtroom as a smuggler and spy acting against the interest of the Republic of the Seven United Netherlands."

An immediate roar went up in the courtroom and Urszula Stephanie's arrogant demeanor crumbled as she sank into a chair. Signe hastily wrote a note to the head Judge requesting an interview with Ms. Stephanie.

Signe and Ted walked out into a surprisingly warm Amsterdam evening. They headed to a nearby bar for several beers while they discussed the details of the case. Then they walked a few unsteady blocks to a nearby back alley *ristaffel* that was crowded with noisy diners. Theo picked it because it had the hot, spicy 'boys' that Signe favored. She liked a little bit of peanut and cucumber, but she craved the chile-spiced vegetables and meats and curry infused eggplant, lamb, and octopus. They ate way too much of the forty boy *ristaffel* and washed it down with several bottles of Grolsch beer.

They walked arm in arm the two miles to the Leidseplein, and found a smoky club with a jazz quartet. They ordered more Grolsch beer interspersed with shots of young genever. Theo pulled out a Davidoff cigar and shared it with Signe. They stayed until the club closed at four a.m. and then took a taxi to Signe's hotel The Rembrandt. Theo walked her to the front door and tried give Signe a good night kiss but completely missed her mouth. Signe staggered to the elevator alone.

In the morning Signe ordered coffee and paracetamol from room service for a vicious, throbbing, bilateral headache. She closed the drapes, put a pillow over her head and went back to a fitful sleep. She had a series of nightmares and in the worst one Svelty and Urszula each with a rusty scythe in their hands chased her over a blasted landscape of burned trees and uneven ground. She was forced to run on the ground and both of them could almost fly. They wheeled and swooped at her missing her shoulders and arms by inches. She finally dove into a dark pool where they couldn't follow.

In the morning, Signe dragged herself to the shower. The superheated water pounding on her neck slowly dissolved her loginess. She had an interview with Urszula but couldn't remember at what time. She forced herself to dress, ordered more coffee and called the Osdorp Courthouse. Her interview was at two p.m. She had forty-five minutes to get there. She put on her makeup and raced to the front door of the hotel asking them to summon a taxi on the way. She arrived at the gate to the Detention Center behind the Courthouse with five minutes to spare. Signe was shown into a sterile light green interrogation room. Urszula Stephanie was sitting in the corner in a ball. Her hair was tangled and she had obviously been crying.

"Ms. Stephanie. I'm Signe Sorensen of the Santa Fe Police Dept. We met after Albina's tragic death. I was at your trial yesterday. Now that you have been convicted, the pressure is off of you in a sense. I am hoping that you can help me solve the murder of Dr. Larry Abramowitz's murder in New Mexico. By the way," Signe lied. "I don't think there is any possibility that you committed that murder. So here goes. Do you know who murdered Dr. Abramowitz?"

Stephanie thought for a long minute and then said, "I really don't have any idea."

"Did you know that for years he had been carrying out clandestine research into compact nuclear weapons, isotopes for assassinations, and compact electric generating stations for use by the Polish underground?"

"I knew nothing of that. My sole function was as a mule. I never knew what I was carrying back and forth. I may have been more important than I know."

Signe was certain she was lying. She thought she might try one back.

"You have already been given a very long sentence (in her heart Signe thought the sentence far too light). I have authorized by the US Government and the Government of the Netherlands to reduce your sentence if you help me solve my case."

"How much could you get my sentence reduced?"

"Depending on the quality of the info by as much as half."

"I can't tell you who murdered him, but I can tell you who bought the info in Poland."

"Who?"

"A general named Leszek Balcerowicz."

"Do you know any of the people in America that were involved in buying the secrets in Los Alamos or sending them to Poland?"

After a long pause, Urszula replied, "Since my job involved transport only from Holland to Poland, I wasn't told about that part of the operation."

Signe was sure Urszula knew the operatives in the United States and that she was bright enough to know that the penalty for espionage at that level is execution.

"I'm afraid you haven't given me enough information for me to reduce your sentence."

"I was afraid that might be true."

"Please contact me if you think of any names that might help me solve my case," Signe said as she rose to leave.

Theo picked Signe up at the Detention Center and raced her to Schipol for a late KLM flight to Denver. She arrived just in time to catch a Frontier flight to Albuquerque. She found herself home at 8:45 p.m. too tired to unpack. She went right to bed.

In the morning she met with Chief Hartford and told him all that had transpired in the Netherlands.

"I think you are beginning to crack this case open," Hartford told her.

"I agree. The European ties are being exposed," Signe replied. "I'm just having trouble following the lines back to the US."

She spent the rest of the day trying to track down her abducted partner, Jack. His last known location was in Slovenia. However, she knew that Jack was traveling with Svelty and her new lover, Arkady Shilkloper. Arkady had worked extensively for the KGB in Minsk. Mateo had set up a stringer there, but when she checked with him he hadn't turned up a trace of them.

Signe went home after a quick supper and was reading quietly when she got a call from Terecita inviting her to Twenty-Nine Waves. Signe threw a black bikini, some lotion, and a cover up in a bag and headed north in her BMW. It was still eighty-eight degrees in the city. At the desk she was directed to hot tub number seven the most isolated of all the private venues deep in the woods. It was a Tuesday night and the Japanese bathing venue was all but deserted. When Signe entered number seven she noticed that the light was burned out. She found the darkness of the woods appealing and began to take off her clothing and guns. She put everything in a neat pile in the locker at the back of the hot tub. She walked naked to the edge of the pool with the bikini in her hand. A low voice spoke from behind her.

"You are even more lovely than I had imagined," the voice husky with desire said. "Turn around slowly so I can see all of you."

As she turned, she searched her memory desperately for the identity of the voice. Nothing came to her. She could see a large ill-defined form in the corner of the enclosure. She also noted that the open side that normally spilled into the woods was covered with almost invisible one inch nylon mesh nine feet tall. Someone had laid a careful ambush for her, Signe noted, and she was naked inside the small enclosure, like a skunk in a live trap. The form in the corner came out of the shadows and caressed Signe's shoulder while pointing a Mauser at her stomach.

"This is the end of the trail, as we say in the west," the voice said with a heavy accent.

Signe had never felt so trapped in her life. She had her mind and her body only to try and outsmart someone who had probably already killed and now wanted to add her to his list of victims. Perhaps she could divert him.

"Why did you have to kill my friend Larry?" Signe asked in a seductive voice.

Her oppressor didn't answer but ran the tips of three fingers over the lower part of her belly. Perhaps I can distract him with his lust Signe thought. She backed up a half a step and began caressing both of her breasts. She lifted them provocatively and then played with her nipples using her index fingers. Her assailant said nothing, but the barrel of the Mauser dropped a few degrees. Slowly Signe put her left foot on the rim of the hot tub then she ran her fingers very slowly down her belly and into her nest of pubic hair. Her assailant reached out and caressed the upper inner part of Signe's left thigh and the gun barrel dropped a few more degrees. She risked turning her back on the attacker and she felt his hand lightly on her ass. She bent her left leg and ran her bare foot slowly and seductively up and down his shin. She stiffened her left arm in front of her and then spun quickly clockwise on her heals. Her fist smashed into her assailant's Adam's apple taking his breath away and dropping him to the floor. She grabbed for the barrel of the Mauser and smashed the butt down on his head with all her strength. He fell to the deck face down and unconscious. Signe raced to her clothing and grabbed the handcuffs off her belt. She quickly cuffed her would be killer before he regained consciousness.

CHAPTER 70

Signe threw on her slacks and blouse and grabbing both of her hand guns, ran through the darkness to her car. She snatched her phone and speed dialed Chief Hartford. He answered on the second ring. Signe explained her situation briefly.

"I'm on my way," Hartford replied.

Signe went back to hot tub number seven, but it was deserted. She began circling the hot tub in wider and wider circles with her flashlight, looking for her assailant. She found nothing. After twenty minutes of searching and finding no sign of her assailant, she had a brief moment when she wondered if perhaps she had imagined the whole thing. In another five minutes Chief Hartford was on the scene with six uniformed officer and the department's two German shepherds, Jasmine and Jethro. Hartford sent a black and white to Terecita Armijo's house to make sure she was all right. The remaining officers set up a perimeter around the hot tub while two officers interviewed everyone in the main building and the hotel rooms. The officers called to say they found Judge Armijo tied up but unharmed. Two hours later nothing had been found at Twenty-Nine Waves.

"Is there any possible way that your assailant could have escaped from the property?" Hartford asked Signe.

"I don't believe so," Signe remarked. "It was so dark I didn't recognize my attacker, but his weak, waivery voice suggests that he is quite old. It took me ten, maybe twelve minutes to get to the car and come back to the crime scene. He would have to regain consciousness, unlock my handcuffs and run or jog to the parking lot, dodging me all the way. I don't think it is very likely, Chief."

"That sounds logical. I'll add more officers to the local search."

The interviews with the Twenty-Nine Waves guests proved unproductive. Someone had checked into hot tub number seven at three that afternoon. The clerk had little memory of the person other than that he was elderly and overweight. He signed in under the name—Thomas Gruber which was obviously an alias. In another hour the twelve officers turned up a body in near by ravine. EMS had trouble getting to the site because of the rough terrain. The techs reported normal vital signs, but the patient was unconscious.

Signe came close and pulled back the sheet. Her assailant was Claus Obermeyer! Ten minutes later the duty officer at the station house called to say that the Mauser used in the assault was legally registered to Dr. C. Obermeyer. Using the keys from the perp's pocket Valerie donned gloves and gown and drove his 1976 Volvo to the station for a thorough search for evidence. Valerie's assistants searched the area of the hot tub for other evidence. They found a pig, like the kind used to transport radioactive material, in the corner of the hot tub enclosure. A Geiger counter placed next to the pig gave off no counts. They also took pictures of the nylon mesh that would have prevented Signe from leaving the area.

It was 4 a.m. Chief Hartford had Signe driven home by an officer followed by another in her car. Signe got right into bed but couldn't sleep after all the excitement. Finally, at 6:45 a.m. she got up and drove to the station. She tried to fit Claus Obermeyer into what she knew about the murder of Larry Abramowitz. She pulled out all her charts and documents and was surprised how well Dr. Obermeyer fit into the picture. As soon as they opened, she called the Santa Fe Institute. Personnel said that Dr. Claus Heinrich Obermeyer began working at the Institute seven years earlier when he was eighty-six. He took a months vacation every year and put Lvov, Poland down as his destination. He had passed all his security investigations for SFI, however the secretary characterized the clearances and lackadaisical since the Institute handled no government secrets. A check of his person to contact in case of emergency listed a Polish name in Lvov that Signe didn't recognize.

She drove to St. Vincent Hospital and found Obermeyer in a bed on the third floor. As she flashed her badge at the uniformed officer guarding the door, she heard Obermeyer's loud voice abusing one of the nurses.

"...I expect my meals to be delivered in a timely fashion and to contain the foods that I like!" Obermeyer said in a loud voice as he pushed his food tray onto the floor.

"Stop that!" Signe shouted back as she motioned the nurse out of the room and invited the uniformed officer on the door to come in.

"I will not and I want out of here!" Obermeyer replied.

"You are under arrest for premeditated murder and the only place you will going from here is to jail," Signe replied.

"You can't hold me!" Obermeyer yelled back. "You can't identify me beyond a shadow of a doubt as the person who threatened you at the spa. If my fat- assed lawyer would get his immensity in here I would be free."

"There is no way for you to know about the hot tub incident unless you were there, Doctor. And you aren't going anywhere," Signe replied.

She took a couple of steps back from the bed to cool off.

As she moved closer again she spoke, "You are going to spend the rest of your life in jail Doctor and the food will be bad. You will be abused in a hundred little ways-sexual, verbal, physical and probably hardest for you, no one will show you any respect. I don't think it could happen to a nicer guy."

"I'm ninety-three years old my very sexy little Detective. There is nothing you can really do to me and I can dream about your naked body every night."

Swallowing her anger, Signe asked, "Did you kill Larry Abramowitz?"

"He was smart but greedy and he had started talking too much. Yes, I had him eliminated. You didn't even consider me a suspect, Signe. You came down hard on my granddaughter, Urszula O. Stephanie. You didn't ever figure out that her middle name was Obermeyer. It could have shortened your investigation by months."

"You realize you are confessing to first degree murder, Sir?" Signe replied solemnly.

"I do. Whatever you do, you can't stop me from thinking and that is all I have done for the past forty years. Long live Poland!"

JEMEZ HIJINKS

Made in the USA
San Bernardino, CA
09 November 2013